THE WILDE TOUCH

BOOK TWO OF THE TOUCH SERIES

STONI ALEXANDER

SILVERSTONE PUBLISHING

This book is a work of fiction. All names, characters, locations, brands, media and incidents are either products of the author's imagination, or have been used fictitiously. Any resemblance to actual persons living or dead, locales, or events is entirely coincidental. The author acknowledges the trademarked status and trademark owners of various products referenced in this work of fiction, which have been used without permission. The publication/use of these trademarks is not authorized, associated with, or sponsored by the trademark owners.

Copyright © 2017 by Stoni Alexander
Edited by Nicole at Proof Before You Publish
Proofread by Carole at Too Thorough for Words
Cover by Johnny & Stoni; Photo by iStock
All rights reserved.

In accordance with the U.S. Copyright Act of 1976, the scanning, uploading, and electronic sharing of any part of this book without the permission of the publisher is unlawful piracy and theft of the author's intellectual property. Without limiting the rights under copyright reserved above, no part of this publication may be reproduced, stored in or reproduced into a retrieval system, or transmitted, in any form, or by any means (electronic, mechanical, photocopying, recording or otherwise) without the prior written permission of the above copyright owner of this book.

Published in the U.S. by SilverStone Publishing, 2017
ISBN: 978-1-946534-02-6 (Print Paperback)
ISBN 978-1-946534-03-3 (Kindle eBook)

To my mother

*Thank you for teaching me to never give up and
for showing me that laughter really is the best medicine.*

1

THE PROMOTION

ALEXANDRA REED TURNED FROM her stoic guest and stared into the lens of Camera One. "I'm Alexandra Reed. For everyone here at *LA After Dark*, thank you for joining us." She smiled. "Good night."

She waited until the director yelled, "Cut!" before unclipping the mic from her suit jacket. The high-powered woman seated next to her burst into tears.

The music exec had just admitted to coercing musicians into signing record deals, threatening managers with blackmail, and accepting several lucrative bribes over the course of three decades.

Alexandra had come prepared, asked the hard questions, and anticipated pushback from the powerful Hollywood record mogul.

Instead, she got a full admission of guilt.

The weekly magazine show was more fluff than substance, so that made the confession even sweeter. Leaning close, she whispered, "You did the right thing."

The segment producer whirled onto the set with a box of tissues, plucked two and held them out. Alexandra wanted to laugh at his sympathetic expression —big, melancholy eyes, nurturing smile. *Who's he kidding?* This interview would reel in humongous ratings.

And Alexandra's reign as Los Angeles's ratings queen would live on for another week.

But her heart tightened at the downward spiral this person's life might take, in part, because she'd done her job.

"Rick wants to talk with you," said the producer. "You go ahead. I'll stay."

"I'm here if you want to talk," Alexandra whispered to the teary-eyed CEO who blotted her mascara-stained cheeks.

Surprisingly, the businesswoman smiled. "I'll probably get a book deal. Plus, my golden parachute is worth more than my salary. When does the show air?"

"Tomorrow night," Alexandra replied.

The exec extended her hand. "You're better than a colonic, Alexandra. Thanks for exorcising my conscience."

With a relieved breath and a satisfied smile, Alexandra pumped her hand before heading toward her boss's office. The tappety-tap of her stilettos on the shiny linoleum went silent when she exited the studio and her feet hit the carpet.

She knocked on her boss's open door. Rick Schwartz glanced up, waved her in, and continued bombarding his assistant with a laundry list of to-do items.

Rick was the best boss Alexandra had ever had. In some ways, he'd been her mentor, too. What he lacked in neatness and organizational skills, he made up tenfold in his keen ability to uncover the perfect story angle. He demanded excellence and integrity. He didn't believe in excuses and, like Alexandra, he knew that garnering the truth demanded persistence, respect, and a knack for storytelling.

"Thank you," Rick said to his assistant before she closed the door behind her.

"You wanted to see me?" Alexandra asked.

"Nice job." Rick's broad grin made her smile. "You got a full confession." He gestured to the chair across his desk, filled with scattered news copy, his beat-up computer bag, and two coffee-stained plastic cups.

Rather than attempting to relocate his things, she leaned against his windowsill.

He glimpsed his chair and offered an apology by way of a sheepish smile. "I've got news." During his pregnant pause, her heart kicked up speed. "Congratulations, you got the job."

On the inside, Alexandra was jumping up and down like a child who wakes to a foot of snow and no school. "Thank you, Rick."

"I recommended you. Brass agreed. A no-brainer. Your contract will get lost in legal long enough for the excitement to wear off." He glanced at his computer screen. "Oh, wow. It's almost Thanksgiving. Feels like September. I anticipate you'll start your new gig late January."

For as far back as she could remember, she'd wanted to be an investigative reporter. "My dream job."

"For the time being, you'll continue hosting LA After Dark and anchor the evening news on the weekends."

"Whatever you need." She grinned. "I'm pretty excited."

"You deserve this promotion. Take the afternoon off. I insist."

Alexandra glanced at the wall clock. "But it's just after one."

"You work harder than anyone I've ever met." Leaning close, he waggled his brows. "Even harder than me, but *shh*, not a word." They laughed. "You're here all weekend anyway. Go play."

With a nod and another thank you, she left.

Since her girlfriends were at work, she'd celebrate alone. After jumping into her BMW, she retracted the rooftop, slipped on her mirrored Prada sunglasses, and rolled out. She cranked up the music of Bishop Briggs's "River" and the singer's sultry voice, coupled with the powerful beat, pounded through the speakers.

Rain had soaked the city all week, but for the moment, the sun smiled down on her. The temperature indicator boasted seventy degrees. After eleven years on the West Coast, she flipped on the heater to take the chill out of her car. *I'm a wimp.*

With time on her side, she took the 10 out of LA, then traveled north on Pacific Coast Highway. Over an hour later, she drove into a posh neighborhood and cut her engine in the driveway of her close friend, Montana Spaulding. Though her pal was shooting on location in Argentina, Alexandra was welcome to swing by anytime. With her tattered Mexican blanket in hand, she let the housekeeper know she'd be out back.

As she rounded the house, she paused to take in Mother Nature's perfect blend of sand and sea, sky and sun. Sparkling sunshine danced on the ocean as the lapping waves kissed the shoreline. On the horizon, shimmering water glistened like diamonds that merged with an endless stream of vibrant blue sky. *This is heaven.*

Before stepping onto the beach, she tugged off her four-inch stilettos. As she made her way toward the water, her toes sank in warm quicksand. This portion of the private Malibu beach was never crowded and on this sunny November afternoon she shared her little patch of heaven with no one.

She laid out the blanket, sat down, and hugged her knees to her chest. The hypnotic rhythm of the sea quieted her overactive mind. She loved the calming aroma of the salty air and breathed deeply. As she stared at the vastness of the undulating water, the tightness running across her shoulders relaxed while her thoughts drifted like seaweed. Without question, this was her happy place.

"Congratulations," she murmured. "You did it."

A tiny smile ghosted across her lips. She'd come a long way since her first internship where she'd done everything from running copy to fetching coffee.

For the past seven years, Alexandra worked between sixty and seventy hours week in and week out. She craved the fast pace and nonstop energy of a newsroom and she thrived on the demanding schedule. The station never slept, which meant Alexandra was never alone. A convenient way to mask her loneliness.

She envisioned a celebratory dinner overlooking the water. A loving toast with the man she adored. A scrumptious meal. A bottle of champagne. A night of doting kisses and passionate lovemaking. Her vision blurred from the unexpected rush of emotion and she blinked away the familiar face with piercing blue eyes.

A couple strolled by, hand-in-hand. She envied their soft laughter and intimate whispers. The man slowed, pulled the woman into his arms, and kissed her. Pain jabbed at Alexandra's heart and she busied herself by fishing her phone from her handbag.

I don't have a boyfriend to share my news with, but I do have someone who won't leave me, unceremoniously dump me, or break my heart. After checking the time—*five thirty in DC*—she dialed. Her mom would be so proud of her.

"Kimberly Mitus Real Estate," answered the receptionist.

"Hi, Jennifer. It's Alexandra. Can I speak with my mom, please?"

The pregnant hesitation sent a shiver through her. "Kimberly has taken…um, uh…a bit of time off."

What? Hairs on the back of her neck prickled. Her mother worked more than she did. Pushing past the concern, she asked, "What for?"

"Best to check with her."

The receptionist's tight tone gave her away. Rather than pressing for information, Alexandra hung up. With shaky fingers, she redialed. Her mom's cell went straight to voicemail. Her brother, Colton, would know. As she called him, anxiety churned in her gut.

"Mitus," Colton answered.

"Hey, what's going on with Mom?"

"I'm in a meeting. I'll call you later."

"Just answer my question, please."

"She's not been feeling well."

"Yeah, that much I got from Jennifer."

"I can't talk now," he said. "Later."

When Colton didn't call her back that evening, she phoned him the following morning. "Stop avoiding me. What's happening?"

"Come home," he said. "Mom has cancer."

2

INCOGNITO

Alexandra tucked her mom into bed and kissed her forehead. She'd learned one thing in the last two weeks. Brain cancer *sucked*.

Always energetic and elegant, Kimberly Mitus had hit a rough patch. *Nothing she can't overcome.* For as long as Alexandra could remember, her mom had been her hero. She'd overcome the horrific loss of a child, the end of a marriage. And she'd beat the cancer ravaging her frail body, too. Alexandra ran a gentle hand through her mom's thinning, dark hair and kissed her cheek.

Her mom's sleepy smile convinced Alexandra of nothing. "I'm going to make a full recovery," Kimberly Mitus said. "No worrying about me. You should return to California right after Christmas. Your life and your new job are waiting for you."

But Alexandra had no intention of leaving. "Have a good sleep. I'll be here until the night nurse arrives. I love you, Mom."

"I love you, my sweet girl." Kimberly's eyes fluttered closed.

Since her return to Northern Virginia, Alexandra had learned little about her mother's condition. Kimberly insisted she'd beat the disease. Her brother, Colton, had been vague. For as long as she could remember, her family had treated her like a child. Even now, their whispers stopped whenever she entered a room. As she tiptoed out of her mom's bedroom, her head pounded from worry.

On her way toward the kitchen of her mom's upscale Old Town condo, she glanced out the living room window. *Another overcast, dreary day.* Not even the ornamented Christmas tree decked in sparkling white lights could lift her spirits.

Alexandra needed to keep busy. She yanked open the stainless steel refrigerator door and loaded her arms with food. Twenty minutes later, she started the slow cooker, stuffed to the brim with chicken and vegetables.

Knock knock.

After spying the familiar nurse through the peephole, Alexandra opened the front door. "Hi, Tamara."

"How's your mom doing?" asked the petite woman with the Haitian accent.

"She's sleeping," Alexandra replied, closing the door. "Another round of radiation today. And the doctor changed her chemo meds."

"I'll make sure she gets extra fluids when she wakes. Now she needs rest so her body can heal."

As Alexandra plodded through rush hour traffic, she hoped her new roommate would be home. The online roommate finder had paired her with a single woman, also in her late twenties, who had a furnished bedroom to rent and would accept a month-to month lease. She'd wanted to stay with her mom, but Kimberly had insisted she live with people her own age.

So far, Mandy had made two brief appearances. Alexandra's move-in day and Mandy's laundry day. The rest of the time, she stayed at her boyfriend's, leaving Alexandra alone night after night. *So much for hanging out.*

She drove into the older Lyon Park neighborhood in Arlington and street parked in front of her compact, brick-front home. In every direction, lights streamed from neighbors' windows. Only her house stood dark. *Alone again.* Feeling bummed, she scooted inside and flipped on lights. As she tossed her coat over the staircase bannister, her phone rang. It was her boss.

"Hi, Rick."

"Hello, hello! Happy holidays, Alexandra! How are you?"

She winced. Rick forced "happy" whenever he delivered bad news. "I think you're about to tell me."

He cleared his throat. "Yeah, I have an update." He paused long enough to worry her. "Because you're under contract with the station, you're not an employee per se. The network isn't under any obligation to grant you family leave, but they did agree to three."

"Months?"

"Weeks."

Her heart sank. After Thanksgiving, she'd returned to LA for two weeks to make arrangements to move back east—temporarily. During that time, she'd also requested a three-month leave of absence from the station. Even with her accrued vacation time and the additional three weeks, she'd still have to return mid-January if she wanted to keep her coveted job.

"If it's any consolation, I'll hold the investigative slot until the end of February."

"I appreciate that, Rick."

"I'm sorry," he said. "On a positive note, the network doesn't want to lose you altogether. If you can't make it back by then, they've arranged a meeting with a DC affiliate. The upside is that you'll continue working. Unfortunately, it won't be a lateral move."

"Who's the General Manager?"

"Max Buchard."

Alexandra's stomach roiled. That bastard never forgot *anything*, including his deep-seated grudge against her.

"Budgets are tight, but this sounds like a decent stop-gap," he continued. "I heard Max balked at the idea, but with ratings in the crapper, he's got no choice. Someone from their station will contact you."

"Thanks for everything."

"How's your mom doing?"

"She's a fighter."

"I hope she makes a speedy recovery."

She ended the call and crumpled onto the musty-smelling sofa. Her throat tightened, tears swimming in her eyes. *No crying.*

She steeled her spine and sent texts to a few close friends. When her phone didn't bing with a reply, she flipped on the television, channel surfed, then clicked it off. Deafening silence surrounded her. *I can't take one more night alone.* With phone in hand, she tapped the Provocateur app and logged in. After scrolling through her private messages, she tapped the one marked *Incognito*.

Dear Ms. Electra,

Thank you for contacting us. We welcome members of Provocateur.

I can reprogram your Silver Towers passkey remotely, so you can gain access to our club at your convenience. We open at five. Your first connection is on the house. For a fee, we'll transfer your membership from Provocateur so you can enjoy the privileges of your elite member status at Incognito.

Once you enter the parking garage, follow the signs for "Private Club" and park near the elevator marked "Private".

Meilleures salutations,

Francois

Assistant to the General Manager

Incognito, A Silver Towers Company

Alexandra had one vice. One dirty, deliciously naughty habit and her best-kept secret. For the past year, she'd been a member of Provocateur, an exclusive sex club in LA, where she lived out her wildest fantasies with masked strangers. Lucky for her, Provocateur had a sister club just outside DC.

The thought of hooking up with a senator or ambassador made her smile. Hell, she'd even screw a regular guy. She wanted to feel his hard flesh sink inside her and melt her thoughts into oblivion. Her insides clenched in anticipation.

She trotted up the stairs and into her shoebox-sized bedroom with rickety furniture that looked like it had been purchased at a flea market. The drab furnishings were a sharp contrast to her sunny and spacious bedroom in California. After flinging open her closet door, she toed off her flats, peeled off her sweater and skinny jeans, and slipped into a black halter dress with matching stilettos. She shaded her lids in a smoky gray, ran a thick layer of eyeliner over that, then layered on mascara. A dab of lip gloss before hiding her long brown hair beneath a shoulder-length platinum blonde wig. She finger-fluffed her bangs and smiled at her reflection.

"Hello, Electra." Her fake southern accent rolled off her tongue. "Play time."

Her body warmed at the thought.

She selected a gold masquerade mask from her bureau drawer, threw on her coat, and left under the cover of darkness.

Fifteen minutes later, she arrived in Crystal City, home to several hotels, dozens of restaurants, and a slew of high-rise condos. But the majority of the towering cement structures housed office space, which went silent after five o'clock when employees filed home like dutiful ants.

Alexandra's mouth went dry. Though excited to check out the club, apprehension tugged at her gut. Would the clientele be to her liking? What amenities did Incognito offer? Would she be able to play anonymously? It wasn't just her reputation she needed to protect. She was a Mitus and in this part of the country, that name was worth its weight in gold.

As instructed, she entered the deserted underground garage

and parked near the lone elevator labeled "Private". Seven o'clock. If Incognito were anything like Provocateur, the club wouldn't come alive until after ten. *Maybe Washington elite are early fuckers.* With an amused smile, she tied on her mask and exited the Prius Colton had leased for her. Shivering from the biting December cold, she pulled the charcoal-colored Silver Towers keycard from her wallet and hurried toward the elevator.

She held the plastic card against the sensor on the wall. The light *should* have turned green and the elevator *should* have opened, but the indicator remained red. She tried again, but nothing happened. *Dammit.*

Her breath clouded and evaporated into the cold air as she dug out her phone. Francois hadn't provided a phone number, so all she could do was message him, then freeze to death while she waited for a reply.

"Screw this." She spun around and bumped into an attractive older man, a black leather mask framing his eyes.

His hollow laugh startled her. "With pleasure," he replied.

"Why, pardon me." Her faux southern drawl oozed from her lips. "My momma always said I should look before I leap. She sure was right."

"Change of heart?"

She flashed the Silver Towers card. "Francois must have forgotten to activate."

"Allow me." He pressed his card to the sensor. The light turned green, the elevator doors opened and, with a grand sweep of his hand, the man gestured for her to step inside. "Age before beauty."

She stepped in, her polite chuckle filling the awkward silence. He held his card against the inside sensor, the light turned green, the doors closed, and they ascended to the twelfth floor.

"The name's Dracule." With a grin, he extended his hand. "What can I say? I have a thing for biting."

Alexandra didn't screw older men, but this one had such a charming personality. Handsome, too, with graying hair and a matching goatee. "I'm Electra." She shook his hand. "Thanks for the lift."

"A southern belle with a spicy name. How delightful! And with a name like that, you must really love your daddy."

Alexandra's chest ached at the mention of her doting father.

The doors slid open and they entered a swanky reception area. In addition to the elegant ambiance, the toasty temperature warmed her icy fingers and chilled cheeks. Unlike the West Coast club where an enthusiastic hostess greeted members, here they waited alone.

Dracule wedged himself between two black pillows on the horseshoe-shaped red sofa. "I'm here for rejuvenation."

"Aren't we all?"

Throwing back his head, he laughed. "True, true." Then, something dark flashed in his eyes and he stiffened. "Aren't you the club's new hostess?"

"No, I'm considering membership."

"My mistake. Someone will be out shortly." His terse tone and abrupt change in body language didn't jibe with the relaxed charm he'd displayed when he thought she was an employee.

She leaned against the reception counter where three tablets were affixed to the marble surface, their screens dark. Two oil paintings of nudes—one man and one woman—hung on the walls above the couch, each basking in the soft glow from the overhead art lights. Holiday decorations included a row of mistletoe dangling from the arched doorframe that opened into the hallway, and an elaborate swag that draped the reception counter. The simplicity worked. She wasn't there to be infused with the holiday spirit.

Across the hall in the bar-restaurant, two unmasked staffers in severe black stood behind a spit-shine bar, drying glasses and chatting. Black linen-covered tables and cozy horseshoe booths filled the room while more framed paintings of naked men and women in artful poses adorned the walls. The club appeared tasteful without being overdone.

First impressions were favorable. Alexandra liked being greeted by no one. Blending into the background while she slipped in and out was more her style. Here, she was nobody in particular, or anyone she desired. Fantasy role-playing came at a high price, but was worth every penny.

A small, balding man waltzed around the corner wearing a pinstripe suit, but no mask. He smiled at Dracule, then flicked his gaze to Alexandra. *"Bonsoir, mademoiselle."*

She hoped her southern accent sounded more genuine than his French one, but she gave him props for trying.

Dracule rose. "This is Miss Electra. I mistook her for the club's new hostess."

"*Monsieur* Dracule, these tablets were installed this week. They replace the host staff for check-in and suite reservation. We sent out several messages to club members."

"Good to know," said Dracule.

The employee addressed Alexandra. "How may we assist?"

"I'm from Provocateur," she replied. "Are you Francois?"

The man's cheeks flamed bright red. "*Oui, Oui.* A thousand apologies, Ms. Electra. I'll be right with you. Have a glass of wine on the house." He pivoted toward the bar across the deserted hallway and snapped his fingers at the wait staff. Both shot to attention.

Dracule extended his hand. "I hope our paths cross again, lovely lady." When she placed hers in his, he pecked it, and left with Francois.

As she slinked out of reception, she glanced down the sconce-filled hallway. Both men entered a suite and shut the door. *That's odd.* While Provocateur's hostess did escort members to their suite, she never entered the room. *Different club. Different rules.*

The bartender poured her a glass of Pinot Grigio. Other than a few cozy couples, the bar and restaurant were quiet.

Five minutes later, the small man bounded in and slapped on a smile. "*Mademoiselle,* welcome to Incognito. *Mes excuses* for my mistake. *S'il vous plait,* let's start over, shall we?"

Alexandra offered her practiced-to-perfection movie star smile. "*Bonjour. J'accepte vos excuses.* Apology accepted." She extended her hand.

Instead of a handshake, he sandwiched her hand inside both of his and tilted his chin. "*Je vous remercie.* Thank you. Tall *and* beautiful. You'll fit in well with our elegant clientele." Releasing his hold, he straightened up and grew an inch.

She handed him her Silver Towers keycard.

"*Merci.* You have an elite membership, *oui?*"

"Yes, I do."

"I'll program at the tablet." He bounded across the hall, reprogrammed her keycard and hurried back to her. "May I give you a quick tour?"

"Thank you, yes." She wondered if he believed her accent. His was terrible.

"This is the lounge," he said. "We offer a delightful dinner menu and stock top-shelf liquor. Across the hall is the greeting room." *He's master of the obvious.*

As they walked down the quiet hall, he explained the club's layout. "We occupy the entire twelfth floor. Sometimes, we turn up the music in the lounge, but Mr. Payne, the club's GM, has soundproofed the walls. I can assure you, you won't hear it when you're in a VIP suite."

She nodded.

"Our eighteen private rooms are available to elite members only." He paused in front of a suite marked "Whips and Chains", swiped his card over the sensor and opened the door. "This playroom comes equipped with the usual BDSM toys." She peeked inside.

The leather pommel horse stood in the center of the room, the straps dangling off its sides. In the corner, a black, leather chair was suspended from thick metal chains. The bed, sheeted in black, came equipped with ankle and wrist straps. An array of floggers, whips, and nipple clamps hung on wall hooks.

At Provocateur, Alexandra liked exploring the balance between pleasure and pain. If she found the right kink partner at Incognito, she'd continue along that path. She needed the pain to keep things real. Pleasure alone was reserved for an intimate relationship…something she hadn't had in years.

The tour continued. "'The Teacher' is popular with adults who like reliving their youth." In addition to a queen bed, this room mimicked a small classroom with a row of desks and a small chalkboard on the wall.

After bypassing "Sleeping with a Senator" because the suite was in use, he opened a door labeled, "The Virgin". Everything, including the furniture, was white. She ran her fingers over her chest to soothe the ache. Role-playing would ruin the tender memory. *I'll never use that room.*

Francois led her around the corner and opened a suite labeled, "The More the Merrier". The spacious area housed several king beds and ergonomic sex chairs. "Based on feedback from our clientele, we made changes," he explained.

The LA club didn't offer an orgy room. Though she wasn't into group sex, a sly smile lifted her lips. Incognito was wilder than she'd expected.

"Some members prefer a group setting," said Francois. "As an elite-status member, you can join in the fun or observe from the theater section." He pointed to a roped off area.

Alexandra had no interest in watching. She was a hands-on type of gal, but the sexy design of the sleek leather loungers caught her eye. "What are those?"

"Tantra chairs," he replied. "They're a big hit."

When they returned to the greeting room, he tapped on a tablet. "As I mentioned, these just replaced the staff. Our sister club in LA still employs hostesses. With a dismissive wave, he said, "Too labor intensive. By checking in here, your connection is notified where he, or she, or they can find you. Feel free to wait here in the greeting room, across the hallway in the lounge, or head to your suite. You can also request a connection through the app anytime, but if you're here and would like to check room availability, use a tablet." Puffing out his chest, he added, "My idea."

"These are great." On first impressions, this club met her erotic needs all while letting her keep a low profile.

"*Merci.* We're open seven days a week from five in the evening until three in the morning. Closed on Christmas Day."

"How is the transfer fee handled?"

"Message me and I'll set up a meeting with our General Manager, Jase Payne."

"Let's set that now. I like your club."

His broad grin was contagious. "*Formidable!* Wonderful! Can you come back tomorrow evening at nine?"

"Yes. Are club amenities listed online?"

Francois tapped the tablet and the "Extras" screen popped up. "What, in particular, can I assist with, *ma chère?*"

"Rejuvenation."

A shadow fell over his eyes. "Excuse me?"

"Dracule mentioned it."

After a pregnant pause, he leaned close, as if he were going to share a fantastic secret. "*Monsieur* Dracule likes a quick nap before his connections. Here at Incognito, we accommodate even the most extreme needs."

The coldness in his eyes belied his words. *He's lying.*

With a tight smile, he tapped the tablet. "If you're interested in connecting with someone soon, I suggest you start your search in our 'New Members' section."

She studied his face for an extra beat before turning her attention to the club's website. "*Merci.*"

"Until tomorrow. *Bienvenue a* Incognito." After a slight bow, he vanished around the corner.

Based on his recommendation, Alexandra clicked on "New Members", filtered the list by "Male" and scrolled through the photos of masked men. But she was too preoccupied with Francois's answer about rejuvenation to pay much attention to the photographs. The journalist in her wanted to dig deeper to find out *what* he was hiding. Whether a curse or a blessing, being suspicious was second nature.

She continued scrolling. *Too happy. Too thin. Too old. Too goofy.* Bam!

Her heart skipped a beat. A gorgeous man stopped her cold. Even though he'd concealed three-quarters of his face behind a black devil mask, those steel blue eyes paired with an undeniable confidence, sent a whoosh of energy straight to her core. *Wow, he's hot.*

Insta-lust worked every damn time. She tapped his profile.

- *Name: Hunter*
- *Stats: 6'2", brown hair, blue eyes, 225 lbs.*
- *Age Range: 30-35*
- *Member Level: Elite*
- *Fetishes: Women*
- *Restrictions: No oral, always masked. No small talk.*

He's perfect. The erotic club would be her new late night escape. She requested a connection for the following evening and hit send. *I'm going to like it here.*

On her way home, she couldn't shake Dracule's comment about rejuvenation. He'd piqued her curiosity, but Francois's shifty reaction had provoked her interest. Her favorite professor at USC had harped on one fact: Everyone guards a secret. As a journalist, your job is to find out what that is and flush out the truth.

3

CROCKETT'S SPY FLIES

Crockett Wilde's long, nimble finger controlled the hovering insect with a light touch on the tablet. His audience remained silent, save for the heavyset man's occasional wheezing. Because Crockett didn't permit cameras inside his lab, his guests' cell phones had been secured in his office safe while they sat cozy as kittens around a conference table. Wilde Innovations's Think Tank housed a white conference table, six white chairs and a wiped-down white board attached to a white wall. No windows. The sole entry point was the white door, which opened into the spacious lab. The simplicity of his white room allowed clarity when thinking, though he also found the space a source of comfort when he couldn't quiet the demons that plagued him.

As Crockett landed the tiny creature on the top of the conference room doorknob, his visitors spun in their chairs, fascinated by its every move. These four individuals from the FBI were the gatekeepers he needed to impress. Not only could their decision bring him one step closer to another significant win for his company, their procuring his devices might help locate his sister and bring her home. That, above all else, motivated Crockett Wilde.

To his left sat his cousin, FBI Case Agent, Danny Strong. A dedicated agent, Danny's expertise with surveillance equipment made him a subject matter expert. Over the past several months, he'd advocated hard for state-of-the-art surveillance equipment. This meeting was step one in the agency's mission to improve operations.

The three lead members for the source selection evaluation panel from the FBI's Criminal Division included the Contracting Officer, Deputy Director of Field Operations, and Surveillance Program Manager.

Though today's outcome was critical to Crockett both personally and professionally, he was neither nervous nor excited. The determination that spurred him forward also anchored him to work late into the evening and on many-a-weekend. He was driven, but his motives were selfish. Staying focused redirected his constant pain and utter frustration. Some called him obsessed but he didn't give a damn what anyone said.

All eyes stayed glued to the stealth Horse Fly as Crockett maneuvered the tiny robot in mid-air before achieving a flawless landing on the Formica. Another tap on the tablet and the Black Fly rose undetected from the corner of the floor. It blended so well with the carpet that the Deputy Director of Field Ops jumped when it hovered next to her.

"Very lifelike," she said, quickly composing herself.

"Thank you," said Crockett. "The insect on the table is modeled after the Horse Fly. The Black Fly is airborne."

Crockett's cousin, Danny, pulled two flying beetles from his pocket and set them on the table. "For comparison. These surveillance devices are what the agency currently uses."

Crockett tossed him an acknowledgement nod. Wilde Innovations's bugs were half the size of the inch-and-a-half beetles. That alone could secure this lucrative deal.

"The one that's been perched on my head is designed after the Moth Fly." Crockett activated the third insect, but it wouldn't budge. With a steady hand on the tablet, he tried again. Still, no movement. *Dammit.* This had never happened with any of his surveillance devices.

"I'll be darned." The Surveillance Program Manager craned to see. "Has that been in your hair the whole time?"

He set the bug on the table in front of him and hoped no one would ask him why he hadn't flown it there. "It's mission critical that these devices mimic real insects. We've camouflaged them as much as possible. The challenge slowed down the prototype, but we worked out the kinks." *Or so I'd thought.*

"Great job," said the Contracting Officer between wheezy breaths.

Signaling an end to the demonstration, Crockett landed Black beside Horse in the center of the table. As casually as possible, he slipped Moth into his suit jacket pocket. If anyone asked him to fly that insect, the most important surveillance opportunity of his career would crash before it got airborne.

"You're welcome to handle them." Crockett picked up Horse and passed it to the Deputy Director. "These UAVs—Unmanned Aerial Vehicles—are sturdier than they look, but if they get crushed underfoot or wheeled by a tire, we lose a $65,000 bug."

"No kidding." She turned the drone over and examined his underside. "I would have guessed these cost six figures."

"They did, but after several iterations, along with retooling the manufacturing, we reduced cost without sacrificing quality," Crockett explained. "Everything we produce at Wilde is American made and assembled."

The Program Manager placed Black in his palm, then removed his glasses to examine the insect up close. "Impressive."

These bugs weren't life-size replicas, but they were as close as Crockett and his innovators could manage, yet still design a powerhouse machine that would act as the undetected eyes and ears of surveillance agents.

While the tiny equipment was passed around and examined against the current working models, Crockett redirected the discussion to better understand the agency's needs. The conversation lasted all of ten minutes. Vague summed up that portion of the meeting.

Crockett rolled back his chair. While today's attendees had shown keen interest, this was step one in a three-part process. And each round would be more grueling than the previous one. Though Crockett had secured a contract for his Spy Flies with another government entity and several law enforcement agencies, doing business with the FBI had always been his primary goal.

Unfortunately, the agency's vendor award could take anywhere from a few weeks to several months. The wheels of bureaucracy moved too slowly. He bit back the rising frustration and forced a smile.

After a round of handshakes, Crockett retrieved their cell phones from his safe, and delivered his guests to the elevator bank. Only Danny stayed behind.

"Thanks for pulling this together." Crockett patted his cousin on the back. "You know the players. What's your take?"

"They were impressed and that carries weight. I know you're pushing for these to hit the streets—like yesterday—but there's a lot of moving parts." Danny paused for several seconds, his expression growing somber. "I've heard back from forensics."

"About the girl's remains?"

"Yeah."

"Let's talk in my office."

The two men, looking more like brothers than cousins with their dark brown hair and bright blue eyes, strode down the hall to Crockett's corner office. After closing his door, Crockett leaned on the corner of his large, somewhat cluttered desk and crossed his arms. His pounding heart thundered in his ears. *Please don't be her.*

With his back to his cousin, Danny stared out the window of the Crystal City building as the steady stream of planes landed at Reagan National Airport. After a moment, he said. "It's not Sophia."

Hope, mixed with the familiar feeling of frustration, leapt from Crockett's guts. "Confirmed?"

Danny turned to face him. "Dental records."

"This is good news."

Danny's phone rang and he silenced it. "I'm sorry."

"Don't be." Crockett pinned him with a hard stare. "That means she's alive."

Danny's brow knotted, but he stayed silent. Crockett knew all too well what his cousin wanted to say. *"Just because we haven't found her remains doesn't mean she's still with us."* But Crockett believed his sister was alive. That single hope kept him from going insane. His fingers ached from gripping the desk and he pushed off the sturdy furniture. "I'm relieved, but we're no closer to finding her."

"It's a big world and a cold case. She was abducted a long time ago, Crockett."

For thirteen years his pain and anger had festered. A sore that wouldn't heal until Crockett found her. "How's Allison?" Crockett purposefully changed the subject to Danny's wife.

"We've been trying to get pregnant but encountered some problems." Concern etched Danny's eyes.

"Nothing serious, I hope."

"We're waiting for test results."

"I'm here if you want to talk." Crockett shook his cousin's hand. "Give my love to Allison and thanks for today."

"You did a helluva job." Danny got two steps from Crockett's door and turned. "Almost forgot. I asked one of our forensic artists to sketch a facial approximation of Sophia from a photo I had of us as kids. Thought you'd want a copy." He handed Crockett a folder, then left.

As Crockett stared at the rendering of his sister, his chest tightened. The artist had captured the innocence in her eyes, something he assumed was long gone. She'd been fourteen when she was taken. His attention drifted out the window. Like clockwork, planes landed every ninety seconds. *Where are you, Soph?*

Had she been forced into a vehicle and driven hundreds of miles from their childhood home? Was she being held prisoner in another country? Or had she been murdered years ago? *Am I chasing her or her ghost?* He wanted to punch his fist through a fucking wall, but he knew, firsthand, the only thing that accomplished was breaking bones.

Even with three different private investigators on retainer, his sister had vanished as if she'd never existed. Shortly after her disappearance, police had found her backpack in a woodsy area near the Wilde home in Uvalde, Texas. She'd been abducted on her way home from high school. Law enforcement had little to go on.

With any luck, he'd be awarded the FBI contract. His army of robotic flies would be deployed and one of the skilled agents would track down his sister. He slid the folder into his computer bag. *I'll never give up on you, sis.*

Regardless of Crockett's constant heartache, he was so damn proud of his team. His hard-working employees deserved his utmost gratitude. But his problem with Moth needed immediate attention. He pulled the tiny robotic bug from his pocket and set it on his desk, then texted his Chief Innovator and second in command, Decker Daughtry. "Man down during demo."

In less than thirty seconds, Decker jogged into his office. "What happened?" His hair, usually tied back in a man-bun, fell loosely around his face.

"No idea. When I activated wheels up, nothing."

"Which one?"

"Moth."

"This is bad."

"I figured that part out on my own." Crockett raked his hand through his tidy hair.

"Tell me they didn't notice."

"We got lucky. I redirected their attention back to Horse and Black."

As Crockett updated him on the three-round procurement process, Decker snatched his phone from his jeans pocket. "I'll work with Engineering and Quality Assurance."

"Try to fly her now." Crockett waited while Decker tapped his screen.

As if the glitch earlier had never happened, the tiny surveillance device lifted gracefully into the air. Decker zoomed her around the room but paused her in mid-flight, to study her wing rotation. "She's fine."

Crockett's jaw ticked. "Like hell she's fine. She had a malfunction."

"Is it possible you *thought* you'd powered her up, but hadn't?" Decker landed the Spy Fly on the conference table.

Crockett let out a grunt. "Winning this contract is top priority. Don't question me like I've never run a damn demo before."

Shuffling from side to side, Decker shoved his hands into his jeans pockets. "Righto. I'll order extensive testing and let you know." After collecting the device, he bolted.

Though Crockett continued working, the nagging concern over Moth's failure gnawed at him. This was a problem he'd never before encountered. *What happened to that bug?*

At six thirty, he closed his office door, changed into his black karate *gi* and left. He'd unleash his mounting frustration on a punching bag.

Plowing through rush hour traffic, he wolfed down two power bars and arrived at the martial arts studio twenty minutes later.

After a quick bow at the entryway of the spacious dojo, he stopped short. Not only was the large room buzzing with activity, several more rows of steel chairs had been added to accommodate parents, grandparents and siblings. *The lower belts are testing tonight.*

Ignoring his aggravation, he shed his running shoes, pulled his black belt from his duffel, and shoved everything else into a wall cubby.

Crockett had been working exclusively with the white belt tiny tots since the class began, so he couldn't duck out. He'd be needed to observe and assist while Sensei tested them. As a part-time instructor, he received a small salary, but forfeited his wages to the karate school's education fund so financially challenged families could benefit from martial arts training.

Working with the children was the one thing that calmed him and, on occasion, made him smile. They were full of enthusiasm and soaked up everything he taught them. Crockett wanted—no, he *needed*—to teach them about self-defense. If his younger sister had taken karate like he had—

"Hello, Mr. Wilde," said Sensei. "Ready for next month's black belt competition?"

Annie Rodele owned and ran Rodele Karate. Students learned Taikido Jitsu, a mixed martial art that incorporated techniques from Budo Taijutsu, Tae Kwon Do, Hapkido, and Ju-Jitsu. Besides receiving excellent training, Crockett liked how she taught her students life lessons, respect, and offered the best self-defense training in Northern Virginia.

"I'm ready to get my butt kicked," Crockett said.

She laughed. "Nah. You're as prepared as you've ever been."

Even as a sixth-degree Taikido Jitsu black belt, there were no guaranteed wins. Time and training had taught him to never underestimate his opponent. "Thank you. Big crowd tonight."

"I want you to lead the white belts," Annie said. "I'll back *you*."

His eyebrows jutted up. "You always handle testing."

"You've been working with this young group since late summer. They're comfortable around you and they trust you."

"I'd be honored," Crockett said.

"It's a piece of cake. Just like class, only smile more." She grinned. "You're going to be featured in everyone's home videos and photos."

He chuckled. "Yes, ma'am."

"Excuse me, Mr. Wilde," said a small voice next to him. Hannah, a dark-haired squirt with bluish-gray eyes, tugged on his karate uniform. Her timid nature had stolen his heart.

Annie smiled at the six-year-old. "You ready for your test, Hannah?"

"Yes, Sensei." Hannah looked a little pasty.

"You'll do *great*." She patted Hannah's back, smiled warmly at Crockett, and took off toward the rowdy group of green belts.

With her hand still gripping the edge of his uniform, Hannah whispered, "I don't want to do this. I'm scared."

He knelt down and offered a reassuring smile. "It's okay and perfectly normal to feel scared or nervous. Sensei has given me permission to lead the test"—her eyes lit up—"so it'll be just like class. All you have to do is follow my instruction. You can do that, right?"

"Uh-huh." She fiddled with the ends of her white belt.

Crockett spied another student entering the dojo. "Isn't Aleesha your partner?"

She nodded.

"Well, she just arrived."

Hannah spun around.

"Why don't you tell her that I'll be working with you guys tonight?"

When she turned back, the color had returned to her cheeks. "Okay."

"Feel better?"

She gave him several quick nods and a tiny smile, then darted toward her friend.

Ten minutes later, the audience hummed with excitement. Standing room only. Phones at the ready. After a brief introduction about the efforts and hard work of her talented students, Annie introduced the young white belt class. She stepped away so Crockett could take center stage on the red mats. His eighteen tots lined up into four rows. Facing them, he bowed. The energetic youngsters bowed back. Next, he walked them through the basics.

"Jab." He thrust his fisted right arm forward.

"Hyah!" they shouted in unison, mimicking his action.

One at a time, he demonstrated the moves for knife hand, front and back kicks, along with heel-stomp kick. Each time they yelled, "Hyah!" with gusto as they followed his every move.

When the test ended, fifteen minutes later, they bowed in unison and Sensei joined Crockett on the mat. "Mr. Wilde, your students are well trained. How do you think they performed this evening?" she asked, projecting so the last row of guests could hear.

"They did a fantastic job and I recommend each student for promotion to yellow belt."

"Congratulations, students!" she said.

The audience applauded while Crockett awarded each tyke with a certificate. The other adult instructors quickly added a yellow strip of adhesive tape to their white belts. As the proud little ones traipsed off the mats, Crockett shook each of their small hands.

"Thank you, Mr. Wilde." Hannah beamed. "That was fun."

Pleased with her newfound confidence, Crockett smiled. "You did a great job, Hannah."

An hour and a half later, Crockett left the karate studio still brimming with pent-up energy and no foreseeable outlet. He tossed his duffel onto the passenger seat and jumped into his truck. Two minutes from home, his cell rang. Kimberly Mitus. He hit the speaker.

"Hi, Kimberly, are you okay?" Crockett tried to hide his concern for the late night call. He worried about his best friend's mom. She'd been undergoing chemo and radiation treatment for brain cancer. Initially, she'd had a tough go of it, but the recent change in her medication seemed to be helping.

"Goodness, yes. I'm checking to see if you're going to Colton's party Friday night."

"I wouldn't miss giving him a hard time about getting engaged. Do you need a ride?" he asked.

"You might not be my child, but you're definitely my favorite." He could hear the smile in her voice. "Thanks, but Alexandra is taking me. Have you seen her since she got back?"

"No," he replied dryly. He hadn't spoken with Alexandra in eleven years, though their last conversation had been branded into his long-term memory.

"I can't wait to meet Brigit," she said, breaking the silence Crockett refused to fill.

"She's good for Colton. You'll love her." He pulled into the garage of his Rosslyn high-rise.

"Alexandra said the *exact* same thing."

Persistent like a Mitus. "I might lose you." He cut the engine in his assigned spot. "I'm parking in my building."

"Thanks for emailing me the photos of your new condo. Beautiful views. Who did I ask to work with you again?"

"Tammy Mackley. I'm sorry it couldn't have been you."

"Me, too." Kimberly sighed. "Maybe you can help Alexandra find a place. She's renting a room in the Lyon Park area of Arlington."

He wanted to laugh. Kimberly led one of the most successful real estate teams in Northern Virginia and she wanted *him* to help find her daughter a place to live. "How are you feeling since the doc changed your meds?" Crockett asked, refusing to take the bait.

She hesitated. "As well as can be expected."

After grabbing his bag, he headed toward the elevators. "I hope they make all the difference." But he knew the truth and his chest ached. "I'll see you Friday."

"Looking forward to it. Good night, dear."

Though he could see right through Kimberly's scheming ways, he couldn't help but crack a smile. As the elevator ascended, he wondered how Alexandra was adjusting to being back east. Though he'd never admit it to Kimberly, Friday couldn't come soon enough.

Once inside his spacious new penthouse, he dropped his karate and computer bags on one of the stacks of still-packed boxes. His old, outdated furniture looked out of place in the elegant space with the phenomenal views of downtown DC.

After a hot shower, he wrapped the towel around his waist and styled his wet hair with a few finger swipes. *Good enough.* His cell phone rang. It was after eleven. Why was his realtor calling so late? *Why is she calling at all?* "Hey, Tammy, what's up?"

"I've made a special delivery."

"What does that mean?"

"Open your front door."

His realtor, Tammy Mackley, stood behind a giant houseplant, its outstretched leaves obstructing his view of her. She set the pot down in his foyer. "My housewarming gift," she said before closing his front door.

"Thanks. This could have waited until morning." *Or never.*

Licking her lips, she fixed her gaze on his bare chest. "Perfect timing. I love a man who's freshly showered." She untied the sash on her overcoat and dropped it on the floor.

His eyebrows shot up. *What the—*

Wearing nothing but stilettos, she hitched her hands on her

hips. "I earned a nice fat commission check because of you and wanted to express my thanks, Tammy style."

After picking up her coat, his gaze floated over her naked body. She stepped close enough to rub her breasts against his chest and he grew hard beneath the bath towel.

Never mind that Tammy Mackley was *Mrs.* Mackley with a husband and two kids. He'd no intention of screwing his realtor, married or not. "No can do." He stepped back.

Her cheeks reddened. She yanked her coat out of his hand and shrugged it on, tied the sash. Clearly, she hadn't expected rejection.

Opening his front door, he said, "You want your plant back?"

"You can shove it up your ass!" On a loud huff, Tammy stormed out.

Crockett closed his front door and laughed out loud as he returned to his bedroom to pull on cotton pajama pants. He'd address his boner later. Padding into his kitchen, he wondered how many men would refuse a late night booty call with such a sexy, willing partner?

Though his shiny, new refrigerator was filled with more than the essentials, he settled for the always-reliable breakfast for dinner. Rather than eat at the center island, he sat in his dining room admiring the twinkling city. The Kennedy Center, the Washington Monument, and the Capitol stood as beacons of strength and power in the nation's capital.

When finished, he checked work emails hoping Decker had stayed late to retest Moth and had determined the reason for her failure. But there were no new messages from his Chief Innovator. He shifted his gaze out the wall of windows that spanned the length of his living area.

Since starting Wilde Innovations eight years ago, he'd never had surveillance equipment fail to operate. *Is it possible I'd forgotten to turn the bug on?* "No way," he said, before turning his attention back to his laptop.

Next, he checked personal emails. One, in particular, caught his eye. From Incognito, the subject line read: Your Connection Awaits.

He opened it and the picture of an attractive woman popped on his screen. Electra, another new member, had invited him to join her in "The Teacher" suite tomorrow evening, nine thirty. *Damn, she's hot.* She had shoulder-length platinum blonde hair, heavily made-up eyes framed in a black mask, and sultry lips made for kissing. He clicked on her name and up popped a sidebar.

- *Name: Electra*
- *Stats: 5'9", 35-24-34, blonde hair, brown eyes, 125 lbs.*
- *Age Range: 25-30*
- *Member Level: Elite*
- *Fetishes: Role Play, light BDSM. Men only.*
- *Restrictions: No oral of any kind. Always masked.*

His boner returned. The beautiful face of this sexy stranger was reason enough to accept her invitation. Two months earlier, he'd agreed to check out Incognito to placate Colton. But even after his best friend had purchased an elite membership for him, he'd forgotten about the erotic club. Sex with strangers wasn't his thing. But as his hard-on strained against his pajama bottoms, he couldn't resist the temptation. Could this alluring mystery woman be the perfect distraction for an hour or two? Before talking himself out of hooking up, he tapped *Accept this Invitation*. An auto-response email dropped into his inbox.

"Congratulations, you're confirmed in 'The Teacher' suite! Electra looks forward to your *connection* tomorrow at nine thirty. Check in using one of our new tablets in the greeting room, then relax on the sofa, enjoy a drink in the lounge, or wait in your private suite."

Embedded within that message, Electra's private note said,

"Hello, Professor. I failed the midterm, but need an 'A' in your course. I'll be by during office hours to see what extra credit work I can do to get my grade up."

He replied to her personal message with one of his own. "You'll have to work very, very hard if you want to earn an 'A' in my course, Electra."

4

THE TEACHER

AT PROMPTLY NINE O'CLOCK, Alexandra sauntered into the busy greeting room at Incognito. Several couples cozied close on the red sofa while the flirty bar crowd spilled into the hallway. Pleased to see more activity than the previous evening, she was relieved everyone wore masks. And dressed to be noticed. She liked.

Before she could check in, Francois scurried into the room. "*Bonsoir*, Ms. Electra. Mr. Payne is expecting you. Right this way, *s'il vous plait.*" He shot her a friendly smile before turning right out of reception. Midway down the hall he rapped on a door marked, "Management". Without waiting, he opened it with a flourish and stepped into the room.

Jase Payne, Incognito's General Manager, slammed his laptop shut, then shot Francois a harsh stare. Alexandra froze in the doorway. Clearly, this was not a good time. When Jase glimpsed her, he broke into a broad grin that revealed a significant gap between his two front teeth.

Pushing out of his chair, he rounded his desk, hands extended. His tight black shirt and snug black pants clung to his compact physique. "Welcome, Ms. Electra." To thwart what she thought might be a bear hug, she stuck out her hand. With his gaze fixed on her, he kissed her knuckle.

Alexandra startled when someone jumped up from the sofa to her right. She couldn't help but gawk. Clothing hung on the young woman's tall, slender frame and her thin hair dangled limply over one cheek. With her head down, she shuffled toward the door, the sudden movement revealing her bruised cheek. Her porcelain skin only magnified the large purple splotch.

Adrenaline spiked through Alexandra. Physical abuse terrified her.

"Sage, are we good?" Jase asked.

After shooting him a furtive glance, Sage stared at the floor. "Of course."

Alexandra's stomach knotted. Her gaunt appearance compelled Alexandra to engage her. "What do you do here?"

Silence.

Sage's eyebrows jutted up. "I'm...I'm sorry. You were talking to me?"

Her sad, gray eyes pierced Alexandra's soul. "Yes, I'm curious about your job."

When Jase anchored his hand on Sage's shoulder, she flinched and lowered her head. "Sage works in the kitchen," Jase said. "I couldn't run the club without her help."

"My goodness, that is great." Alexandra's strained smile accompanied her twang, but her skin crawled from the sugary tone of Jase's voice.

As the jumpy employee tied on her masquerade mask, Jase removed his hand. "I worry about our little Sage. She walked *smack* into the swinging kitchen door."

Back in LA, Alexandra had earned a television Emmy for her six-part series about three women who'd escaped their abusers. Was Sage really accident-prone or had someone hit her? *The signs are there.* Her attention darted between Sage and Jase, but neither said anything more.

"Sage, I'll walk you to the kitchen," Francois said. The two left, shutting the door behind them.

Jase's steady stare sent a shiver through her. "Please, make yourself comfortable." After tapping the seat across from his desk, he eased into his executive leather chair.

She folded into the plush seat.

"Would you like a glass of wine?" He tucked his shoulder-length dirty blond hair behind his ears.

"No, thank you. I can't stay. I'm meeting a connection." *And I prefer to screw them sober.*

"Excellent. I'm delighted when new members jump right in. I think you'll be pleased with our diverse clientele. If you don't like what you see or have a concern, let me know. I stay connected to my clientele, especially the elite ones."

Should I ask about rejuvenation? Her gut said no. Instead, she plucked the money order from her tiny clutch and slid it across his desk. "My transfer fee."

As Jase eyed the check, she glanced at the portrait hanging on the wall behind him. The dark-skinned woman's haunting expression tore at Alexandra's heartstrings. A sheer red scarf draped her nude back like a shawl as she glanced over her shoulder. Though the club boasted a generous art collection, this portrait seemed different. *She's so young.*

"Would you prefer a monthly payment plan or do quarterly installments better meet your needs?" he asked. "The interest rate is about the same for either—thirty-five percent."

What? "I'm not following."

"Unfortunately, this is half of what's owed. Our prices are higher than Provocateur. To keep your *elite* status at Incognito, the transfer fee is $10,000."

Her stomach dropped. Though she wanted to scream, "That's all I've got!" she folded her hands in her lap. "Monthly," she uttered. What choice did she have? Life would be so much simpler

—and affordable—if her tastes weren't so eclectic or if she didn't have intimacy issues and could handle being in a relationship.

Jase pushed out of his chair. "I'll get the paperwork in order. In the meantime, I hope our club provides you every pleasure."

Before leaving the office, Alexandra glanced over her shoulder at the pretty young girl in the portrait.

CROCKETT SET THE BLACK devil mask on the passenger seat of his gray Ford F-150 limited edition and started the engine. Pulling out of his underground garage, he punched speed dial. He'd never had masked stranger sex, so a brief conversation with his closest friend and one-time business partner would set him right.

"Hey," said Colton. "Still at work?"

"I'm on my way to Incognito," Crockett said.

"First time?"

He blew out a breath. "Yeah. Feels a little weird."

"Once you meet her, you'll get over it. Even if she says she's on the pill, use a condom. The club provides them, but you've got your own, right?"

Crockett squeezed his front pants pocket. "Got 'em."

"What are you doing about your accent?"

"What accent?" Crockett turned onto the main road.

"Your Texan one. It's subtle, but you should hide it."

"Colton, I'm going to screw this woman, not chat her up."

After chuckling, Colton said, "Change your speech pattern, then."

"Is that the lengths you used to go to?"

"Years ago, someone stalked me, so I made adjustments. When our Crockett Boxes roll out next month, you might find yourself in the spotlight. You don't need your sex life overshadowing your career, especially if you're trying to do business with the FBI."

He stopped at a red light. "It might be my name, but you're the face of Crockett Boxes. Thanks for the pointers."

"I hope she works out."

Crockett ended the call and continued two blocks past his Crystal City office building, parking in the garage beneath the Silver Towers high-rise. After tying on the mask, he exited his truck.

As the elevator whisked him to the twelfth floor, he buttoned his tweed sports jacket. *I'm Hunter. Say the damn 'r'. Hunterrr. Hunterrr. This is crazy.*

The doors slid open and Crockett entered the swanky club. First impressions were favorable. Dim lighting, while a sultry jazz musician crooned quietly from invisible speakers. Classy portraits of nudes hung on the walls. The club was busier than he'd expected on the Tuesday before Christmas. A few well-dressed masked members flirted on the horseshoe-shaped red sofa. None of them were Electra.

After checking in on the tablet, a pop-up alerted him that his connection hadn't yet arrived, but he could indicate where he'd be waiting. He selected the lounge, settling into an empty booth tucked in the back of the restaurant. Four giant candelabras anchored each corner while flickering candles adorned the black linen-covered tables.

Within seconds, an unmasked waiter took his vodka martini order. He relaxed into the cushiony seat while singles, couples, and small groups mingled in the bar on the other side of the room.

The server delivered his drink, collected the cash. The chilled cocktail slid easily down his throat and he enjoyed another sip before setting the glass down.

A masked brunette in a low-cut dress slid into the booth. "You're looking good." She curled her fingers around the glass and sipped his martini. "I would love to get to know you better."

No small talk and no boundaries, either. "Maybe another time. I'm waiting for my connection."

"In the mood for a threesome?"

"Can't say that I am." Freewheeling sex wasn't his thing.

Her smile faded as she slid out of the booth. "If you change your mind, I'm a good time," she said and headed toward the bar.

A statuesque woman sashayed into the lounge. Her elegance stole his breath. *Jesus, it's her.* Electra wore skinny jeans, thigh-high brown suede boots and a white cardigan sweater that spotlighted her protruding nipples. His cock twitched. *No bra.*

In those heels she had to be six feet tall. He loved a leggy woman. He pushed out of the booth, slipped a hand into his pocket and waited. She pivoted in his direction. As they eyed each other everything around him faded to black. The only thing that mattered was the sultry blonde gliding his way. Suddenly, the strangest feeling came over him. Like *déjà vu. Here comes Lady Luck.*

Heads turned in her direction. The closer she got, the faster excitement coursed through his veins.

Her hair swished against the top of her shoulders while her hips swayed back and forth. With her eyes pinned on his, she sauntered close enough for him to catch a whiff of her flowery fragrance.

"Electra. I'm Hunter. It's a pleasure." He extended his hand.

"Hello, Huntah. The pleasure's all mine." Her southern accent surprised him. When she pressed her hand into his, her chilly fingers cooled his internal inferno. Behind the mask, her whiskey-brown eyes twinkled.

Damn, she's hot. "Can I buy you a drink?"

"No, thank you." She stepped into his personal space as if she already knew him. "I'm meeting my professor and don't want to keep him waiting."

He hardened.

With a light grip on his bicep, she directed him down the

corridor to a suite labeled, "The Teacher". She flashed her Silver Towers keycard over the wall sensor. The light turned green and he pushed open the door. "After you."

"Office hours start shortly." Her sultry voice sent another shock of adrenaline to his groin. "You get situated. I'll be right in."

He appreciated Electra's all-business attitude. Like him, she wasn't interested in small talk or getting to know him. That worked. He wasn't there to make friends. He was there to fuck, plain and simple. One look at her and he was up to the task.

When he stepped into the suite, she closed the door behind him. Bathed in flickering light, several faux candles had been placed around the room. The front half of the room resembled a college classroom. Professor's desk and chair faced a row of student desks. The back half of the room housed a queen bed covered in taupe linens and four fluffed pillows. A microfiber loveseat stood flush against the far wall. The open night table drawer revealed a variety of condoms, neatly arranged in their boxes. In the corner were two bathrooms marked "Teacher" and "Student".

Behind the desk hung a variety of sex toys. Handcuffs, paddles, a flogger, a crop and nipple clamps. Before sinking into the chair, he placed the crop on the desk alongside the neat stack of copier paper and pens. Until now, sexual role-playing seemed absurd, but *game-on* based on his raging hard-on.

Electra tapped on the door, stuck her head inside. "Hello, Professor." Her smile flamed in his chest.

"Electra, come in. Here to discuss your midterm?"

"I am." She closed the door, slipped into the student chair and crossed her legs. "My failing midterm grade makes getting an 'A' in your class impossible."

"You should have thought of that before you opted not to study. I don't offer extra credit work." Crockett pushed out of the chair and walked around the desk, then leaned his backside against the corner. His hungry gaze floated over her beautiful masked face, her full breasts, and down those amazing legs. "You should have come to me for help before the test."

"This is going to ruin my chances of getting into grad school." She rose and sashayed toward the door. "I'd have done just about anything to improve my grade."

Crockett couldn't wait to anchor those swaying hips and drive himself inside her. He marveled at how sincere she sounded. Was Electra an actress? "Wait."

As she slowly turned, the tips of her erect nipples stole his attention.

"Maybe I can assist with some private tutoring. One-on-one."

Her breath hitched and she breezed close, her alluring scent of wild flowers drawing him in. "I need personalized help *now*, Professor. What can I do to thrust my grade to the top?" With a devilish gleam in her eyes, she arched her back, thrusting her fantastic cleavage dangerously close to his mouth.

Desire made his dick throb and he removed his sport coat. He wanted to pull her into his arms and drive himself deep inside her until they both surrendered to the ecstasy. "I should take you over my knee and spank you for being such a bad student."

On a breathy gasp her lips parted. "The perfect punishment," she murmured.

"You'll have to come twice weekly. And you must agree to whatever lesson I'm prepared to teach you."

She briefly closed her eyes, then pinned him with a smoldering stare. "I'll do it if I can assure myself an 'A.'"

"No." He brushed his hand across her sweater, his fingers grazing her hard nipple. "I'll promise a passing grade *only*. Anything more, you must earn."

"How many sessions will I need?"

Her sexy moan roared in his ears. "That's up to you. How fast of a learner are you?"

"Very." She nibbled his lobe and palmed his crotch. "I catch on quickly."

"Good." As he unfastened a button on her sweater, his fingers brushed against her cleavage. "We have a lot of ground to cover in a short amount of time."

A husky groan ripped from her throat when she curled her fingers around his forearm. "You keep your office warm, Professor."

"I like it scorching hot." He continued unbuttoning her sweater. "How do you like it, Electra?"

"Hard," she said, dragging her fingernails down his back. "And fast."

Sliding next to him, she sat on the desk and slowly unzipped her boot. Before she could tug it off, he pushed off the desk, faced her, and slowly removed it. Her sockless feet were toasty warm and her toenails were painted a holiday red. *She's hot.*

He unzipped and removed her other boot, then placed her bare foot against his erection. She gripped the desk, flexed her long toes against his hardness. "I'm eager to learn. What will you teach me today?" Ever so slowly, she ran her tongue over her lower lip, then bit down on the soft, pink flesh.

"Lesson one. Failure equals punishment. For starters, I'm going to spank you."

Damn if she didn't tremble. "Yes," she whispered. "Please."

"Stand," he commanded. Stepping away from her, he snapped the crop across his hand. "And show me your tits."

As if she had nothing but time, Electra unbuttoned and pulled her sweater off, exposing her perfect breasts, her hardened nibs ready to be sucked. "Is that better, professor?"

Hell, yeah. Crockett was there to release his need. She didn't want nice and easy. She wanted raw and uninhibited. That worked. Grabbing her around the waist, he placed his mouth over her firm and plumped nipples, licking and biting until her knees wobbled. On a low growl, he pulled away and straightened up.

"Time for your punishment, Electra."

Even in the candlelit room, he couldn't miss how the blacks of her pupils bled over the caramel brown. Her breath came in short gasps, her fingertips kneading his back.

She wiggled out of her jeans and hitched her hands on her bare hips. Naughty Electra hadn't bothered with underwear. Sparks flew between them in the charged air. She stroked her hairless pussy, teasing him with her nimble fingers and raw moans. But when he ran his fingers along the length of her cunt, her juices soaked him. A groan shot out of her. Driven to fuck her, his cock ached.

"Turn around. And hold on," he bit out. Even to him, his voice sounded sinister. Like she'd awakened his inner wild.

With her palms on the desk, she bent over, offering her beautiful, round ass. First, he ran his hand over her smooth skin and between her legs. Then, he bit her flesh.

Her yelp morphed into a long, gritty groan.

"My favorite kind of coed. Dripping wet."

He snapped the crop over her firm ivory flesh. Once. "What did you learn?"

She moaned. "I need to study."

Again, he flicked the crop across her pinkened skin. "And?"

"I should come to you with questions."

This time, he put some force behind the smack and her throaty moans made thought impossible.

"I'm going to enjoy tutoring you, Ms. Electra. You're a fast learner."

Her shoulders rose and fell, her jagged breath roared in his ears. "Fuck me *now* before I explode."

"You're in no position to bark orders." He tossed the three-pack of condoms on the desk. As he removed his clothing, she turned and watched him with keen interest. "What did you do instead of study?"

"I partied." Still gripping the desk, her hungry eyes perused every inch of his naked body. Twice. Then, her lips curved up.

"Your cock is huge, Professor. I can't wait until you're balls deep inside me."

"You're eager. I like that." He sheathed himself in a condom, pressed his shaft against the crack of her beautiful ass, and reached around to pinch her hard nipples. "Define partying."

"I went to a frat house and fucked a couple of guys."

"You're a dirty girl, Electra. Did you have fun?"

"Yes, for hours and hours."

"Do you like fucking?"

"Yes. I. Do."

He anchored his hand on her hip and nudged her legs apart. "If you liked screwing those frat boys, you're going to love getting fucked by me."

"Ohgod, yes, Professor, I am." Her breath came in gasps. Her body shook.

With his shaft in hand, he pressed the head against her slickened core. Then he slid his cock back and forth over her opening until she begged for mercy.

"How do you want to be punished?"

"Hard and fast."

With his head poised at her opening, he reached around and fondled her fantastic tits, squeezing and pinching her nipples. She shot him a primal stare over her shoulder while her throaty moans made his knees weak.

"Please, *please*, take me, Professor. I need you inside me when I come."

He took himself in hand and tunneled inside her hot, tight sex. She felt incredible. Her throaty cry made his balls tighten. Through gritted teeth, he bit out, "You come when I let you. Do you understand me? I'm in control. Not you." The harder he thrust, the more intense her cries and whimpers.

She bent farther over and spread her legs wide. On his next thrust, he sank to her end, pleasure spiraling through him. The reality of everything faded away as the ecstasy built.

"Yes, ohmygod, yes, I'm trying not to come, but damn you feel —oh, oh, fuuuuck—*so* good," she rasped.

Their gritty, raw sounds filled his ears as he waxed his speed, driving himself to her end, again and again. "Harder, Professor," she cried out.

"Come for me, Electra." This time he smacked her ass with his hand.

"Oh, hell, yes." Crying out, she convulsed and shook as the orgasm ripped through her. "I'm coming," she hissed.

He slammed balls deep into her and released. Waves of pleasure pounded through him. He groaned through gritted teeth, the intensity stealing his breath, his thoughts, his mind. For several euphoric seconds, the intense pleasure filled him with hope. Every agonizing moment disappeared in a fog of ecstasy and he enveloped her in his arms. Still panting, he let the goodness wash over him. Whatever savagery this woman had evoked helped exorcise his demons.

As Crockett caught his breath, her delicate back distracted him. He wanted to drop tender kisses along her skin. But this was nothing more than a hookup in a swanky sex-play club. He'd done his job. Made sure she'd come. In the world of stranger sex, he hoped he'd done right by her. But why should he care? For all he knew, he'd never see her again. Somehow, pleasuring this woman mattered.

While Crockett wanted to stay inside her heat, Hunter didn't cuddle or engage in *anything* tender, so he withdrew. She turned to face him, wrapped her arms around his neck and rubbed those fabulous tits and engorged nipples against his chest. Would she break her rule and kiss him? Kissing this sexy goddess would be heaven.

Still catching her breath, she murmured, "Did that boost my grade?"

He wanted to laugh. *She's good.* Unable to stop himself, he smiled. "Only marginally. Next time, nipple clamps."

On a soft gasp, she rose on tiptoes and twirled her tongue in his ear. "I can't wait. Thanks for the fun fuck."

He'd no idea whether her interest in using the nipple clamps meant in the next ten minutes, in an hour or sometime next week. Since he wasn't about to blunder through a question, he excused himself into the bathroom. When he returned, she was gone. *Damn.*

But she'd left a note on his sports coat. "Until next time, Professor."

With a satisfied smile, Crockett dressed and left the club. *Next time* couldn't come soon enough.

5

STUCK WITH MAX

ALEXANDRA'S BLOOD BOILED. HER former boss, Max Buchard, had kept her waiting for over an hour. *On purpose.* Her stomach growled again. She rummaged through her handbag and spied a stick of gum. *Yes!*

But it was so old she couldn't separate it from its wrapper. She gave up and tossed it into the trash. Her meeting, with the pompous TV station manager, had been at eleven. She'd made the incorrect assumption she'd be out by eleven thirty and grabbing a sandwich with the DC lunch crowd.

She needed to take this gig for more reasons than a paycheck. Being an out-of-work journalist was the kiss of death. So, she'd do what the network recommended. *I've endured Max before. I can do it again.*

Four years ago, Alexandra had applied for the weekend anchor position in the mid-sized northern California city where she worked. Max, then her news director, had pressured her to withdraw her candidacy. She refused. His decision to promote another woman was overruled by the station's GM and Alexandra got the job. The other candidate filed harassment charges claiming she'd had a sexual relationship with Max in exchange for that anchor spot. Not only had Max vehemently denied any sexual misconduct, he blamed Alexandra for the entire fiasco.

A young man with a shiny complexion zoomed around the corner. "Alexandra Reed?" She glanced up at him and smiled. Had to be an intern. "Max will see you now."

Painting on a smile, she followed him through the newsroom toward the corner office. While one reporter paced with phone to ear and a copy girl scooted by on the way to production, a handful of reporters worked at their desks. Even though it had only been two weeks, she missed the excitement of working in a newsroom. If she felt at home *anywhere*, it was here. Her anxiety morphed into excitement.

"Go on in," said the young man.

She heaved in a breath, steeled her spine and pushed open Max's door. With any luck, he no longer clung to his grudge.

Max stood with his back to her, facing the window, while he spoke on his cell phone. Alexandra waited, squinting against the bright afternoon sunlight.

"Good job covering the White House press briefing, honey," Max said. "Since you're playing with the big boys, I'll coach you on some more substantive questions. 'Who designed the First Lady's gown for the state dinner?' doesn't pack the punch you need to be taken seriously."

Goose bumps covered her arms. The conversation sounded like so many she'd heard Max utter. Even after all these years, his patronizing tone chilled her blood. She cleared her throat.

"I'll see you in ten—" He turned and shot her a cool glance. "Let me call you back." He slipped his phone into his pocket, didn't bother to shake her hand. "Our paths cross again, Alexandra Mitus."

Mitus? He knows I use Reed professionally. She really didn't want to meet with him and forced a pleasant smile. "Hello, Max."

In addition to packing on the pounds, he'd colored his salt and pepper hair to midnight black. No longer wrinkled, his face reminded her of a baby's rump. His attempts to conceal his age had only exacerbated it. But the one feature that hadn't changed was Max Buchard's smug expression.

He eased into his executive chair and leaned back. Across from his desk, she perched on the edge of a Kindergarten-sized seat and peered up at him. In every way possible, Max exerted his authority.

After he pontificated about the differences between the West and East Coast markets, he rested his clasped hands on his protruding belly. "Rick Schwartz forwarded me one of your magazine shows. Cozying up to those A-listers got you big ratings."

She bit her lip to force herself to stay silent. *My journalistic integrity got me those ratings.*

"But watching your demo reel gave me an idea," Max continued. "We need something to jump-start our dwindling viewership. Launching a news magazine show could be our ticket out of last place. Congressmen, senators, hell, a segment with POTUS and his family would rocket our numbers sky high and get me noticed." He broke eye contact to stare out the window for several seconds. "Capitalizing on your popularity in LA could work. Would you consider hosting my show?"

Absolutely! She sat tall, trying to make up for the difference in chair size, but she didn't want to show her hand, especially since the network had forced his. Max was the Big Kahuna and she needed *this* job in *this* market. So, she played it cool. "Whatever you think is best."

This Max appeared affable and more relaxed. Had he changed? Learned his lesson? Buried the hatchet? A tiny seed of hope took root.

"Also, I'm not averse to letting you cover the White House," he said. "For now, keep all this under wraps."

Her heart leapt at the thought. *The White House.* "Of course."

He checked his watch. "Thanks for stopping by. I run a tight ship of hardworking professionals, so prepare for 'nose to the grindstone' at the start of the New Year."

Alexandra struggled out of the tiny chair. "Thank you for your time." Trying to sound casual, she added, "By the way, I don't use Mitus. I still use Reed, professionally."

"Yes, I remember. Like an elephant, *I forget nothing*." His eyes narrowed. "Thought you'd want to capitalize on the famous Mitus name. In this neck of the woods, that packs one hell of a punch."

"I'll keep that in mind."

Pushing out of his chair, he looked down his nose, though they stood eye-to-eye. "I have an off-site meeting. I'll walk you out." As he rounded his cluttered desk, he grabbed a weighty stack of papers. "Take these." He shoved the pile at her. "No one here has time to flush out these possible leads. My gift to you."

Alexandra's cheeks heated while her hope fizzled. She glanced at the disheveled papers cradled in her arms. Rookie reporters would sort through the pile, hungry for a story or news tip. Surely there was a journalist more junior than she who should be assigned this job.

With the meet and greet over, Max escorted her out. A few minutes later, she stood alone on the busy sidewalk as Washingtonians whisked by.

After grabbing a sandwich at Phillips Cafe, she tooled around the nation's capital. Even though the one-way streets turned her around, she loved the vibe of her new city. As she drove past the Newseum, a long line of children, walking in pairs, traipsed inside. She hoped something in that museum would spark an interest in journalism for one of those kids.

Later that afternoon, Alexandra ran on the treadmill in the gym of her mom's condo building, then cooked dinner. While she and Kimberly ate, Alexandra mentioned how the network had found her a temporary assignment. But she didn't mention her new boss by name. Why ruin her mom's day? Like Max, Kimberly forgot nothing.

Years earlier, when Max had insisted Alexandra withdraw her application for weekend anchor, she'd consulted her mom. Kimberly suspected Max might have been up to no good and encouraged her daughter to stay the course.

After setting down her fork, Kimberly regarded Alexandra for several seconds. "That sounds like a rookie job. Float your resume with the local competition."

She was all too familiar with her mom's cocked brow and unblinking stare. "Working forty hours will be a piece of cake." Alexandra smiled. "Plus, this arrangement lets me spend time with you."

Kimberly stared at her half-eaten plate of pasta. "I'm doing fine, as you can see."

Sadly, though, Alexandra knew differently. Her mom needed help dressing. And the nurses doled out her daily meds after Kimberly had taken the wrong chemo dose one evening, then vomited all night long.

Alexandra blanketed her mom's hand with her own. "We haven't hung out together in a long time. I've missed that. Plus, my life in LA isn't going anywhere." Rising from the table, she stacked their dinner plates. "How about this? When you have a clean bill of health and go back to work, I'll get out of your hair and return to California."

Although Kimberly's lips lifted, her eyes grew sad. "Deal."

As Alexandra loaded the dishwasher, she blinked back the moistness from her eyes. She wanted to scream, *tell me the damned truth*, but Mituses never discussed anything with her. Even now, Alexandra didn't dare discuss her mom's ill health for fear of upsetting her. She made a mental note to talk to Colton. No doubt, Kimberly had confided in him.

Ten minutes later, her mom dozed on the sofa, the unread Washington Post blanketing her chest. While waiting for the night nurse, Alexandra curled into the comfy recliner and watched the evening news. When it ended, she perused the pictures of masked men on Incognito's website.

While at Provocateur, she'd enjoyed a variety of kink partners. And she had every intention of doing the same thing at her new club, too. Until Hunter. As she stared at his photo, his steely blue eyes sent a rush of heat down her neck, her chest. Her insides clenched. *That man can screw. And talk about eye candy.*

The overwhelming need to be in his arms had her squirming in the chair. Not only was he hot, he was fantastic at taking care of her needs. *And damned good at role-playing, too.*

She tapped the "Request a Connection" button. *One more time, then I'll branch out.* Three rooms were available the following evening. After choosing the "Pick-Up", she sent him a personalized message.

"Hello, Hunter. Meet me in the lounge where we'll begin our exciting evening of wild fun. Where does our evening end? It ends in me."

She sent the invitation, tidied up the kitchen and roused her mom to help her get ready for bed.

Kimberly woke confused and swatted Alexandra away. "I don't want your help. You need to give me space."

Alexandra sat on the floor next to the sofa. "I want to help you, Mom."

"No, no." Kimberly pushed herself into a sitting position. "I'm independent."

"I know that, but we all need a little assistance every now and then."

"No! I don't!"

Alexandra flinched. Her mother never lost her cool.

Knock, knock, knock.

Alexandra welcomed Tamara in. "She's having a rough time, tonight," Alexandra said while hanging Tamara's coat in the front closet.

"What's going on?" asked the nurse.

"She's resisting me."

"I see this a lot. Your mom isn't ready to give up her independence. I help her in ways she doesn't realize."

"Like?"

"I ask her which nightgown she wants to wear. I let her choose between water or juice." Tamara's rueful smile reflected Alexandra's feelings. "It helps that I'm not family. If it's any consolation, she talks about you and your brother all the time. Cancer is a tough one."

"I can't help her if she's fighting me on this. What would you suggest?"

"Speak to her oncologist."

"Maybe you could fill in the blanks until I do that."

The nurse shook her head. "I can't discuss details about Kimberly's health."

With a light hand on the nurse's shoulder, Alexandra said, "Of course. Thanks for taking such good care of my mom."

"Tamara, is that you?" Kimberly called.

"Coming, Miss Kimberly," called Tamara.

The two women entered the living room.

"Hello, Tamara." Kimberly's sleepy voice sounded hoarse. "Ali, you can go now."

Alexandra whipped her head toward her mom. Kimberly hadn't called her that since elementary school. Was she regressing to an earlier time? Losing her grasp of reality? She kissed her mom's cheek. "I love you."

"I love you, too."

Hugging herself to quell the sudden shaking, Alexandra threw on her wool coat and left. *I need some answers. She's sicker than she's letting on.*

Alexandra drove home in silence. After turning down her quiet street, she hoped to see lights pouring from her house. Per usual, darkness greeted her. She parked, hurried inside, and turned on every light on the first floor.

With a glass of Cab in hand, she sat at the wobbly dining room table and phoned her brother. When she got voicemail, she sent him a text. "Mom had a hard time tonight. I need to talk to you. Call me!" She stared at her phone, hoping for those three little dots.

Several minutes later, her brother still hadn't replied. After refilling her wine glass, her phone binged with a message from Incognito.

"Congratulations, you're confirmed! Hunter looks forward to your connection at ten o'clock, Thursday evening. Once you arrive, please check in using one of the new tablets in the greeting room."

Hunter had included a personal message. Her lips curled as she read it. "Get a good night's sleep, Electra. You'll need it."

6

THE PICK-UP

Alexandra awoke with a start. Bathed in sweat, she threw back the blankets and flipped on the table lamp. *I haven't had that nightmare in years.*

In it, a man slapped a woman with dark hair and terrified eyes, then grabbed her shoulders and shook her. Instead of cowering, Alexandra ran screaming toward the lady. Decades later, the faceless man remained a mystery.

Trying to slow her thundering heart, she breathed deeply. When that didn't work, she padded to the bathroom for water. It was almost five in the morning. After snuggling beneath the covers, she closed her eyes. But the image of the timid club employee with the bruised cheek crashed into her consciousness. Her eyes flew open. *Poor Sage.*

For reasons she couldn't explain, physical abuse was a known trigger for her nightmares. *I'll bet a hundred people at the club have seen that poor woman and turned a blind eye to it. Well, not me.*

Years ago, Alexandra had reported on the brutal murder of a young woman at an LA shelter. Following that, she spent six months following the lives of three female residents who struggled to break free from their abusers. Though the story had gutted her, she'd wanted their voices to be heard. In the process, she'd exorcised her own demons and the ongoing nightmares that had haunted her since childhood.

Or so she'd thought.

The only other time her nightmares had stopped was when she'd dated Crockett. Hoping to soothe her heartache, she rubbed her chest. Though she'd never stayed overnight at his place, she'd felt safe and loved. *Until he dumped me.* She did not look forward to seeing him at Colton's engagement party. *I've avoided him for eleven years. I can avoid him tomorrow, too.*

Desperate to stop daydreaming about Crockett Wilde, she tossed off the covers and started her day.

Later that evening, Incognito was aflutter with activity. After snagging the last two barstools in the crowded lounge, Alexandra searched the sea of masked faces for Hunter. Though eager to see him, she'd arrived early to talk to Sage. So often, battered women lived in fear. If Sage had been a victim of violence, Alexandra doubted the frail employee would admit to it. But that wouldn't prevent Alexandra from speaking to her. Despite being concerned, her motives were selfish, too. She wanted the nightmares to stop.

As the bartender poured her Chardonnay, Alexandra asked if Sage was working.

He leaned over the bar to better hear over the chatter and music. "Who?"

"Sage. She works in the kitchen. Tall, slender." She wanted to add *jumpy*, but didn't.

"I don't know anyone by that name, but I'm kinda new. Would you like me to ask around?"

She wanted to snoop without a target on her back. "No worries, I'm seeing her tomorrow." With a nod, the bartender moved on.

Someone's shoulder brushed against hers and she turned. Dracule was all smiles.

"We meet again, lovely Electra. I'm delighted to see you." Mistaking her polite expression as an invitation to join her, he set her small clutch on the bar and slid into the seat. The one she'd saved for Hunter.

"Why, good evening, Dracule." Alexandra oozed southern charm. "Thank you again for helping me the other night."

"Of course. How do you like the club?"

Members became loose-lipped after a few drinks, so Alexandra did her best to avoid small talk. Before she'd become the savvy and uber-private Electra, one of her Provocateur partners had confided he was married. She had dumped him on the spot. Another time, over drinks, a partner told her she looked familiar, like someone he'd seen on TV. She'd dropped him, too.

The barkeep set a napkin on the bar in front of Dracule. "Excuse me, sir. Beverage?"

"No, thank you, my good man. I'm passing through."

"The club's fantastic," Alexandra said, resuming their conversation. "What about you? Were you sufficiently *rejuvenated* the other night?"

His smile faltered. "Are you here for the ambiance or did someone catch your eye?"

He didn't answer my question. With a sly smile, she sipped her wine. "Both."

Pausing, he rolled up his sleeves, exposing a tattoo with the initials "CM" on the inside of his left wrist. After leaning his wrist on the bar, he stroked the black ink. "Someone I lost years ago." Alexandra did not want the conversation to become personal, so she stayed quiet. "My son." Dracule's voice cracked, his shoulders slumped.

She'd no idea why he'd confide something so personal to a complete stranger and wondered if he was trying to garner sympathy. Either way, she felt obliged to say something. "I'm sorry for your loss."

He swiveled on the stool and sandwiched her hand between his. "Thank you, my dear." He leaned toward her.

Goose bumps crawled up her arm and she tugged her hand away to sip her wine. Feeling like someone was watching her, she glanced over her shoulder and her heart skipped a beat.

Hunter's broad physique filled the entryway and her insides turned to molten lava. Except for the black masquerade mask, he looked like he'd come straight from work. Dressed in a dark tailored suit, a white dress shirt and bold pink tie, his taste was as impressive as the apparent quality of his duds. His confidence carried him, but his swagger sent her pulse soaring. Damn if she wasn't excited to see him.

"Electra." Hunter stood behind their barstools. As she swiveled toward him, she peeked up through her lashes. The possessiveness in his eyes seared her like a tinder fire, but when he eyed Dracule, his expression turned icy. "I don't share what's mine. Find another woman to cozy up to. This one's taken."

Her insides tingled. Had anyone else made that bold claim, she'd have bolted. But Hunter's words had the opposite effect. What kind of hold did this sexy stranger have over her?

Dracule slid off the stool. "No worries, fine sir. Miss Electra and I were just having a friendly conversation."

Francois rushed in, almost crashing into Hunter. "*Bonsoir, Monsieur Dracule.* Sorry to have kept you waiting. Your room is ready, *s'il vous plait.*"

"Lovely to have seen you," Dracule said to Alexandra. Without addressing Hunter, he left.

Alexandra rose. "Excuse me, Huntah. I'll be right back." She had to know. She followed at a respectable distance, keeping her eyes on the target. Like before, Francois ushered Dracule into the room at the end of the hallway and shut the door behind them. *That's too weird.*

She returned to the bar and eased into the stool beside Hunter. "Good evening."

A few seconds passed before he faced her. "Don't let me stop you from connecting with that man."

Though she owed no one an explanation, she wanted—no, she needed—Hunter to know she had no interest in Dracule. Running a hand down his arm, she leaned close. His virile scent wafted in her directed and she inhaled. "I'm curious about the special treatment he receives."

Behind the mask, his eyes widened. "You don't strike me as someone who'd care. Trying to keep up with the Joneses?"

She stared into his eyes, the undeniable pull tugging her closer. She desperately needed his mouth on hers, something she'd never wanted from a hookup. "He gets escort—" She pursed her lips. "It's nothing…never mind. Let's start over."

He signaled to the bartender. "Vodka martini, dry," then asked if she wanted another glass of wine.

"No, thanks." The devil mask he'd worn the other night had concealed most of his face, but tonight, his simple black mask showed off his squared jawline and high cheekbones. Dark whiskers covered his cheeks and chin. She loved a sexy, handsome man with a few days of facial hair. Were the hairs rough or soft? Would they burn or tickle? Caressing his face would be too intimate, so she settled for stroking his windblown hair. Even that simple touch sent her heartbeat skyrocketing.

As she fiddled with his hair, his breath hitched. Her insides thrummed with desire, her pussy slickened with need. His piercing gaze had her squirming in her seat.

When she finished, he grasped her hand and pressed her palm to his mouth. Her nipples pebbled, the ache between her legs throbbed. As much as she wanted to kiss him, she would not break that rule. Kissing was reserved for lovers. And this man was not her lover. *Not my lover.*

"Do I meet with your approval?" He released her hand.

God, yes. "You'll do." Curling her fingers around the wine glass didn't replace the loss of his touch.

"Are you attending the tech convention?" he asked.

"Excuse me?"

Leaning in, he rested his lips against her masked cheekbone. Unable to control herself, she moaned. "We're in the 'Pick-Up' suite," he whispered. "Time to play."

Right. Of course. She swiveled toward him and entwined her hands on her lap. "I travel a lot for my job."

He eyed her sheer cream blouse, lingering over her fuchsia bra and black mini-skirt. Tonight she'd dressed for him.

And he'd noticed.

After checking her out, he covered her bare thigh with his large hand. Shock waves traveled up her leg. The throbbing between her legs hindered her ability to think clearly.

"Pink is my new favorite color." His hand vanished beneath the black fabric. His moan, slow, deep and filled with promise, turned her insides to jelly.

Though she wanted to reposition herself so he'd have easy access to her sex, she crossed her legs, instead. After pulling out a lipstick from her tiny handbag, she popped off the top and slowly spun the tube. Then, with her eyes on his, she placed the hard stick to her lower lip and ran the dark color back and forth. His lips parted and a low growl shot out of him.

The server set his drink on the napkin and Hunter dropped cash on the bar. "This covers mine and the lady's. The rest is yours."

With a grateful smile, the bartender collected the money.

"Thank you for the drink," she said.

He flashed her a smile, sipped his martini, then placed his hand on the back of her barstool. "Are you staying in the hotel?"

She wanted his hand on her body, not the damn furniture. Frustration tinged her tone. "Yes. You?"

"I am. We're expected to attend a team-building exercise at

Casino Night. I skipped out. That ballroom is so packed, I couldn't hear myself think."

"What do you do?" She held her breath, hoping he wouldn't answer her question honestly. Nothing killed a fantasy more than the truth.

"As little as possible," he replied. "You?"

Relieved, she smiled. He'd stayed in character. "When I travel I like to see where the evening takes me."

"I know where I'd like to take you." His deep voice rumbled through her. His self-control and confidence had her feeling dizzy. Then, his large hand wrapped the back of her neck.

Her body hummed with desire. Every nerve fiber, each cell, vibrated and came alive. This man had completely undone her and they hadn't even left the lounge.

As they stared into each other's eyes, her breasts felt heavy. She could barely think, distracted by the heat between her legs. He stroked her bare thigh. Up and down, back and forth. The scent of his arousal had her hungry to have him and she released her breath in a long, low hiss.

"Where is that, Huntah?"

"To bed."

Oh, yes. "I'm not that type of girl." When she sat tall, her protruding nipples caught his eye and he grazed one with the back of his finger. Shuddering in a deep breath, she wanted him to pinch them, hard. *More. I need more.* "I don't even know your name."

Behind the dark mask, his eyes turned stormy. "All you need to know is that I will bring you nothing but intense pleasure for hours. Why tell you my name if you won't remember your own when I'm done fucking you?"

He's a sex god. Quivering with anticipation, she set down the wine glass. She wanted to run to their suite and devour him. *Now. Right now.* But she knew better than to give in to the need so quickly. The building pressure between her legs meant a sweeter release later.

With a long finger, he moved her blonde hair away from her ear, pressed his mouth to her lobe and whispered, "Take a walk on the wild side." Then, he bit her lobe. She gasped from the quick shock of pain.

"We shouldn't. We're strangers."

A devilish smile reached his eyes and he held her gaze for several seconds before pushing out of the chair. "And we'll keep it that way. Turn left out of here. My suite is right down the hall. I'll leave the door cracked." He brushed his lips against her ear. "So much fun awaits us. Don't be long."

He exited and Alexandra sucked down a deep breath. With her heart pounding in her ears, she waited a few moments before following. No need to let on how excited she was to play with him.

As promised, he'd left the door ajar. Several flameless candles illuminated the room and she crossed the threshold.

Hunter waited in the corner chair. Naked.

With her heart pounding a frenzied rhythm, she shut the door. Several seconds passed while he devoured her from head to foot. Then, he rose. Beyond his devastatingly handsome face, sculpted body, and jutting erection, there was something about him that stole her breath. Even if she'd wanted to, she couldn't have looked away. He commanded her full attention simply because he existed.

With a slow and deliberate cadence, he stalked toward her. Even masked, his hunger was palpable. He was going to fuck her. And she was going to love every damned second of him.

The longer he stared into her eyes, the more she ached for him. Anticipation swirled in a cyclone of need. Grateful he wasn't wearing cologne, she indulged in his musky scent. From his bulging thighs and massive chest to the sinewy muscles running down his arms, she soaked up his physical perfection.

When he reached for her, she became his.

With his eyes cemented on hers, he unbuttoned her blouse. His breathing remained slow and controlled while hers roared in her ears. He removed the blouse and cupped her breasts, still hidden behind the silk bra. His breath hitched. Instead of walking around her to remove her pencil skirt, he reached around, forcing her flush against him. A shiver of excitement ran through her. The skirt dropped.

Again, she'd not worn panties and he caressed her ass. On another moan, she closed her eyes.

For that brief moment, she popped out of role-playing. *What does he think? Does he find me sexy? Am I pretty enough?* Why did she care? She'd never once wondered about her sex-play partners. But this stranger—this alluring, breathtaking man—was different.

When he kissed her bare shoulder, she trembled in anticipation.

"Touch my cock." His deep voice, coupled with that commanding tone, sent zings of energy straight to her pussy.

As she caressed his thick, hard shaft, wetness trickled out and she thumbed the head with its juices.

"Fuck, you feel good," he bit out.

She wanted him to throw her on the bed and take her. Being with him was the ultimate escape, but also the ultimate illusion.

Through the silky bra, he caressed her breast, then lowered his face to bite her other nipple through the thin material. She cried out. A few tender strokes to her swollen clit and she'd come undone, shattering into a million pieces.

"I like that," she murmured, but her voice didn't sound like hers. It came out in a whoosh of breath, raw and unfiltered.

He slid the straps over her shoulders and with one flick of his hand, unhooked the bra. The garment fell away, exposing her breasts. Though her jagged breath came fast, his remained slow and controlled.

His gravelly groan ripped through her and she fought the urge to drop to her knees and suck him. Even in her heightened erotic state, she would never break that rule. His cock, thick and hard, strained against her soft touch.

His mouth found her nipple and, while he sucked and bit her sensitive flesh, he snaked his arm around her ass and pulled her close. Then he laved and nibbled the other. Whimpering, she rolled her head back, exposing her neck. Pleasure cascaded down her like a waterfall and she bathed in it.

And then, he stepped away. Her eyes flew open, her hand dropped, and she wondered if she'd done something wrong.

"Get in bed," he said. "Lie on your back. I'm going to fuck you."

Relief washed over her and she gave him a saucy grin. "Hard, I hope."

"Very hard."

Yes. Pivoting slowly, she sashayed to the sleigh bed. Crawling in, she remained on all fours. He ran his hand over her round ass, then slapped it. She yelped. "So good."

"Naughty Electra. Picking up a stranger in a hotel bar. I'm going to enjoy driving myself inside you."

"Me, too."

"Fuck," he growled as he cupped her sex. "You're dripping wet. I bet you taste so damn good."

A moan shot from her throat at the thought of him eating her. "Finger me."

"No, you'll come," he said as he caressed her bottom. "It's too soon. You need to wait for it."

A thrill ran through her. *Who is this man? My deliciously sinful addiction.*

She lay down on her back and shot him a smirk. One by one he placed nipple clamps, a black leather flogger, his tie, and a three-pack of condoms on the purple satin sheet.

When he straddled her, his cock stood erect and proud. "Arms over your head, wrists together."

After complying, she studied his face while he bound her with his silk tie. Though desire flamed in his eyes, his touch was gentle. And suddenly, she was back to wondering who he was and what he looked like without the mask. Blinking rapidly, she pushed away the intimate thought and focused on the reason she was there. Sex with a stranger.

Eyeing his long, thick erection, she couldn't wait for him to bury himself deep inside her until he fucked her sore. Pain kept things real...and in perspective.

His every stroke, his every caress heightened her state of anticipation until she begged him to relieve her suffering. Each time his fingers reached the apex between her legs, they brushed the edge of her unshaven pussy. Squirming and panting, she clamped down on her lower lip hoping the pain would slow the build. "Your long, sexy legs stay unbound so you can wrap them around my back while I fuck you into tomorrow."

First with his fingertips, then with the leather strands of the leather flogger, he caressed her breasts and stomach. Back and forth over her sensitive skin until her breathing became erratic and her coos and whimpers thundered in her ears. And when he attached the nipple clamps, she cried out.

"Pleasure and pain." His husky voice rumbled through her. "You control how much of each you receive. Your words guide my actions. Do you understand?"

"Yes," she said, steadying her breathing to help manage the pain.

After rolling on a condom, he slipped on a cock ring that featured a pleasure nib for her, but didn't enter her. He ran his fingers over her smooth sex, then slid two fingers inside. "A beautiful woman inside and out." He thrust, slowly, sending euphoric shock waves pounding through her. Unable to hold still, she writhed on the bed fighting against the release.

"Fuck. Me. Now." She bent her legs.

"You dictate my pace," he said, planking over her.

When he plunged inside, she arched and cried out, the

intensity of that initial thrust sending waves of pleasure through her tight core. "Hard and fast."

Again and again he slammed into her, the clit stimulator on the ring titillating her sensitive pearl. With every move, the nipple clips sent delicious pain straight to her sex.

Intoxicated from all the feels, her eyes rolled back in her head. She didn't want to block him out, she wanted to watch him watching her, but she couldn't keep them open.

The heightened pleasure of his thick cock expanded her insides. The musky smell of his skin and the raw sounds he made as he moved over her had her speeding toward orgasm.

He must have felt her tightening around him because he stilled. Frustration crashed through her. Was he going to deny her this release?

While supporting his weight with one hand, he removed the nipple clamps. Again, she whimpered, this time from sheer relief. With his mouth over one nipple, then the other, he laved her nibs with his warm tongue. When finished, he said, "Wrap your legs around my back."

She did as instructed and he stared into her eyes. A darkness fell over his handsome face. "You come when I give you permission. Do you understand?"

Mesmerized by his need to control her, she nodded her agreement.

"I'm going to take you slowly for my pleasure. If you start to come without telling me, I'm going to punish you. Is that clear?"

"Very. And what about you?" she asked.

"Ladies first."

A brief smile crossed her lips. Ready to begin again, she arched into him. He rewarded her by moving inside her. Supporting his weight on one arm, he slid his other beneath the small of her back and continued to thrust slowly. Each time he rubbed the cock ring over her clit, she moaned. The way he sucked and nipped her nipples had her bucking beneath him, but when she tightened her legs around his back, he let out a long, luxurious groan.

"You're going to squeeze the orgasm out of me," he ground out. "You feel amazing."

Just hearing his throaty voice and knowing she could bring him the ultimate pleasure, triggered the start of her release, low and deep in her belly. Between pants and cries, she fought against the urge to close her eyes. She wanted to watch him while she came. He slipped his large hand beneath her ass, pulled her even closer and thrust fast—but not deep. The cock ring teased her clit and she imagined his tongue licking her folds and penetrating her core. As she gazed at him, the orgasm tore through her with such intensity she couldn't see, couldn't think, couldn't breathe. Crying out, she stared into the eyes of the sexiest kink partner she'd ever been with. While convulsing and shuddering beneath him, the only thing she missed was his mouth on hers and their tongues tangling in an erotic dance of their own.

When finished, she relaxed into the mattress, boneless.

He withdrew so quickly she winced. "You didn't tell me you were coming, Electra. I'm going to punish you while I come inside you. Roll over."

The incendiary look in his eyes sent a rush of heat through her. His unexpected aggression aroused her. She could understand the sting from a crop or the pinch of a nipple clamp. But she'd never made peace with the heartache of abandonment. She didn't want a man's love. Love hurt in a way that screwing never did. Sex with strangers was a reliable way to quiet the hedonistic monster that lived inside her.

With her wrists still bound, she rolled onto her knees and presented her ass to him. To her surprise, he kissed her back so tenderly emotion tugged at her heart and she closed her eyes to block it out. With his lips pressed to her skin, he whispered, "You are beyond breathtaking."

She didn't know what to say or how to react. His kind nature seemed out of context. Did his true nature accidentally slip out?

With a soft caress between her legs, he found her opening. The head of his penis replaced his fingers and he slipped back inside but without the cock ring. Slowly he began thrusting until he reached her end. And then, *whack*! He smacked her bottom, the sting shocking her back to reality.

"Yeah, baby, you feel good. Now I'm going to fuck you *my* way."

As he thrust faster, his soft kiss and gentle caress became a mirage in her rear view mirror. She'd not felt a man's tender touch in a long, long time. Eleven years to be exact. The farther west the plane had flown, the harder she'd forced herself to forget. By the time she'd landed on California soil, she'd convinced herself that she no longer cared. But in her heart of hearts, she knew the truth. Neither time nor distance could sever true love.

Another sharp sting of his hand on her ass smacked her back to the present. But he caressed her skin to soothe the sting. With firm hands on her hips, he thrust hard. Again and again. "Fuck," he growled.

Even though he was taking her for his own pleasure, the strength in which he gripped her hips and controlled her movement aroused the hell out of her. Between moans, she inhaled the thick aroma of sex. She craved his hardness, his commands, and his punishments. Her erotic stranger doled out glorious pain. But his relentless fucking didn't feel like a scolding.

"Yeah," he said and went balls deep.

Moaning through his orgasm, he shuddered as her core clenched around him and she came again, relishing in the ecstasy that replaced her never-ending loneliness.

7

THE SHOCKING TRUTH

No one would guess Crockett was running on two hours of sleep, having returned home after three in the morning. Normally he'd be dragging, especially after a full day at work. But he was energized, thanks to Electra—his *very* seductive and addictive kink partner.

But his workday wasn't without its frustration. He'd spent the last two hours trying to get Moth to replicate her failed flight, but like she'd done with Decker, she'd responded to his every command with flawless precision.

As he wound his way up Colton's long driveway, his thoughts turned to Alexandra. Though Kimberly had showed him every demo tape she'd sent home over the years, he hadn't seen her in over a decade. Not because he hadn't tried. Alexandra was a Mitus and they were a stubborn lot.

He parked in the driveway, cut the engine. Carrying a bottle of champagne and a vibrant holiday bouquet, he admired the lit wreaths hanging from the windows of Colton's beautiful Great Falls mansion as he headed toward the front door. Time to celebrate his best friend's engagement. *Smile. Show time.*

The therapist who had counseled his family after his sister's abduction had explained that there would be times when they'd have to act *as if*. As if they were happy, as if they gave a damn, as if life mattered. She taught them constructive ways to release their anger so they wouldn't take it out on some numbskull who cut them off in traffic, or a spouse during a disagreement, or a coworker who needed mentoring and not a harsh reprimand. He and his parents had stuck with therapy for a year, but when it became apparent Sophia wouldn't be found anytime soon, they stopped going. Managing their anger and frustration became their new norm while they limped forward a broken family. In the end, martial arts had saved Crockett. No one got hurt when he beat the hell out of a punching bag.

On occasion, something would make him happy. Fleeting, yes, but real. Those moments were not without conflict. How could he feel joy when his little sister's whereabouts were still unknown? How dare he have fun when she could be buried in some shallow grave after meeting a horrific death, or in some third-world country serving some drug lord? And even though he could hear her sweet voice telling him that she'd want him to be happy for her sake, the frustration that lived in the pit of his stomach never left. He'd feel *joy* the day Sophia returned safely home and not one day sooner.

Tonight, however, he'd get to see Alexandra. *My Goth Girl.* Eleven years ago, he'd ended their relationship with a heavy heart. For her sake. Hoping they could start anew, he rang the doorbell, then let himself into the foyer, thick with people. "Merry Christmas!"

Colton slapped him on the back. "Glad you could make it." With a smile, he added, "You look good, bro. Showering helps."

Best friends since their freshman year at Harvard, the two men couldn't be more different. Colton had long, wild hair while Crockett kept his short. Colton had found his way to kink years ago and that seemed to quiet his raging soul. Crockett released his aggression in the dojo. The one commonality they shared was their intense passion for business and for success. If Crockett could have chosen a brother, Colton would be that man.

Chuckling, Crockett extended the bottle of Dom Perignon. "For toasting or to share with the fiancée. Congratulations on the big news."

"Thanks. Great vintage." Colton grasped the bottle. "I never thought about marriage until I met Brigit. It's all about finding the *right* woman. You next?"

"Hell, no."

"For me?" Colton asked, pointing to the bouquet.

"You're a smart ass, you know that? Where's Brigit?"

"Consoling my sister."

The knot between Crockett's brows deepened. "Did something happen with your mom?"

"All things considered, Kimberly's doing well. She's reviewing her will." Colton's voice cracked and he cleared his throat. "That upset Alexandra."

"Totally understandable. I'm sorry."

"Thanks." Colton threw an arm around Crockett and the two men headed toward the kitchen. "So, how often do you talk to my mom?"

"Every week."

"No wonder she calls you her favorite."

"Not me." Crockett glanced around for Alexandra. "That baby sister of yours has always been her golden child."

As Colton set the champagne on the island, Crockett said hello to the kitchen staff. Movement on the screened porch caught his eye. Alexandra and Colton's fiancée rose from the sofa and hugged. Though the women had been sitting in the dark, he recognized Alex right away.

And he couldn't look away.

"How long has it been since you've seen Alexandra?" Colton asked.

"Eleven years. She'd just graduated high school."

The two women scooted inside. "Too cold." Brigit's teeth chattered and Colton pulled her close.

Crockett had liked Brigit immediately. Petite, blonde and crazy smart, she was Colton's equal in every way that mattered. But more than that, she made him happy.

Alexandra's eyes grew wide. "Crockett." Her blue lips quivered.

Blood pounded through his veins. *She's gorgeous.* Large, caramel eyes blinked up at him. Dark brown hair flowed over her bare shoulders. Her elegant red holiday dress showed off her womanly curves, but her breathtaking beauty captured his heart.

"Hello, Goth Girl." As they stared into each other's eyes, he felt like he'd come home. And eleven long years compressed into mere minutes. He remembered how her eyes sparkled when she smiled at him, or that her sweet kisses could soothe his karate injuries. And how she'd undo him with her passion.

He smiled. Her gaze slid from his eyes to his mouth, then back into his eyes. The corners of her lips lifted. Then, a flash of anger shadowed her pretty face.

She flicked her head and squared her shoulders. Alexandra Mitus in defense mode. His heart tightened. That rigid posture had been his last image of her. *She's still pissed at me.*

"Thanks for talking, Brigit," she said, her attention still locked on Crockett. "Excuse me, I'm going to check on Mom." She walked away. Before vanishing around the corner, she glanced back at him.

He grinned. *Not that angry.*

SAFELY OUT OF VIEW, Alexandra heaved in a shaky breath while trying to appear nonchalant. But she was on fire. Crockett Wilde had shorted her mind. She hated the power he had over her. Always had. *My god, he's gorgeous.*

From the moment she'd laid eyes on him, at fourteen, he'd

rocked her world. The summer after she'd graduated high school, they'd fallen crazy in love, or so she'd thought.

Seeing him now had awakened the best memories and the worst feelings. Clearly, time had been good to Crockett Wilde. Gangly no more, his massive, sculpted body was eye candy for her lonely soul. She'd always found him handsome, but when he'd pinned her with those baby blues she knew she was in trouble. His chiseled cheekbones and strong jawline made looking away impossible. Like years ago, his undeniably sexy accent wove a ribbon around her heart.

Stop!

Pasting on a cheery smile, she bypassed Colton's mingling guests, then scooted down the hallway in search of her mom. She'd not anticipated the depth of her emotion when coming face-to-face with Crockett. Breaking into a cold sweat, she ducked into her brother's office, sank onto the plush sofa, and gripped the cushions until her fingers turned ghost-white.

Even though Colton and Crockett were best friends, and Crockett like a second son to her mom, she'd managed to avoid him—for years. Even Houdini would have been proud of her vanishing act. When she traveled home, Kimberly would invite Crockett to swing by. Alexandra would scramble to come up with a lame excuse as to why she'd have to leave. Once, he dropped in *seemingly* unannounced. As soon as she heard that Texan lilt, she'd hightailed it upstairs. Her excuse? A sudden and violent case of food poisoning. Her mother had given her a piece of her mind when he'd left. But she could *not* see him. The excruciating pain from their breakup had been worse than when her beloved daddy had walked out after the death of her brother, Cain. Daddy had broken her heart, but Crockett had ripped it beating from her chest and stomped it. *Never, ever again.*

Tonight, she'd expected he'd be there. How could he not be? He was like family. What she hadn't anticipated was her gut-wrenching reaction. Her body shook and her heart palpitated.

Crockett Wilde was the one man, the *only* man, who could evoke such intense passion. Buried deep beneath her frustration and anger laid her true feelings. She loved him. No one measured up. No one mattered. Only Crockett.

Steeling her spine, she glanced around her brother's spacious office. Deep breaths and a Mitus determination helped steady her. Colton's quiet workspace was the perfect man-cave. Mahogany-paneled walls made the large room both stately and cozy. The only item on his massive antique desk was a framed picture of him and Brigit. True love. Inwardly, she sighed. Maybe Colton had broken their curse. Mituses weren't lucky in love.

Lack of sleep from her marathon tryst with Hunter, along with her work challenges and her mom's health issues, had left her frazzled. Adding Crockett into the mix was too much. Suddenly, she was struck by the strangest thought. *I've seen him since I've been back. No—that's ridiculous.*

A few moments passed. She composed herself enough to leave the sanctuary of her brother's office and headed for the door. Colton's voice, followed by Crockett's unforgettable and way too sexy laugh, sent her flying behind the door of Brigit's office, which was an offshoot of Colton's. No way could she face Crockett again.

Like a child playing hide-and-seek, she peeked through the opening of the door hinge.

"I keep my best bourbon in here." Colton opened his credenza, pulled out a bottle of Pappy Van Winkle and poured two glasses.

After tapping Colton's glass, Crockett tossed back a mouthful of bourbon. "Congratulations on your engagement."

"I want you to be my best man."

Alexandra could not take her eyes off Crockett. His grin made her heart pound faster. *He's more gorgeous than I remember.*

"I'd be honored." Crockett leaned against the furniture. "Set a date?"

"We're working on that."

"By the way, thanks for the membership to Incognito."

Alexandra's mouth dropped open. *Incognito?*

"I haven't been to that club in years, but I thought that would be the right place for you," Colton said, relaxing on the arm of the sofa. "How'd it go?"

A shiver ran through her. *Colton was a member?*

"Having sex with a masked stranger isn't my thing, but I figured, why the hell not? Swanky club. Membership must have been costly."

"You needed a break from work."

"Well, I'm hooked now."

Colton laughed. "No wonder you look so good. You're *finally* getting laid."

Crockett's smile shot Alexandra's heart into her throat and the haunting feeling she'd seen Crockett came racing back.

"You're an idiot, you know that."

"How many partners?" Colton asked before sipping his drink.

"Just the one. She's so damned hot. I know these are casual hookups, but there's something about her—"

"Don't get attached. She's there to screw a stranger."

"I can't stop thinking about her." Crockett tossed back the whiskey.

Oh. My. God. No. No. No Way. She knew exactly how he felt. *It can't be.* But there had to be more than one tall, well-built man with short, dark hair and glacial blue eyes at Incognito. *Not electric blue eyes. Not his eyes.*

Reality punched her in the gut and she couldn't catch her breath. She'd been with him until the club closed at three that morning. They couldn't get enough of each other and she hadn't been able to shake him from her thoughts all day.

"Your connection could be married with children for all you know," Colton said.

Nope, not married. No children.

"For the time being, my mystery woman is my escape."

Oh, Crockett, if you only knew.

"Glad you're having fun." Colton poured more liquor into their glasses. "While I'm thinking about it, can you check in on Alexandra for me after the holidays? I'll be at the Francesco Company for the rollout of Crockett Boxes."

"Whatever you need, but I'm not sure she'll welcome my company."

"Ancient history." Colton stashed the bottle in his credenza. "She looks phenomenal."

Heat bloomed in her chest. *Right back atcha.*

"Fortunately, her Goth Girl days are behind her." Colton stifled a chuckle.

Oh, be quiet, Colton!

"Alexandra Mitus will always be my Goth Girl," Crockett said before they left.

As soon as her brother closed his office door, Alexandra crumpled onto Brigit's sofa. Hunter from Incognito was Crockett Wilde. Her Crockett. *No, he's not mine.* She hugged herself, but couldn't stop trembling. When the room started to close in, she folded over so blood would rush to her head. *Breathe. Deeply.* She hadn't passed out in years.

After crushing on Crockett all through high school, they'd spent an amazing, inseparable summer together. But when she'd told him she didn't want to go to USC, he'd sent her packing. Over the years, she'd tried to forget him, but she couldn't. She hadn't just given him her virginity; she'd given him her heart.

She'd been back less than a freakin' month and yet somehow she'd found him *and* had her fun with him. *I really need to broaden my taste in men.* Surely there was someone else in the DC metro area worthy of a romp between the sheets. *Never again.*

The lightheadedness passed. She pushed off the sofa, tugged on her crimson cocktail dress, then marched out to find her mom. Determined to stay clear of Crockett, she mingled with Colton's staff, all the while keeping him in her sights. He never approached her nor did he glance her way.

Below the simmering exasperation, her heart felt heavy. Why was he ignoring her, especially after telling Colton she looked *phenomenal*? And why in the hell was she giving him a second thought? The last thing she needed was for him to figure out she was his kink partner.

Toward the end of the scrumptious five-course dinner, Colton stood and announced his engagement. After a round of applause, he added that his closest friend and one-time business partner had agreed to be his best man.

"Let's have a toast," someone called out.

After kissing Brigit, Colton tossed his best man a nod. "Crockett, the floor is yours."

With champagne flute in hand, he rose. "Colt, Brigit, I speak for everyone," Crockett began. "We wish you both a lifetime of love and happiness. You're a lucky man to have found such an amazing woman who not only puts up with you, but makes you a better person."

As laughter filled the room, he shifted his attention down the table and cemented his gaze on Alexandra. Their fiery connection sent her blood coursing at a frenetic pace.

While staring into her eyes, he raised his glass. "Here's to your forever love." As guests sipped their bubbly, Crockett flashed her a sinfully sexy grin.

And she melted. Flat-out melted.

8

BAIT AND SWITCH

THE NEW YEAR BROUGHT Alexandra's first day at the new job. While she waited in reception, butterflies fluttered in her stomach.

A pretty olive-skinned woman with a super large baby-bump waddled over. "Alexandra Reed?"

"Yes." Alexandra collected her laptop satchel and rose from the sofa.

"Welcome. I'm Sapphire, one of the news reporters. Max asked me to help you get situated."

As Sapphire escorted her down the hallway, Alexandra caught a glimpse of the newsroom, abuzz with activity. Her first-day jitters settled down as she spied a handful of reporters at their desks, banging out stories on their laptops or talking on the phones.

Sapphire veered into the conference room and eased into a chair. "Max wanted to welcome you himself, but he's out of the office until later this afternoon."

Alexandra sat across from her and the two chatted about their broadcasting careers.

"Once we're done here, I'll introduce you to the team and take you on a tour," said Sapphire. "After lunch, you can join me for an off-site interview."

"What's your beat?"

"Human interest with a focus on neighborhood communities. Because we inundate our viewing audience with political stories, they embrace the features. My stories air during the midday broadcast. On occasion, Max runs them during prime time. He can spot a ratings magnet."

Doubtful.

"Anyway," Sapphire continued, running a soothing hand over her large belly, "Max wants you to take over my assignment while I'm on maternity leave."

What happened to the White House gig or hosting the news magazine show?

Sapphire continued, "Just so there's no confusion, I work for the station's *cable* outlet."

Oh, no. Her gut churned. This job was like her first gig after college. Her smile waned as she struggled to hide her disappointment. "I see."

"Max wants you to work with Stacy. She's been slated for our news magazine show, still in development."

Alexandra's eyebrows shot up. That sounded promising. "Is she the producer?"

"No, the show's host. Max wants you to mentor her since you hosted *LA After Dark.*"

That son of a bitch! Her blood pressure spiked. Max had dangled *her* the show, then pulled a bait and switch. Per usual, he was sticking it to her. But what choice did she have? She needed to keep her hand in the game while dealing with her mom's health.

Covering local news on a cable station was one thing; mentoring a newbie would require extra time outside of normal working hours—time she'd earmarked to spend with her mom.

"Max said you'd be a terrific coach." Sapphire leaned forward. "Stacy's pretty green."

With the message delivered, the coworker introduced her around the office. They grabbed a quick lunch, headed to the Metro, and boarded the train.

Alexandra was determined to move past the disappointment and focus on the job at hand. "Who are you interviewing?"

"I've been working on a piece for our annual contest," Sapphire explained. "We pick a topic—this year it's technology—and turn to our viewers for nominations. Not only is it our biggest ratings draw, the community loves the local angle. We whittled down the several hundred nominees to twenty. Then, our viewers vote and the top three are featured in a special program. This one's called *DC's Brightest Tech Star*. I've interviewed the third-place winner. We're meeting with the second tech genius today. The gentleman who won first place has been ignoring me, but I'm persistent." Sapphire waggled her brows.

The two women exited the train station, headed into the office building and completed their interview with the least-talkative person Alexandra had ever met.

Later that afternoon, while Alexandra sat with Sapphire at her desk, Max entered the newsroom with a busty redhead. Though he shot Alexandra a cool glance, he headed straight for his office and shut the door. The young woman bounced over and dropped her handbag on the desk next to Sapphire's.

"I'm Stacy B-L-U-N-K. Pronounced like the wine. *Blanc*. Max said I need a mentor." She rolled her eyes. "I hear you're it."

Gritting her teeth, Alexandra extended her hand.

"Shaking is for old people. I'm a fist-bumper."

Oh, great. Alexandra dropped her hand.

After providing her entire journalism history—which took all of thirty seconds—Stacy explained that Max had personally selected her for the fast track. She was slated for the next available on-air position, even if the meteorologist slot opened up before the news magazine show aired.

Up until that moment, Alexandra had been under the guise

that meteorologists were trained professionals who could speak proficiently about the plethora of weather systems. *Welcome back to Max's fucked-up world where his dick reigns supreme.*

Though Alexandra envied Stacy's position, she didn't envy Stacy. She lacked the critical experience needed to survive in the cutthroat world of broadcast news. Given Stacy's inflated ego, Alexandra got the impression she didn't want help. She wanted camera time.

Stacy trotted off and Sapphire pushed slowly out of the chair. "I need a quick bio break."

When she returned, she grabbed her cell. While waiting for the person to answer, she whispered to Alexandra, "My water broke." Sapphire spoke softly into the phone, then hung up. "My husband will be here shortly."

"You're so calm. What can I do?"

"Finish my tech story." Sapphire handed her a folder.

Alexandra helped Sapphire with her coat. Five minutes later, Sapphire's husband arrived and they left.

After grabbing a cup of stale coffee from the break room, Alexandra settled into Sapphire's chair. She opened the folder, read her notes and preliminary news copy. Scanning the page marked *Competition Winner*, her eyes popped wide.

The winner of *DC's Brightest Tech Star* was the thirty-three-year-old founder and CEO of Wilde Innovations—Crockett Wilde.

9

ROGUE BIRD

Crockett skimmed the in-house report, smacked his laptop shut, and shoved out of his chair. After spending the holiday week with his parents and extended family in Texas, he was ready to jump back into the fray, head first.

What he hadn't expected was a shit-ton of problems right out of the gate. *This is the biggest load of crap.*

Crockett had anticipated a few viable conclusions as to why Moth hadn't flown during Round One of the FBI Demo, but the results staring back at him catapulted his frustration to a whole new level. The extensive testing led all three of his teams— Hardware and Software Engineering along with Quality Assurance—to conclude that Moth failed due to human error. In this particular case, they cited him as the individual responsible for the error. *No way.*

Like a pilot completing his pre-flight checklist, Crockett always performed the same exact series of tasks to ensure each demo went off without a hitch. Over the years, he'd honed that list and could recite it in his sleep. Turning on a surveillance device was at the top. *Jesus, this pisses me off.*

Muscles running the length of his shoulders felt like stone and he rubbed the back of his neck. No relief.

Decker tapped on his open office door, strolled in, and set down the cardboard tray of coffees. "Happy New Year. How was your holiday?"

Forcing down the surmounting anger, Crockett lifted out a coffee and sipped. A thick sugary taste coated his tongue and he fought the urge to spit out the hot drink.

"Dude, that's mine." Decker tugged out a different cup and handed it to Crockett.

How Decker could drink that syrupy crap was beyond him. "How was your time off?"

"I worked some," Decker said.

"Me, too. I hope we were in the minority. I close Wilde so employees can take a break from work."

"Work is my chill. Plus, I was the fun uncle for my eight nieces and nephews. After five days of chaos, I was ready to roll out."

"Don't like kids?"

His upper lip twisted into a grimace. "They're okay. You?"

"I teach eighteen of 'em. I love the little squirts."

Decker gulped a hearty sip. "Did you see QA's assessment of Moth?"

Crockett's pleasant expression plunged like an anchor off the side of a vessel. "I read the report."

"I was hoping you hadn't, yet."

"The results are dead wrong."

"Moth checked out. So did the software. I spoke with Larry myself."

"Is he in yet?"

"No idea."

"Let's go pay our QA Director a visit." Crockett was halfway to Larry Berry's office before Decker caught up with him.

Effective December first, Larry Berry ran Wilde's Quality

Assurance Division. Over the past five years, Larry had made steady career progress. He'd started as a QA Analyst, then got bumped to manager. Though Larry had the personality of a bucket of fucking hair, Crockett promoted him because he got the job done.

After the debacle with his former QA Director, Ruth Lizzard, Crockett welcomed the man with zero personality. While Ruth had been his sharpest director, she'd also caused him more disruption than all his other employees combined. So, in October, he'd terminated her for her continued sexual improprieties and sexual harassment.

The thought of her left a nasty taste, which he swallowed down with the robust espresso. He and Decker walked into Larry's office to find him hunched over his phone, typing a text.

"Larry, we need to discuss your report on Moth," Decker said.

Ignoring them, Larry continued texting.

"Larry." Crockett's firm tone made his director jump.

Larry set his phone face down on his desk. "Happy New Year. What brings you by?"

Crossing his arms, Crockett said, "Moth's failure."

"Everything checked out," Larry said while smoothing his thick moustache.

Up went Crockett's eyebrows. "It's inaccurate."

"What Crockett means," Decker interjected, "is that we need to review your analysis."

Larry shot Crockett a cool smile. "No problem." He shifted his attention to his computer. Several clicks later, he said, "You've got it. Let me know what questions you have. My results are final."

"Based on what?"

After glancing at Decker, Larry turned his full attention on Crockett. "We found no problems with the software. The hardware checked out." He shrugged. "It was a one-off. Happens to everyone."

What the hell kind of answer is that? A malfunctioning robot during a customer demo was unacceptable. Was Crockett the only one with alarms going off in his head? Deciding to change topics, he asked, "How are you adjusting to your new position?"

Larry's expression flattened. "No complaints."

"Have a good holiday?"

"Kids drove me nuts. Wife dragged me to too many stores." He shrugged. "Good otherwise."

"I'll let you get back to work." Without waiting for a response, Crockett headed back to his office to drill down into the details of Larry's findings.

After reading the analysis, he wanted to fling his laptop across the room. The QA team had cleared Moth of any physical anomalies. Moth's software was a flawless match to that in Wilde's propriety Software Development and Deployment System —SDDS. On paper, Moth had performed with the same degree of precision ever since he'd plucked her from his Maryland manufacturing facility two years ago.

Crockett bit back a grunt. When it came to his customers, or in this case his prospective ones, he brought his A-game each and every time. But, based on the available information, everything did point to human error. *Did I turn on Horse and Black, but forget Moth?*

He decided to refocus his efforts by completing his business plan for the year. Goal number one: Winning the FBI contract. Though a shred of doubt had slithered into his psyche, he wouldn't alter his vision based on his mistake. *Alleged mistake.*

A boisterous voice severed his concentration. He glanced up as his assistant, Ellen Tate, rushed into his office. "You have a vis—"

The cyclone of energy whizzed past her. "Hey, babe!" Maverick threw out his arms.

Chuckling, Crockett leapt out of his chair and rounded his desk. Good thing he welcomed the man barreling toward him because his afternoon had just gotten hijacked.

Rather than shake Crockett's outstretched hand, his longtime friend bear-hugged him. After loud back slaps, Crockett grabbed his shoulders. "What the hell are you doing here?"

Maverick's wild blond hair and whiskered face, along with his wrinkled denim shirt and tattered jeans, had all the earmarks of a weeklong binge. Former Harvard housemate and business associate, Ashton Hott partied hard, chased women harder, and worked until he conked out at his desk. He didn't get his nickname by accident. He'd earned it.

Just because Crockett didn't smell the stench of stale booze didn't mean his friend hadn't spent the last week jet setting around the globe welcoming in the New Year with a different gal in each country.

Ellen cleared her throat. "Ashton's pop-in will disrupt your schedule." Loyal and efficient, she guarded him and his daily agenda like a Rottweiler.

Maverick slung his hand over Ellen's shoulder and hauled her close. "This is my go-to guy, Ellen. Why would he turn me away like a stray cat? The man loves me." Maverick batted his eyelashes. On a laugh, Ellen smacked his chest.

"I'll clear the next hour, take notes at the R&D meeting, and bring you two some coffee," Ellen said.

"Got any food around here?" Maverick winked at her.

Though she rolled her eyes, her smile never dropped. Maverick was annoying as hell, yet everyone loved him. Crockett's dutiful assistant whizzed out.

"Sit." Crockett returned to his desk chair and leaned back. "Or are you not done entertaining the masses?"

Maverick laughed. "I like to bring the heat."

When his friend's smile fell away, Crockett suspected the unannounced visit was more than social. "Back from Iraq?"

"I haven't left yet." Maverick's eyes narrowed. "When did I tell you my location?"

"I've known you long enough to read between the lines. I knew it was the Middle East. I drew my own conclusion."

Maverick's bright eyes grew serious. After pushing off the back of the leather chair across from Crockett's desk, he retrieved an oversized duffel from outside the doorway and slammed it onto the conference table. The loud metallic clatter of the bag's contents had Crockett pushing out of his seat.

Shouldering past Maverick, he unzipped the oblong bag. "What the hell happened?" His $150,000 surveillance bird had been reduced to a pile of scrap metal.

"Happened during beta test—"

"Wait." Crockett grabbed his cell phone and called Decker. "Maverick's here with a dead bird." He hung up as Ellen set the refreshments on the credenza. After peering into the duffel bag, she lifted her gaze to Crockett. "That's not good."

"Yes, thank you, Ellen," Crockett said.

Decker flew in and gaped at the bag's contents. "Oh, no, not Eagle. Which one is she?" He dropped his tablet on the leather chair.

"Third generation," Crockett replied. "Looks like version 3.2.6, but you'll have to confirm if you can find her ID."

Ellen shut the door behind her.

"I haven't seen you in a while, Decker," Maverick said. "I like the man-bun. Maybe I should grow one."

"We need details." Crockett had no patience for small talk, not when he had what could be another drone fail on his hands. Before sitting, he removed his suit jacket and rolled up his sleeves.

"I'll take notes." Decker spun a chair at the conference table, grabbed his tablet, and sat.

"I met my team this morning at oh-seven-hundred for a test flight," Maverick said.

"At your airpark on Maryland's Eastern Shore?" Crockett asked.

"Yes. Every device goes through rigorous testing there, then again at the final destination prior to deploying the aircraft."

"Was she the only one you tested?" Crockett asked.

"No. We ran another bird—Falcon—and several Spy Flies through their paces. Those we'd purchased several months ago. We just got Eagle last week." Maverick poured himself a mug of coffee and shoved half a cinnamon bun into his mouth.

Decker looked pasty white. This equipment breakdown was something Wilde Innovations had never experienced before.

After wolfing down the rest of the pastry, Maverick leaned against the credenza. "Two minutes into flight, she quit responding to pilot instruction and went rogue."

"Ah, hell." Decker glanced at Crockett.

"She buzzed us, then, about twenty-five feet in the air, she dropped," Maverick said. "I've been working with your drones for what—over five years—and I've never witnessed *anything* like this."

With his jaw clenched, Crockett shoved out of his chair. Again he peered inside the duffle as if the answer could be plucked out.

"We collected everything we could find and I hauled ass here," Maverick continued. "This is some crazy shit. I swear she acted like she'd been hijacked."

"Smart move coming here." Crockett fought the urge to pound his fist through a wall. "Footage?"

"Of course." Maverick sipped the hot java. "I'll forward you the video along with the corresponding ground-to-air audit trail. If I hadn't been there, I wouldn't believe it myself."

"Was your ground pilot new?" Decker asked. "And what kind of device did you pair with Eagle?"

"Penelope's no stranger to Wilde products. She operated Eagle via one of several military-spec tablets dedicated strictly to our missions. And no, she wasn't joking around. This was a pre-flight inspection for a top-secret mission overseas. I don't screw around when it comes to my Birds or my Flies."

"This breakdown couldn't be happening at a worse possible time." Crockett's phone rang. "I've got to take this." He answered. "Danny, what's going on?" he asked, trying to soften his gruff tone. He shifted his focus out the window at the office building across the street.

"Congratulations! You made it past Round One."

Crockett sighed. "Great."

"You don't expect me to believe that, do you?"

"You caught me in the middle of a meeting."

"The Director is pushing hard for this, so Round Two will be in seven to ten days. The CO will contact you with your timeslot."

Dammit. "Thanks for the good news." Crockett hung up and shifted his attention to Decker. "We're headed to Round Two in about a week. You'll be joining me, in a suit."

Decker's expression brightened. "Why don't you look like we just got one giant step closer to *the big win*?"

Maverick's brow puckered. "What's going on?"

"Later," Crockett replied.

Decker snapped his tablet closed, then hopped up and over to the open bag. "Can I take her?" He zipped the bag.

"She's all yours," Maverick replied. "I hate to lose a bird—"

"I'll make you whole," Crockett said.

"Thanks, brother." Maverick shot him an appreciative smile. "When can I expect my new flyer?"

"I'll want to be there when you test her," Crockett said.

"Roger that."

"I'll take you to Saul's office to schedule delivery or pick up from our manufacturing facility." Crockett extended his hand. "Thanks for coming here to tell me yourself."

"Try not to sweat it." Maverick hugged him. "I know you. You'll figure it out. That's what you do. You've had my back for fifteen years. Nothing's changed."

Crockett managed a dry smile. "One hell of a start to the new year."

Decker tried lifting the bag off the table, but it didn't budge. His neck muscles strained and his face grew red. "Hey, babe, let me get that for you." Maverick shot Crockett a playful glance as he shouldered the hundred-pound device.

After Maverick dropped the bag in the lab, Crockett escorted him to Saul's office. The three men concurred that the fastest way for Maverick to secure another bird was to pick it up from Wilde's manufacturing facility in Jessup, Maryland.

"I'll call you when we schedule a test flight," Maverick said. "Thanks for letting me barge in."

Crockett escorted Maverick to reception. "Not sure I had a choice, but in all seriousness, you had a *legitimate* reason."

"You're never going to let me forget that, are you?"

"Interrupting my eight A.M. midterm to tell me you lost your virginity could have waited. I had to defend myself to that prof."

The two men laughed before Maverick heaved open the door to Wilde Innovations. "Those were the days. Study and get laid. God, I miss that."

"Did you hear about Colton?" Crockett walked to the elevator bank and jabbed the down button.

"He invited me to his engagement party, but I was out of the country. I thought he was joking. I mean, hell, I thought he'd be the *last* of our motley crew to get hitched."

The elevator doors slid open to reveal a single occupant. An attractive blonde. Maverick slapped Crockett on the back. "Gotta fly." And with that, he strode into the elevator and winked at Crockett as the doors closed.

First, a crippled Fly. Now, a Bird goes rogue. What the hell is going on?

As soon as Crockett opened the glass door, Ellen accosted him. "You have a visitor."

He glanced around the empty reception area. "I've been gone ten minutes. Now what?"

"A reporter from Cable News Fifteen."

Other than his receptionist, the room was empty. "I don't have time," he said to Ellen.

"She said to tell you she's a Mitus."

Alex. His heart kicked up speed. "What does she want?"

"Well, *you*." His assistant smirked. "You won a geek contest—her words, not mine—and she wants to talk with you."

"No damned publicity."

"She's waiting in your office," Ellen called over her shoulder as she walked away.

Alexandra had gone out of her way to avoid him during Colton's party. That much was obvious. He'd assumed that after eleven years she would have been cordial. Not friendly. Friendly would have been asking too much. Cordial would have worked. But she'd been meat locker cold. *So what, now she needs something and expects me to jump? Think again.*

He'd give her two minutes. He didn't have time for an interview. Even if it was his Goth Girl.

When he stepped into his office, she pivoted toward him. No longer a teen, the woman before him took his breath away. Regardless of how he felt about her, this visit wasn't personal and she was not his. "Hello, Alexandra."

"Thank you for seeing me."

Had she worn her hair down on purpose knowing how much he loved that? She looked stunning, even in a simple brown dress. Damn her for barging in and bringing the heat with her. "Speaking to me now, are you?"

For a split second, her eyes danced with that familiar spark. Then, she cleared her throat. "I'm here on business."

"Wilde Innovations doesn't grant interviews. I'll show you out."

Alexandra had been rooted behind his desk eyeing the framed photos lining his bookcase. She lifted one and glided toward him. Her intoxicating wild flower scent brought back a rush of memories. The way she'd press her body into his before she'd kiss him breathless or the passion in her touch when they'd make love. His heart thundered in his chest. One lingering glance at her mouth and his cock twitched. *Perfect lips.* Truth was, most everything about her was pretty damned amazing. *I've missed her.*

"I thought I knew you once," she murmured.

He snapped out of his thoughts. "No small talk?"

"We don't do small talk." She turned the photo toward him. "I learned about your sister—*your sister*—from my research on the tech winner of some lame tech contest."

He puffed his chest. "I didn't win a *lame* contest."

"Oh, I see." Her eyebrow arched in defiance. "So, now it's an important one?" She stood dangerously close. "You knew every little thing about me, but I have to read the following quote in an article about you. 'My life's work is committed to finding my sister, Sophia, abducted when she was fourteen.'"

She narrowed her eyes, steeled her spine. But when she gazed into his eyes, he glimpsed her sadness.

"Let's sit," he said.

Still clutching the picture frame, she sashayed past him and eased onto his sofa. Her feminine scent wafted in his direction. When she crossed her killer legs, he had to look. If this were some kind of power game, that simple move gave her the clear advantage.

"How have you been?" He joined her on the sofa.

She set the picture on her lap, then tapped the glass with her fingernail. "I'll answer your questions when you answer mine. Why didn't you tell me you have a sister who'd been abducted?"

He appreciated that she spoke of Sophia in the present tense, like she was still alive, somewhere on this giant globe. But any comfort he felt from Alexandra's thoughtful reference fell away as he recalled the most gut-wrenching period of his life. "The short answer is Kimberly."

Without displaying the slightest reaction, she said, "I'd like to hear the long answer, *please.*"

His chest tightened. The last time she'd said, '"please" she'd asked him to make love to her, one last time. As he peered into her soulful brown eyes, he knew he would make love to her again, if she asked.

"You were sixteen when Sophia was abducted," he said. "You were a quiet teenager who hid behind your Goth."

"Go on."

"Your mom was concerned that if you learned what had happened to Sophia you'd become more withdrawn or afraid to leave the house."

Alexandra placed a soft hand on his shoulder and the warmth from her fingers seeped through his dress shirt. "I'm so sorry this happened to your sister and to your family. I wish I'd known."

Even after all the years, the familiar way her long fingers caressed and kneaded his muscles sent blood pumping through him. He studied her face. The tiny upturn of her nose. The depth of compassion in her eyes. It would be effortless to pull her into an embrace.

With a tender pat, she let go. "It's time for me to hear the entire story."

"Are you here as Alexandra Mitus or Alexandra Reed, the journalist?"

Her breath came out in a harrumph. "Does that matter?"

"When it comes to my sister, I don't give a damn about ratings or market share or net profit. And I don't give a fuck about some contest."

On a huff, she crossed her arms. "You would if it helped bring her home, Crockett."

Lifting the photo from her lap, he stared at his then two-year-old sister. His gangly eight-year-old self stared back. He'd just finished building the perfect Hot Wheels track and had lined up his cars—in an *exact* order—for the big race. Sophia had plunked down in the middle of his track, demolishing his set-up, and grabbed two cars. Somehow, his mom had captured the annoyance on his face and the gigantic smile beaming from hers. Sophia had idolized him. Bugged the hell out of him, actually.

Now he would do anything, give anything, to find her and bring her home.

He didn't talk about the abduction because he wanted to avoid the anger that burned in his gut. That kind of fury would land a guy in prison if he ever found the son of a bitch who took his sister. Peering into Alexandra's eyes soothed his anger, but ignited a different kind of flame.

As she waited, determination, not pity, shone from her eyes and that, above all else, spurred him forward.

"Sophia was abducted on her way home from school, freshman year of high school. I was at college and didn't find out until the next day. My parents were so frantic my mom had to be hospitalized for a short time. When my dad called, I was in class, so he told Colton. Broke down with Colton is more like it."

Feeling like his lungs were being crushed, Crockett returned the picture to the shelf. With his back to Alexandra, he said, "Colton was the one who told me."

"I'm so sorry."

Leaning his rump against his desk, he faced her. "I wanted to drop out of Harvard to help my parents. They were a mess. But they insisted I focus on my studies. I couldn't have gotten through that ordeal without your brother, plus a few other close friends." He crossed his arms over his chest.

"The police had to do their job, which meant investigating all of us," he continued. "Without question, we were cleared. When they refocused their energies, the trail had gone cold. With my permission, Colton confided in Kimberly. Your mom told me to never give up hope, then treated me no differently than before Sophia's abduction. She has this amazing way of making me feel as if I'm one of hers."

A sweet smile touched Alexandra's eyes. "She has a soft spot for you. Always has." She paused. "Sophia has been gone a long time."

Their silence hung heavy.

"Thirteen years," he said, finally breaking it. "I built Wilde Innovations around improving surveillance equipment in the hopes of finding her and bringing her home."

Alexandra's eyes had misted. "I wish I'd known. My family has kept so much from me. Thank you for answering my question." Clearing her throat, she fished a business card from her handbag and circled her cell phone number. "I would make your sister's abduction the centerpiece of the story. It's the driving motivation behind your company. How can you ignore the elephant in the room?"

That was damned ironic coming from Alexandra Mitus. Wasn't everything they'd once shared the real elephant?

Alexandra squared her shoulders and rose. "By *not* discussing Sophia, you're missing out on an opportunity. Someone watching the piece might know something. People come forward for the strangest reasons." She slung her handbag over her shoulder. "You might have won this tech contest, but it's her story. And you need to tell it."

Following a quick tap on Crockett's door, Decker moseyed in with coffee. "Hey, oh, sorry." With a nod to Alexandra, he set Crockett's drink on his desk. "Nectar from the gods."

"This is Alexandra Reed," Crockett said. "She's interested in doing a story on us. Decker Daughtry, my Chief Innovator."

The two shook hands. "If Crockett agrees to do the story, I'd like to interview you, too," she said.

"Good luck with that, Ms. Reed. Crockett never grants interviews."

Alexandra's jaw clenched, her cheek muscles working overtime. Like a Mitus, she did not handle disappointment well.

Decker sipped his drink, then shifted toward Crockett. "A few of us are working late, boss. We're hungry."

Chuckling, Crockett pulled out his wallet. "That's my cue." When he tugged on a credit card, a different one slipped out and landed on the floor.

Decker picked it up. "Silver Towers. Is this some kind of executive-only credit card?"

After snatching back the card, he glanced at Alexandra. "Something like that."

She skewered him with a piercing stare and the air between them grew charged. Hunger and need poured into him. Something had shifted in her, but damned if he knew what. Though he wanted to ask her to dinner, he wouldn't. Better to keep his distance and stick with her business agenda.

Decker cleared his throat, severing their steamy connection. "Hey, man, do you want me to order you something? We're getting Chinese."

"I can't stay," Crockett said. "I'll walk Alexandra out, then grab my credit card from you."

"Hot date?" Decker asked.

"Yes, with eighteen tiny tots who just graduated to yellow belts." A brief smile crossed Crockett's face. He couldn't help himself. Those little ones brightened his spirits week in and week out.

"Wow, you still study martial arts," she murmured. "You must be like a what…twelfth degree black belt?"

"Sixth degree."

"That's awesome."

Decker's brows shot up. "You two have a history?"

"Place the food order," Crockett said. "I'll be back in five."

As Crockett helped Alexandra with her coat, her bewitching scent surrounded him and he breathed deep. He'd missed so much about her. In silence, they left his office. Once in the elevator, he asked where she'd parked.

"Down the street, but you don't need to walk me to my car." They stepped outside and a cold wind gust had Alexandra shoving her hands into her coat pockets.

"Like hell I don't."

"Thank you," she whispered. "Now I understand why you were always so attentive about my safety."

"Sophia was only half the reason."

When she arrived at her Prius, she slipped inside, leaving the door open. The tiniest hint of a smile danced in her eyes. "What was the other reason?"

Nice try. "You know."

The subtle shift in her expression revealed a lot. She hadn't forgotten how much he'd adored her. "Thanks for being upfront with me, Crockett. I hope you'll do the story, for your sister's sake."

"Lock yourself in, Goth Girl." He closed her car door and she started the engine.

As Alexandra drove away, a fleeting sense of loss squeezed his chest. A bitter reminder of the last time he saw her before she drove out of his life.

Crockett returned to his office and changed into his karate *gi*. On his way out, he grabbed his credit card from Decker.

"So...you and the reporter have a past." Decker's playful tone made Crockett laugh. "She's got a thing for you. I can tell."

"And here I thought your area of expertise was technology. Who knew you were a romance expert, too? She wants me to do the interview. That's all." Crockett's abrupt tone signaled the end of the discussion about the leggy, gorgeous, and very driven Alexandra Mitus.

En route to karate, he weighed the pros and cons of doing the interview with Alexandra. While working with her should be a pro, he also had to add that to the cons. Staring into her eyes felt like medicine for his suffering soul and spending time with her would only remind him of what they once had. On the other hand, she had a point about the publicity.

Still undecided, he parked, but before going inside, he requested a connection with Electra for later that evening. Being around Alexandra had churned up a tornado of need. Fortunately, he had a new and satisfying way of releasing it.

The earliest he could get to the club would be ten o'clock, so he reserved the only available suite—"Master's of the Universe". Since the name spoke for itself, he sent the invitation without a note and strode into the building.

On his way past Annie Rodele's office, he glanced through the interior window. Annie sat behind her desk with little Hannah perched on her lap. Hannah's parents sat in guest chairs. Annie glanced up and waved him in.

"Mr. Wilde!" Hannah scrambled off and threw her arms around his legs.

He tossed a nod toward Hannah's parents and patted her back. "You ready for class, Hannah?"

Hannah's dad rose and extended his hand. "Hannah raves about you."

Though the munchkin wouldn't detach, Crockett leaned over and shook her dad's hand. "Crockett Wilde. Hannah's a pleasure to work with."

"I'm glad you're here," Annie interjected. "Close the door."

"Hannah, come here, honey," said Hannah's mom.

The little sport climbed onto her mom's lap as Crockett closed the door.

"Hannah needs to take a break from karate," explained Annie.

Crockett leaned against the windowsill. "I'm sorry to hear that."

"My dad got laid," Hannah announced.

Crockett's eyebrows jutted up as he glanced at Hannah's parents.

Though his cheeks reddened, Hannah's dad smiled. "Not quite. I got laid *off*, so, we're cutting back."

Hannah's eyes filled with tears. "I don't want karate to end."

Hannah's mom explained that while she worked, they wanted to be conservative with their spending.

Without hesitating, Crockett said, "Karate is important to Hannah and she's a good student. Why don't I cover the next six months and we'll reevaluate then?"

Annie Rodele's mouth dropped open.

"We can't let you do that," said Hannah's mom.

"Please. I insist." Crockett pushed off the sill. "Annie, we'll discuss offline."

Hannah's dad stood and shook Crockett's hand. "That was unexpected and incredibly generous of you. I don't know how to repay you."

"If Hannah continues to study martial arts and she enjoys it, that's the best repayment."

With tears in her eyes, Hannah's mom set her daughter in the chair and hugged Crockett. "Thank you."

"I don't want to say goodbye," Hannah said.

"Mr. Wilde is going to pay for your lessons for a little while, so you can keep taking karate," said Annie.

The child's eyes grew wide. "Really?"

"Yes, I am, Hannah." Crockett crouched down. "I believe in you and think you should stick with karate for as long as you like it."

Beaming, she threw her arms around him. "Thank you, Mr. Wilde. You're the best teacher, *ever*."

With a smile, Crockett stood. "All righty, Hannah, did you bring your *gi*?"

With a big smile, she pointed to the duffel bag on the floor.

"Where can Hannah change?" asked her mom.

"Right here." Annie closed the blinds. "Pull the door shut when you leave."

Crockett and Annie left. Amidst the kids scurrying about, they headed for the dojo.

"Week in and week out I preach acts of kindness," Annie said. "You've exceeded my expectations."

"Most families hit a rough patch. I'm glad to help them out in a small way. She's a sweet kid and I believe in self-defense. I'll bring you a check tomorrow."

After bowing into the dojo, they entered. Annie patted his back. "You're a good man, Crockett Wilde."

"Thank you, ma'am."

Crockett taught his class, then spent another hour sparring in the Black Belt room. Drenched in sweat, he left the dojo. Appreciating the chilly evening, he jumped into his truck and headed home as a light snow started falling.

After a quick shower, Crockett threw a New York strip steak into a cast iron skillet and a potato into the microwave. He wolfed down his dinner and headed out. Electra hadn't responded to his invitation. If she didn't show, he'd have a drink and leave. The flakes were falling fast, so he flipped on his wipers and drove to the club.

Strolling through the greeting room and into the lounge, he settled into a booth. A prompt server took his vodka martini order. While waiting for his drink, he checked his phone. Still nothing from Electra.

Ten minutes later, she sauntered into the lounge and squeezed in at the bar. A moment later, Crockett's phone binged. The subject line of the message from Incognito said, "Try Someone New."

Electra's rejection included a personal note. "Hunter, thank you for the invitation, but it's best we don't see each other again."

Damn. I should have known. I'm not her only connection.

10

CHASING SAGE

Though Alexandra desperately wanted to spend another wild evening with Crockett, she couldn't risk it. The blonde wig and southern accent could only fool him for so long. Besides, screwing the winner of *DC's Brightest Tech Star* would buy her no points. If Max somehow found out, he'd fire her. Then, he'd trash her reputation. Hosting the cable station's most watched show could open doors for a network opportunity. The faster she could distance herself from Max, the happier she'd be.

So she'd typed the note, tapped the reject button. *He'll move on.* Sadness snaked its way around her heart.

Alexandra had come to the club for a different reason. To find Sage. No pressure, just a few chill questions. If her suspicions were wrong and Sage was accident prone, maybe the nightmares would cease. At this point, she had to do something. She was turning into a zombie.

After work, her roommate hadn't come home *again* and her mom was asleep by eight. She hadn't made any friends at the news station and, other than Colton, she knew no one.

Except Crockett. And she wasn't hanging out with him.

"Excuse me, sir," Jase said to the masked man seated next to her at the bar. "Your room is ready."

Alexandra glanced at the club's GM. *Jase, too?* The two men strode out. She followed. Using his keycard, Jase and the member slipped into the same suite that Francois had used.

A chill swept through her. *What the hell? Is management screwing its members?*

She moseyed down the hallway. Each door displayed a gold engraved nameplate, except the one they'd just entered. This one had no identifier.

The explanation could be simple. Maybe Incognito operated differently from Provocateur, offering special amenities to a select few. On the other hand, Jase could be up to no good. Curiosity, paired with her insatiable need to dig and dig and dig, had turned her into an award-winning journalist. Like the relentless child tugging on mommy's shirt, that tiny voice insisted she plow deeper. Something wasn't right at Incognito.

Then, again, this wasn't the first time her overactive imagination had run rampant with suspicions that led nowhere. *I need a drink.*

She slinked back into the lounge and sat at a table near the arched entryway. A female server with black and purple hair bustled over. "Good evening, ma'am. What can I get you?" She smacked her gum like she worked in a diner.

"Sparkling water, please."

The attendant's shoulders sagged, probably because her tips depended on racking up a drink bill. "Could I interest you in a menu?"

Alexandra sighed. "Ever have one of *those* days?"

As if she'd asked the magic question, the gal nodded. "Lately, all of 'em."

"What I'd like is a gallon of mint chip ice cream, a bottle of wine and a family-sized bag of potato chips."

The server's laughter brightened her eyes. "How about a giant piece of chocolate fudge cake?"

Alexandra smiled. "You know, water isn't going to cut it. I'll have a glass of wine. What do you suggest?"

"We have a great Pinot Grigio, but it's pricy."

"On your recommendation, I'll take that."

The waitress perked up. "I love your accent. Are you from South Carolina? No, wait, Tennessee."

"Nowhere in particular. I moved around like a gypsy. How 'bout you?"

"From Pennsylvania. Live in Maryland."

"Is the Maryland to Virginia commute as maddening as I've heard?"

As the waitress rambled about beltway backups, tension tightened her voice. "I'm running on no sleep, too much caffeine, and I'm trying to quit smoking. This nicotine gum isn't cutting it." She paused to catch her breath. "I'm Wendy, by the way."

Alexandra smiled. Maybe this chatty employee could help her. "Hi, Wendy. I'm Electra. Have you worked here long?"

Wendy cracked her gum. "I'm an old timer at six months. From what I've heard, *churnover*—as I like to call it—is pretty high." She leaned down. "The GM is a tough ass, but a girl's gotta work, right? This place is crazy wild. Before this gig, I had no idea kinky shit like this happened in clubs." The color drained from her face and she pointed to herself. "Sorry. Me and my big mouth."

"No worries. I won't say anything. But I could use your help. A woman named Sage works in the kitchen. I wanted to say 'hey'."

Wendy shrugged. "Don't know her."

Opening her purse, Alexandra pulled out five twenties. "Find her and this is yours."

The waitress's eyes popped wide. "I'm on it." Wendy beelined toward the kitchen.

I hope this works.

A moment later, Dracule strolled into the club, checked his

watch and glanced down the hallway. When he peered into the lounge, she waved. *Time to find out about rejuvenation.*

Sporting a toothy grin, he sauntered over. "What a pleasant surprise. May I join you?"

"Please." She slid out the catty-corner chair with her stiletto. "We really must stop meeting like this."

Chuckling, he unbuttoned his suit jacket and sat. "Waiting for that handsome young man? The one who *doesn't* share?"

"I'm appreciating the ambiance." She winked. "Before I get busy."

He threw back his head and laughed, a little too hard. "Perhaps one of these evenings…ah, well…wishful thinking."

Not happening. "Wouldn't that interfere with your rejuvenation?"

A shadow darkened his face and his eyes narrowed. "You are persistent."

When she leaned forward, he ogled her cleavage. "It sounds kinky. I mean, that's why we're here, isn't it?"

"I hate to disappoint, but rejuvenation is my word for *connection.*" His finger glanced the side of his nose.

Francois had told her it was his code name for a nap. *You're a terrible liar.* "I see," she said, tilting her head. "Well, you certainly look rejuvenated." She pinned on a smile and hoped he bought it.

Jase paraded into the room, spotted Dracule and bounded over sporting an exuberant smile. "Good evening. How is everyone doing?"

"Why, hello, my good man!" Dracule said.

Jase shifted his attention. "Is everything here to your liking, Electra?"

"It most definitely is." The twang elongated her vowels.

"I'll have your contract completed next week with incentives for early payoff," Jase said.

Heat infused her masked cheeks. How dare he mention her debt in front of Dracule? She rose and stepped close enough to catch a whiff of alcohol on Jase's breath. "Please keep my financial obligation between us," she whispered.

"My apologies," Jase replied. "I'll be more discreet going forward." Then, Jase patted Dracule's back. "May I steal you from your lovely companion?"

Dracule stood. "Lovely as always to see you, Electra." The two men headed into the crowd and she sat with a huff.

Drugs, gambling, prostitution, money laundering? Club management was up to something.

Seconds after they left, Wendy slid the glass of wine in front of her. "No one named Sage works in the kitchen." The server nibbled her fingernail. "I saw you talking to the GM. Did you tell him about my comment?"

"Of course not. I kept my word." Alexandra offered the hundred dollars. "Thanks for asking around."

"I can't take your money. I couldn't find your friend."

"For your efforts and your silence." Alexandra shoved the money into her hand.

"Thanks, I could really use this." Wendy stashed the cash. "Describe her. I'll keep an eye out."

"Tall, gaunt, flyaway hair and very shy."

"Got it. Thanks for the tip." The waitress left.

After a long pull of the chilled wine, Alexandra tried to relax. Since moving back east nothing had gone as planned. Nothing. She tossed back another hearty sip and eyed the members milling about in their fancy duds and flirty smiles. *Maybe I should join a matchmaking service. No, that would suck.*

At the top of the hour, couples scattered toward their suites. A woman strolled in. Baggy black clothes hung on her wiry figure and her melancholy eyes were framed in a purple mask. She locked eyes with Alexandra, her sullen expression sending shivers down her spine. When the woman turned to leave, Alexandra spied her bandaged hand and wrist. *That was disturbing. Oh, hell, that was Sage. Go!*

Snatching her purse, Alexandra bolted into the hallway. Sage had whizzed past Jase's office and ghosted around the corner. Alexandra hurried to catch up, but as soon as she rounded the bend, Sage ducked inside an alcove midway down the hall.

Alexandra's pounding heartbeat throbbed in her temples as she raced past members, finally reaching the spot where Sage had disappeared. Tucked inside the nook were two closed doors marked, "Linen Closet" and "Private". Alexandra jiggled the locked handles. With clammy palms, she dug her keycard out of her clutch and held it against the linen closet's wall sensor. The solid red light refused her access. She tried to gain access into the room marked "Private" with the same disappointing results. *Why lead me here if I can't get in?*

"What are you doing?" a deep voice growled behind her.

Panicked, Alexandra whirled around. *Hunter...Crockett!* An explosive hunger lurked in his bright eyes, framed by the black leather mask.

Her heart fluttered. All the logic in the world couldn't slow the rush of emotion hurtling toward her. "Hello, Huntah."

As if stalking his prey, he halved the distance, forcing her to tilt her chin. She gobbled down his delicious scent in deep, calming breaths. Draping herself over him would be the perfect remedy to everything that ailed her.

"Snagging extra soap or do you need a fresh towel?" Though he had tamed his accent, this time she heard it. His deep voice, paired with that subtle lilt, dripped with sex appeal. The timbre rumbled through her and found a home in the deepest part of her heart.

Gorgeous. Sexy. Off-limits. *Get it together.* "No, I saw someone I've been concerned..." Her hands landed on her hips. "Are you stalking me?"

He turned rigid, his playful expression fell away and his eyes narrowed behind his mask. "No, I'm not. If you knew me, you wouldn't have asked that."

Her stomach plummeted. *Oh, no. I've insulted him.*

"Have a good evening." Crockett turned to leave.

The door marked "Private" swung open. Out of the corner of her eye, she glimpsed Jase.

She yanked Crockett into an embrace and flung herself against the wall, as if he'd pinned her there. Then, she kissed him. With everything she had. Because the passion needed to be real. As soon as her mouth melded to his, she didn't have to fake a thing. She curled her hand around the back of his neck and pulled him flush against her with the other. In seconds, his erection pressed against her tummy. Her clit throbbed in anticipation as desire washed over her.

On a deep growl, he ground against her.

A quiet chuckle interrupted their passionate embrace. "You do know we have private suites, right?" Jase asked.

Breaking the incendiary kiss, Crockett pulled back, but his eyes remained fixed on Alexandra.

"If you're into the full-blown make out session in the hallway, I think you'd enjoy our 'High School' suite." Though Jase cracked a broad grin, his smile felt more like a warning. He flicked his attention to Crockett. "We've not met. I'm Jase Payne, General Manager."

Crockett rose to full stature, dwarfing Jase in his shadow. "Hunter."

Their handshake seemed charged with an excess of testosterone.

Alexandra was the first to admit she didn't understand the opposite sex, but this introduction had all the markings of two lions staking claim on a pride. Crockett's stance screamed, "Don't fuck with me."

Then, the shadow covering Jase's eyes lifted and he threw an arm around each of their shoulders. "Come with me. I'll personally find you a room."

11

IRRESISTIBLE

CROCKETT TAPPED HIS FINGERS on the black leather armrest and studied Electra. Women baffled him, but this one set the bar so high a pole-vaulter couldn't clear it. For the second time in three minutes, she'd peeked out the door of their suite and peered down the hallway. Calm, cool and collected had morphed into fidgety, jumpy and obsessed.

He'd been enjoying a martini when he'd spied her at a table with Dracule. Despite her earlier rejection, he'd followed when she'd flown out of the lounge. Was he stalking her? *Hell, no.* Hunting her down? *Maybe.* Ensuring her safety? *Dammit, yes.* For some unknown reason, he wanted to protect her from Dracule. And Jase was scum sporting a slick suit and a slicker grin.

Since kissing was taboo, she must've had a damn good reason for shoving her tongue in his mouth.

"Since the GM booked us this room, I'm going to use it," Crockett said, breaking the silence.

She pivoted in his direction. "I don't...it's just that, I can't...I'm not available."

Tripping over her words seemed unlike her. "I didn't ask you to stay. Keep in mind if *I'd* fake kissed *you*, you might not have played along like I did. Lucky for you, I'm a good sport."

One tentative footstep after another, she inched toward him. "Thanks for doing that."

Crockett removed his Crockett & Jones dress boots and pushed out of the corner chair. With his gaze cemented on hers, he slipped out of his sport coat and draped it across the back of the chair. "I've been burning the midnight oil, so shut the door on your way out. I'm going to nap." He rolled up his shirtsleeves.

"You're into rejuvenation?" Surprise tinged her voice.

What happened to her accent?

Instead of eating up the space between them, he slid his hand into his front pants pocket and stood his ground. "Rejuvenation, nap, snooze, whatever. The next time you find yourself in a pickle, my tongue is off limits."

On a chuckle, she edged a little closer.

Her sweet sound touched him in a way he hadn't felt in a long time. And he had the craziest desire to say something funny again, so he could hear her playful giggle.

Crockett was not a game player. Never had been. Tonight, though, this game of cat and mouse seemed to be propelling her toward him. If he flat-out told her to leave, would she throw herself on him? They had the room and nothing but time. And she was so damned hot. The thought of caressing her silky skin and sinking inside her heat rocketed blood straight to his groin.

One controlled step at a time, he closed the space between them until they stood inches apart. Though her flowery scent drew him in, he fought the urge to secure her in his arms and kiss her soft lips. *Time to call her bluff.*

"Electra, good luck with your—what did you call it? Rejuvenation? And I hope you find the key to the linen closet."

Her mouth dropped open. With a firm grasp on her arm, he escorted her to the door. "Out you go." He twisted the knob and pulled.

ALEXANDRA SMACKED THE DOOR closed. "I'm not leaving." Despite rejecting his invitation to connect, fate had thrust them together. No way could she walk away from him.

He turned toward her. "Then you can watch me sleep."

His intensity seared her. She was standing in "The Virgin" suite with the one man who'd taken hers. Masked in the illusion that sex between them meant nothing, could she risk stealing one more hour with him? And was she emotionally capable of reliving something that had once meant so much to her? Even she had her limitations. Sex with Crockett in "The Virgin" suite topped the list.

The energy swirled around them, the undeniable need to be with him kept her feet anchored to the floor. *Don't let him go.* She flung her arms around his neck and kissed him, like she meant it. Because, by God, she did. She'd already broken her "No kissing" rule. No going backwards now. Hungry for his mouth on hers and the way his tongue wound around hers, she anchored her arms around his hard body. His breathing roared in her ears. His delicious baseline scent filled her lungs. She ground against him and let her body say what she could not.

Ravenous to be with him, she clawed at his clothing, desperate to get to his flesh. To feel his heat, his need.

Clothing. Gone in seconds.

His piercing gaze lit her insides on fire. Every nerve, every cell screamed out for him. For eleven long years she'd imagined being with him. And only him. She needed his hard body rooted in her soft one.

His guttural groan ripped through her. Their tongues clashed. He bit her lip. She scraped her fingernails down his glorious back. His intensity thundered through her, leaving her thrumming with need.

He broke the kiss, his breath coming fast. His magnificent

chest expanded on every inhale. She wiped her mouth, already raw from his ferocity.

"You're a virgin," he uttered. "We need to slow this down."

She didn't want the role-play. She wanted him. She wanted to lose herself in everything Crockett Wilde, indulge in him without his knowing. Years ago, she'd readily given herself to him and she wouldn't defile the loss of her innocence by pretending.

Just because she knew the truth didn't mean she'd play her hand. With a sultry smile, she curled her hand around his shaft and rubbed her thumb over its sensitive head. "Maybe you're the virgin, Huntah."

The gleam in his eyes wasn't wasted on her. He banded his arms around her, stroked her ass. "I'll play this any way you want, Electra."

"No talking," she blurted.

Her body heated, not from his intensity, but from the realization that he might figure out who she was. Though ludicrous and far-fetched, she didn't want to risk being discovered, or losing out on this…on him.

"Kiss me again. And then take me. I need you inside me." She skewered him with a hard stare.

A gritty groan was his only response.

Anchoring one hand on the back of her neck, he threaded the other around her waist. And then, he kissed her.

They were incapable of going slowly. Their need cycloned through them, whirling them into a frenzy. Like two halves of a whole, their bodies said what they could not. Locked in a ravenous embrace, she half-stepped, half-dragged him toward the sofa. He allowed himself to be directed because his entire focus was on her. One hand fondled her breast, her nipple. The other stroked her slickened core.

She could barely stand by the time they reached the sofa. Trembling and panting, her body throbbed with the need to release the pent-up energy. But she refused to give in to it, yet.

When she pushed him onto the sofa, he smiled. His undeniable beauty sent a rush of heat blasting through her. Above all else, that smile—*his* smile—undid her. Always had. Always would.

Despite her attempt to conceal her feelings, she smiled back. Not because she wanted to, but because she couldn't control herself around this man. He deserved a slap across his gorgeous face for dumping her and sending her three thousand miles away when all she'd wanted was to stay with him. And love him.

And his damn dick bobbed up and down like it was waving at her.

She had to sheath him before she did something really stupid and climbed onboard. "Condom."

He started to rise, but she nudged him back. "Don't move. I'll do it." She sashayed toward the night table.

"My pants pocket."

She collected the three-pack and, on her way back to him, ripped open a packet. Seconds later, she'd covered him in latex and straddled him.

Crockett Wilde was devastatingly handsome. Totally naked. And about to get fucked.

With her hand around his shaft, she rose up, placed his head at her opening, and slid down on his thick cock. She cried out from the pleasure as her body molded around his shaft. He fit like he was meant to be there.

Their first time had been romantic and tender. Crockett had taken control, because she'd been both innocent and naïve. But this time, she would take charge. She needed to keep things in perspective. They were in suite twelve of an erotic club. And he thought he was screwing a blonde named Electra.

Once again, their mouths found each other and, as she glided on him, her body sang with ecstasy. Her strangled mewling swallowed by his intense kisses. He consumed her, ate her alive. And she melted into him.

"Oh, yeah," she whispered, her breath jagged. "You feel amazing, Cr—" *Ohmygod.*

His eyes popped open. He gripped her hips, stilling her movement. *"What?"*

"Crazy good, Huntah." As a quick distraction, she raised her arms over her head, arched her back, and thrust her nipples inches from his mouth.

"You are so sexy." He placed his mouth over her plumped nib, suckling and biting one at a time. His groans and growls made her wetter, the climax whirling toward her at a reckless pace.

Gliding faster, she rode him until the ecstasy of being with him became too much and the orgasm started deep in her belly. Her muscles clamped around his shaft. "Oh…oh, yes, that feels… oh, yeah, like that. Just like that."

Her fingernails dug into his flesh, the pleasure almost unbearable. "I'm gonna come."

He covered her husky cry with his mouth, grabbed her hips, and thrust to her end. Groaning and shuddering through her orgasm, she raked her nails along his shoulders.

A fuck is a fuck, but not this one. This was wild and raw and amazingly satisfying.

"Oh, yeah, I'm coming." When he emptied himself inside her, she devoured his grunts and groans with another explosive kiss. She could not get her fill of this man. Never could.

Floating back to earth, she stared into his heavy-lidded eyes. Serenity had replaced the ferocity. The corners of his lips lifted. His happiness tore at her heartstrings. Time for another goodbye.

She wanted to stay connected to him; to stare at his face, to drop kisses on his soft lips and chiseled cheekbones. But Electra would never linger. Moving slowly, she lifted off him. Rather than sitting next to him, she stood. "I should head out."

As if he had nothing but time, he soaked up her body with his heated gaze. He either liked what he saw or he wanted more.

Either was acceptable. Once hadn't been enough. Did he feel it, too? When their eyes met, the air crackled. She felt the insatiable tug she'd always felt whenever she was around him. She wanted to go to him again and draw his body into hers. And never *ever* let go.

"I'm not going to invite you to connect again, Electra, so this is goodbye."

His words cut like a knife slashing through her soul. Unfiltered pain pierced her heart. Taking a step back, she crossed her arms. Sex with strangers satisfied a need without the emotional attachment. And she'd been damned successful at it, until now.

Until Crockett.

As she tried to cope with what was happening, she bit her lower lip to redirect her pain.

"Tonight I was your alibi for whatever sleuthing you were doing," he said. "Good luck with that and thanks for a fun evening."

Again, he was rejecting her. She had to get out of there, away from him. "Goodbye, Huntah." She forced herself to walk away. Muscle memory kicked in. She collected her clothes. Only once she had locked herself and her runaway emotions behind the bathroom door, did she allow a single tear to fall.

12

THE BIG REVEAL

Damn. How could this sexy stranger evoke so much raw passion? The distraction of the club had been good for Crockett, but he wouldn't return. He didn't have the desire or the time to become a player in a sex club. *Goodbye, Electra.*

With clothing in hand, he entered the other bathroom. After flipping on the light, he shut the door and stared at himself in the mirror. Her fingernails had left red streaks down his shoulders. *No effin' way.*

Years ago, Alexandra had scratched his shoulders during lovemaking. In the aftermath, she'd soothed his reddened skin with tender kisses. Her long dark hair had tickled his face while he'd suffocated in her floral scent. She'd smelled of wild flowers in a spring meadow. *Like Electra.*

He palmed the vanity to steady himself. Then, he remembered how her laughter had touched him. That, along with her familiar flowery scent and now, the love scratches. *Jesus, it's her.*

Find her! He cleaned himself up, threw on his clothes, and hurried out. As he'd expected, she was gone. He strode to the elevator. *Come on. Come on.* The doors opened and he dashed inside.

He did a three-sixty in the parking garage. Though packed with cars, he was alone. *Dammit. Where is she?* As he pulled onto the snow-covered street, a silver Prius spun out twenty yards ahead of him. Freezing snow had turned the pavement into a sheet of ice. The compact car skidded to a halt in the middle of the intersection. Ripping off his mask, Crockett parked at the curb and jumped out. He shuffled to the car and flung open the door.

A shaken Alexandra, still masked and wearing her blonde wig, gaped at him with scared brown eyes.

Crockett breathed. He'd found her. "We've got to get you out."

"Can you push my car out of the road?"

He glanced up to see a van fishtailing down the hill toward them. With lightning speed, he unbuckled her, yanked her from the car and carried her across the slick road. They reached his truck just as the vehicle slammed into the driver's side of her Prius, spun around, and continued sliding down the street.

"Ohmygod," she whispered, pressing her hand to her chest. "I can't breathe."

She trembled from head to toe. When he set her down, he gripped her arm to keep her from slipping. "Are you hurt?"

Gasping, she blurted out, "I'm going to pass out."

He flung open the passenger door of his truck and helped her onto the seat. "Face outward, drop your head to your knees, and take slow, deep breaths."

While she hunched over, he rubbed her back. Comforting her helped slow his own racing heart. *She's safe.*

After a few moments, her tremors subsided and she lifted her head. "Thank you. I'm okay now and should get going."

She's still using that ludicrous accent.

Her feet hit the ground and she slipped on the shiny street. Again, he grabbed her arm before she hit the icy pavement. "Get going? In what? We don't even know if your car is drivable."

"Please help me push it out of the intersection."

The street was quiet, but that van had come barreling out of nowhere. No way would he put either of them in jeopardy of getting T-boned. "I'll call a tow truck."

"How am I supposed to get home?"

"I'll drive you."

"*What?* I'm not accepting a ride from a stranger."

He forced down a laugh and fought the urge to roll his eyes. How much longer could she keep up this ridiculous charade? With cold fingers, he pulled out his phone and found a twenty-four hour tow company with a twenty-minute ETA. He grabbed her purse from the passenger seat of her car, turned on her hazards, and returned to his vehicle.

"We'll wait in my truck." With a firm hand on her arm, he offered his assistance.

She wouldn't budge. "No."

Rubbing his gloveless hands together, he said, "Get in the truck." If he was freezing, she must be a block of ice.

Her blue lips quivered. "I'll wait here for the tow truck."

"Get in the truck, *Alexandra*. And lose the damn accent. You aren't from Texas. I am."

Her shoulders sagged as she climbed in. After situating himself in the driver's seat, he started the engine. "How long have you known?" she asked.

"Twenty minutes."

Her left eyebrow hitched, ever so slightly. "What gave it away?"

"Your laughter. Your perfume." *Your love scratches.* That he'd keep to himself. Reaching behind her, he untied her mask, then set it on her lap. "Much better." He needed to kiss her. And he wanted her to take off that blonde wig.

"How long have *you* known?" he asked, then flipped on the heater.

"Colton's engagement party."

"That explains a lot."

"What we once shared is ancient history," she murmured. "No

more Incognito either. As soon as you complete the interview for *DC's Brightest Tech Star*, we can go our separate ways. That part we've got down."

Though she'd meant to zing him with her sharp words, he wasn't fazed. She was trying to push him away. And he understood why, too. So, he stayed silent, letting her have the last word.

Crockett fixed his attention on the steady stream of falling snowflakes. And breathed. The image of the vehicle careening toward them sent aftershocks through him, but he shoved the thought away. *I've got her and she's okay.*

He didn't try to mask the silence with small talk. Based on her creased brow, he doubted their conversation would be friendly anyway. Just having her by his side felt so damn good.

Ten minutes later, the tow truck pulled up. He opened the door, turned back to her. "Stay here. I'll handle this."

After speaking with the driver, he snapped a few photos of her car and climbed back in. "He'll tow your car to my mechanic. I'm guessing you'll need body work." He shot her a smile. "*You* don't need any body work. *You* are perfect. I'm talking about your vehicle."

His pulse quickened at her full-on grin. "Thank you for pulling me out of the car, Crockett."

He'd always loved the way her lips puckered when she'd murmur his name. In the past, he'd have jumped at the opportunity to kiss her. But not tonight. Tonight, she'd drawn a firm line in the sand. So, he'd start with baby steps.

"I want you safe," he said and her eyes softened. "The driver told me we could get seven-to-ten inches, so let's get you home. I'll email you the photos for your insurance company. If they won't deliver your rental car, I'll drive you to pick it up. Do *not* drive until the roads have been plowed." He tapped his GPS system. "All righty, where do you live, Alex?"

Melancholy crept into her eyes. "You were the only one I ever let call me Alex."

Beneath that tough, independent exterior was the shy, sweet Goth Girl he'd fallen deeply in love with.

After she gave him her address, Crockett weaved his way through unplowed icy streets toward her Arlington neighborhood. It was almost one in the morning when he turned onto her picturesque street. Lampposts mounted in front of every home bathed the snow-covered houses and tiny front yards in shimmery white light.

"That's weird," she murmured.

He shot her a glance. "What's wrong?"

She yanked off her wig, unpinned her hair and ran her fingers through it. "Every light is on. My roommate's home." She directed him to the brick-front house that shone like a beacon on an otherwise dark street.

With no available parking spot, he double-parked out front. As she exited his truck, she slipped and, again, he caught her. "We need to get you snow boots or you're going to break your neck."

As they approached the house, the wailing vocals of Jimi Hendrix's "Purple Haze" blasted into the silent night. They stepped into a smoky living room that reeked of marijuana.

Partygoers sprawled on the sofa, lay on the floor, and sat on the lower stairs. Empty beer bottles lined the coffee table along with two bottles of Jack Daniels and an empty bottle of tequila. Candles dripped hot wax onto the side tables and fireplace mantel.

Alexandra's mouth fell open.

"Hey, roomie!" A pigtailed woman wearing footie pajamas jumped off the sofa and threw her arms around Alexandra, almost knocking her over. "Who's this cutie?" The roommate eyed Crockett. "I'm Mandy, Alexandra's roomie." She snorted a giggle. "Duh, right?"

"I'm Crockett."

"My boyfriend, Ben, thought we should crash here during the storm." She pointed to a man sitting at the small dining room table with his back to them. She swayed, then giggled. "We're partying. You wanna beer? How 'bout some weed?"

"No, thanks," Alexandra said.

"Hey, guys, listen up!" Mandy shouted over the slurred chatter and deafening music. "This is my home girl, Alexandra. And this is her man, Crockett. They're gonna join our slumber party. Whoo hoo!"

A chorus of hellos echoed through the room.

Mandy's boyfriend rose. As Ben lumbered over, the linebacker-sized man had a glassy look in his eyes. He was as tall as Crockett, if not taller. And the stench of dope clung to his stained wifebeater and ripped, baggy jeans. When he homed in on Alexandra, she threw Crockett a furtive glance.

"Hey, baby. You're gorgeous." Ben gawked at Alexandra. "Mandy, have you been keeping me away from this hottie on purpose?"

And that's when Crockett spied the lines of cocaine and crack pipe on the dining room table. Time to get Alexandra the hell out of there.

Eyeing the crowd, Crockett counted seven men, five women. He'd no idea what drugged-up condition they were in, but he felt confident he could handle the situation.

When Ben tried to kiss Alexandra, she shoved him away. "Change into something sexy and join us," he said, ogling her chest.

Mandy glared at her boyfriend. "Ben, stop."

"We aren't staying," said Crockett. "We just—and I mean *just*—got engaged. We're celebrating at my place."

Alexandra whipped her head toward him at the same time Mandy squealed. "Do you have a ring?" She grabbed Alexandra's hand, then frowned.

"She literally said yes outside in the snow," Crockett

continued. "Ring shopping happens when the roads get plowed."

"Aw, how romantic," cooed a chorus of women.

Crockett pulled out his phone. "How about a picture of the two roommates to mark the occasion?"

Ben squeezed in between them and Alexandra grimaced as he groped her shoulder. His fingers brushed the swell of her breast and she jerked out of his hold. After snapping a few photos that included the lines of coke on the table, Crockett clasped Alexandra's hand. "We'll be back."

Making the assumption her bedroom was upstairs he headed in that direction. At the bottom of the staircase, he gestured for her to go first. He couldn't keep her safe if he couldn't see her. The three people lounging on the lowest steps made no attempt to move, so she picked her way through with him in tow.

Once inside her small bedroom, she tugged her hand from his. "What the hell was that?"

"That was me giving you a legitimate reason to leave without causing a scene," he said. "Did you happen to see what Ben was doing before he got up to grope you?"

She crossed her arms. "No, what?"

"There were several lines of coke on the table. And a pipe for freebasing. You can't stay here."

"What? Why not? I'll lock my bedroom door and go to sleep."

"You might be snowed in for a day or two. If a neighbor smells the dope or can't take any more of the blaring music, they'll call the police." He paused, hoping the weight of the situation would sink in. Mituses had thick skulls. "What would your producer say if you got hauled to jail for drugs?"

"I don't do drugs!"

"Yeah, well, tell the police that and see how much sympathy you receive. You report the news, Alexandra. You of all people know innocent people can get lumped in with the guilty."

On a loud huff, she vanished into her small walk-in closet, emerging a few moments later with two zipped duffel bags bulging at the seams and a hanging garment bag. Either she couldn't decide or planned on never returning.

She shoved the duffels at him. "Happy?"

"No, I'm rarely happy." He slung both bags over his shoulder. "You ready?"

"Where are you taking me?"

"My place."

She snickered. "I don't think so. I can stay with my mom."

"I'm not driving to Old Town in this snowstorm."

"I can move into Colton's guesthouse."

"Not tonight." He stepped toward her door and glanced back. "Pretend like we're in love."

"I'm not that talented."

Her smart mouth made him chuckle. "The longer you stall, the icier the roads get."

Before heading downstairs, she grabbed her toiletries from the bathroom. As they picked their way around the bodies on the stairs, he eyed the dining room table. The lines were gone. Sizing up the group, he placed a protective hand around her shoulder. "We're outta here."

Ben rose from the arm of the sofa, his hazy stare locked on Alexandra. "What's the rush? Party with me, baby. P-a-a-a-r-t-a-a-a-y." He held out his hand.

Crockett eyed Ben. *Six two or three, two fifty. Burly. Probably stoned, drunk and high on coke. I've got this.*

"Not tonight," Alexandra said. "I want some alone-time with… my fiancé."

Ben cocked his hands on his hips and stepped too damned close to Alexandra. *Jesus, he stinks.* Crockett pulled her flush against him, preparing to shield her with his body.

"Stay." Ben's eyes grew beady. No smile, harsh tone. *He's turning aggressive.*

No one seemed interested in Ben, save for one average-sized guy smoking a joint on the sofa. Crockett could manage two, though he'd no idea what drugs they'd taken or how combative this crowd could get. He couldn't turn his back on Ben, so he stepped backwards hoping Alexandra would walk toward the door. She did, but Ben moved around them with more speed than Crockett expected.

Whack! Ben slapped his hand against the front door, causing everyone to jump.

"Step away," Crockett said.

"Get the hell outta here. But she stays. Me and her are gonna have some fun."

Crockett squared his shoulders, prepared to either throw the duffel bags off or use one of them if Ben pulled a knife. "Get out of our way."

"Or what? You gonna make me, pretty boy? Fuck you. This is my place. You do as I say."

"Ben," Mandy said. "They don't want to stay, honey."

"Shut up," Ben said, his glare still cemented on Crockett. "The bitch stays." Ben's fist flew toward Crockett's face, but Crockett blocked it.

Both duffel bags hit the floor. Crockett grabbed Ben's wrist and twisted until Ben buckled onto the hardwood. Crockett jammed his boot into Ben's shoulder while applying pressure to Ben's twisted wrist. Trapped beneath the weight of Crockett's boot, Ben laid there, face down, his arm wrenched in the air.

"Motherfucker, that hurts," Ben said. "You're a fuckwad, you know that?"

Alexandra flung open the front door and hurried outside.

With his boot shoved into Ben's back, Crockett growled, "I don't give a damn what you want." He released his grip on Ben, shouldered the bags, then left, slamming the door shut behind him.

Grasping Alexandra's arm, he guided her down the snow-covered path and opened the passenger door. Before climbing in, she stared into his eyes. He'd seen that fiery look before.

"Are you okay?" he asked, taking the garment and cosmetic bags from her.

"Yes. You?"

"I'm fine." Fury coursed through him. He'd wanted to punch that asshole senseless. But he'd learned to manage his anger by controlling his actions. And he'd achieved his primary goal. Get Alexandra out of that hellhole.

Crockett set her things on the back seat and settled in behind the wheel. After a quick glance at his passenger, he started the engine, flipped on the windshield wipers, and drove. "That is one messed-up guy. I take it you'd never met him."

"No, I hadn't. I'd only seen Mandy twice before tonight. She pretty much lives with him."

As Crockett meandered out of the sleepy neighborhood, his sense of calm returned. He'd rarely had to use his martial arts, but it always served him well. And for that he was grateful.

Though Alexandra didn't know it yet, Crockett would accompany her when she went back to get the rest of her things. Ben had been humiliated in front of his friends and Crockett had a feeling he'd want to retaliate by hurting Alexandra. He tightened his fists on the steering wheel. She could never return there alone. And no way in hell could she *ever* stay there again. His guts churned at the thought.

In the darkened truck, Crockett peered at his beautiful passenger. Though she appeared somewhat shaken, she'd fared well. Truth be told, he could stare at her for hours. He used to tell her she was the most beautiful girl on the planet. She was every bit a woman and more breathtaking now than she'd been back then.

The GW Parkway hadn't been plowed, so Crockett proceeded with caution, as did the other vehicles on the dark road made brighter by the snow. "You doing okay?"

"I've been living alone and wishing my roommate would spend more time there. After seeing that crowd, I dodged a bullet."

By the time he pulled into his penthouse parking spot, it was after two thirty in the morning. When he cut the engine, the last remaining traces of fury rolled off him. She was safe. Nothing had happened to her and nothing ever would. He'd make sure of that.

"Your black belt moves were pretty hot, Crockett. I've never seen anyone react that fast." Alexandra shot him a sly smile as she exited the truck.

He lifted her bags from his back seat and strode toward the elevator. That was the first compliment she'd given him in eleven years. Given the sultry look in her eyes, it wouldn't be the last.

13

THE SLEEPOVER

In the quiet of the night, Alexandra stared out Crockett's floor-to-ceiling windows. Lamplights twinkled across the Potomac River while the nation's capital slumbered beneath a blanket of cottony white. She wished the picturesque landscape could calm her rattled nerves. But the whirlwind of activity had frazzled her and she hugged herself.

After everything Crockett had done for her in the past two hours, she owed him a debt of gratitude. But she needed to keep things real. *This isn't the beginning of anything. Yes, he's a good guy, but he's not my good guy.* She rubbed her chest, but the ache wouldn't go away. In her heart of hearts, she wanted to throw her arms around him and tell him how much she'd missed him. *Snap out of it. He ended things a long time ago.*

He stood beside her. Their shoulders brushed. This time she trembled for a very different reason. His confidence and magnetism excited her. The man he'd become didn't just own the condo; he owned the space, the air, and every damn move he made. And he owned her, too. How long could she conceal *that*?

"I envy your view," she murmured.

"It is *spectacular*." Crockett's deep timbre sent sparks flying through her. She turned to find him studying *her*. A few seconds passed, the familiar zing of attraction skittering through her. He offered her a steaming mug. "Drink this. It's a hot toddy."

The kick from the whiskey burned a welcomed trail to her stomach and the hot liquid soothed her nerves. She had no contingency plan and was desperately trying to come up with something—anything. Tonight, she'd crash on his sofa, then seek refuge at Colton's or her mom's until she could find another place to live.

His delicious scent surrounded her and she breathed him into her soul. Why did he have to stand so closely? She should have moved, but she didn't. Couldn't. Her feet kept her anchored in place. He'd removed his suit jacket and tie, sipped what might be whiskey from a lowball glass.

"Is that helping?" he asked.

Is what helping? His arm pressing hers? The way his steely gaze soothed her soul? How her heart leapt every time he smiled at her? Or that her insides turned to jelly from his deliciously sexy accent?

Arching a brow, he peered into her mug. *Oh, of course. The drink.*

Her cheeks warmed. "Yeah, it's great. Thanks. I could use a shower." *So lame.*

After grabbing her duffels, he guided her around the stacks of moving boxes. "Moved in a few weeks ago. Unpacking hasn't been a priority." They entered his bedroom. He flipped on a small desk lamp, snatched a pair of flannel pajama bottoms. "Make yourself at home."

"No, you stay. I…I don't want to put you out."

"I'll shower in the hall bath." Stepping close, he stroked her cheek with the back of his finger. "I want you in my bedroom."

Those words undid her. Her body hummed from the gentle way he caressed her skin. But she stepped back, severing their connection. While he didn't appear affected by their chaotic evening, she wanted to bury her face in his chest and sob. But Mituses were pros at concealing their emotions, so she forced a grateful smile. "I won't be long."

"Fresh towels in the linen closet. You seem to have a thing for those and, lucky for you, mine isn't even locked." With a playful wink, he closed the bedroom door.

Sucking down a jittery breath, she crumpled onto his bed and dropped her head in her hands. To say she was a wreck was an understatement. A kaleidoscope of emotions swirled through her.

Spinning out on the ice had scared the hell out of her. Her roommate's lunatic boyfriend had freaked her out. If Crockett hadn't jumped in twice to rescue her, her evening would've ended in disaster. Those heroic efforts, coupled with their steamy connection at Incognito, had her quivering for a very different reason. The rush of emotion tumbled from her and she drew her knees to her chest and rocked.

Their explosive connection tore at her heartstrings. When she'd had the opportunity, she didn't leave him at Incognito. To further complicate things, she couldn't get enough of him when she stayed. Their passion had always been off the charts, but now she was making up for lost time. Gritting her teeth, she glanced around the room, cluttered with moving boxes.

Crockett's king bed was unmade, the navy blue sheets and dark comforter a rumpled mess. She imagined them lying together, her legs entwined around his while he kissed her breathless and moved inside her. A burst of energy surged through her. *Enough! I can't keep going down that path. It's a dead end.*

She had to suppress this constant craving. A steaming hot shower would calm her shattered nerves. After stripping off her clothing, she walked into his bathroom. *This is bigger than my bedroom.* The Jacuzzi, spacious enough for two, caught her eye. Her mom had mentioned that Crockett and Colton had launched an innovation that could rock the telecom world. Based on his new digs, the world had been rocked.

Showering had helped. Feeling less anxious, she pulled a sweatshirt from her bag and—*crap*. In her mad dash to leave, she'd forgotten sweat pants. Even her favorite yoga pants were missing. She tugged on the top and rummaged through Crockett's drawers until she found a pair of drawstring shorts. *These'll work.*

Even though she was in a strange apartment in a new city, being there felt right somehow. Like she belonged. For the first time since she'd moved back, her loneliness lifted a little. Crockett had always had that effect on her. She padded out of his bedroom and down the hall.

"In here," he called.

Crockett stood at his kitchen island cracking eggs into a bowl, shirtless. *Oh, boy.*

"I'm a big fan of breakfast at three in the morning. Hungry?"

Starving, but not for food.

His cotton drawstring pants hung low on his hips and his thick thighs stretched against the soft fabric. He hadn't shaved. Earlier, when she'd kissed him, his scruffy whiskers had scratched her face. And she'd loved the raw burn. *Are you trying to torture me?*

He tossed a nod toward her bare legs. "Are you cold? Do you want pants?"

"I'm fine if you don't mind my wearing your shorts."

With a sly smile, he said, "I'll suffer through it."

Keeping a safe distance, she stood across the island admiring her host. The man standing before her had the body of a god. Over the decade, Crockett had filled out in all the right places. Long and lean, like a runner, but ripped and taut, like a weight lifter. *He's built like a tank.*

As he moved about the kitchen, her heart fluttered wildly in her chest. Even after learning his true identity, she couldn't keep her hands off him at the club.

Why did all roads *always* lead to this one man?

With his gaze cemented on her, he rounded the island. The closer he got, the faster the butterflies whirled. She imagined his firm grip and his hard kiss as her body bowed to his. She wanted to say something—*anything*—but words failed her. All she could do was stare back.

He switched on the stovetop burner, grabbed a pan, and poured in the scrambled eggs. His bare arm brushed against hers and shock waves scurried through her. She *could* have moved away. She *should* have moved away. But, like earlier, she didn't.

Heat seeped through the thin layer of her worn college sweatshirt. How would he react if she slinked her hands over his biceps? She peeked at him and her breath caught. Long red scratches marred his shoulders. "Wow, you've been clawed."

"And I loved every second of you." His deep voice rumbled through her and her insides clenched.

Me, too.

The Crockett she'd once fallen deeply in love with flashed her a grin. "But, I *could* use your magic touch."

Those words punched her gut. In an attempt to diffuse the storm brewing beneath the surface, she grabbed a spatula to push the eggs around in the pan.

During the summer they'd dated, he'd swing by to see her on his way home from karate after work. Kimberly would heat a plate of leftovers, then disappear into her home office. Crockett would tell her about his latest sparring injury, then insist her *magic touch* would make the pain go away. Without fail, her kiss magically healed him, every single time.

She lowered the heat on the stove, but couldn't regulate her own internal thermostat. Why did Crockett have to bring up their past? "Do you want antiseptic cream?"

Their eyes met. "Where's the fun in that?" He studied her face and her cheeks burned under his intensity. His commanding presence enticed her toward him. As if under a spell, her lips parted, her breath came in short bursts, and her fingers tingled, desperate to stroke his scruffy face.

Bing!

Saved by the toaster. As she slathered the crispy bread with butter, she squeezed the knife to steady her tremble. When he turned away to pour coffee, she admired his backside. Before she could check herself, she sighed. The wingspan of his broad shoulders paired with that long, muscular back and tight ass rocketed her sex drive into the stratosphere. Then she spied two familiar freckles on his shoulder blade and the bittersweet memory came racing back.

They'd been at the neighborhood pool and had returned to his place to make sandwiches. He hadn't bothered to put on a shirt and she'd drawn a smiley under the freckles. Next to that she'd penned: 'CW + AM Forever'. It had been silly and immature, but he hadn't minded. He'd been the sweetest boyfriend…until he dumped her.

I've gotta get out of here. One night, then I'm gone.

With their plates loaded with food, they ate side-by-side at his dining room table while the snowplows lit up the sleeping city across the dark river. But Alexandra stayed keenly aware of Crockett's close proximity. His every breath and sideways glance reminded her she was with the one man she'd fought so hard to forget.

They fell into a familiar rhythm, like two halves of a whole. He set his fork down to sip his coffee. She paused to drink her water. She crossed her legs. He shifted in his chair. By the end of their meal, their shoulders rose and fell in sync. Despite facing the window, Crockett turned his chair so he could see her without craning his neck.

His solicitations comforted and unsettled her. Regardless of her deep-seated feelings, she needed to keep him at arm's length. Her heart was already breaking over her mom. She couldn't fall for him again only to lose him again. He'd dumped her once. Chances were good he'd do it again. Torturing herself was pointless. She wasn't staying. When her mom got better, she'd return to California.

Plus, she needed him to do the interview. *DC's Brightest Tech Star* would bring in the ratings and get her noticed. Then, she could circulate her resume and get the hell out from under Max's thumb.

She'd show her appreciation by cooking him dinner and buying him a tube of antiseptic cream for his shoulders. *Wow. That's pathetic.*

"I'll crash on the sofa," he said. Ignoring her protests, he escorted her to his bedroom, and retrieved a pillow and blanket from his walk-in closet. "Get some sleep." He closed the door, leaving her alone.

A sharp pain sprang from her chest. Feeling like he'd abandoned her, she flung open the door. In the darkened hallway, he turned.

"Thank you for tonight," she said.

A satisfied grin spread over his face. "Are you thanking me as Electra or Alexandra?"

Both. Smirking, she said, "Goodnight, Crockett."

He tossed her a nod, then retreated toward the living room. Fearing another nightmare, she left the door ajar and the desk lamp on. Exhausted, she curled up in his bed. Surrounded by Crockett's delicious scent, she closed her eyes and remembered happier times.

She'd met Crockett Wilde when Colton had invited his freshman college roommate home for Thanksgiving. Alexandra's attraction to him had been immediate and intense. Normally quiet, the fourteen year old had been so tongue-tied she'd barely uttered a word during his entire visit. Beyond Crockett's obvious good looks, his easy laugh, Texan charm, and sexy accent made her heart pitter-patter and her cheeks flush.

After crushing on him for four, long years, she wanted him to see her without her dark disguise. So, when her mom hosted a party to celebrate everyone's graduation—hers from high school, and Colton's and Crockett's from Harvard—Alexandra traded her

Goth look for a chiffon dress and heels. She washed away the black hair color, pulled her brown hair into a sweeping ponytail and went makeup free. Despite feeling totally naked and completely vulnerable, she had to do it. Even if Crockett hadn't cared, her mom had been ecstatic. That, alone, had been worth the effort.

But her plan *had* worked. Crockett had noticed her. They spent most of the afternoon and evening together. And when he told her he'd landed a tech job in Northern Virginia, and wasn't returning home to Texas, she'd made up her mind on the spot. She would give him her virginity before she left for college in August.

In true form, Crockett had been a gentleman. He asked her out on a date—then another and another and another. When they did finally make love, she fell, hard. But in true Mitus fashion, she kept her feelings tucked deep inside. That summer they became inseparable—until he sent her packing and broke her heart.

She rolled over and hugged the other pillow. As she drifted to sleep, she imagined snuggling in Crockett's strong embrace.

Alexandra woke with a start. Adrenaline spiked through her as her eyes darted around the unfamiliar room. Then, her consciousness kicked in. *I'm at Crockett's.* And her thundering heartbeat slowed.

Another nightmare. The faceless man and dark-haired woman had argued, but then as nightmares often go, the woman morphed into a different lady—a blonde drenched in makeup. The man kissed her. For some reason, that upset Alexandra. The man wasn't supposed to be kissing that lady. She wasn't his mommy. *What the hell?* The dream made no sense. *I'll need sleep meds to get through this bout of nightmares.*

Confused and frustrated, she tiptoed toward the kitchen for a glass of water.

"You okay?" Crockett asked.

She startled. "Ooh. Yeah, sorry. Didn't mean to wake you. Just grabbing some water."

"I'm a light sleeper." After flipping on the stovetop light, he filled a glass with filtered water from his refrigerator and handed it to her.

Guzzling the cold liquid helped, but she couldn't shake the disturbing image. "Thanks."

He furrowed his brow. "What's wrong?"

"Nothing."

"At Wilde Bed & Breakfast, we have a tell-the-truth policy." He paused. "Let's try this again. What's really going on?"

Tell him. "I had a nightmare."

IN THE KITCHEN, ALEXANDRA'S eyes had been wild with fear, but when he settled her on the sofa, beneath the warm blanket, her quaking subsided. He sat beside her. "Talk to me."

She paused to gather her thoughts. "I met an employee at Incognito," she said, tucking her leg beneath her and pivoting toward him. "Her name is Sage and I'm concerned she's being abused."

Her trigger. Time to listen.

Though concerned for Alex, he stayed silent hoping she'd continue.

"She's skittish and she flinched when Jase Payne, the GM, touched her. She had trouble making eye contact. When I asked her a question, she deferred to him. All the classic signs are there."

"And you want to help her?"

"I want to talk to her, at the very least. She also had a nasty bruise on her cheek. And last night, her hand and wrist were wrapped in gauze. I think Jase struck her."

"So, that's why you were snooping around?"

"Yeah. She led me to that door in the alcove, but she disappeared before I could speak to her. Jase said she works in the kitchen, but a server checked and no one knows her."

"Maybe she's a chambermaid and doesn't want to admit to changing the bed linens."

"There's more," she murmured. "Something is going on at Incognito that makes me suspicious."

From the many stories Kimberly told him about Alex's tenacity as a journalist, he knew she went full-tilt until she'd flushed out the truth. "Go on."

"Before I do, you can't say anything to anyone."

He wanted to blurt, "Who would I tell?" Instead, he extended his hand like he was conducting a damned business deal. "You have my word."

Though they shook like two professionals, he stayed connected for an extra beat before letting go. So much passion flowed between them. How could she deny the obvious? Or was he imagining something long gone?

"Some members don't check in via the tablet."

Seriously? That's all she had? "That's not required, is it?"

When she moved to the window, her curvy ass distracted him. After barely digesting that she'd moved back east, seeing her float around his new home was surreal. With her back to him she said, "Management *personally* escorts them into a room."

Crockett joined her at the window as the bright orange sun crested over the horizon. "Like white glove treatment?"

"No. They go into the room with the masked member."

"Are you positive?"

"Yes."

He hitched a brow. "That's a little odd. Who does this?"

"Jase and Francois, his assistant."

"How long do they stay in there?"

"I've never seen anyone come out. Once, I spied Jase exiting from the door marked 'Private' next to the linen closet."

Nodding, he said, "So that's why you mauled me in the alcove."

Her cheeks pinked. "Since Sage had led me there, I didn't want him to suspect anything."

"Good to know, Nancy Drew. Honestly, Alex, I don't know why you'd care if management escorts club members into their suite. It is strange, but not criminal."

"One of the men—the older gentleman, Dracule—calls it *rejuvenation*."

He shifted his attention out the window. "Maybe that's how he feels...you know...after."

Brushing the flyaway hair from her face, she hitched her hand on her hip. "Men are being escorted into the same unmarked room on a regular basis. I've seen it every time I've been there."

"It is odd, but I'm not sure that's reason to suspect the worst." He kept his voice steady, on purpose. Inciting her was the last thing he wanted to do.

Her shoulders dropped. "You don't believe me."

"I did *not* say that. Is it possible you're gunning for a story where there is none?"

"*Crockett*—" She crossed her arms. "Granted, I am suspicious about most everything, but there is something bizarre going on at that club and I'm *not* talking about the sex play. Plus..." Fear banked in her eyes. "Seeing Sage has triggered my nightmares. I'm hardly sleeping."

Dammit. He wrapped his arms around her and kissed her forehead. "I'm sorry." Her flowery scent surrounded him and he tightened his hold.

When she pressed her body to his, memories of *them* flooded his thoughts.

Over a decade earlier, she'd confided terrifying dreams that had haunted her since childhood. Then, a month into their relationship, the nightmares ended. She credited him, though they'd never spent the night together. "I feel safe with you," she'd said. Those words had stayed with him all these years.

Then, two weeks before she left for college, she told him she was going to withdraw. "I don't want to leave you." Going to journalism school at USC had been her primary goal. Though she wasn't a chatty teen, she had been vocal about *that*. For days, he struggled with his decision, but in the end, he couldn't stand in her way. Especially since his sweet Sophia never had the opportunity to follow her own dreams.

When he'd reminded Alex that she'd wanted to attend USC and study broadcast journalism since forever, she still wouldn't back down. She wasn't going to leave him. The "let's be friends" and the "you should date other people" talks also backfired. She was staying. And his heart broke for what he knew he had to do.

Breaking up with Alexandra had been gut-wrenching for them both. Being the bad guy had sucked. This time, he wouldn't let her leave without telling her how much he loved her.

Were her suspicions about Incognito his opportunity to prove he wasn't the bad guy? That her happiness had always mattered to him? And that he'd be willing to do anything to prove that? "I have an idea."

She lifted her face, her eyes brimming with hope. "I'm listening."

"I'll do one better. I'll show you."

14

HATCHING THEIR PLAN

Though the side streets hadn't been plowed, Crockett had no trouble trucking through the six inches of packed snow. He rolled over the tire tracks of those brave enough to venture out ahead of him. Even at half-past eight, there was more traffic than he'd anticipated. As he pulled onto the plowed main road, Alexandra's ringtone blasted from her handbag.

"Hello."

After listening, she said, "I *am* working on a story, Max. I'm conducting an interview." Her staccato tone caused him to glance over.

"You want me to cover *what?*" After a longer period of silence, she replied, "Got it. Arlington Hill." She hung up and growled.

Even angry, her husky groan had always aroused him. Sometimes he'd say something just to coax her into making that raw, gritty sound. And today was no different. She still affected him in the best of ways.

With his eyes on the road, he said, "Snowstorms around here are always big news."

"It would appear that way." After thumbing around on her

phone, she dialed. "I'll have to postpone that trip to your office. I need a rental car."

"Hang up, Alexandra."

"What?"

"After last night's spinout, you're not driving in this. It can take days for trucks to plow the side streets."

"I'll call a taxi or car service."

"Like hell you will. I'll take you to Arlington Hill." He eased the truck to a stop at the red light and fixed her with a hard stare. This issue was non-negotiable. Despite his plan to get to the office early to analyze Maverick's downed Eagle, helping Alexandra trumped that.

She studied him like he'd grown a second nose. With that strong Mitus independent streak, he expected she'd fight him on this. Instead, her expression softened. Her sweet smile sent a bolt of energy powering through him.

"Thank you. You're right. I don't want to drive in this."

He wanted to hug her. Alexandra Mitus never showed vulnerability. "Let's get to work."

When she tucked her chin, her cascading hair shadowed her pink cheek. "I'm embarrassed."

The light turned green and he moved forward. "What for?"

With a quick toss of her dark mane, she shook it off. "Nothing. Never mind."

Her pain became his. Refusing to let it go, he murmured, "Tell me."

"I have to cover the kids sledding." Her last word caught a tremble.

She wants me to respect her as a journalist. "Snow is a hot topic. Even Washington politics takes a back seat. You'll see."

"My career has taken a major step backward, but it's okay." Squaring her shoulders, she pursed her lips. "I sound like a spoiled brat. I'm sorry."

As he turned onto a residential street, he glanced over. "I understand. You gave up a lot for your mom."

"I love her and Colton so much. I hope my being here is helping."

"Kimberly is thrilled. Everyone missed you." *Me, most of all.* He searched her face for a sign, the tiniest clue, a flicker of hope that there was something between them besides a few nights of passion or her relentless need to unearth the truth and save a woman from suspected abuse.

She ran a soft hand over his shoulder and adrenaline powered through him. "Thank you for the ride."

Her touch could slay him. And she probably didn't even know —or care. *One effin' step forward and two back.* This woman would be his undoing.

He parked in the older Arlington neighborhood filled with quaint brick homes and a small dog park. Leaning over, he eyed her rubber boots. "No four-inch heels today."

"I grabbed them last night before we made our great escape." With the cutest smile, she lifted her leg to show him. "I love my Hunter rubbers. They're super-dependable." Her eyes popped wide. "Oops."

"I'm familiar with Hunter *and* his dependable rubbers." The air grew electric as they stared into each other's eyes. When her breathy sigh floated between them, he leaned close. Her lips parted and she flipped her attention to his mouth. "Watch out for ice patches." He slipped on his Maui Jim's and exited the truck.

As soon as she stepped out, he was waiting. Snow boots or not, he wrapped his hand around her slender arm. Just another excuse to touch her, but falling in plain sight would add insult to injury.

"Thank you." She slipped on her dark shades as they trudged into the cul-de-sac. "It's so cold. Hard to believe I used to spend hours outside sledding when I was a kid. No snow days in Uvalde, huh?"

She remembered. "No, ma'am. Big news when the temp dipped below forty." He surveyed the area. "Where's your camera crew?"

"Someone's meeting me here."

He led her through the well-stomped footpath between two brick homes. As the expansive hill appeared before them, she gasped. "What the—"

Even at eight forty-five in the morning, there were dozens of children sledding down the ginormous hill while several dogs romped in an impromptu pack.

"Welcome to your story, Goth Girl."

"Alexandra Reed," someone called.

With her hand positioned over her sunglasses to shield the snowy glare, she stared and stared. Then a giant grin erupted on her face. "Gavin!" Her hand shot into the air, and she waved at the tall man with long dreads trekking toward them.

Although he had two large bags slung over each shoulder, she threw her arms around his neck. "What a shock!" she said.

"Good to see you, doll!" Gavin threw his burly arms around her. "You're looking fab as always." After setting the camera bags on a cushion of packed snow, he hitched his hands on his hips. "Max never said a word."

"No surprise there. I can't imagine he enjoys having to utter my name."

Laughing, Gavin extended his hand to Crockett. "Gavin Aviato."

"Crockett Wilde." The two men shook hands. "Good to meet you. How do you two know each other?"

"Alexandra and I worked together in California. We made a great team—called ourselves Mutt and Jeff. I moved when my partner—now husband—Bruce returned to DC."

Alexandra grinned. "Congratulations. That's so awesome."

Gavin ungloved his hand to display a wedding band. "The old ball and chain."

They laughed.

Gavin eyed Crockett. "You snagged yourself a handsome one, girl. Lord knows Bruce and I tried fixing her up, but our gal was too picky for her own good."

"Oh, no, he's not my—" Alexandra blurted.

"I'm an old friend," Crockett said. "Alex needed some help navigating through the snow."

"I've got her if you need to head out," Gavin said.

"I'll be a while," Alexandra said to Crockett. "Gavin, would you mind dropping me off at Crockett's office in Crystal City? He won our *DC's Brightest Tech Star* contest."

"Congrats. That's a big ratings boost for our station. I'll team with you on that, if you want, Alexandra."

"Like old times," she said. "Only, Crockett hasn't agreed to the interview."

"Ooh, honey, you *know* I love a man who plays hard to get," Gavin said and Alexandra laughed.

"All righty, then, I'll take off," Crockett said.

"Hellooooo," someone hollered.

Not bothering to turn around, Gavin cringed. "I've got teacher's pet in tow. In addition to being an award-winning cinematographer, I can add chauffeur to my list of accomplishments. Max had me pick Stacy up."

"Is she a reporter?" Crockett asked.

Alexandra sighed. "She covers the White House."

"Brace for insanity," Gavin whispered. "And God help us."

With one hand gripping her hip while the other shielded her eyes from the sun, Stacy appeared beside Gavin. "How long will this take? I've *got* to get to POTUSville."

Shaking his head, Gavin ignored her. "I'll set up here, Alexandra."

Eyeing Crockett, Stacy broke into a grin. "Stacy B-L-U-N-K. But pronounced like the white wine. If we're setting up a shot, *I'll* interview him."

"Wait in the truck," Gavin said.

"Look, Gavin, I neeeeeeed to leave." Stacy stomped her foot, but her heel got stuck in the snow mound. As she yanked it out, she flailed her arms to keep from falling. "How long is this bullshit going to take? There are issues on the Hill that require *my* attention."

"I thought you said you covered the White House," Crockett said. "That's not Capitol Hill."

"Oh, yeah, right. Whatever."

Crockett glanced at Alexandra, who'd pinched her lips together. He needed to get to the office, but maybe he could buy himself a few points by taking the whiner off her hands so she could work. "I'll drop you off."

Grinning, Stacy grabbed his arm. "Ooh, you're made of steel. Are you Superman?"

He ignored her fawning and wrapped his hand around Alexandra's shoulder. "I'll see you later."

She eyed Stacy's vise grip before shooting him a little smile. "I'll be by."

The sparkle in her eyes lit his insides on fire. *So beautiful.* "Have fun in your Hunters, GG." *My Goth Girl.* He hadn't called her that nickname in years, but damn it felt right. Like a secret handshake.

Alexandra made his day when she mouthed, "Thank you."

He tossed Gavin a nod and set off toward his truck with a very chatty Stacy B-L-U-N-K in tow. Stacy clambered into the truck and draped her white parka over her lap. His car wasn't that warm. Her two-sizes-too-small sweater clung to her oversized breasts like a second skin.

"How do you know Alexandra?" she asked as he drove out of the neighborhood.

"Miss Reed was interviewing me for a story before she got called to Arlington Hill."

"I've only been at the station for a few months, but I'm already trending," Stacy said. "People are starting to notice me." She pulled the giant clip from her hair and red waves tumbled down her shoulders. "We should go out for drinks sometime."

"I'm seeing someone."

"If things don't work out—and I only mention that because I *personally* like leaving my options open—call, *anytime*. It's a good policy. Don't you agree?"

No, I don't. Crockett cracked his window to get a breath of fresh air.

She touched his arm. "I'm on every social media site, so it's super easy to find me. B-L-U-N-K."

Crockett drove over the 14th Street Bridge and into DC. "How'd you get the White House gig? Isn't that earned through experience and seniority?"

"Can you keep a secret?"

"If you mean, 'Are you capable of keeping a secret,' then the answer is yes."

Giggling, she tossed her hair off her sweater. "Max, the station director, has taken me under his wing."

Crockett squeezed the steering wheel. His sister was God knows where. Alexandra was interviewing some seven year old about a snow day and this chick with no solid broadcasting experience was spending her days at the White House. *Life is effin' unfair.* "Hope that works out for you."

"I'm not worried. Max has assigned Alexandra to be my mentor."

Oh, Jesus, that's gotta suck for Alex. "You're lucky. She's an Emmy-winning journalist."

She dismissed him with a wave of her hand. "Whatever that is."

"Seriously? Google it. You do know what Google is, right?"

Stacy laughed. "Of course I do, dummy!"

He pulled up as close to the White House as security would allow. Which meant she'd have to walk a couple of blocks. He threw the truck into park.

"Can you get any closer? I'm in heels."

"Not unless I want to get shot."

Her ear-piercing squeal sent a shiver down his spine. "Your accent is super sexy. Where are you from?"

"Texas."

"Where do you work?"

"Wilde Innovations."

Her mouth fell open. "No shit."

"And I need to get there."

"Oh, right. What do you do at Wilde?"

"Innovate."

On a snort, she opened the door. "See ya, Tex. Thanks for the ride." She slammed his door, turned and slipped, crashing flat on her ass on a mound of snow.

She doesn't know my name but she's ready to sleep with me. Shaking his head, he pulled into traffic and headed back toward Virginia.

LATER THAT AFTERNOON, CROCKETT pushed out of the chair in his Think Tank and scraped his fingers down his whiskered cheeks. His six-person innovation team had reconfigured the specs around their night vision goggles, but they couldn't come to a consensus on the rework.

He drew an arrow on the white board. "Ergonomically, this is the stronger choice, but the cost of this one"—he starred a different configuration—"aligns with our budget."

"We hear you," Decker said. "But the less expensive one has a wonkier plastic."

"The first prototype gets my vote," said the lone female on the team. "We can't sell the less expensive one with a note that says, 'fragile'."

"We've reached an impasse," said another. "I don't think either of these will work."

Crockett studied the calculations that covered every inch of the white board. "We've got to go back to the basics. What have we overlooked?" A knock on the door interrupted his train of thought. "Come in."

Ellen poked her head in and eyed Crockett. "Before I head out for the evening, I need to speak with you."

"Make a run for it," Decker said.

Laughter lightened the intense mood.

Crockett glanced at the time on his tablet. It was after five. "We'll finish this tomorrow," he said to his team. "Thanks for your efforts."

Talking amongst themselves, the group filed out, and Ellen squeezed into the room.

Decker rose. "I'll re-analyze the plastics formula after a caffeine hit."

"Alexandra has been waiting for a while," Ellen said.

"Show her to my office, please."

"Yes, sir." But his assistant didn't budge.

"Everything okay?" Crockett asked.

"No." She shut the door. "I just got off the phone with Charles Bowen."

Decker smiled. "We love Charlie."

"And fortunately for us the feeling is mutual," Ellen said.

Charles Bowen was the Under Secretary for Science and Technology at the Department of Homeland Security. Not only had DHS been one of Wilde's first Spy Fly customers, Bowen had personally spread the word within the agency. In total, DHS owned over two thousand unmanned aerial vehicles manufactured by Wilde Innovations.

Crockett felt another headache coming on. "What did he say, Ellen?"

"He's had some device failures," she said.

"Some?" Decker scraped his fingers over his forehead.

"He said you can call him on his cell tonight until ten."

"I'll call him now," Crockett said. "Please let Alexandra know I'll be another ten minutes. Thank you, Ellen."

With a tight nod, his efficient assistant buzzed out.

"Let's get this over with," Crockett said. "Shut the door." Crockett dialed and put his phone on speaker.

"Hey, Crockett, I had a feeling you'd be calling me right back," Charlie said.

"Absolutely," Crockett replied. "I've got you on speaker. Decker's with me. What's going on?"

"I'm hoping you can tell me," Charlie began. "CBP—Customs and Border Protection—called me. Two new Falcons failed. One never got off the ground. The other crashed. This is a first, Crockett. Batteries checked out fine. The units are on their way back to you. Have you come across other failures like this?"

"Of the twenty-five hundred birds we've shipped so far, we've had one other recent report. My team is troubleshooting it. Getting yours back will accelerate our efforts. I'm sorry for the impact this is having on your operations. We'll get it squared away ASAP."

"Secret Service had a problem with three Spy Flies," Charlie said. "I don't have details yet but thought you'd want to know. We rely on your devices, so let's get this resolved."

"Thanks for the call, Charlie. I'll be in touch." Crockett ended the call. "What a cluster—"

"This can't be a coincidence," Decker said.

"We'll have to delay certain product shipments until we isolate the problem. This could cost us hundreds of thousands of dollars in lost revenues." He slammed his fist on the table. "Dammit this pisses me off."

Decker rose. "This time I'll oversee QA's analysis."

"Keep me updated," Crockett said. "Switching topics, I want to show Alexandra our Spy Flies."

From the doorway, Decker spun on his heels. "Seriously? That project is Eyes Only."

"I trust her." Crockett pushed out of the chair.

Decker's frown was a clear sign he did not approve. "You sure about this?"

Hitching an eyebrow, Crockett said nothing.

"Fine," said Decker. "Give me ten to ready the lab for an intruder—I meant, outsider."

Decker's pushback didn't surprise Crockett. He trusted the media less than Crockett did. But he believed she wouldn't exploit him for professional gain. He was sharing this information with Alex, not Alexandra Reed the journalist, and he'd make that clear before he showed her the tiny drones.

As Crockett strode down the hallway, he forced Charlie's disturbing news to the back of his mind. Alexandra deserved his full attention.

On and off throughout the day, he'd wondered whether she'd be returning home with him that evening. He assumed she'd move in with Kimberly or Colton. Though he wanted to insist she stay with him, seeing her float around his penthouse in his old gym shorts would give him a perpetual hard on.

He found Alexandra staring out his window with her phone jammed against her ear. Her brown corduroys hugged her ass, the stark white camisole shone through her sheer black blouse.

"I can help you tomorrow afternoon, Stacy." While listening, she twisted a chunk of dark hair. "The President's recent trip to Russia is more topical than what the First Lady read to the elementary school class." After listening, she added, "No, I didn't say tropical. I said *topical*."

"I'm sorry—who?"

"Yes, your new friend *Tex* is right. I did win an Emmy. No, I won't give you his number. Gotta run."

After hanging up, she sighed. "Something has got to give. I'm babysitting a bubblehead. I need a story I can sink my teeth into."

"Hey," he said.

As she pivoted, he eyed her long legs and lean torso. He

couldn't resist a leggy woman, but no one did it for him like Alex. No one. Her rosy cheeks gave her a girl-next-door look. "Hi."

Her phone call had revealed plenty. Not only had she held her ground with that twit, but she desperately needed a meaty story. Though he detested publicity, he'd help her out. She deserved a break. Plus, her skills weren't being utilized. *DC's Brightest Tech Star* would provide her with the right stage to showcase her talent. But he'd wait until the right moment to tell her. Maybe even earn himself some extra points. "How was Arlington Hill?"

As she recounted her interviews, her left eyebrow arched when she emphasized certain words and her smile favored one side. He'd forgotten how much he loved those endearing imperfections.

"And we finished our day with a story about two brothers," she said. "The younger has special needs and the older designed a sled so he can play in the snow." Her eyes softened. "It was touching."

Her sweet smile made him want to kiss her breathless. Instead, he focused on the reason for her visit. Help her track down some Incognito employee named Sage, then flush out her rejuvenation hunch. "Let's continue where we left off this morning," he said. "Ready to see my lab?"

Her face lit up. "That would be great." Her phone rang and she glanced at the screen. "*Finally*. It's Colton. Do you mind if I take this?"

"Go ahead."

She answered. "Hey, did you get my message?"

As she listened, her shoulders sagged. "Oh, okay. I understand." More silence. "When will you be back in town?"

She turned toward Crockett. "I'm with him now. Hold on." She held out her phone.

"Hey, man," Crockett said. "How's the rollout going?"

"A few snags, but overall, great," said Colton. "You two joined at the hip?"

Crockett flipped his gaze to Alex. "Alexandra wants to do a story on Wilde Innovations."

"She's got an uphill battle. You don't grant interviews."

"No, I don't. What's goin' on?"

"I need a favor," Colton said. "I understand Alexandra can't move back into her house. Brigit and I are redesigning the guesthouse at the mansion. It's a gutted mess. Could you put her up?"

"What about Kimberly?"

"That won't work. She doesn't want Alexandra to know how sick she is."

"No worries. I've got this."

"Thanks. We'll be home in a few days."

The call ended. Crockett stood transfixed. Even in her anxious state, Alexandra's beauty captured his heart.

She rubbed the back of her neck with slow, deep strokes. Heat infused his chest. He imagined those long fingers raking down his back while he was rooted deep inside her. He blinked away the fantasy to focus on *her* needs.

He hated that she was stressing over where to live, especially when he had plenty of room. But moving in with him spelled trouble and complications. How was he supposed to keep a safe distance if she lived under his roof and paraded around in his shorts? Having her there would be pure temptation. Even he only had so much willpower.

And what about his feelings? He couldn't risk getting emotionally attached, only to lose her again. Hadn't he learned his lesson the first time around?

His buzzing phone interrupted his angst. "All set," texted Decker.

"Let's head to my lab."

As Alexandra drew close, he wanted to pull her into his arms and kiss her until they both succumbed to the need. Instead, they walked side-by-side toward his lab. He heaved open the heavy glass door and she crossed the threshold.

Six of the seven workstations were cloaked with black cloths.

"Welcome to Wilde lab," said Decker.

"Thanks for prepping the room," Crockett said.

"Time for a combo caffeine-sugar hit from Mimi's. I'll grab you two something." Decker left them alone.

She surveyed the spacious room. "Why bring me here if I can't see anything?" Then, the V between her brows disappeared and she hitched her hands on her hips. "Why don't you show me what's lurking beneath the sheets?"

His body tensed while the air grew thick with anticipation. She was tempting fate with that question. He palmed the small of her back and guided her toward the table where the Spy Flies waited. Her body heat seeped through her silky blouse and his need surged.

"The primary scope of our projects is top secret surveillance for military and law enforcement," Crockett explained.

"I understand."

"You confided in me and I want to help you," he said, stopping beside the uncovered table.

Her simple smile made him smile. "Thank you."

As they stared into each other's eyes, he fought the urge to kiss her. "These are our latest surveillance creations," he said.

"Wow, I'm impressed." Damn if her sultry voice didn't make his balls ache.

His Spy Flies—Horse, Black, and Moth—were lined up, ready to fly.

"Have a seat." Once she eased down, he sat next to her and picked up Black. "These are the eyes and ears when agents and law enforcement can't gain access to a facility or other POI—point of interest."

He had her hold out her hand and he set the insect on her

palm. After studying it, she examined its underside. "This is phenomenal."

"Thank you." Pride filled his heart. For years, he'd measured his life in terms of Sophia. Despite all the innovations, all the success, and all the wealth, he still felt like he'd failed. Because his sister was still missing. For a fleeting second, Alexandra filled the gaping whole in his heart.

Over the next several minutes, Crockett demonstrated the Flies' abilities using a tablet to control the bugs.

"Who currently uses these?"

"I'm not at liberty to say, but we have a contract with one federal agency and several law enforcement organizations on the state level." He slid over the tablet. "Give it a try."

Alexandra did her best to maneuver Black but crash-landed the insect belly up.

"Good job," he said. "It takes practice."

Decker returned with a cardboard tray of coffees and a bag. "We can always count on Mimi. She heated the croissants." Then, he cast a serious eye on Alexandra and the atmosphere grew chilly. "This project must be closely guarded from the public."

Normally easygoing, Decker had turned into a pit bull. "She understands," Crockett said, coming to her defense.

"I wouldn't betray Crockett or do anything to jeopardize his business," she said.

Decker and Crockett exchanged glances. *Let it go.*

After another look around the room, disappointment tinged her eyes. "Given the secrecy of your work, there's no point in my interviewing you or your team."

"She has a point," Decker said.

Wanting to assure her, Crockett laid a steady hand on her shoulder and gave a quick squeeze. "We have other innovations I'm prepared to discuss *if* I agree to the interview."

She shot him a relieved smile. "I hope so. I would love the opportunity."

If she was using her charm to change his mind, it was working.

"Geez, you two, get a room." Decker grabbed a coffee out of the tray and pulled a pastry from the bag. "I've got work to do." He trotted out.

A pink hue blossomed on her cheeks. "Tell me about your plan."

So pretty. He rose, collected the bag and cardboard tray. "Let's talk in private."

Together they entered his Tank and he shut the door. "We're not ready to erase the white board. Can I trust you not to run a story about this?"

Without hesitation, she extended her hand. "Again, you have my word. For the record, I don't understand any of that. Chemistry and I were not best buds."

He shook it. "Thank you." Unable to control himself, he blanketed her hand with his other one.

A seemingly innocent gesture rekindled his desire. Being alone with her heightened his senses. Her beautiful scent filled his nostrils. Her breath hitched, then, fell in line with his. The longer he stared at her angelic face, the more he wanted to haul her into his arms and kiss the hell out of her.

The air crackled between them. Her light brown eyes bled black. Her lips parted. The slightest pull and she'd come crashing against his chest. He'd strip her bare and take her on the hard Formica tabletop. *Get a damn grip.*

As if she could read his thoughts, she tugged her hand away and eased into one of the chairs at the conference table.

In those seconds, he'd begun to harden. Their blazing connection, their dangerously close proximity, and her inability to conceal her need drove him wild. He sat at the head of the table and crossed his legs.

He needed to focus his efforts on his mounting problem at work, not help her sleuth around the club. *Make time for her.* After clearing his throat, he said, "I'm proposing we return to

Incognito to track down this woman and get to the bottom of rejuvenation."

"Using your flying insects?"

"Yes."

Twenty minutes later, with the pastries eaten and their coffee long gone, Crockett believed their plan could work. Only one thing remained unclear.

"How far are we willing to go to ensure no one at the club catches on to what we're doing?" he asked.

Her provocative gaze sent another surge of energy through him. "All. The. Way."

"We'll have to pretend like we're there to play, especially if Jase has surveillance throughout the club. Can you pull this off, Alex?"

"Huntah." Electra's sexy southern lilt caught him by surprise. "I wasn't planning on faking a thing."

15

THE GUT-WRENCHING TRUTH

Alexandra's senses had been thrust into overdrive by Crockett's scrumptious baseline scent and wicked-hot gaze. His commanding presence had her quivering in her seat. Damn him for making her panties wet. If she didn't bolt from that cozy room, she'd rip off his clothing and have her way with him.

On. The. Spot.

Her new partner in crime would help her get to the bottom of whatever was going on at Incognito. Maybe put an end to her string of nightmares, too, if she could find the elusive Sage. But, by agreeing to help her sleuth around the club, he'd tied himself to her. Night after night. Even sex-crazed, emotionally unavailable Electra would have to work hard at *not* falling in love with him all over again.

The idea of being with him was too provocative, too exciting. She had to put distance between them. Jumping up, she flung open the door. But his undeniable pull kept her feet firmly in place. She turned back. The intensity of his bright eyes sent a zing of energy through her.

Like a heroin addict desperate for a fix, she wanted him in the absolute worst way. But their *connections* would be part of a contrived plot to fly under management's radar. *Lusty sex to blend in. That's all.*

"Thank you for agreeing to help me." *Chicken. Tell him how you really feel.* "I need to call my mom." *And beg her to let me live with her.*

Crockett pushed out of his chair. "Let's stop by and check on her."

Her heart warmed. She loved that he cared.

As they walked through the quiet lab, the dark windows reflected their images. Some couples looked like they belonged together. *Are we one of them?*

In heavy rush hour traffic, Alexandra called her mom.

"Hello, sweetheart!" Kimberly sounded perkier than she had in days.

"Hi, Mom. How are you doing?"

"Perfect timing. My new chef made a pot roast and I'll barely put a dent in it. Can you join me?"

"Sure. I'm bringing someone." Silence. "What's the matter?" Alexandra asked.

"I'm thrilled you're making friends, but I'm not up for entertaining."

"It's Crockett."

"*Our* Crockett?" Kimberly's smile burst through the receiver. Could her mom be any happier?

Grateful she hadn't put the call on speaker, she peeked at him. "Um, yeah."

"Tell him the chef's a delight."

"Why?"

"Crockett hired him to cook dinner for me three times a week."

Wow. "Do you need anything from the store?"

"I'm good, thanks. When can I expect you?"

"Hold on." Turning to Crockett, she asked, "How far away are we?"

"Ten to fifteen."

"Te—"

"I heard him. See you shortly." Her mom hung up. Alexandra wanted to scream. Was the universe conspiring against her? Why did all roads continue to lead to this one man?

"All set?" He rolled to a stop at a yellow light on King Street.

"Thanks to you, Kimberly has dinner waiting for hungry mouths." She gulped. That didn't even make sense, but it sounded deliciously dirty. Downright naughty. And dripping with possibility.

In the darkened vehicle their eyes met, the swirling energy dizzying. Her breathing roared in her ears. Or was that his?

Her body palpitated with desire. She wanted to rake her teeth over his scruffy jawline or press her mouth to his. Desperate to kiss him, she leaned over.

The car behind them laid on the horn. Startled, she flung herself against the seat as Crockett powered through the green light. Mortified, she turned away and stared out the passenger window. *Have some self-control.*

"I'll drive you around until the plows dig us out." His calm voice carried none of the inner turmoil she wrestled with.

Her eyebrows flew up. Was he trying to kill her with kindness? "I don't want to inconvenience—"

"Enough, Alex. I'm helping out so Kimberly doesn't stress over you." His firm tone clarified his motive.

I'm a charity case for Mom's sake.

"Speaking of Kimberly, are you going to filter what you tell her about your living situation?" he asked.

Chewing her options, she clamped down on her lower lip. Never before had she censored conversations with her mom, but he brought up a good point. "I can't tell her my roommate's boyfriend is a nut job. She'll worry or worse, call the police."

"Let's not poke the Ben bear. And, for the record, she's your *former* roommate."

"I *still* need a place to live."

"According to Colton, you're living with me."

After a breathy sigh, she said, "Well, he's not the boss of me."

"Don't tell him that. He thinks he's the boss of *everyone*."

She laughed. *He knows my family so well.* "I can't tell her my car was hit, either. She'd freak out." She'd reached one solid conclusion. *Keep mum with Mom.*

They found Kimberly in high spirits, her energetic mood uplifting. Were the chemo and radiation killing the cancer? Could her mom be turning a corner?

After Crockett carved the beef, they served themselves at the kitchen island and sat at the small oak dinner table. Alexandra's knee brushed Crockett's. Their eyes met. He flashed a smile. Her cheeks warmed. Kimberly peered over her glasses and smiled like she'd won the effin' lottery.

Crockett raised his wine glass. "Kimberly, here's to your health."

So thoughtful.

As they dug in, Kimberly asked a question that made Alexandra's eyes grow moist. "So, Alexandra, tell me what made *this* day special?"

Bittersweet childhood memories tore at her heartstrings. "You haven't asked that in a long time, Mom."

Kimberly's eyes softened. "Some things are worth reliving."

"I was reunited with Gavin Aviato. He's a cameraman I teamed with in California. He's the best of the best."

Kimberly tilted her head toward Crockett and waggled her eyebrows. Subtlety wasn't her mom's strong point. She wanted Alexandra to mention something about *Crockett*. So, she added, "And Crockett offered to drive me around since I'm not comfortable navigating the icy roads."

Her reward? A beaming Mitus grin. "That's a relief. Thank you, Crockett."

"Kimberly, I'm hoping you can help me with something," he said. "A reporter wants to interview me for a story."

As Kimberly hitched a brow, she asked, "On what?"

"Me."

With precise movements, she set down her silverware, then tapped her fingernails on the table, one at a time. "You never grant interviews."

"I thought I'd make an exception."

"Why?" Kimberly asked.

"The journalist is your award-winning daughter."

Kimberly's eyes slid from one to the other, then her face burst with happiness. "That's wonderful! What a fantastic surprise."

"Crockett won *DC's Brightest Tech Star*," Alexandra said.

"When will it be on? I'd love to see it," said Kimberly.

"I've been told late spring. I'll let you know."

Though subtle, a shadow fell over Kimberly's eyes. "If you interview him right away, will it air sooner?"

Panic churned in Alexandra's guts. Was her mom sicker than she'd let on? "Crockett hasn't even agreed to do it."

"He wouldn't have brought it up if he wasn't going to do it!"

Wide eyed, Alexandra fidgeted in her seat. "I'm not sure the air-date can be changed. Why the rush?"

Kimberly smacked her palm on the table. "I ask the questions around here!"

Alexandra startled, then composed herself. *She never flies off the handle.* "I'm worried about you. Maybe I should move in here for a little while."

On a huff, Kimberly threw her napkin on the table. "Absolutely not."

Mixing meds with the wine was a bad combination. She rubbed her mother's back. "Can I get you some tea?"

Jerking back, Kimberly pushed out of her chair. "What is the matter with you, Alexandra? We're having a nice dinner, thanks to

Crockett, and you're treating me like I'm an invalid. I don't want tea! I want normal conversation. Just go!" And with that, her mom left the room. Several seconds later, she slammed her bedroom door.

Alexandra stared at her plate of half-eaten food. Appetite gone, her head throbbed. Embarrassed that her mother had yelled at her, she didn't know what to say to fill the uncomfortable silence.

"I'm sorry," Crockett said after a moment. "Why don't I clean up?"

"Her behavior has been erratic." Shaking her head, Alexandra added, "I don't know what to do. Do I go to her? Do I call the service to confirm the night nurse is on her way?"

Crockett rose. "Let's give Kimberly some space. She might come back out. If she doesn't, you can check on her."

As they put away leftovers, Alexandra flipped on the TV. The familiar cadence of the news broadcasters comforted her. When finished, she excused herself.

With a heavy heart, Alexandra tiptoed down the hallway and tapped quietly on Kimberly's bedroom door. No answer. She cracked open the door. All the bedroom lights were on and her mom was asleep beneath the comforter.

As she started to leave, Kimberly stirred. "What a nice surprise. What brings you by?"

A shiver flew down her spine. She needed to tell Colton about Mom's erratic behavior and memory blips. And she needed some damned answers.

Alexandra sat on the edge of the bed. "Just wanted you to know how much I love you."

Kimberly smiled. "My sweet angel. Are you here for the weekend? Be sure to visit your brother and Crockett, too, while you're in town." Her eyes fluttered closed.

Unable to tear herself away, Alexandra watched her mom sleep while her heart wept.

At some point, Crockett caressed her back. She'd no idea how long he'd been standing next to her. "The nurse is here," he said.

After debriefing the caregiver on Kimberly's volatile and confusing behavior, she and Crockett left. Once outside, she took in the night sky. *Shouldn't Mom be getting better? Was her reaction from mixing alcohol with her meds?* Alexandra had too many questions, but no answers. Frustration replaced sadness.

Ever the gentleman, Crockett opened the passenger door to his truck and she climbed in. "Guess you're stuck with me for another night," she said after he'd pulled onto the main road. "I'll call the roommate finder in the morning and request a new search."

"Alex—"

"Don't. I appreciate everything, but it's best that I not stay with you while I'm in town. You're already helping me follow up on some insane hunch. And yes, I know I'm probably wrong about the club. And you're probably right about rejuvenation. Who isn't rejuvenated after sex? And so what if some employee got smacked around by her employer? How is that even my problem? It's not." She massaged her shoulder, but the knotted muscles wouldn't release. "I have no idea what's happening with my mother. I have nowhere to live. Colton asked me to come home, which I was happy to do. Then he flies out of town for work and you're stuck babysitting me. When are those two going to treat me like an adult?" She pounded her fist on the door handle. "*Ouch!*"

Crockett turned off the busy road and parked in a quiet, residential neighborhood. He leaned over and clasped her injured hand in his. "Where does it hurt?"

"*Everywhere.*"

He dotted her palm with tender kisses, massaged the side of her hand where she'd smacked his door handle. "Better?" He stared into her eyes.

She slammed her eyes shut, but an avalanche of emotions flowed over her, smothering her under its weight.

"Look at me."

Her eyes fluttered open. "It still hurts."

"Where?"

"I can't tell you."

Moving in a small circle, his thumb caressed her skin. "Yes, you can, GG."

Her body tensed. "No, Crockett. *Don't*. I'm not that person anymore. Goth Girl doesn't exist."

Her hand throbbed. Somehow, Crockett knew the exact spot and he kissed it. A soft, tender gesture that contradicted the intensity in his eyes. Her breath caught while blood whooshed through her. She wanted him. On her. In her. Desperate to forget reality, she needed the ecstasy to swallow her whole.

Breaking eye contact, she wiggled her hand away. Screwing at the club in a masked disguise was one thing, but she had to keep her physical and emotional distance from this powerhouse of a man.

"Tell me where it hurts." His deep voice plucked her from her angst and she turned to face him.

"My heart." The truth. Her next breath came a little easier. "It's breaking for my mom. I'm dying inside and yet I'm supposed to act like everything is okay. Well, it's not. She won't talk to me, won't let me in. It's a Mitus thing. You wouldn't understand. And don't think you can kiss *that* problem away."

"Trust me to do that and more." He cupped her chin in his hand and tipped her face towards him.

Panicked by his intimate words and loving touch, she jerked away. "Please, can we drop this? I don't want to talk. I want to fuck. Isn't that what we're doing together? *Fucking?*"

On a growl, he dropped her hand and steeled his back. His height and width dwarfed her. Gripping the steering wheel, he stared straight ahead, then threw the gearshift into drive.

"Wait." She pressed her hand on his thigh. "I'm sorry. That was me venting. You've been wonderful. Amazing, really. Thank you for everything, Crockett." Her rueful smile was her feeble attempt to shove away the sorrow.

"Dammit, Alex." He shoved the gearshift back into park. With his hands clutching both sides of her face, he leaned over and kissed her. One worshipful kiss that shorted her brain and turned her insides into molten lava.

"Ohgod," she moaned. "That might have helped, a little."

He kissed her again. Her eyes fluttered open. Large blue orbs blinked back. Her heart skipped a beat. She wanted to get so lost in those eyes, in all of him. But she couldn't. No way would she allow herself to become emotionally involved with him again.

"Let's go home." With all the confidence and ease of a man in complete control, he slipped back into traffic.

CROCKETT'S HEAD ACHED. THOUGH he knew what needed to be done, he did *not* want to be the one to do it. But someone had to tell Alex the truth. He had no idea what history haunted the Mitus family because Colton never talked about his past. When they'd been freshmen, Colton mentioned his twin had died and his father had left shortly thereafter. That was all he'd ever said. Not wanting to pry, Crockett asked nothing. And neither Kimberly nor Alex spoke about Cain or Wilson. The only reminder that their brother, Cain, had existed was a single framed picture in Kimberly's home office. The three young Mitus kids sat smooshed like sardines on a worn, leather recliner, their giant smiles a somber reminder of happier days.

If Kimberly had her reasons for shielding her daughter from the truth when Alex was a child, he could understand that. But she was a grown woman. *A news reporter, for God's sake.* If anyone could handle the truth, he believed Alex could. *Why in the hell does it have to be me?*

He pulled into his condo garage and parked in his spot. As they rode the elevator to his penthouse, Alexandra glanced up at him.

"We should go to Incognito tonight," she said.

"No."

She blew out a breath. "I need—"

"A hot bath and a strong drink." He hitched a brow. Not that he didn't want to sink balls deep into her while she ground against him, but tonight was not that night. Her hunch and her need to help Sage could wait.

They entered his home and, as he strode toward the bathroom, he flipped on lights. After turning on the water in the Jacuzzi, he went in search of her. She stood in front of his gas fireplace, mesmerized by the roaring flames, looking somewhat lost.

"Let's get you into the tub."

She flicked her gaze to him. "I don't want you to see me naked."

He would have laughed, but her tone and expression were so serious. "Alex, please."

"If you're joining me, put on a mask."

She's a mess. "I'm going to make you a hot toddy, but I'm not going to fuck you."

She rubbed her chest, over her heart. "I can't make love."

There it is. Did she realize she'd just given herself away? She could handle meaningless screwing but not the deep, emotional connection they'd once shared.

"No sex. Period." He was done talking. Grasping her hand, he brought her into the bathroom and stripped her out of her clothing. Though he wanted to pull her into his arms and run his hands over her beautiful curves, he stayed focused on the task. Grabbing the bag of Epsom salts from the bathroom closet, he dumped some into the steaming water.

"I'm not injured," she said while tying up her hair.

Like hell you're not. "You're tense. This soothes aching muscles." As he helped her into the tub, he forced himself *not* to peek at her beautiful breasts, her phenomenal ass, those toned legs and that beautiful back. "Push this if you want jets." He tapped a button on the porcelain. "I'll be back with your drink."

"*Ouch, ouch.* Hot." As she eased into the water, she shot him a quick smile. "It feels good."

He made her tea, added a shot of whiskey to the mug, and returned to the bathroom. Her eyes were closed and he paused to admire her. Beyond the obvious attraction, she looked peaceful. He hated that this feeling would be short-lived.

His head pounded in his temples and he ground his teeth together. He had to make the call and then, he had to tell her. She deserved to know the truth. Kimberly and Colton might treat her like a child, but this breathtaking beauty before him was every inch a woman.

She opened her eyes, studied his face. "What's wrong?"

He forced a smile, hoping to hide his angst. "Here's your hot toddy."

"I know you're doing this because I'd be homeless if you didn't put me up. So, thank you. But you don't have to go out of your way for me."

He kissed the top of her head. "Try to relax. I'll be back in a few." He closed the bathroom door to the saddest brown eyes.

Guilt filled him with dread. He'd lied to her, too, all those years ago. Even though he'd broken up with her for her sake, he was no better than anyone else trying to protect her.

He poured himself a whiskey, tossed it back, then called Colton.

"Everything okay?" Colton asked.

"Yeah. Not really. No."

"Do I need to cut my trip short and come home?"

"No. Kimberly is pushing Alex away. This isn't right. Alex deserves to know."

"Mom insisted."

"When do you listen to anyone?" Crockett asked.

"She's dying."

"Yeah, that I'm aware of."

"I want to respect her wishes," Colton said.

"You know I'm not one to overstep, but if you'd been with us tonight, you would understand. The treatment isn't working and neither is Kimberly's charade. Besides, Alex doesn't have a place to live, she's having issues at work, and she's worried sick about your mother, who she thinks is going to make a complete recovery."

"How will telling her the truth make things better?"

"It won't. But I'm going to tell her. Unless you want to fly home tomorrow and do it yourself. Believe me, my head is pounding over this one."

After a pregnant pause, Colton spoke. "I trust you. But this is going to kill her."

"I'll be here for her." Crockett ended the call.

Heaving in a breath, he strode down the hall and into his bedroom, tapping on the bathroom door before gently pushing it open. The mug was empty, the jets were blasting, and Alex had finally relaxed against the porcelain, her sweet eyes closed. *This sucks.*

When she opened them, her serene expression tore through him. He was about to shatter her world. And he wouldn't blame her if she hated him for it.

"I feel better," she said. "Do you want me to re-heat the water so you can soak?"

"I'm good," he said, holding up a towel. He hated being the bad guy.

She rose and stepped out. He wrapped her and before he could check himself, he hugged her.

Pain slashed his heart open. In some ways he was reliving the loss of Sophia. The disbelief. The immeasurable heartache. The loss of control. The overwhelming helplessness. But tonight wasn't about him or his damned feelings.

He found her a pair of his sweat pants with a drawstring. Even so, the pants hung low—too low—on her womanly hips. This exercise of dressing her was proving to be more of a challenge than he'd realized. Her moment of serenity both comforted and aroused him. Maybe he should throw her on his bed and fuck her until morning. Mind his own damned business and let Colton tell her. *No, it's got to be done.*

"I'm sleepy." She slipped his large sweatshirt over her head.

She's adorable. "So am I."

She plodded out of his bedroom. He didn't want to follow her. But he had to. She crashed on his sofa and pulled up the blanket. As he eased onto the far end of the sofa, he lifted her feet, and placed them on his lap.

"Do you want to watch TV?" she asked.

Why the hell couldn't her family have been honest with her? "I talked to Colton tonight."

She struggled to keep her eyes open. "Uh-huh."

"I told him I was going to tell you the truth."

Her eyes flew open and she jerked her feet off his lap. "About what? What have you been lying to me about?" She lurched forward, her back ramrod straight.

"Your mom isn't well."

Pain flashed in her eyes. "I know that."

"Her behavior tonight…"

"She shouldn't have been drinking. It didn't mix with the change in meds."

"Her brain cancer is terminal." He hated himself, the words tasting like poison as they spilled from him.

"*What?*" She flung off the blanket and sprang to her knees. "No, you're wrong. She told me herself, she's going to get better."

Nausea spread through him like a wildfire. "She has Gliosarcoma."

"I don't know what that is!" Her panic surged through him. "What are you saying?"

For what felt like the longest moment, he couldn't answer.

Then he said, "This type of cancer doesn't respond well to treatment. She isn't going to get better. She's dying and you deserve to know the truth." Pain pummeled his chest. "I'm so sorry."

She stared at him with disbelieving eyes. He didn't crowd her or hug her. She needed space to process the unthinkable. The unimaginable. He'd turned her world upside down.

Her gut-wrenching wail came from the deepest, darkest part of her. Then, she flew off the sofa and with both hands gripping the sides of her head, paced in front of him. "No, no, no, no, no."

She repeated the words, like a chant. He jumped up. She froze and stared into his eyes. Then, he put his arms around her.

Words escaped him as the horror washed over her face. She pounded her fists against his chest. "Nooooo! No way! You're *wrong*!"

Hauling her against him, he hugged her tightly. "I've got you. I'm right here."

Rearing back, she glared at him. "Why are *you* telling me? What business is this of yours? You aren't a Mitus. You have no idea what you're saying!" She spun away from him and crumpled to the floor, sobbing uncontrollably. "Ohmygod, ohmygod. Please, no."

He dropped by her side and pulled her into his lap. She tried resisting, but he wrapped his arms around her and wouldn't let go.

Crockett hadn't shed a tear since the day he'd learned his sister had been taken. He'd learned about the abduction from a Mitus. This moment didn't feel like he was returning the favor. A tear streaked his cheek, but he wiped her tear-stained face instead. He wanted to take all of her pain, but he couldn't. No one could.

16

DON'T SHOOT!

"Hello." With his cell phone to his ear, Crockett rolled onto his back and stared at the ceiling. In the pre-dawn hour, the tiniest glint of light filled the sky and his bedroom.

"Hey, babe." Maverick's booming voice cut through the silence.

"Easy, man, you'll wake the dead."

Alexandra bolted upright. "Is it my mom?"

"It's okay," Crockett said. "It's work. Go back to sleep."

"Jesus, you're with a woman. You never said anything."

"What's going on?" Crockett asked as Alexandra laid her head on his chest. He switched the phone to his other ear, wrapped his arm around her, and pulled her close. She felt phenomenal wedged against him. Skin on skin.

"Weather conditions are good. We're a 'Go' for running aircraft tests today."

"Time?"

"Five forty-five."

"Not *now*. What time are you *flying?*"

"Oh, right. Eleven hundred at my airpark."

"I've got a meeting I can't miss. Expect me closer to eleven thirty. Thanks for the heads up." Crockett hung up.

Alexandra didn't budge, her soft, steady breathing an indication she'd fallen back to sleep.

Last night, after she'd calmed down, she'd asked a lot of questions about Kimberly's cancer. He'd told her everything he knew, which wasn't much. When she'd asked how long her mother had, he'd answered honestly. "Colton told me three-to-six months, but the oncologist said everyone is different."

Her sadness had turned to anger. She'd threatened to give her brother a piece of her mind. He'd let her rant. When the anger had burned off, soft, quiet tears of acceptance and understanding had begun to flow. In the end, she'd thanked him for doing what her family could not.

When he'd tucked her into his bed, she'd asked him to stay. So he did. She'd snuggled into him and conked out. He'd laid awake for a while, holding her in his arms and listening to her breathe. This was the first time they'd spent the night in the same bed. Damned if he didn't want it to be for a different reason.

Her beautiful essence surrounded him. He didn't want to leave her, but he had a full day ahead of him and a major work crisis to deal with. Moving slowly, so as not to disturb her, he rolled away, then slunk out of bed. Before walking into his bathroom, he turned back. *Peaceful and so beautiful.*

After brushing his teeth, he turned on the shower faucet and stepped into the glass-enclosed marble stall.

Inasmuch as he wanted her in his bed every night, he was a realist. Sex happened at the club. But even if they did start sleeping together at his place, she would return to California once Kimberly had passed. Her move back east had always been temporary. He'd anticipated seeing her, but he'd never envisioned she'd be the one woman he'd hook up with at Incognito. And he'd certainly never expected she'd be living with him.

What didn't surprise him was the way he felt whenever she was near and every time their eyes met. Or how she belonged in his arms. Or that he'd do whatever it took to help her and keep her safe.

He turned off the water and dried himself. The body shop had repaired Alexandra's car and his mechanic had run diagnostics to ensure the vehicle was road-ready. Crockett had arranged for his cousin, Danny, to meet them at her home that evening. Unbeknownst to her, he was moving her out.

Even though she'd probably contacted the housing agency and requested a different place to live, he didn't want her moving in with another stranger. *Too risky.* Since she'd walled herself in emotionally, he'd create a no-pressure living arrangement. The lengths he would go were over the top, but he'd waited a long, long time for a second chance. No way in hell would he let her slip through his fingers.

After raking his hands through his damp hair, he stepped into his bedroom. Bedroom lights on, Alexandra bent over, making his bed. *Ah, hell.* Though she'd slept in his gym shorts and a T-shirt, her long legs hijacked his attention. A rush of heat swept through him.

She turned. Her gaze roamed down his naked body—pausing at his junk—then back up. "Good morning. Thanks for last night."

Ignoring his thickening shaft, he stepped close. She, however, glanced down.

"If you're comfortable driving, I'll drop you at my mechanic's," he said. "Your car is ready."

Her breath hitched. "I'll be okay."

He braced his spine against the need to haul her into his arms, throw her on his just-made bed and love her for hours. "Most of the roads are drivable. Be careful on the side streets."

As she peered at his chest, she shuddered in a breath. She lifted her arm and, for a second, her delicate fingers hovered inches from his skin. A groan shot out of him. Hell, he wanted her so fucking badly.

Without shifting her gaze, she ran her long, elegant fingers through her hair. And his jutting cock banged against her T-shirt. This living arrangement was proving to be one hell of a challenge. He wasn't embarrassed he had a boner. He was agitated he couldn't start his day by sinking inside her and finding pleasure in all things Alex.

Grunting out his frustration, he walked to his dresser, pulled on black boxer briefs and a white undershirt. He had to get out of his bedroom in the next five minutes or all bets were off. Sitting on his bed, he tugged on black dress socks, then retreated into his closet to dress.

"I'm going to get ready for work," she called.

We need different sleeping arrangements. Or I'm going to have a permanent case of blue balls.

On the way to his mechanic's, he told her he'd be at the Eastern Shore all afternoon, but would meet her at her home after work. "My cousin, Danny, will be joining us. We're moving you out."

"*What?* Where will I live?"

"With me." She opened her mouth to protest. "Meet me at your house at five. Don't go in without me."

After making sure her car checked out, Crockett thanked his mechanic and left. He thought twice about paying her bill, but decided against it. Her auto insurance company covered the majority of the cost. And he didn't want his good intentions to be misconstrued. She was an independent woman who could take care of her financial obligations.

On the way to his off-site meeting in DC, he called his assistant. "Ellen, I'm sorry for the early call."

"One second, Crockett." He listened while she said goodbye to her high school-aged son. "I'm back. What can I help with?"

"After my off-site meeting, I'm heading to Maverick's airpark on the Eastern Shore so I won't be in all day."

"You have three afternoon meetings. I'll reschedule."

"Thanks. I need your help with something. Please order a

bedroom suite and have it rush delivered. Use my personal credit card. You know the store I like. Henredon furniture or the equivalent. A display model would work."

"For the master bedroom?"

"No, guest room. Room size is fourteen by sixteen. Something tasteful and neutral."

"I've got to jot this down." After a pause, she said, "Go on."

"Queen bed, bureau, and two night tables."

"I'll purchase a wall mirror for over the bureau. You'll need lamps and bed linens. I'll handle everything."

"I'll be at my karate competition all day Saturday, but the concierge can let the deliverymen in."

"*This* Saturday?" Ellen asked. "That's gonna cost you."

"Whatever it takes."

"Got it."

"Thanks, you're an angel." He ended the call.

Since his parents were planning a spring visit, he needed furniture, but he wanted this expedited for Alexandra.

After his client meeting, he texted Maverick. "On my way." He headed east, eventually jumping on Route 50 toward Maryland's Eastern Shore.

His phone rang and he hit the speaker button. "Hey, Decker. Tell me you've isolated the reason for the random device failures."

"Sure did," Decker replied. "And since that only took me ten minutes, I used the extra time to solve global warming *and* I've devised a plan to end world hunger and—"

"You pulled another all-nighter, didn't you?"

"No, but I'm holding it together with caffeine. I've got the QA team teed up and I'm overseeing the project going forward. Charlie's downed craft will arrive in the next day or two. I need to go over a few things with you. You got time now?"

An hour and a half later, Crockett pulled into Ashton Hott's airpark. He and Decker had outlined a plan for analyzing the problem and a different one for freezing the sale of further UAVs until the issue had been sufficiently resolved. That major setback had knotted his guts.

Exiting his truck, he slid on his shades, pulled on his parka and headed toward the lone hangar on Maverick's private property. The front door flew open and Maverick stepped outside. Though the temperature hovered at forty-three degrees, the bright sun and lack of wind were the perfect weather conditions to test his crafts.

"You made great time." He shook Crockett's hand. "Who's the chick?"

Crockett laughed. "Couldn't wait, could you?"

"Hell, no. You're a total workaholic."

"With good reason."

"I know that." Maverick's expression softened. "So, who is she?"

"An old friend."

Grinning, Maverick added, "With benefits."

"It's complicated." Crockett pulled on his leather gloves.

"Aren't all women? So, does your gal have a name?"

"Alexandra Reed."

"Why does that name sound familiar?" Maverick asked, knotting his brow.

"Alexandra Reed *Mitus*. Colton's sister."

"Ah, hell. She left la-la land?"

"Temporarily."

Maverick slapped Crockett's back. "I hope it works out. You've had a thing for that woman for—"

"For fucking ever."

The two men laughed.

"C'mon in," said Maverick. "I'll grab my team."

The metal structure resembled a Quonset hut. Maverick opened the front door and they walked inside. The open space housed one large conference table with several chairs, and enough vacant floor space to line up the crafts on the cement flooring.

Crockett admired the Eagle, three Falcons, and six Spy Flies like a proud papa. After introductions, Maverick's eight-person team collected their assigned aircraft and set off for the landing strip three hundred feet from the building.

Over the next three hours, Maverick's ground pilots put each of the devices through a series of rigorous tests. The aircraft soared, hovered, dove, glided and landed without a glitch. This group of aircraft had responded with the precision expected from a Wilde Innovations's product. Even so, the angst surrounding the failed aircraft still hung over his head like a threatening storm cloud.

After each drone passed its final test, Maverick paired his pilots to fly the crafts in tandem. The majority of his personnel used military-grade tablets, two directed the crafts via cell phones, and one used a hand-held transmitter base.

When the rigorous flights had been completed, Maverick signed off on each one and shot Crockett a grin. "You've got some damned good products, brother. I'd be a paper-pusher dreaming of this life if it wasn't for you."

"Thanks. You were born for the thrill of action. Hell, you live for danger. You would have found your adventure without me. But I am relieved they flew as directed."

As the team headed back toward the building to ready the craft for shipment, Maverick pulled Crockett aside. "Relax. These babies performed flawlessly. My rogue Eagle was a one-off. You've got nothing to worry about."

But Crockett knew differently. "Thanks for including me today," he said and extended his hand. Per usual, Maverick bear-hugged him instead. "You're like a damned teddy bear."

"Aw, shucks, that's what all the girls say," said Maverick.

"I've got to get back."

"Meeting your girl?"

Crockett smiled. "Yeah and I'm running late."

ALEXANDRA PARALLEL PARKED IN the only available spot on her block. Glancing down the street at the darkened house, relief washed over her. She'd been worried the partygoers would still be there, but the streets had been plowed and the mild temperatures had turned the remaining snow into a slushy mess.

Ten minutes after five. *Crockett's late.* She shoved her hand into her bag to fish out her cell, but it wasn't in its usual spot. After digging through the contents, she confirmed the phone was missing. And it wasn't in her coat pockets either. "Dammit. I left it at work or at the mechanic."

Since the house was dark, she let herself in and flipped on the living room light. The room was neat; the drunken fools long gone. Eager to get packed, she trotted upstairs and into her bedroom. Though anxious about moving in with Crockett, she would not miss this place.

Tossing her coat and handbag on the bed, she pulled her suitcase and carry-on bag out from beneath her bed. To save time, she'd leave everything from her closet on hangers. Working quickly, she opened bureau drawers, grabbed her undergarments and loaded up the suitcase. The last drawer was filled with several masks. As she set those in the bag, the stairs creaked. Her blood ran cold.

"Crockett?" She stilled. "Is that you?"

A shadow darkened the staircase wall and her heart rate skyrocketed. Ben appeared, beer bottle in hand. His lascivious grin sent adrenaline spiking through her. Standing in the doorway, he blocked her only escape route. "I've been waiting for you."

Though she tasted the panic, she hitched her hands on her hips. He glanced at her chest. "Get lost, Ben."

"Relax, baby." He stepped into the room and set the bottle on the bureau. When she tried to run past him, he grabbed her and shoved her against the wall. "You're not going anywhere." He pressed his palms to the wall, sandwiching her in.

She gagged from the stench of stale beer mixed with his pungent body odor. "My boyfr—fiancé—will be here any minute. You'd better let me go."

"Let's get to know each other." His eyes turned dark and he licked his lips. "I'll bet you taste good."

WHEN CROCKETT TURNED DOWN Alexandra's residential street, he sensed something was wrong. Besides the fact that Alex hadn't responded to his calls or texts, the lights were on in her home. Just because he'd told her to wait, didn't mean she'd listened. He slammed on the brakes, double-parked out front, grabbed the duffel bags and jumped out of the truck. As he strode toward the front door, Danny jogged down the sidewalk.

"She went in without us," Crockett said.

Though Crockett wanted to believe Ben wouldn't be there, he anticipated the worst-case scenario, hence his armed cousin. It wasn't like he couldn't take on the thug himself, but he knew his limits. Firearms being at the top of the list.

As they reached the front door, Danny said, "I've got a second weapon—"

"*NO!*" Alexandra shouted. *"Let me go!"*

Her scream sent Crockett throwing open the door and bolting up the stairs.

"Wait!" Danny yelled, but Crockett was already at the top.

"Well, lookie who's here," Ben said as Crockett sprang into the room. "Now it's my turn to kick your ass." Charging Crockett, he took a swing.

While ducking Ben's right hook, Crockett thrust his head into Ben's torso, yanked Ben's feet up, sending them both crashing to the floor. Crockett wrapped his hands around Ben's throat and pressed his thumbs against his Adam's apple.

"Crockett!" yelled Danny. "*Stop.*" Crockett tightened his hold. Ben's face turned tomato red. "Let him go!" Danny exclaimed.

Releasing his grip, Crockett pushed off Ben and rose. "Lucky for you, I brought back up. If I hadn't, I would have fucking killed you."

Danny aimed his Glock at Ben. "Roll over, face down. Clasp your hands behind your head."

Ben flattened on the hardwood and did as he was told. "Jesus, don't shoot me."

After holstering his weapon, Danny cuffed Ben's wrists behind his back and frisked him. In addition to a wallet, Danny pulled out a vial of crack and a baggie of marijuana.

"Get on your knees, then sit with your back against the wall," Danny commanded.

As Ben got into place, Crockett knelt next to Alexandra who'd scampered into the corner, her eyes big as full moons, her mouth agape. She threw her arms around him. Though she was safe, his heart beat a frenetic rhythm while she trembled in his grip. "I've got you."

"Hey, man," said Ben. "This is my girlfriend's roommate. We were just catching up."

Alexandra scrambled to her feet. "Catching up?" Her eyes narrowed. "You held me against my will, for starters."

"Whoa, whoa, whoa, we was just talkin'," Ben said.

"You want to press charges?" Danny asked her.

"You bet I do."

"Press charges?" Ben asked. "For what?"

"Ms. Mitus said you held her against her will," Danny said. "That's a federal charge of kidnapping."

"Fuck me," Ben said, his shoulders sagging.

As Danny phoned for back up, he flipped open Ben's wallet.

"Run a check on a Benjamin Jenkins." He read the driver's license number to the FBI analyst. "And send a cage car."

Crockett needed to put his fist through a wall. "You got this?" he asked his cousin.

"Yeah, time to get Alexandra out," Danny replied.

Without making eye contact, she entered her closet. He followed. They worked in a chilling silence, focused on the task at hand. He'd deal with her reckless behavior later. For now, he needed to get her the hell out before he killed that motherfucker.

After filling the duffel bags with shoeboxes, he flung them over his shoulder. Then he grabbed handfuls of hangers and draped the clothing over his arm. Loaded up like a pack mule, Crockett exited her closet.

He and Alexandra went downstairs and outside to Crockett's truck. Using his key fob, he retracted the cover, then laid her clothing in the bed. Rarely overcome by emotion, Crockett was still too angry to speak.

"I'm sorry," she said, breaking the silence. "I made a terrible mistake based on an incorrect assumption." She placed her duffel bag next to the clothes. "The house was dark. Ben must've been in the basement. I put you and Danny at risk." Rubbing her arms over her wool coat, she tilted her face to his. "I messed up, Crockett."

He stroked her arms. Had to confirm she'd stopped trembling. "You placed yourself in a dangerous situation and scared the hell out of me."

With a sweet smile, she leaned up and kissed his cheek.

"It's going to take a helluva lot more than a peck to get back on my good side." Grasping her hand, he headed toward the front door.

"Alexandra! Hey!" Mandy bustled down the sidewalk. "Ben's here. You guys wanna grab some dinner?"

"I'm moving out," Alexandra said.

"*What? Now?*"

"Your boyfriend is being arrested for kidnapping. Fortunately, Crockett and—"

"What?" Mandy gaped at her. "Kidnapping who?"

"Me," Alexandra said. "He's crazy and dangerous."

"Ben has talked about you nonstop," said Mandy. "I'm so sorry."

"Mandy, you might want to change your locks and get yourself a new boyfriend," said Crockett. "Alex, let's finish packing."

Mandy stared at him, her face ghost-white. "Yeah, wow. I...I don't know what to say." In silence, she followed Alexandra and Crockett inside and upstairs.

With his cell phone pressed to his ear, Danny asked, "How long until back up arrives?" He listened, then said, "Got it. Thanks." After hanging up, he addressed Ben. "Mr. Jenkins, you have an outstanding warrant for conspiracy to distribute narcotics across state lines. My buddies at the DEA will be paying you a visit in your jail cell."

"If you need additional evidence, I snapped these the last time I was here." Crockett showed Danny the pictures on his phone. "We interrupted quite a party."

"I can see that." Danny eyed the photos. "Forward those to me."

Alexandra handed Mandy her house key.

"The cage car is here." Danny unholstered his gun. "Please get up, Mr. Jenkins. We're going downstairs."

Once Ben had been loaded into the back of the car, Danny said goodbye to Crockett and Alexandra.

"I'm so sorry," Alexandra said.

"Are you okay?" Danny asked.

"Yes," she said, but Crockett wasn't convinced.

Crockett hugged his cousin. "Thanks for doing this. Jesus, I owe you. I would have killed that son of a bitch."

With hands on his hips, Danny turned his full attention on Alexandra. "*You.*" He pointed. "Stay out of trouble." Danny climbed into his SUV and drove away.

"I'm beginning to think that's an impossible task," Crockett said to her. "Follow me home. Are you capable of that?"

She swallowed. "Yes."

"I have a second assigned parking spot. Park to my right."

"Thank you, Crockett." She hugged him. Though still angry, he hugged her hard. *She scared the living hell out of me.*

She stepped away and he shot her a stern stare. "On the way home, you might want to figure out a *proper* way to thank me."

17

HOME

AN EXPLOSION OF CLOTHES, shoes and masks covered the floor of Crockett's guest room, which now looked like a ladies boutique. *How can one woman wear all this?* The space had been empty, but then, so had his life.

Enter Alexandra. Chaos everywhere.

He hated leaving her, especially after her traumatic run-in with Ben, but he wouldn't break his commitment to his kids. Plus, he needed to take out his aggression on a punching bag. Kneeling next to her, he peered into her eyes. "You sure you're okay?"

"Positive." She glanced at his black *gi*, her gaze hovering over the V exposing his chest. Her sharp inhale landed in his groin. "Club later?"

"Absolutely." Breaking their steamy connection, he tapped the Incognito app on his phone. "There's a suite available at ten."

"Book it." Determination replaced the lingering fear banking in her eyes. "If you stand in the hallway, outside the lounge, you'll be able to see Jase and Francois escorting men into the suite."

"Which room is it?"

"Left out of the greeting room. Last one on the right before turning the corner. It's the only one that's unmarked."

"Got it. Where will you be?"

"I'll meet you in the lounge. If you see Dracule hanging around, don't scare him away. He might prove himself useful. He's king of rejuvenation."

"I don't trust that weasel." He offered her a spare house key and underground parking garage door opener.

"Thank you." As she hooked the key onto her keychain, the atmosphere turned electric. Just like that, his home had become theirs.

Before he could check himself, he stroked her back. The pull to touch her too powerful to ignore. If she were his, he'd kiss her senseless.

Fuck it.

His mouth was on hers, his pent-up energy impossible to contain. Her throaty moan spurred him forward. Her lips parted. When his tongue slipped inside, she fisted his hair and pulled. But leaving her wanting more would send a stronger message, so he stopped. Abruptly. Like kissing her hadn't fazed him. Everything about Alex, including her wild eyes and rapid breathing, had turned him hard. But he had to leave. *Now.*

He stood, grateful the *gi* jacket hid his boner. "I'll be at Rodele Martial Arts if you need to reach me."

A tiny whimper floated from her lips, her gaze still fixed on his. Then, she broke eye contact and blinked, several times. "Oh, my phone is missing. I left it at work or with the mechanic."

He sighed. That explained why she hadn't responded to his earlier texts. "Alexandra, what am I going to do with you?"

As she arched her eyebrow, the corners of her mouth tugged up. That answered that question.

ALEXANDRA HAD FORCED HERSELF to keep it together, but Ben had terrified her. With a glass of Chianti in hand, she soaked in the

Jacuzzi. The scalding water temperature relaxed her knotted muscles, while her thoughts drifted to Crockett. When left with a moment to daydream, that's where her mind strayed. Though devastated over her mom, and frustrated about her job, Crockett had been her lighthouse in a stormy sea. Being in his home, surrounded by his things and knowing that he would return here, day in and day out, planted a seedling of hope in her heart. *Maybe I could let down my guard and give this a second chance.*

Fear slammed her chest. Her eyes flew open. *So much for my moment of Zen.* She stopped the jets and exited the tub. Being in a relationship with Crockett wasn't going to work. Especially for the short run. History had proven that.

The doorbell chimed. Alexandra wrapped herself in Crockett's bathrobe and hurried down the hall. After spying an attractive woman through the peephole, her heart dropped. She'd assumed he didn't have anyone special in his life. Had she assumed wrong? She opened the door.

The woman's megawatt smile fizzled. "I'm here to see Crockett Wilde." She eyed the oversized man's robe.

"He's not home. Can I help you?"

Her jaw ticked. "I'm Tammy, his realtor."

Seemed late for a pop-in. "Do you have copies of anything you need to leave with me?"

"No, my visit is personal."

Alexandra had no idea what this woman was up to, or whether Crockett was screwing his realtor, but she didn't have the time or the patience to deal with her. "I'll tell him you dropped by."

Tammy's eyes narrowed. "And you are?"

"With Crockett." Her heart bloomed at the thought. "So, if he never thanked you, let me. You found us a fantastic place to live."

"You can't be that important. He never even mentioned you." As the agent tightened her raincoat sash, Alexandra spotted a diamond wedding band.

"Would your husband appreciate this late night *personal* call?"

"Why, you little bitch."

Arching her eyebrow, Alexandra said, "I call it like I see it. Please, no more surprise visits." She closed the door, flipped the deadbolt, and marched into the kitchen. *I might have overstepped. Nah. She wasn't right for him anyway.*

She didn't know if Crockett would grab something to eat before Incognito, but when she was done with him, he'd be famished. She pulled up "Mayhem" by artist Imelda May and, as she sliced mushrooms, peppers, and onions, her spirits lifted for the first time since she'd returned. She couldn't remember the last time she'd cooked dinner for a man. After sautéing the chicken with the vegetables, she added rice to the steamer and set the timer.

With him in mind, she dressed in a lacy push-up bra, low-cut cashmere sweater, and black leather skirt that brushed against her thigh-high boots. On went the blonde wig, then a heavy dose of eye makeup. Lastly, she tied on a black and pink masquerade mask. Eager to sleuth and play, she headed to the club.

On her way, she wondered how she'd get Sage to open up about her bruises. Anticipating she'd have one hell of a time even locating her, Alexandra refused to get discouraged. Somehow she'd find that timid employee. She parked and headed upstairs.

Cozy club members lined the red sofa, so, as they agreed, she moseyed into the lounge. Wall-to-wall people made it impossible for her to slink over to the bar. Instead, she snagged a booth tucked in the corner.

Seconds later, the familiar server with purple-streaked hair appeared. "Hey, good to see you."

"Wendy, right?"

"Yup. I'm good with faces, or in this case, masks, but can't remember names. No offense. I've got over thirty cousins and I still get them confused."

"I'm Electra."

"Yes, you are. We've got a great new red wine. How 'bout a glass or maybe a spritzer?"

"I'll take a top-shelf manhattan with an extra cherry."

"I'm impressed. Being a southern belle, I figured you'd want something sweet with a cutesy pink umbrella sticking out of it."

Alexandra laughed. "Even us southern gals like the burn of bourbon now and again."

"Sorry. My big mouth gets me into more trouble. Some guy I waited on the other night said something to Francois about a comment I made." She glanced over her shoulder. "Now I've got a target on my back." Wendy zoomed off and returned with her drink but said nothing more.

Fifteen minutes later, Crockett walked in. Her heart leapt. The quarter zip black sweater stretched against his bulging pecs. Black pants showed off his strong, muscular thighs. And a black mask framed those piercing blue eyes. *Simple, elegant and smokin' hot.*

When his eyes met hers, heat shot through her belly, settling between her thighs. With a cool smile, she slipped out of the booth to greet him. As he approached, he studied her like she was a priceless work of art. Inches away, his clean scent wafted in her direction.

"Evening, Electra." Brushing his mouth against her ear, he whispered, "Chicken was delicious. Can't wait for dessert."

His husky voice rumbled through her sex-starved body. Desperate to touch him, she curled her hand around his hard bicep. "Good to see you, Huntah."

"May I join you?"

"Please." She slipped back onto the bench. Instead of sitting across, he slid next to her. Close enough that their legs touched. Her body came alive. She'd craved him all day. Before she could check herself, she caressed his thigh.

A raspy groan shot out of him.

"Good workout?" she asked.

"Not as good as the one I'm going to have."

Her nipples tightened and she glanced at his mouth. "Naughty, naughty, Huntah." But a whisper of a smile danced on her lips. *I can't wait, either.*

Wendy approached the table. "Good evening, sir. Can I bring you a beverage?"

"Vodka martini, dry."

"Right away." She left.

"I don't need a drink," he murmured. "I need you."

"Patience." She stroked his forearm. "Did you see management escort a man to the suite?"

"No and I watched from the hallway. How long do we have the room?"

"An hour."

"Then you owe me an hour. *At home.*"

"Huntah, that seems a little forward. I hardly know you."

The waitress returned with his martini. "Wendy, do you think you could find Sage?" Alexandra asked.

Crockett pulled out two Ben Franklins. "One for you. Keep the change from the second. Electra is anxious to see her friend."

After quickly stashing one of the bills, Wendy flicked her gaze toward the kitchen. Her grateful smile dropped and she cleared her throat. "Thank you, sir. I'll see what I can do."

Jase sidled over. "See what you can do about what?"

"Um...I..." mumbled Wendy.

"Book us more time in our suite," Crockett said.

While fidgeting under Jase's scrutiny, Wendy refused to look at him. *She's intimidated, too.*

"Good," said Jase before addressing Wendy. "If it's booked, let me know. I'll see what I can do."

"Yes, sir." Wendy peeked at Alexandra before ducking into the crowd.

"Electra, Hunter. How are you enjoying your evening?" Jase asked.

Crockett's expression hardened. "Jase."

"Electra, may I have a word?"

"Could you excuse me, Huntah?"

Crockett pushed out of the booth so Alexandra could slide out. Then he sat back down and sipped his drink.

Jase stepped close and she whiffed his liquor breath. "I come bearing good news. Your five-thousand dollar debt has been paid."

Had she heard him correctly? "Pardon me?"

"You don't owe Incognito anything. You're free and clear."

"Paid by whom?"

"Anonymous." When he drew back his lips, his grin resembled a snarl. "Congratulations."

Her stomach dropped. This grand gesture didn't feel like a random act of kindness.

One of the wait staff approached Jase. After speaking with the employee, the GM excused himself and hurried off. Alexandra slipped back into the booth. Pressing the cocktail glass to her lip, she took a hearty sip. And another. Anxiety pressed in on her.

"What did he want?" Crockett asked.

"An anonymous member paid my five thousand dollar debt."

Crockett's upper lip twisted in a snarl. "I don't need three guesses to know who did that. That horny old man will want something in return."

A sudden chill from within made her shiver. *Yes, he will.*

HELLO, DETECTIVE

CROCKETT EYED THE POLICE officer's uniform hanging on a hook in the "Frisk Me" suite. "Good thing I'm an undercover detective."

She sashayed close. "Not into the costume?"

He cupped her chin, kissed her soft lips. "If you need it, I'll wear it."

"I need you."

Time to indulge his woman in the ultimate escape. "You'll have to work for it, baby." He shot her a cool smile.

A soft moan escaped her lips. "Don't I get a phone call?"

"No, you don't. You're in *my* interrogation room and you'll do as I say."

"Mmm, yes, sir," she purred.

Compared to the other suites with their cozy beds, fluffed pillows and quality linens, this room was bare-bones. Half the room was set up for a police interrogation. A metal table was secured to the floor with steel supports surrounded by four aluminum chairs. A lone bulb in a metal shade dangled from the ceiling over the center of the table. The other half of the room resembled a jail cell with a full size cot, on a metal frame, stark white linens, and two plain pillows.

"Sit." He spun a chair around.

As soon as she did, he swung another chair around, straddled the hard seat and eased down.

Her gaze swept over his face and down his chest. "Why'd you bring me here, officer?" she asked, batting her lashes.

"It's *Detective*. And I ask the questions." He leaned close. Her eyes turned black with passion. "You were seen leaving the jewelry store at the time of the robbery, Ms. Electra."

"Yeah, so? That doesn't mean anything."

He interrogated her about the missing bag of loose diamonds. As the story unfolded, she came alive. Her voice dropped. Her erect nipples pressed against the low-cut sweater. She sat tall, crossed her legs. The mini skirt rode up her beautiful thighs and he resisted the urge to stroke her silky skin.

Every subtle action—the way she ran her tongue over her lower lip, a lingering glance, her sharp intake of breath—churned his growing need.

"If you've hidden the diamonds, I'll find them. I need to perform a cavity search." Her breath caught and her deep, throaty groan made his balls tighten. "Remove your boots."

She slowly unzipped one and removed it, held it upside down and shook it. "No jewels hidden here." She repeated the action for the other boot. "Satisfied?" She smirked at him.

"Hardly." Unable to resist, he stroked her beautiful thigh. Up and down. Twice. Then he pushed out of the chair and kicked it aside. "Stand up. You probably stored the diamonds in your bra."

With a gleam in her eyes, she rose.

He stepped close and grazed her nipples with the back of his hand. Her gritty groan sent desire pounding through him. With care not to disrupt her mask or her wig, he helped her remove the cashmere top.

She arched toward him, letting her head fall back, revealing her swan-like neck. Despite her body language, her jagged breath, and how her sultry gaze stayed locked on his, he'd make her wait. He'd continue the fantasy to a frenzying state so that when he finally took her, she would shatter beneath him.

"Take off your bra." His gaze stayed locked on hers until she dangled the frilly undergarment. "No diamonds here, either."

He lowered his head to taste her pert nibs. Heat infused him as he sucked and bit one, and then the other. Her sexy sounds pounded a trail straight to his cock.

"Turn around," he ordered. When she did, he stroked her beautiful bottom before unzipping her butt-molding skirt. It, too, dropped to the floor. "Remove your thong."

Rather than pulling the undergarment down, she slipped her thumbs inside the lace, bent over at the waist, and slowly dragged them over her beautiful ass. With a hungry glint in her eyes, she glanced over her shoulder. He smacked her ass and she yelped.

"Turn back towards me and open your mouth."

"Yes, sir."

Instead of waiting for him, she lifted his hand and slid his index finger into her mouth. With her sultry gaze cemented on his, she sucked and licked. Shock waves traveled up his arm. After withdrawing his finger, she murmured, "I can't wait to suck you for real."

Need thrummed through him. "You're a sneaky one, but I'll find them," he said, staying in character. He pulled out a latex glove from the box on the wall, snapped it on and coated his fingers in lubrication. "Bend over. Do you understand what I'm about to do?"

She moaned. "Yes, sir. Completely."

With his ungloved hand, he stroked her long, lean thigh until his hand bumped against her ass. A soft hiss escaped her lips. Heat flushed his amped-up body and he smacked her ass. On a yelp, she lowered herself onto her elbows.

"If you don't want me to check every cavity, tell me."

"I want it. I need it. *Please.*"

Wild, naughty Electra. He stroked her anus, eliciting a series of shudders and moans. "Do. Not. Move."

Though she obeyed his command, her body trembled with need, her shoulders rising and falling with each jagged breath.

He slipped a finger inside, drew it out. Again, he circled her opening. Small, gentle motions designed to tease, to torment, to excite. She ground out a dark, edgy groan, then bit out, "I love how you do that."

Using a tender touch, he slipped two fingers inside. He thrust gently, again and again, until her husky groans made his knees go weak. "No diamonds, there, either," he said, removing his fingers. "You're a sneaky one. But I'll find them." He pulled off the glove and dropped it in the trash. "Put your foot on the chair, Ms. Electra. I have one more search to complete."

Without hesitation, she set her foot on the chair. Moving painstakingly slow, he caressed her thigh, moving higher on each upstroke. Up went his hand until he reached the apex between her legs.

"Oh, Detective."

Her eyes fluttered closed. Her breath came hard and fast, her coos thundering in his ears. He caressed her pussy, slipped two fingers inside. She ground against his thrusts, groaning and mewling.

Her erotic sounds undid him.

He thrust with merciless strokes, but as soon as he rubbed her engorged clit, her insides tightened around his fingers, so he withdrew them. She was too close to orgasm. "No diamonds there. But I'm not done searching you."

He snaked one hand around her waist and pulled her flush against him.

Her hardened nibs beckoned for his mouth, so he obliged. He sucked for his enjoyment, bit and pinched them for hers. Her knees buckled and she grabbed him to keep from falling.

He was done playing. No more talk of diamonds or jewelry heists. Time to fuck. First, with his mouth. He hauled her into the jail cell. "Lie down and raise your arms over your head. You're a flight risk and I'm going to make sure you stay put."

After he cuffed her wrists to the bars at the head of the bed, he eyed her long and lean body. Hot, naked and all his. "I can't wait to pleasure you. Spread your legs."

The wicked glimmer in her eyes reminded him of a feral cat. "Is this how you're going to get me to open up?"

"Whatever it takes."

Planking over her, he laved her breasts.

"Bite me."

A quick tug of her tender flesh and she responded by jerking on the restraints. As he trailed a path down her body, she responded to his every touch, every pinch, each bite with a shudder or a moan.

By the time his mouth had reached the apex between her legs, she'd lifted her masked face to watch. "You feel amazing."

When he kissed her inner thigh, she murmured, "I shouldn't need your mouth on me as much as I do." Those last words came out in a whoosh of a whisper, as if she were sharing a fantastic secret.

"This is a critical part of the interrogation."

As soon as he tucked a second pillow under her head, she bent her knees and spread her legs. With a tender flick of his tongue on her most sensitive area, he began. The build was slow and sensual, but when she'd lift her ass off the mattress, he'd slow back down or stop altogether. He'd take her right up to the edge, then deny her.

"Please, I'm begging you," she whispered, her body shaking with desire.

As he slipped three fingers inside her, he stroked her clit with his tongue, hard.

"Yes, oh, so good." Her erratic breathing and bed thrashing

signaled her orgasm. He threw his arm across her hips to secure her, forcing the energy straight to her core.

"*Oh, Huntah,*" she cried, the orgasm rocking her.

In seconds, his mouth found hers and he kissed her. Pleasure spiraled through him. "Do you want me to uncuff you?" he asked between kisses.

"No," she gasped out. "Hurry."

He stripped off his clothes, fished a condom from his pocket and rolled it over himself. He was done role-playing. He planked over her and, with his shaft in hand, drove himself inside. More than the euphoria, he felt complete. Even at this sex club, he couldn't deny how right they felt coupled together.

Her smoldering gaze met his. He smiled. Couldn't help himself. She was too pretty, too sexy, too delicious. The smell of their arousal hung heavy in the air.

For several seconds he stared into her eyes, drowning in everything Alex. "Deeper," she said and wrapped her beautiful legs around his back, anchoring him in place.

He couldn't thrust slowly. Slow had left the building thirty minutes ago. Even patient Crockett had his limits. Wild Hunter was filled with explosive energy. He gritted his teeth, his hands owning her supple body. "I've got to fuck you, baby."

"Ah, yes."

He claimed her with a rough, hard kiss while he wrapped her in his arms and thrust, hard and fast, again and again. "I can't get enough of you."

"Take me. I need you. I need this."

The orgasm shot out of him, curling his toes and shorting his mind. The love in her eyes took his breath away. She might not be able to say the words, but she couldn't hide her true feelings. Not from him. Even in a kink club they'd managed to eke out a tiny slice of heaven, if only for a fleeting moment.

"Without the evidence, I can't hold you, Ms. Electra." He kissed her and withdrew. "You're free to leave, but know this: you've been the highlight of my law enforcement career."

She laughed. "I have to hand it to you, Detective. You're phenomenal at your job. I'm tempted to take up a life of crime just so that you'll search me again."

With a grin, he removed the handcuffs. "You don't need to break the law to get me to do this to you again. All you have to do is ask and I'm all yours."

"I'll keep that in mind." She kissed him.

He pushed off the cot. "I'm going to hang out for a few extra minutes. Catch a glimpse if I can."

Her grateful smile turned him into putty. "Thank you for doing that for me."

When they finished dressing, he handed her his phone. "I don't like you being without one."

With his phone in hand, she kissed him and left the suite.

Though they'd role-played, this connection felt different. Crockett wasn't one to dwell, but he believed they were making progress. *Slow and steady.*

He left the suite and powered down the hallway, moving through the loitering couples. After ordering a whiskey at the bar, he walked across the hall and eased onto the red sofa. If Jase or Francois paraded past, he'd spot them. But almost twenty minutes into his stay, he hadn't seen any suspicious activity and decided to call it.

As he approached the elevator, the doors slid open. Crockett stepped aside. Two masked men breezed by. Dracule had arrived at eleven forty-five on a weeknight. And this time he'd brought along a squirrelly-looking buddy.

This should be interesting.

Dracule walked through the greeting room, stood in the hallway and glanced in both directions. The other man waited by the reception counter adjusting his mask and fidgeting. *A first-timer.*

A moment later, Jase hurried over and shook the other man's hand. When Dracule's guest offered Jase cash, Jase refused the money and whispered a reply. The guest shoved the money back into his pocket and the three men walked in the direction of the unmarked suite. As Alex had predicted, Jase tapped his card over the sensor, pushed open the door, and gestured for them to step inside. He followed and closed the door behind him.

Crockett wasn't sure what was considered *normal* behavior at an erotic club, but he had to agree with Alex. He couldn't think of a legitimate reason for Jase to join them. If those two men were going to be intimate, they didn't need the GM tucking them into bed.

Several moments later, Jase rounded the corner, coming from the opposite direction, and disappeared into his office. *She's right. He's up to something.*

Exhaustion settled on him. He needed sleep, preferably with a leggy brunette wrapped around him. He punched the elevator button, the doors slid open and he got in. As they closed, a thin, masked woman, with her arm in a sling, appeared. Assuming she wanted to get in, he stabbed the open button, but too late. "Sorry," he said to no one.

As he drove out of the parking garage, he blurted, "Oh, Jesus, that was Sage."

19

THE INTERVIEW

CROCKETT COULD NOT GET a damned break. Decker's analysis of Maverick's rogue Eagle concluded a non-specific one-time anomaly. AKA: Inconclusive findings. Crockett didn't buy that load of crap. On a resounding grunt, he smacked his laptop shut.

Decker startled, but kept staring out the window of Crockett's seventh floor corner office. "Pretty much everyone is staring at their phones. It's a wonder they all don't get hit by a bus."

Crockett joined him at the window. Snarled traffic moved in tight bundles from light to light while throngs of bundled pedestrians skittered beneath a gray sky.

Things didn't come easily for Crockett, but that never slowed him down. He'd dig deeper, concentrate harder, revisit and reexamine problems until he got to the root of the issue. He'd burn the midnight oil and work weekends. And he believed the pulse of his success came from collaboration. That was how Crockett Wilde rolled and nothing would change that; not even the recent equipment failures.

But now wasn't the time to get into the details of the report with Decker. That conversation would result in a heated stalemate. Alexandra was interviewing members of his team for her tech story and he wanted to ensure his most valued employee had a good attitude. No need to piss Decker off, especially since he was against the interview in the first place.

"Alexandra Reed is due here any minute," Crockett said.

"Yeah, I saw your email," Decker replied. "Not loving your decision."

"We won a contest. Time to put on our game faces and show the viewers a few gadgets they'll think are cool. Ten minutes after the program airs, people will forget about it. If we refuse, the media will hound us because they'll think we're hiding something."

"We *are* hiding things," Decker said.

"Right, but we don't want to draw attention to that, *especially* now. If a reporter—and that includes Alexandra Reed—finds out about our device failures, we've got a whole new set of problems. Maverick is loyal. Charlie Bowen from DHS is staying quiet for now. If word gets out, we aren't the only ones the media will hound. Let's do the feel-good interview and move on."

"Got it," Decker said, but his curt tone belied his answer. "What tables do you want covered?"

"All but the NVGs. Take out two of the original mini-drones and set those on the same table. Can you stay in the lab with them?"

"No problem."

Crockett's intercom buzzed. "Yes."

"Are you in there?" Ellen asked. "Never mind. You answered. Sorry, I'm a little out of sorts."

"What's wrong?"

"I'm not comfortable in front of the camera. Ms. Reed is here. Do you want me to—"

"I'll handle it."

"Yes, sir." The line went dead.

"I'll cover the tables." Decker trotted out.

While Ellen could have escorted Alexandra and her team into the lab, he needed to see her, even if just for a moment.

When he'd gotten home the previous evening, she'd already crashed on his sofa. This morning she'd left for work before he had a chance to tell her about Dracule and Sage. He needed her in his bed, his arms, and his life. Not on his damned sofa.

As Crockett powered down the hall, his heartbeat kicked up. As he entered reception, she turned to greet him. Her beauty and confidence sent energy pinging through him. Though she'd stepped onto his turf, she commanded the space. She might be his Goth Girl, but the journalist standing tall before him carried herself with confidence and grace. *A class act.*

She extended her hand, but the sparkle in her eyes defied the barrier she'd created with her stiff arm. He shook it. The familiar and welcomed current traveled up his arm. "Alexandra, good to see you."

"You as well, Crockett."

"Gavin, welcome to Wilde Innovations." Crockett shook the cameraman's hand.

"How've you been?" Gavin asked.

Crockett shot Alexandra a quick glance. "All things considered, pretty good. You?"

Gavin split his attention between him and Alex, the faintest smile curling his lips. "Doing great."

Crockett then met Gavin's assistant, Tom, and Millie, the makeup artist.

"We'll conduct the interviews in the lab," Crockett said. "Right this way."

Alexandra fell in line as he escorted the news team down the hall. "You look beautiful, Ms. Reed," he murmured.

A pinkish glow colored her cheeks. "Thank you."

As they approached the double-etched glass, Decker emerged. No smile. In fact, he greeted everyone with a scowl.

"You're in good hands with Decker." Crockett regarded the group. When he eyed Alexandra, her lips curved. "I'll be back." Her smile did it for him, every single time.

THIS INTERVIEW WAS ABOUT something much more important than a ratings winner, so Alexandra would tread lightly where Decker was concerned.

Decker rubbed his palms on his worn jeans. "Crockett considers the lab sacred space. We all do, so if a table is covered, it stays covered. If you're cool with that, in we go."

Alexandra nodded. "Totally on board."

"I'm a look-don't-touch kinda guy myself," Gavin said.

As soon as Decker received verbal agreement from the others, he heaved open the door and they entered.

"Great space. Good lighting," said Gavin. "If it's alright by you, I'll set up by the window next to the uncovered table." After a tight nod from Decker, Gavin and his assistant took off toward the corner.

Decker's cool demeanor didn't concern Alexandra. But she did need him to be in the right frame of mind. Savvy viewers picked up on the slightest nuances and any negativity could tarnish the segment. While this was a feel-good story about a local company with international reach, she wanted the audience to understand the true motivation behind everything the team created.

First up, Crockett's Vice President of Operations, Natalie Floyd. She breezed through makeup and settled into the chair across from Alexandra. Poised, personable, and intelligent, Natalie's no-nonsense but congenial answers set the stage. Alexandra liked her strong work ethic and quick wit.

Though Decker agreed to be interviewed, his guarded nature made him appear as if he was either trying to hide something or he didn't like being in front of the camera. Alexandra continued to ask open-ended questions until she elicited Decker's driving motivation. His loyalty to Crockett.

"I started working for Crockett as an intern while I was an undergrad at Maryland," Decker said. "I have the freedom to be as creative as my imagination will allow. Crockett and I don't always agree, but we find common ground and go from there."

Interviewing Decker gave Alexandra insight into Crockett's right-hand man and, while she didn't appreciate his chilly demeanor, she understood it. Decker Daughtry was Crockett's friend and greatest ally.

Next up was Crockett's assistant, Ellen. She kept wringing her hands and pursing her lips while Millie applied her makeup. By the time Ellen settled into the hot seat, she'd turned a pasty green.

"I can't do this," Ellen whispered. "I don't even like having my picture taken."

"Why don't we chat for a few?" Alexandra asked. "No camera, no interview. Tell me about yourself."

Ellen shot Gavin a furtive glance. "What about your cameraman?"

Gavin moseyed over. "I'll watch the playback while you two ladies get acquainted."

"Thanks, Gavin." Though Alexandra hadn't teamed with Gavin in years, she knew he was rolling tape. If the conversation didn't go well, the footage would get scrapped. But Alexandra's gut told her that once Ellen relaxed, she'd be great.

Crossing her legs, Ellen swept her hand over the leg of her pants suit. "Not much to say about me. I'm married with four children."

"And you work here full-time?"

During their conversation, the color returned to Ellen's face and she stopped fiddling with her bracelets. As she spoke about each of her children, she smiled, the softness in her eyes matching her sweet tone.

"What do you do for *yourself*?" Alexandra asked.

"I work at Wilde!" Ellen laughed. "Magic happens here. It's an exciting environment and even though I'm not a creative type, I feel like a part of the team. I've been an executive assistant for over twenty years and Crockett is a dream to work for."

"How would you describe your boss?"

Ellen's sincere smile said it all. "Honest, driven and insanely smart. But success hasn't gone to his head. He's grounded and steady. I've worked for some real hotheads." She shook her head. "Plus, if one of my children is sick—or all of them, like when they got the flu last winter—Crockett tells me to take care of my babies and not to worry about a thing." She smiled. "He doesn't even dock me vacation time. That man is a gem."

Alexandra called over her shoulder, "Gavin, are we good?"

"Got it all," Gavin said as he set the camera down.

With a smirk, Ellen pointed at them. "You two are sneaky."

Alexandra laughed. "I like to call it *'efficient'.*"

"Great job," Gavin said.

Next up? Wilde Innovations's Quality Assurance Director, Larry Berry. Larry flirted shamelessly while Millie applied his makeup and joked with Tom as he clipped the mic. He announced how excited his wife and kids were about seeing him on TV and how he'd become a mini-celebrity in his neighborhood. But when Gavin started rolling, Larry straightened up, cleared his smoker's throat, and lost the animated gestures. After a brief introduction, Alexandra asked a few basic questions. Larry's easygoing nature made him a natural in front of the camera.

"What's involved in leading Wilde's QA team?" Alexandra inquired.

"Nothing leaves this camp without my seal of approval." Larry's gritty timbre was a sharp contrast to his relaxed personality.

"Can you expand on what's required to earn that seal?"

"Absolutely." Larry caressed his moustache before launching into a high-level summary on the ins and outs of testing code following the software engineer's stringent requirements. "If my team approves, products move to the beta stage. But if we find the slightest glitch, back it goes."

"What types of glitches would send a product back to the drawing board?"

"I can't discuss specifics. What I can say is that my team catches each and every problem before the products fly."

Off-camera Decker grunted. Alexandra flicked her gaze in his direction, acknowledging she'd heard him. Had Larry meant fly out the door or was he referring to the Spy Flies? Either way, his answer would have to be edited. Changing tactics, she asked, "How long have you run the Quality Assurance team?"

"I got promoted last month and I've got giant shoes to fill. My predecessor, Ruth Lizzard, deserves *all* the credit. Her commitment and dedication ensured every single product worked as expected. And in mission-critical situations, there's no room for failure."

Crockett hadn't listed Lizzard as an available interviewee. She made a mental note to check with him. "What does the future hold for you, Larry?"

He grinned. "This is the year to make things happen. The sky's the limit."

"Got it," Gavin said.

"Great job, Larry." Alexandra shook his hand.

She loved crafting a well-rounded story. Ellen's warm nature contrasted Natalie's straightforward and polished persona. Decker rounded out the interview with his creative genius and steadfast loyalty. And Larry contributed an affability that made him instantly likable. Everyone brought value and perspective. And hopefully increased viewership.

Out of the corner of her eye, Alexandra spied Wilde's handsome CEO and her heart flipped. He'd been leaning against a cloaked table, looking fashion magazine ready. With a hand in his pocket, his relaxed stance contradicted the fierceness radiating from his eyes.

She rose, the attraction tugging her toward him, but she folded her fingers around the edge of the table to anchor her in place.

"Great interview, Alexandra."

Her heart swelled from his compliment. "Thank you." For more reasons than she cared to admit, doing right by this man mattered.

Though he smiled, his eyes did not. "I need to borrow Larry for a moment."

Ignoring his boss, Larry ambled toward Millie. "Hey, Mill, can you remove my makeup?"

"Now," Crockett said.

Anger flashed in Larry's eyes. "Sure thing." He and Crockett stepped out of the lab.

What's that all about?

"I caught Larry's comment about products 'flying,'" Alexandra whispered to Decker. "Even though he could have meant 'out the door', I'll work with the editor to cut that. No worries."

"Thank you." The tightness around his eyes faded. "I'm headed downstairs for coffee. Can I get you anything?"

"No, thanks." She tossed a nod toward the cloaked tables. "We won't peek."

"I trust you," Decker said.

Maybe she'd cracked Decker's guarded exterior. Millie and Tom joined Decker, leaving her and Gavin alone in the lab. With his full attention on Alexandra, Gavin chuckled.

Up went her eyebrows. "What?"

"You and Wilde have it baaaad for each other. And I mean bad."

She crossed her arms. "Oh, that's ridiculous. I do not. He doesn't, either. I'm a professional. We have a job to do. Why would you even say that? I'm insulted, Gavin. I mean, *really*!"

He burst out laughing. "You dizzy from that speech? I've known you for a long time, Reed, and I have never—and I mean, *never*—seen you blush. I can't wait to tell Bruce. It was the damn cutest thing."

She shoved her finger in his face. "I. Do. Not. Have. A. Thing. For. That. Man."

He raised his hands. "Whatever you say, doll."

Leaning against the table, she whispered, "That obvious?"

Gavin cleared his throat and Alexandra flicked her gaze to the swinging door as Crockett powered into the room. *I do have it bad for him.*

After makeup, Crockett took the hot seat. Since he'd returned from speaking with Larry Berry, something was off. Nothing he said, just a general feeling she had. Brushing it aside, Alexandra began with general questions about the business he'd built from the ground up.

"All of our surveillance equipment is designed to enhance operations for our armed forces, law enforcement, and first responders," he explained.

Alexandra asked about the items on the lab table and Crockett lifted a helmet equipped with night vision goggles. "This is an example of a current challenge we've been tasked to improve. Military, law enforcement and first responders rely on night vision goggles or NVGs. The infrared light gives them a clear advantage in the dark, but the challenge centers on the weight the goggles add to the helmet." He offered to place the helmet on Alexandra.

Gavin panned the camera to Alexandra as Crockett lowered the helmet onto her head. "It's heavy and the weight isn't distributed evenly," she said.

"Within as little as an hour, neck muscles strain against the weight of the goggles." Crockett took the helmet from her and set it back on the lab table, then lifted one of their two prototype designs so Gavin could get a close up. "We've been focused on reworking the goggles. These are much lighter, which means less neck strain. Right now, they're cost prohibitive. The goal is maintaining integrity without scrimping on quality. All while staying within the client's budget."

After Alexandra wrapped up her questions on the NVGs, Crockett rounded the table for a show-and-tell about mini-drones.

"Wilde Innovations holds a patent for one of the first initial military-grade mini-drones," he said. "But this little flyer took hundreds of iterations until we got it right." He added, "In the beginning, we crashed more than we landed."

His pride for his team was evident and he credited others for his successes. He was driven, intelligent and direct. But he was humble and as motivated today as he had been when he first began. When she asked him a few questions about his career in the early years, he became more introspective.

"Everyone on the team, especially those who've been with me since inception, put blood, sweat and tears into those early projects. I've grown along with my business and believe that work-life balance is key to our success. Though I rarely follow my own sound advice."

Despite the fact that she'd interviewed famous, wealthy celebrities and lots of successful business magnates in her career, this interview mattered the most. Not because of her personal feelings, but because of his.

The driving force behind his organization centered on someone he loved. If the interview helped another family or somehow eased his pain, she would consider it a success.

"Crockett, what was your primary motivation behind Wilde Innovations?"

Pausing, he broke eye contact. She waited, her heart hammering in her chest. *Make this story personal, Crockett. Tell them.*

Several more seconds passed. *Dammit.* She'd have to cover with another question.

He steeled his spine. A flicker of misery shadowed his

normally bright eyes. "My sister, Sophia, was abducted when she was fourteen. Although she's been missing for thirteen years—almost half her life—I remain optimistic she'll come home to us one day. Everything we create at Wilde is with her in mind. It's my goal that improvements to surveillance will help bring her, and others who've been abducted, home."

She breathed. He'd done it. Alexandra wrapped the interview. When Gavin stopped filming, she extended her hand. "That was fantastic, Crockett. You and your team did an outstanding job."

Instead of shaking her hand, he held it. Heat infused her body. Though she should have shook his hand and released, she gave him a little squeeze before letting go. Millie moved in and removed Crockett's makeup.

"Crockett, who can I speak with about shooting footage at your manufacturing plant?" Gavin asked.

"We have stock you can use," Crockett said.

"Great." Gavin handed Crockett his business card. "My cell is the best way to reach me. Congrats on a solid interview. Alexandra, we're gonna take off."

"Did ya'll drive together?" Crockett asked Alexandra.

"I drove alone," said Alexandra.

"Can you stick around for a few?" Crockett asked.

"Of course." Out of the corner of her eye, she spied Gavin's smirk.

"I'll escort you guys out," Decker said to Gavin and crew.

"Meet me in the Tank," Crockett said to him.

On a nod, Decker led Gavin, Millie and Tom out.

"Let's talk in private." Crockett gestured toward the back of the lab.

They walked into the isolated room. He shut the door, pinned her with a steely gaze. Suddenly, the air became electric. Her heart pitter-pattered, her body warmed.

"You're a natural, Alex," he murmured, his deep voice rumbling through her. "Talking about Sophia is very difficult for me."

The need to touch him overpowered her and she caressed his muscular arm. "Thank you for pushing through. You did a great job. When it airs, I hope someone comes forward with information on Sophia."

"It's a long shot."

"You sound like you've lost hope."

"I never give up on someone I love." His gaze turned fiery. He gripped her shoulders. Fierce blue eyes pierced her. "Last night I came home to an empty bed."

His words rocketed through her. His touch ignited her need. "I crashed on your sofa." Her words sounded hollow, pathetic. She leaned toward him, that familiar and powerful attraction taking hold.

He said nothing. But their increased breathing, now in sync, filled her ears. Seconds passed. Though desperate for his mouth on hers, she didn't move. The energy swirled; her lips tingled. *Kiss me, Crockett.* Her heart dipped when he released her.

"After you left the club last night, I saw Jase escort Dracule and a male companion into that unmarked suite." His jaw ticked. "And I'm pretty sure I caught a glimpse of Sage."

"*What?* Why didn't you wake me?"

He hitched a brow. "Because I wouldn't have wanted to talk."

Warmth spread down her chest and she moaned, quietly, under her breath.

"Did you have another nightmare?" he asked.

She swallowed. "Yes, but knowing you were down the hall helped."

He shook his head. "I don't need a roommate, Alexandra."

"Crockett, I...um...it's not a good—"

This time he stopped her with a tender kiss. "Don't fight this," he murmured.

More. Her body hummed with need. And again, his mouth brushed against hers...

Tap! Tap!

Decker plowed in, almost crashing the door into them. Alexandra jerked back.

"Whoa, okay." Decker squeezed in, coffee cup in hand, and shut the door. "This is tight."

With a smile in his eyes, Crockett eased into the chair at the head of the table. "Sit."

Alexandra and Decker sat across from each other.

"Other than Larry's slip up, the interviews went well, don't you think, Alexandra?" Decker sipped his drink.

"What slip up?" Crockett asked.

"Larry said his team catches each and every problem before the products fly," Alexandra said. "He could have meant 'fly out the door', but I'll make sure that's cut."

"He also mentioned Ruth," Decker said to Crockett. "More like gushed."

"Ah, crap," Crockett replied.

"Who is she?" Alexandra asked.

"Someone I terminated," Crockett replied. "I'm not concerned about his 'fly' comment, but don't include Ruth."

"I'm glad you were there, Decker," Alexandra said. "Anything else?"

"No," Decker said. "I was against this interview, but you did a good job."

Progress. "It was a pleasure interviewing you, Decker. I admire your loyalty."

"Decker, I need your help," Crockett said. "I have an off-the-record task for you on the dark net."

This didn't sound like a request. Decker waited.

"There's a members-only sex play club here in Crystal City called Incognito." Crockett's voice rumbled from the depths of his chest. "Some men ask for and receive something called 'rejuvenation'. See if you can find out what that is."

"My mind is blown," Decker said with a sly smile. "I would never have guessed you—"

"This information does not leave this room," Crockett said.

Decker dropped his playful expression. "Of course not. Just to set expectations, this could take awhile. It's not like there's a Google in the dark web and a few clicks later, I've got an answer."

"Don't use any of Wilde's computers. Purchase one if you don't want to use your own. I'll reimburse you from my personal account."

"I've got one at home I can use."

"After I walk Alexandra out, let's discuss your report on Maverick's Eagle," Crockett said.

"It'll have to wait. Charlie's crafts arrived in Jessup." Decker stood and opened the door. "I'm headed there now."

"Keep me posted," Crockett said. "Good luck."

"We need a lot of that," Decker said and left.

"What did he mean?" she asked.

A shadow fell over his eyes. "Nothing."

He's not telling me something. Rather than force the point, she rose. "I should go. Thank you for—"

He moved so fast, she was nestled in his arms before she could refuse him. But when he kissed her, refusing him was the last thing she wanted to do. Her nipples firmed, her insides tightened and she threaded her hands into his hair.

Groaning into him, she pushed her tongue into his mouth, electricity pulsing through her. He squeezed her ass, holding her tightly against his thickening shaft. She ground against him, the need between her legs making her lightheaded. When he bit her lip, she whimpered.

Knock, knock, knock.

Crockett released her just as the door opened and Ellen popped her head in. Her eyes shifted from one to the other and her face turned puce. "Oh, goodness me. I thought you were with Decker."

Though Crockett said nothing, his eyes flashed with annoyance. *What was he thinking? That he'd bend me over the table and take me here?* A zing of energy hit her between her legs and she caught a moan before it escaped.

"Ashton Hott is waiting in your office." Still red-faced, Ellen hurried out.

"We'll address our unfinished business later," Crockett said. "I'll walk you out."

"I know the way." She wanted to stroke his whiskered cheek or kiss him goodbye, but she couldn't give in to her emotions. "Thank you for allowing me to interview you and your team." Feeling like a ticking bomb, she spun on her heels and left. How much longer could she keep him at arm's length? She wanted to let herself fall, but she couldn't handle the pain of losing him all over again when she left.

Since the parking garages near Crockett's office building had been full, she'd parked several blocks away. On the trek back to her car, gray clouds gave way to dark, stormy ones. Seconds later, heavy drops splattered the sidewalk, the wind whipped around her, and the rain pelted her. Drenched, she ducked into a nearby coffee shop.

While waiting for her Chai tea, she spied Larry Berry and a woman, snuggled on a loveseat tucked in the corner. After paying, Alexandra headed toward the back of the cozy cafe to say hello. But Larry and the blonde had vanished. On the coffee table in front of the loveseat were their drinks, nearly full and still steaming.

She glanced outside. Sheets of rain blew sideways and traffic had come to a standstill. *He sure was in a rush to leave.*

20

THE COMPETITION

Alexandra smiled at the young child seated on the bleachers in front of her as she and Kimberly waited in the crowded high school gym. Her mom had been in good spirits all through lunch. And she seemed stronger, too. Though Alexandra knew the gut-wrenching truth, she clung to hope. *Maybe the chemo and radiation treatments are working after all.*

"This is exciting," Kimberly said as she unbuttoned her coat. "Where's Crockett?"

Alexandra leaned around the little girl who'd been standing in front of her. The child's mom noticed. "Hannah, please sit down. The lady behind you would like to see, too."

"It's okay," said Alexandra. "She's fine."

The child spun around. "My teacher is competing. Do you study karate?"

"No, I don't." Alexandra smiled at the munchkin. "I've never been to a karate competition. What can we expect?"

"Today is the first round of a national tournament," Hannah's mom explained.

"It starts with this regional competition," Hannah's dad said. "Virginia, Maryland, DC."

"Pennsylvania and Delaware, too," added Hannah's mom. "The event lasts all weekend and is divided by belt rank and age group."

A squirmy Hannah beamed. "My teacher is sparring. He's super strong." She threw her tiny arms up into a Hercules pose. "Grrrr."

Alexandra laughed.

Kimberly pointed. "There's Crockett."

Several members of the black belt class filed into the gym and began stretching on the mats in the far corner.

Hannah's mom turned around. "Are you a friend of Mr. Wilde's?" she asked Alexandra.

As Alexandra smiled, her cheeks warmed. "Yes, we are."

"He's my teacher!" The child beamed. "And he's the best!"

Alexandra and Kimberly laughed. "Sounds like you like your teacher," Kimberly said. "We're fond of him, too."

Here we go. "How long have you been studying karate?" Alexandra asked.

"I'm a yellow belt," Hannah said, then fiddled with her hair.

Hannah's mom placed a soft hand on her daughter's shoulder. "Hannah started over the summer. As you can see, our six year old has a lot of energy."

"Mr. Wilde is so generous." She leaned toward Alexandra, cupped her hand next to her mouth and whispered, "He paid for my lessons."

Wow. What's that all about? Alexandra glanced at the child's parents.

"Okay, Hannah," said her mom. "That's enough, young lady. Why don't you—"

"She's darling," interrupted Kimberly. "Hannah, what is it about Mr. Wilde that makes him the *best?*"

Staring at her mom, Alexandra raised her brows. Could she be more obvious?

"He's fun and he's nice," Hannah explained. "At first, I was scared but he always says 'good job'. And we get high-fives at the end of every class." She continued wiggling. "He's been studying karate for a lo-o-o-ng time."

Hannah's dad pulled his daughter onto his lap. "Sorry. She's quite a chatterbox."

"It's lovely meeting one of Crockett's students and his parents, isn't it, Alexandra?" Kimberly patted her daughter's thigh.

Alexandra smirked at her mother. *Why do I feel like Hannah isn't the only child in this conversation?*

Refocusing her attention, Alexandra watched Crockett stretching on the mat in his black *gi*. Confidence radiated off him. And then, as if he could feel her eyes on him, he peered into the crowded bleachers. Their eyes met, her heart flipped. Even across the room, energy crackled between them. She gave him a little wave and he tossed her a nod.

Hannah leaped up and waved. "Mr. Wilde!" When Crockett waved back, she jumped up and down.

Kimberly leaned over and whispered, "I wish *you* were that excited to see him."

Alexandra laughed. "I would be if I were six."

An hour into the event, Crockett rose. From the second he stepped onto the mat, Crockett Wilde owned that space. Though his opponent was a physical match, Crockett dominated. To say he was self-assured was an understatement. Based on the intensity in his eyes, his rival didn't stand a chance.

After facing each other, the two black belts bowed and the sparring began. Crockett moved with the speed and grace of a cheetah and attacked with the same ferocity. He outsmarted and outmaneuvered. Laser-focused, he never once took his eyes off his adversary.

Though Alexandra abhorred physical violence of any kind, she sat transfixed. Impressed and in awe, her opinion of him shifted. Sweet, patient Crockett Wilde morphed into a beast, determined to win. Second to none.

There was power and precision in every kick, every punch,

every shout, yet he moved with cat-like speed when confronted with those of his opponent.

She knew so little about him outside of their interview and their sexual romps at the club. Yet, he'd given her a place to live, shared his bed, even. He'd pulled her from her car during the snowstorm and he'd agreed to help her pursue a hunch with his very expensive surveillance equipment.

And he had the courage to tell her the truth about her mother when her own family wouldn't.

For as long as she could remember, Alexandra had locked herself in an emotional prison to avoid the heartache of abandonment.

Crockett used his pain to fuel him. His aggression aroused her. His zeal appeared to have no limit. For that brief moment, she wondered how her life would change if she let go of her fears and loved him. When she was eighteen, loving him had changed her for the better but losing him had changed her for the worse.

Could she push past her fear and take a chance on loving him again?

Crockett handily nailed his first opponent, then returned to his seat, grabbed his towel, and wiped the sweat from his brow. While Alexandra applauded, Hannah jumped up and down with gusto. Kimberly nudged her daughter. "He wants to see that level of excitement from you," she whispered.

He'd seen that all right. Electra never held back.

"I have to use the restroom," Kimberly said.

Alexandra helped her mom down from the bleachers, then waited for her in the busy high school lobby.

Crockett rolled out of the gym. And her heart rocketed into her throat. She wanted to run to him, throw her arms around his neck and tell him the damned truth about how she felt. She adored him.

"Congratulations! You were great." She squeezed his bicep. Had to touch him, for just a second.

He kissed her cheek. "Now that my lucky charm is here, I can really kick some ass." When she gazed into his eyes, she knew with complete certainty that he was the one. The reality of her feelings terrified her.

Kimberly sidled next to her daughter and slipped her arm through the crook of her elbow. "Crockett, you are sensational!"

"I'm glad you're here." He kissed Kimberly's cheek. "Gotta go." He flashed a smile and jogged toward the gym.

Kimberly squeezed her daughter's hand as they headed slowly back to their seats. "He's a good man, baby girl."

"I know he is, Mom. But my life is in LA."

"No, Alexandra. Your *career* is there. Your *life* is where your heart is."

She kissed her mom's cheek. "You make it sound so easy."

As soon as they returned to their seats in the stands, Hannah announced, "Someone tried to take your spot, but I told them you were here first."

"Thank you, Hannah," said Alexandra. "I'm glad we're watching this with you."

"Can I sit with you?"

Before Alexandra could answer, Hannah squeezed between her and Kimberly.

"Hannah Marie!" Hannah's dad scolded. "Do you want to leave?"

The child gaped, her eyes big and wide. "No, Daddy!"

"Come down here, now."

"She's fine, really," said Alexandra. "We love having Hannah sit with us."

"Send her back if she becomes a bother," said Hannah's mom.

Hannah sat quietly while they watched the competition. When Crockett handily beat out his second opponent, Hannah jumped up, threw her tiny arms into the air and cheered. Kimberly laughed, seemingly thrilled to be around such an exuberant child.

As the tournament continued, Crockett appeared to draw

strength from the matches. His aggression increased every time he advanced. As did his technique. He seemed to have the ability to sum up his rival as soon as he stepped onto the mat. Had he learned to contain the anguish of his loss and unleash it during a competition?

Before today, Alexandra had never viewed him as a fighter, but her opinion of him changed when his third opponent limped off the mats pinching his bloodied nose.

"Hannah, is Mr. Wilde like this in class?" Alexandra asked.

She shook her head, sending her hair flying. "Nuh-uh, but in the black belt room he's like grrrrrrr." She scrunched her face and closed those little hands into boxing fists.

Kimberly burst out laughing. "Too cute."

"You look scared." Hannah clasped Alexandra's hand. "He's okay."

Alexandra released her breath. Was it that obvious, even to a youngster?

Crockett's final competitor charged him as soon as the sparring began. His frenetic movements prevented Crockett from going on the offense and gaining the upper hand. When Crockett absorbed a powerful kick to his torso, then another to his head, Hannah clapped her mouth and squeezed Alexandra's hand.

This challenger was going at Crockett hard, striking him again and again. Crockett finally exploded in a burst of jabs, spins, and kicks that dropped his opponent to the mat. When the timer buzzed, the two men bowed. Alexandra breathed. They stood like soldiers awaiting the judge's decision. The audience fell silent, the tension palpable.

When Crockett was declared the winner, the gym erupted in applause.

Though Crockett would advance to the semi-final event the following month, he left the mat drenched in sweat, out of breath, and clutching his side.

Hannah threw her arms around Alexandra's neck. "He won, he won, he won!" the little one shouted.

When Hannah sat back down, Alexandra spied her mom wiping a tear from the corner of her eye.

"That man is going to need some TLC and I expect you to take extra special care of him." Kimberly shot her daughter a stern look.

Alexandra's lips curved. For once, she agreed.

The emcee invited the winners of each category onto the mats for their trophies. After the presentation and a few brief announcements, he closed the event. Friends and family slowly made their way toward the floor, while others filed out.

"Let's go see him!" Hannah exclaimed, then tugged on Alexandra's hand.

"I'm going to help my mom, but I'll meet you down there shortly." Alexandra smiled at Hannah's mom. "I have a feeling you're going to beat us there."

With her mom's cane draped over her arm, Alexandra supported Kimberly down the bleachers. When they reached the bottom, her mom took her cane and they ambled toward Crockett.

After witnessing his unrelenting determination, precise technique, and physical prowess, Alexandra was a little star struck.

Hannah and her parents, along with several others, crowded around Crockett. As soon as he spied her, he didn't look away. What passed between them couldn't be denied, couldn't be ignored. If he could face his fears, could she? How would she deal with the unrelenting heartache when she returned to California? *It would kill me to lose him again.*

Her heart bloomed at the tender way he kissed Kimberly's cheek. Then, he kissed hers. "I hope you both had fun, all things considered."

"You were phenomenal!" Kimberly raved. "My blood hasn't pumped that fast in quite some time."

Crockett laughed, then winced. "You and me both." He smiled at Alexandra. "Did you like?"

"Very much," she said.

"I see you met one of my best students." Crockett winked at the tiny tot.

A beaming Hannah grasped Alexandra's hand. "Is she your wife, Mr. Wilde?"

"She ought to be," murmured Kimberly.

"No, she's not, Hannah." Crockett shifted his gaze to Alexandra. "What do you think we should do about that?"

21

CHILDHOOD SECRETS

A FTER HEARTY HANDSHAKES AND hasty goodbyes, Hannah's parents headed out, their precocious daughter in tow.

"I was hoping you'd join us for dinner, but I already know the answer," Kimberly said.

Crockett raked his hand through his damp hair. "I need to go home and nurse my wounds."

"Why don't you help him, Alexandra?"

Why, Mom, why? "And how will you get home, Mom?"

"Taxi. I can call a friend. My broomstick."

Crockett laughed, winced and again, clutched his side.

"I'll take you home and, if you have leftovers, I'll plate one for Crockett," Alexandra said.

Kimberly's face lit up. "The chef made me a delightful salmon almondine last night. The sooner we leave, the quicker you can bring Crockett something to eat." She patted his shoulder. "You deserved the win. Great job."

"I'll walk you out," Crockett said.

After tucking her mom into the passenger seat of Kimberly's white Mercedes, she said to Crockett, "You did a fantastic job clobbering those guys."

He chuckled. "I took a beating. Take your time with your mom."

"I'll see you later."

He pecked her cheek. "I look forward to it."

As she stared into his eyes, his energy drew her to him. In a very non-Mitus move, she leaned up and kissed him, then slipped into her mom's vehicle.

He flashed her a grin and she drove out of the parking lot.

After dinner, mother and daughter relaxed in the living room. Alexandra sat on the floor in front of the fireplace, the flames warming her back. Kimberly was propped on the sofa, tucked beneath a throw, nursing a coffee.

"Thank you for insisting I go today," Kimberly said. "I loved watching Crockett compete. That little girl reminded me of you. Friendly, outgoing, and *so* talkative." Kimberly's laugh made Alexandra smile. She wished she could record her mom's laughter for when—. Pain slashed her heart.

Though Alexandra had promised herself she wouldn't broach the subject of her childhood, her mom had created an opening and time was running out. "I don't remember much about being a kid. I was happy and then really, really sad. For a long time. And then I wore a lot of black."

"Oh, that Goth was dreadful. But you had a right to express yourself and I didn't interfere." Kimberly sighed. "I hope one day you'll be a mom. Being yours and Colton's and Cain's has been my greatest joy. It's also been the hardest job. I've had to make tough decisions that affected both your lives."

This was her chance. "Like what?"

"Baby girl, you were the sweetest child. I chose to protect your innocence." Kimberly broke eye contact, briefly. "But you deserve to know the truth."

Alexandra's mouth grew dry.

"What do you remember about Colton's twin?"

"Cain was loud and funny. He talked all the time. I remember him answering for Colton, too." Alexandra smiled. "And he didn't like to get his hair cut." Then, her expression turned serious. "I have this memory of him having a black eye. He got it defending Colton, so you didn't punish him for fighting."

A rueful smile touched Kimberly's eyes. "He was such a wild little boy. And yes, he was very funny."

"You never talk about him."

"It's too painful. But I think about him every day." After pushing upright, Kimberly squared her shoulders. "Do you remember your father?"

A sliver of a smile crossed Alexandra's lips. "I do. Like, when he'd read to me in the big chair. Or we'd have tea parties. I was Daddy's little Princess."

Kimberly's eyes grew sad. "Those are wonderful memories. Perhaps it best we leave them intact."

Alexandra pushed off the floor and knelt next to her mom. "I need the truth."

Her mother hesitated and Alexandra held her breath. "Your father adored you. I hope you'll be able to reconcile your feelings for him once you hear what I'm about to tell you."

Her guts pinched. "I'll try."

"Wilson became greedy. His obsession with wealth turned him into a monster. When you kids were little, he got mixed up in several illegal business deals and owed tens of thousands. He hid everything from me. I found out about it when the men broke into our home to rob us as a way of recouping their losses. I told you Cain drowned in the bathtub, which he did. But he was murdered." The color drained from Kimberly's face, the tears pooling in her eyes.

Alexandra's pulse shot up and she hugged her mom. "*No!* Oh, no, no!" The truth was worse than anything she'd imagined. "Mom, let's not do this. It's too much."

"No." She swallowed her grief with a deep breath. "You should know everything."

"There's more?" Alexandra sat on the sofa beside her mom and covered her legs with the throw, but she couldn't quell the shaking.

Kimberly nodded. "Your father was a terrible philanderer. He didn't think I knew…" Kimberly tossed off the blanket and, using her cane for support, pushed off the sofa. With slow, deliberate steps, she walked to the fireplace and pivoted. Strength and determination shone in her eyes.

"While your father loved you and Cain, he despised Colton. Back then, Colton was shy because of his stuttering. Instead of being patient and supportive, Wilson viewed Colton as weak and bullied him. Colton grew to fear him. Cain, on the other hand, was bold, brazen even, and Wilson favored him above everyone else. Even you."

Alexandra struggled to maintain her composure, her head reeling. "So, that's why you and Colton had secrets."

"It is. Colton knew too much and you, nothing. I needed to ensure that one of my babies' childhoods remained intact. Wilson's sudden departure affected you deeply. I tried to be both a mother and a father, but you missed him."

Alexandra broke into a cold sweat and she kicked off the blanket. "I'm sorry for what you and Colton had to suffer through. Thank you for protecting me."

"As a teen, you retreated behind your Goth. Crockett was the only one who could reach you." A tear slid down Kimberly's cheek. "The summer before you left for college, you blossomed."

Alexandra's vision narrowed and she threw her head between her legs before she passed out.

Returning to the sofa, Kimberly rubbed her back. "I'm sorry, honey."

"I'm glad I know," Alexandra muttered, her head still tipped down. "Is there more?"

Kimberly didn't reply.

Alexandra repositioned herself, lying on the floor with her legs draped over the sofa cushion. Kimberly laughed, then apologized. "You haven't gotten light-headed in years."

Alexandra studied her mom's tired face. "You didn't answer my question. *Is there more?*"

"Isn't that enough?" Kimberly asked.

"I have nightmares that have haunted me since childhood." She shuddered in a shaky breath. "A faceless man hits a woman and I run screaming and crying toward her."

Anger flashed in Kimberly's eyes and Alexandra worried that she'd upset her. "I remember those. You'd wake screaming. Do you remember what I used to tell you?"

Alexandra shook her head. "Not really."

"Dreams clean out the clutter. When we wake, our minds are clear to take on the day."

But her mom's wringing hands sent Alexandra's stomach plummeting. "Oh, God, no," she whispered. "That wasn't a dream. He hit you, didn't he?"

"Your father was a monster." Kimberly's hushed delivery sent a chill down Alexandra's spine. "One night you woke up and saw him attack me. You were wild with fear."

Alexandra started shaking, the tremors jolting her like earthquakes. She didn't want to believe it, but the truth was impossible to ignore. Her amazing, doting father was an evil bastard. She choked back a sob as tears flowed down her temples.

The nightmare finally made sense. And the other one, too. The man kissing a lady that wasn't *his* mommy was her child's brain wresting with the fact that her father was kissing a woman that wasn't *her* mommy. *I saw him with another woman.* Nausea blurred her thoughts while her heart thundered in her chest.

"Everything changed the day I found the courage to boot the son of a bitch out. You, Colton and I forged a new family. A loving, peaceful one." Kimberly smiled. "Though I miss Cain terribly, I'm thankful you and Colton survived the horror of Wilson Mitus."

"Why didn't Colton tell me?"

"He was a tormented little boy. After Wilson left, he became your protector, then time and our love healed him."

Her heart broke for her mom and for the brother she adored and admired. Silence hovered, the harsh reality sinking in. When she felt like she could move, she curled up next to her mom on the couch. "I'm sorry for the hell you endured. I resented the secrets I knew you both were keeping, but now I understand why you kept them. What happened to Wilson?"

Kimberly stiffened. "He vanished. Recently he attempted a hostile takeover of the Francesco Company and Colton almost lost Crockett Boxes."

"*Wow*. Where is he?"

"Wilson is an executive at MobiCom in Northern Virginia."

"Thank you for telling me the truth, Mom. Talking about this wasn't easy." Alexandra hugged her mom.

"It was necessary." She hesitated. "I won't always be around forever to protect you, my angel." She patted Alexandra's leg. "Now, let's talk about Crockett, shall we?"

ALEXANDRA DROVE HOME IN a stupor. Though grateful for the truth, the conversation with her mom had wrecked her.

It was after ten. She'd stayed later than expected and hoped to find Crockett sprawled on his living room sofa. The roaring gas flames greeted her with silent waves along with a note on his dining room table. "Wake me."

She glanced down the hallway and into his dark bedroom. Was his open door an invitation for her to go in? *Let him sleep.* She turned away. The disappointment of not seeing him, of not being near him, of not touching him left her feeling empty and alone.

After storing the leftovers in the refrigerator, she poured herself a glass of wine and sat at the dining room table, admiring the panoramic view. How much did Crockett know about

Wilson? Was he privy to the Mitus secrets? The resentment she'd harbored against her mom and Colton disappeared. Not only had they each endured a world of pain at the hand of her father, they'd sheltered her from the abominable horrors. For as long as she could remember, she envisioned a day when she'd be reunited with her dad. That dream fizzled, but the loss remained. She'd idolized a man who had abused the two people she most adored.

Maybe the alcohol contributed to the building emotion, but when she downed the last sip, the rush of grief and anger came thundering out in a tornado of heartache.

CROCKETT WOKE WITH A start. Pushing past his tired muscles and aching bones, he got out of bed. Wearing only the cotton pajama bottoms he'd fallen asleep in, he found Alexandra curled on his sofa, her head bowed in her hands, sobbing. Though her cries were muffled, he'd heard her in his dreams.

She's upset about Kimberly.

Sitting beside her, he put his arm around her and kissed the top of her head. Rather than ask her if she was okay—which she wasn't—or ask what was wrong, he just stroked her back until her weeping subsided. When she lifted her tearstained face to his, he kissed her. One tender kiss because he could not resist. Even sad, her beauty astounded him.

After grabbing a handful of tissues, he waited while she dried her eyes. Somehow, Alex made nose blowing cute. Her teeth chattered, so he covered her with a blanket.

"For the first time in my life, my mom talked to me like an adult," she said. "Now I understand why she and Colton sheltered me."

He tucked her hair behind her ear. "Did you get the answers you needed?" His side ached where he'd been kicked, so he shifted, trying to get comfortable.

Awareness flashed in her eyes. "I'm sorry. I'm so selfish. Did you soak in the bath? Have you eaten?"

"No and breakfast."

"That's not enough food. We packed up most of dinner for you." She threw off the blanket and beelined toward the kitchen. Five minutes later, he was enjoying salmon almondine, mixed vegetables and wild grain rice.

"You want to talk about your conversation with Kimberly?" he asked.

In a quiet voice, Alexandra relayed everything she'd learned about the *real* Wilson Mitus. His heart broke for a family he loved as much as his own. But he also admired Colton and Kimberly for their inner strength and sheer determination.

When she finished, Crockett's guts had knotted. He'd also been keeping information from her, for what he believed was her own good. He opened his mouth to confess, but she held up her hand. "You have been there for me and now it's my turn. Let's go soak your sore muscles."

He joined her in the bathroom. With the Jacuzzi filling fast, she poured in Epsom salts. Her gaze traveled over every inch of him, but when her eyes met his, he hoped his grateful smile conveyed what he couldn't say. Because the next thing out of his mouth would be the truth.

"I'd say you fared pretty well," she said after examining him thoroughly. She ran the pads of her fingers over the bruise on his side. "That's gotta hurt."

"I've had worse."

After the crystals dissolved, he removed his pants and climbed in. While the jet blasts beat against his aching muscles, she massaged his shoulders. He should be comforting her, but instead, he leaned against the porcelain and accepted her loving touch.

When the water cooled, he got out. She eyed his saluting hard on and waggled her eyebrows. "The gift that keeps on giving," she said with a sparkle in her eyes.

He couldn't contain his laugh and groaned from the shooting pain. After helping him dry off, she suggested he get into bed.

He had to tell her. Though he ran the risk of losing her, she wasn't his to lose. Not this time. Maybe if he told her the truth, she would forgive him for what he'd done.

"I have a confession," he said, and watched her playful expression fall.

22

UNMASKED

"**N**OT YOU, TOO?" SHE whispered.

Since Crockett hadn't planned for this, he had no strategy. Winging things wasn't his style, but based on the worry in her eyes, he didn't want to drag this out. After pulling on the pajama bottoms, he clasped her hand. "Let's sit by the fire." Though he had a fireplace in his bedroom, he didn't want to tell her in his bed. Beds were for lovemaking and for sleep. Not for drudging up the past.

After pouring himself a scotch and refilling her wine glass, he sat on the floor by the hearth. She sat on the edge of the ergonomic leather chair and set the wine glass on the side table. Leaning forward, she clasped her legs to her chest. He hoped his words would eliminate her scowl and the anxiety in her eyes.

"I know you loved me once," he said, keeping his voice low and steady.

She bolted upright. "Please, not tonight."

"What you don't know is that I loved you, too. So much. And that's why I had to let you go."

In a flash, she flew out of the chair. "Crockett—"

He held up his hand. "Let me say this."

Her deep inhale was followed by a slow, audible hiss. "Alright."

"I met you Thanksgiving weekend freshman year. The only thing you said all weekend was that in four years you were going to journalism school at USC. Do you remember that?"

A tiny smile lifted the corners of her mouth and she sank back into the chair. "I remember a lot about you from that weekend."

"Good, then you might recall that the day you told me you loved me, you also told me you were withdrawing from USC. More than anything, I wanted to tell you how deeply I'd fallen in love with you. But I couldn't."

"You loved me?"

"Yes, very much, which is why I couldn't be the reason you didn't follow your dream."

Her eyes softened, but she stayed quiet. He studied her face, the cute way she'd haphazardly tied her hair in a ponytail and how it hung lopsided, and then he caught a glimpse of hope springing from her deep, soulful eyes. *Don't hold back.*

"One weekend during sophomore year, I'd come home with Colton. You were still wearing dark clothing and Goth makeup and you rarely spoke. Something I said made you giggle. Your belly laugh lit up your face and the room. It touched me, too."

"I remember your surprised expression made me laugh harder."

He tipped the lowball glass into his mouth and swallowed down some scotch. "The day of our graduation party, I checked with your mom to confirm the gorgeous woman in the flowery dress was you. The transformation was astounding. Eleven years later, you're breathtaking. But it's your inner beauty I love most. That summer was bittersweet for us both. I fell in love with someone I knew would be leaving. The end was inevitable."

She slid off the chair and scooted close, but faced the fire. "Can I say something now?"

"Go ahead."

"I had a crush on you from the moment I met you. After four

years of hiding behind my Goth, I decided to take a chance. On you." She tilted her face and peeked through her lush lashes. "I didn't expect to fall so hard."

"Ending something that good killed me," he said, "but I didn't see how a long-distance relationship would benefit either one of us. Every time you came home during college, Kimberly made sure I knew you were in town. But you wouldn't see me."

"I couldn't. It hurt too much."

"When I realized it was you at Incognito, I went after you. Sophia's absence haunts me every day, but life becomes bearable when you're by my side." He tossed back another sip. "I don't give a damn about what those men are doing at Incognito, but it's important to you, so I've made it a priority. That woman—Sage—I haven't thought twice about her, but you care, so I'll do whatever I can to help you shake the nightmares. You needed a safe place to live, so I moved you in with me. But dammit, Alex, I need more. A lot more."

"Crockett." She murmured his name like a prayer.

"I need to tell you what I couldn't say all those years ago." He clasped her hands, stroked her skin with his thumbs. "Eleven years ago, I wasn't in a position to make you mine, but I'll do whatever it takes now. I see the way you look at me, the way you find excuses to touch me, and how connected we are, even at the club. I adore you, Alexandra, but if you don't feel the same way, now would be the time to put it out there."

ALEXANDRA WAS CONVINCED SHE'D misheard him. Was now the time to admit her true feelings? Tell him she'd never stopped loving him. Admit she'd dreamt of a life with him. Though the room was toasty warm, a shiver ran through her. She wasn't ready to talk, but she might be able to show him. "I used to be good at making your pain go away. Where does it hurt?"

"Where *doesn't* it hurt?"

She kissed his cheek. "Here?"

"That helped."

"And here, too?" She kissed his other cheek, then his earlobe and his neck. When her mouth found his, she knew she'd come home.

Despite the trembling, she needed to take this next step. But her deep-seated fear of abandonment had crippled her. She hadn't made love to a man in eleven years. Sex, yes. But sex and lovemaking weren't the same thing. Letting Crockett into her heart would leave her vulnerable, but she needed to be close to him. In every way possible. She needed to push past her fear and take this next step.

Moving off him, she stood. Though her heart raced and she had to keep reminding herself to breathe, she peeled off her sweater, then her pants. Once naked, she helped him remove his pajama bottoms.

"You're shaking," he murmured. "Let me hold you."

"After, you can hold me all night." His knowing smile boosted her confidence. "Would you be more comfortable in bed?"

"The only place I want to be is inside you." His voice had dropped. His huskiness made her heart pound faster and her insides clench with need.

"I don't want to hurt you."

"Then don't leave me," he murmured.

God, his honesty was stirring up a maelstrom of emotion. "I haven't done this in a long time."

When he stroked her breast, his fingers grazed her nipple. Excitement shot through her. "Condoms are in my night table."

While she wanted to feel his hard, thick shaft without the thin layer of latex, she wasn't ready for that level of intimacy. *Small steps.* She retreated into his bedroom and returned with a packet, which he rolled on.

As she straddled him, she watched for signs of pain. If

Crockett was uncomfortable, he hid it well. "I want to make love," she murmured. "But I'm afraid. I have no mask to hide behind. I'm vulnerable and so are my feelings." She gobbled down a jittery breath.

"Let me love you, my sweet, beautiful Alexandra. Let me show you how much you mean to me. Trust this. Trust us."

Losing him had been unbearable. Would loving him now result in more heartache? The adoration in his eyes mirrored everything she felt for this man. *No regrets.*

One simple kiss unleashed a decade of waiting and hoping and wanting. She let go and got lost in everything Crockett. The build was slow and tender. The kissing never stopped, nor did their touching. Neither could look anywhere but into the other's eyes, into their bared souls. She loved Crockett Wilde with her entire being and she felt his love tenfold.

When their lovemaking ended, she lay by his side, sated and happy. The flickering firelight danced in his eyes, the outpouring of his love undeniable.

After dotting her face in worshipful kisses, he smiled. "I've missed you so much."

She propped herself on her elbow, kissed his shoulder, his chest, his cheek, and when her lips touched his, she smiled.

He slipped his hand behind her neck and pulled her close. One soft, doting kiss turned into many. "I'm still in pain," he murmured.

"Then I'll stay up all night and kiss you better."

23

THE FORENSIC SKETCH

Crockett reached out for her, but she was gone. Though groggy, his eyes flew open. He'd dreamt she'd left him and moved back west. *Not happening.* Dismissing the thought, he stretched...and groaned. His sore muscles and battered body felt the full impact of his bouts the day before. *Hell, I ache.*

The sublime image of Alexandra gliding over him sent a surge of electricity pulsing through him. Her soft curves, silky skin and look of love erased his anxiety and soothed his pain. Pushing slowly out of bed, he padded into the bathroom. Upon exiting, he pulled on a T-shirt and sweat pants, grabbed the gift box from his closet shelf, and left in search of his Goth Girl.

Their rumpled clothing lay on the floor by the fireplace and warmth flooded his chest. He'd waited years for last night. *Well worth it.*

Alexandra stood at the counter, scooping coffee into the filter, wearing yoga pants and a long-sleeved shirt. All he wanted to do was hold her close and tell her how deeply he loved her.

"Good morning." He set the gift on the island and wrapped his arms around her. Her beautiful scent surrounded him. Nuzzling her neck, he breathed deep. No perfume, no lotion. Just Alex. Though subtle, her muscles tensed.

Instead of leaning against him or turning to face him, she stepped away, severing their connection. Her tight smile didn't touch her eyes. "How are you feeling?"

He studied her face, trying to make sense of her chilly behavior. After last night, he'd assumed that their relationship had taken a step forward. Unmasked sex. No role-playing. Beautiful lovemaking. But today, she couldn't push him away fast enough. "What's wrong?"

"Nothing." She spun around and finished making coffee.

Bullshit. He grabbed the bottle of ibuprofen and swallowed down four. Yesterday's injuries were screaming today. His body hurt in more places than his brain could absorb. He pulled out the carton of eggs and a large skillet.

Ten minutes later, they ate in silence side-by-side at the breakfast bar. He'd not anticipated the day would begin like this.

Maybe the food helped. Or the coffee. Maybe the silence did the trick. Could have been his groan when he got up to refill their mugs. When he delivered her hot drink, she offered a timid smile. *That's a start.*

With a grunt, he sank onto the stool.

"Are you in pain?" she asked.

He didn't need a damned nursemaid. He needed her to talk to him. "What pains me is that you won't be honest with me."

"I'm sorry, but I can't do this."

Not good. The tightening in his chest had nothing whatsoever to do with his physical injuries.

"Coming home has reopened old wounds," she said. "My life is one big lie. My father—whom I adored—is a monster. My mother is dying. 'Everyone knows, but don't tell Alexandra.'" She set down her mug. "For over a decade I kept my distance from you. Last night I learned the truth about why you let me go. I'm grateful you would do that for me, but it doesn't eliminate the heartache. I've loved two men and both rejected me. Wilson Mitus didn't leave me, per se, but tell that to the six-year-old child inside me that he abandoned."

He swiveled toward her.

"Playing Monday morning quarterback is easy," she continued. "You're back in my life—more like, we're inseparable. *DC's Brightest Tech Star* is my one decent story. You're helping me at the club. I live with you. I made love—*made love*—to you last night. And this morning you want to pick up where we left off. I'm not eighteen. I have a dark side. Making love is what normal people do. I hook up with masked strangers because I'm not capable of having a close, intimate relationship with a man. I'm scared to give my heart, even to you. "

There it is.

"Last night I finally got the truth," she continued. "I'm still reeling from what I learned about my childhood and while I'm elated you're back in my life, I'm not the naïve teenager who was once ready to chuck everything for a man. We have the same challenge we had back then. I live there. You here. Wilde Innovations appears to be closely aligned with certain government and military agencies. You have a manufacturing plant; you employ a lot of people. I have to be a realist. You know, eyes wide open."

"I understand and I agree."

But she furrowed her brow. What about that answer didn't she like? He did not understand this woman.

"Last night I slept in your bed, curled up to you like my life depended on it," she continued. "I can't even escape into my work because my career has completely derailed." She shivered. He reached out to stroke her shoulder.

She jerked away. "Please, that's not helping. I think it would be best if I moved out."

Never had anyone infuriated him more. Never had he felt so

much passion toward one woman. If she needed space, he'd back off, but there was no way in hell she'd be moving out.

"I bought you a present," he said. She stared at the gift, then at him. "Open it."

"Did you hear nothing of what I just said?"

"Do you know what gets me out of bed every fucking day?" he asked. "Guilt. While I was having a great time at Harvard, my sister was taken. The pain and anger and terror are indescribable. Then, I fall in love with this amazing girl. But I have to end the relationship. I might be stupid, but I'm sure as hell not selfish. I lost my sister and then I lost you. Now you're back and I'm happy, but drowning in guilt. I have no right to feel this way. No right." He pushed out of the chair and dropped his plate in the sink.

With trembling fingers, she lifted the lid and pulled away the tissue paper. "You got me gloves." Her words were barely audible, as if he'd crashed in on some private moment. With a tender smile and gentle hands, she slipped them on.

"You needed them. Like we need each other."

She approached him and peered into his eyes. "They're beautiful and elegant and perfect. Thank you for this thoughtful gift. Last night *was* special and that terrifies me."

He wrapped his hands around her soft shoulders. A tornado of need ripped through him. She was right. Their lives were so entwined he couldn't see where his ended and hers began, but he'd tread lightly. *I won't lose her again.*

With all the strength he could muster, he kissed her forehead and let her go. Sadness bled from her beautiful brown eyes. She wasn't as good at concealing her emotions as she'd want him to believe.

"Last night was the best thing that's happened to either one of us in years." He threw his hands up in surrender. "But if we're back to masked screwing at the club, then book us a suite. Small steps, I get. Please don't move out."

ALEXANDRA WANTED TO TELL Crockett how much she loved him. Instead, she retreated into the hall bath to drown her feelings in a scalding hot shower. As the water pounded her, she imagined him joining her. His hard body would meld so perfectly into her soft one.

Feeling encouraged by his "small steps" suggestion, she dried off. Wrapped in the towel, she walked into the guest bedroom to dress and her jaw fell open. The room had been furnished, down to the elegant golden-beige comforter atop a queen-sized bed with four fluffy pillows covered in maroon cases.

Her heart melted. *He did this for me.*

After dressing, she emerged and found him working at his dining room table. One of his Spy Flies soared around the room while a second hovered mid-air in the center of the table. He glanced up and shot her a smile.

The familiar zing of attraction skittered down her body. She slipped into the chair closest to him and watched him operate all three insects simultaneously.

"I have a product presentation tomorrow at the FBI," he said. "It's important, so I'll be here all afternoon prepping." He landed the insects in a line and gazed over at her. "You look pretty."

She'd dressed in leggings and a long sweater, twisted her hair into a ponytail. Nothing special, yet he'd taken the time to notice. "The guest furnishings are beautiful. You didn't purchase that for me, did you?"

"I put a rush on the order so you'd feel at home, but I hope you never sleep in that bed without me."

"I'll keep that in mind." With a light hand on his shoulder, she pecked his scruffy cheek. "Thank you for being so thoughtful." Hesitating before she rose, she gazed at his handsome face. "I'm going to visit my mom."

"Give Kimberly a hug for me."

Alexandra shrugged on her parka and collected her new leather gloves from the kitchen. As she headed toward the front door, she glanced over at him. He'd been watching her, a ghost of a smile on his lips.

"Bye," she called and left. Halfway to the elevator, she stopped. "I'm a brainless idiot." She strode back to his penthouse and into the dining room.

"Forget something?" he asked.

She stood close enough to touch him, but she didn't. "Do you know how I feel about you?"

"I do."

"I'm afraid of getting close to you again. I'd be devastated if you left me."

"Yup, that I'm aware of."

"And I like masked sex, role-playing, and sometimes I like it wild."

"If the 'it' you're referring to is sex, then yes, I know that, too."

"And I live in California. I'm only here for a short time and I—"

He leapt out of his seat, sending the chair crashing on the hardwood. He clutched her in his arms and kissed her, hard. Moaning into him, she thrust her tongue into his mouth and he responded by stroking it with his.

She clawed his back and pulled him so close, she couldn't breathe. But she didn't need oxygen. She needed him.

Their wild, passionate embrace lasted an eternity. She broke away, her mouth sore, her body thrumming, and her heart desperate to be heard. Caressing his face, she murmured, "Let's slow this down. I can tell you're in pain."

"I'll grab a condom," he uttered between kisses.

"No," she murmured. "I want you in my mouth."

"Oh, Alex." With both hands cradling her face, he kissed her. The depth of his passion made her throat constrict, the emotion teetering on the edge of exploding out of her.

She entwined her fingers in his and headed toward the sofa.

"My bed."

Hand in hand, they walked into the master suite. The bright light of day couldn't mask her fear, but she desperately wanted to take this next step with this amazing man. Slowly, they disrobed each other.

Because she hadn't found the courage to tell him, she'd show him how much he meant to her. Clasping his hand, she led him into bed. They lay together, but when she planked over him and peered into his eyes, his turned dark with desire. Soft kisses and tender touches bowed to a firestorm of desire. She dotted a trail of kisses, starting with his handsome face, down his hard chest and six-pack abs until she reached his protruding cock.

Caressing his shaft, she licked the smooth, pink head. Then, with light strokes and a hungry mouth, she let herself go. His excitement seeped into her mouth and she throbbed with desire. His moans morphed into groans of raw need. And when she unleashed a frenzy of energy, he exploded in her mouth.

In the aftermath, he murmured his appreciation and kissed her breathless. "I love you, Alexandra and I've missed you so damned much."

I love you, too. Unable to tell him, she settled for, "This. You. Us. Feels right."

He wanted to love her, to satisfy her, but she refused him. Not because she didn't want his affections, but because she needed to do that for him. Just him. After showering together, they dressed. Crockett returned to his work at the dining room table and Alexandra put on a pot of coffee for him before slipping into her coat.

"Okay, this time I'm actually leaving." Alexandra glanced at the sketch Crockett had pulled from his backpack. "Is that Sophia?"

"Yes. It's an age-generated rendering of what she *might* look like. You never met her, did you?"

"No. She was at a sleep-away camp when your parents visited."

Alexandra could not tear her gaze from the picture. "Do you have a photo of her?"

"Probably in one of these boxes. Why?"

Alexandra peered into Crockett's eyes. "There's something about this woman that's vaguely familiar."

That's all the push he needed. With a kitchen knife in hand and determination brimming in his eyes, he opened box after box, rifling through each.

After checking every box in the living room, they moved into his bedroom and split up their search. "What am I looking for?" she asked.

"A stack of high school graduation pictures."

Sweaters and ski clothes filled the first two boxes, but in the third, Alexandra found a journal. As she lifted the worn notebook, a photo of Crockett slipped out. He was in his high school cap and gown, surrounded by friends. Flipping through pages for more photos, she spied another snapshot. When she removed it, the lone journal entry caught her eye.

I miss my beautiful Goth Girl. But she's gone.
Gotta move on.

Alexandra's heart dropped. He'd made the ultimate sacrifice by letting her go. Not only had he lost Sophia, he'd lost her too. In that moment, she despised herself for refusing to see him all those times he came by.

"You found it." Kneeling next to her, Crockett shook the book. Several more snapshots fluttered out.

"Here she is." Crockett handed her a graduation photo of his family. "That's Sophia at twelve. Two years before she was taken."

Alexandra's stomach dipped. She stared at the photo of the pudgy middle-schooler with a mouth full of braces and oversized glasses. "This doesn't look anything like Sage."

His eyes popped wide. "The woman from the club? What made you think Sage might be my sister?"

She sighed. "Never mind. I...I'm sorry I said anything."

The hope in his eyes fizzled and he tossed the stack of photos and journal on his desk. "It's okay. I'm going to get back to work."

"Can I see your pictures?"

"Sure." He pecked her forehead on his way out.

Pain slashed through her. The burden of his commitment to find his sister weighed heavily on his shoulders.

After collecting the photos, Alexandra sat cross-legged on the bed. As she flipped through snapshots, she found one from *the* summer party her mom had thrown after she graduated high school. That event had changed her summer and ultimately her life.

Alexandra had goofy-posed with her mom and Colton. There was another picture of Colton and Crockett each holding a bottle of champagne along with their Harvard diplomas, gigantic grins plastered on their handsome faces.

She smiled at the photo of a blushing Alexandra sandwiched between her brother and Crockett. She'd spent four years sneaking peeks at Crockett, but he'd never noticed her until that fateful day. Sure, he'd always been polite and friendly, but in a you're-my-best-friend's-little-sister kind of way.

Then, during the early afternoon of their graduation party, she spotted him checking her out across the lawn. The next time she spied him, he and her mom were staring at her. Five minutes later, she caught a glimpse of him moseying over and her heart had pounded out of her chest. When he told her how pretty she was, she couldn't stop grinning, though she'd known she must have looked like a fool.

Bolstered by that compliment, she decided to try to have an actual conversation with him. Since she had no idea what to talk about, she asked him about his new job. The party had continued until late in the evening, but all she remembered was Crockett's blue eyes pinned on her—for hours. And how much he had smiled...at her. When he asked her out, she couldn't believe her ears. Somehow she managed to squeak out, "Okay, that sounds like fun."

Unable to sleep, she kept saying to herself: *I have a date with Crockett Wilde.* Surprisingly, her mom had consented to let her go out with someone four years older, but only because it's "our Crockett".

If her mother had known all the things she'd wanted to do to "our Crockett", she would have locked her only daughter in the house and barred her bedroom window.

The next morning, Alexandra stacked her Goth clothing in the donation pile her mom kept in the basement, thrown away her dark makeup, and gone shopping for a sundress.

Smiling at the memory, Alexandra continued flipping. There were group shots of Crockett with friends and family at his own high school graduation. One particular photo made her jaw drop.

In this close-up, Sophia wasn't smiling and she'd removed her clunky glasses. Sad, gray eyes stared back. Clutching the photo in her hand, Alexandra flew down the hallway and into the dining room.

After glancing up from his laptop, Crockett did a double take. "You okay?"

She held out the photo of Sophia. "We need to talk."

THAT EVENING CROCKETT ROLLED into Incognito with a guarded sense of hope. While he had no expectations that Sage was his sister, he couldn't dismiss Alex's comment, either. *What if* kept him pushing forward for thirteen years.

Alexandra's voice had quivered when she'd shown him the photo of Sophia. She'd insisted the woman at the club—who looked nothing like his sister—had the same gray eyes. "It's not *just* the color." She'd jabbed at the picture for emphasis. "I don't know what it is exactly, but I've seen *these* eyes before."

As he and Alexandra had planned, Crockett arrived at the club first and went directly into the "Master's of the Universe" suite across the hall from the unmarked room. After snapping off the night table lamp and plunging himself into darkness, he dipped his hand into his sport coat pocket and retrieved Horse. Even with his phone set to dim, there was risk associated with what he was about to do. The surveillance cameras in the greeting room, the lounge, and the hallways were mounted in plain sight. If Jase did monitor the private suites, drawing attention to himself and Alex was the last thing he needed, especially if Jase was doing something illegal.

He cracked open the door, nudged the tiny creature outside, and shut it. Still fully clothed, he slipped beneath the linens and, using his phone, activated the insect.

When the foot traffic from passersby quieted, he zoomed Horse across the hallway and landed him flush against the upper doorframe of the unmarked suite with the camera pointing toward the greeting room. If Jase or Francois entered the suite, he'd fly the bug inside.

At long last, he and Alex would know what the hell was going on inside that room.

JUST PAST TEN O'CLOCK, Alexandra entered the club. Her part in their scheme was simple. Alert Crockett when management escorted a member into the unmarked suite. She sashayed into the busy hallway, leaned against the wall outside the lounge and waited. Ten minutes passed. Another five ticked by. No sign of any rejuvenation activity. Then, Dracule stepped off the elevator.

Yes! Painting on her best Electra grin, she waved. That horny old geezer couldn't get to her fast enough. "Why, hello, lovely Electra."

"Hello, yourself." She'd worn a black, strapless bustier dress and his gaze roamed hungrily across her chest. "Here for a little late night fun?"

His leer sent a shiver down her spine. "Absolutely. Life is short. Make every moment matter."

I've heard that before. She studied his masked face, but nothing came to mind. Dismissing the *déjà vu*, she agreed.

As if Jase had been watching, he joined them. "Two of my favorite members." He glanced from one to the other. "Say the word and I'll arrange a suite to accommodate a more *intimate* setting."

"Thank you, my good man. If Electra were interested, she would have made her intentions known."

You got that right. "Enjoy your evenin'." Alexandra forced a smile. As soon as they headed down the hallway, she sent the cued up text from her phone. "Now."

The two men vanished into the unmarked suite. She hurried toward "Master's of the Universe" and pressed her keycard against the sensor. The light turned green and she entered. After slipping beneath the linens, Crockett pulled out an ear bud and handed it to her. She shoved the tiny device into her ear.

"I have a kitchen emergency." Jase's gruff voice was void of the usual charm. "Those idiots can't fucking boil water without causing a goddamn inferno. I have to pass you to Sage tonight."

"Oh, Christ, not that little bitch." Dracule's harsh tone sent a shiver down Alexandra's spine. "I'll slap her if she bites me again."

Poor Sage.

"I dealt with her myself. She won't misbehave." Jase hurried toward the back wall. A concealed panel slid open revealing another dimly lit room.

Oh, my God.

Dracule stepped over the threshold and the door shut behind

him. Crockett zoomed the bug forward, but it crashed into the closed panel.

"Dammit," Crockett muttered.

Anxiety churned in her guts. The room was a pass-through, but to what? Her mind raced with possibilities, none of them good.

Jase hurried out and Crockett flew Horse with him. "Crack open the door," he whispered.

As soon as she did, he zoomed the tiny surveillance bug into their room. "You were right," he murmured.

Dread made her blood run cold.

24

EPIC FAIL

CROCKETT'S IMPENDING PRODUCT PRESENTATION at the FBI was the gateway to the biggest opportunity for Wilde Innovations and he needed to keep his head in the game. But he'd tossed and turned all night, even with Alexandra snuggled in his arms.

If a grown woman had to resort to biting a member, something extreme was happening at Incognito. But until they could gain access into that back room, he had to focus on the task at hand.

Round Two with the FBI.

As he and Decker approached the Department of Justice on Pennsylvania Avenue in northwest DC, Decker bit out a grunt. "What's *she* doing here?"

Crockett flicked his gaze to the entrance of the gray government building that covered most of the city block. Ruth Lizzard, Wilde's former QA Director, chatted away on her phone. He'd terminated her employment last fall for sexual misconduct and had zero interest in speaking with her.

"Hopefully not vying for the same business we are," Crockett replied. "Do you know where she landed?"

"Director of Software Development for No Man's Land."

"That drone manufacturer has been trying to break into the federal space for years."

"Looks like they found the right person to blow that door wide open."

Ruth Lizzard ended her call and marched in their direction.

"Ah, crap," Decker grumbled.

"Hello, boys." Ruth Lizzard did not crack a smile. "Here to wow the FBI with your little critters?"

"I heard you joined Chavez's company," Crockett said, taking control of the conversation. "How's that working out?"

She grinned. "Ray's a dream to work for. We're rolling out some fantastic products. Just between you and me, the FBI was totally impressed."

But Crockett wasn't. "Good for you."

"Best of luck, kiddos," she said. "You're gonna need it." With a smug smile, she flicked her blonde head and strode off.

Lizzard made his skin crawl. She'd been an outstanding employee until she'd attempted to screw her way into an executive position. When he'd refused her, she'd gone after Decker. So, he'd terminated her and hadn't thought twice about her. Until now.

Swallowing down the bitter taste, he and Decker entered the building's waiting area. Danny Strong exited through security and shook both men's hands. "Good to see you."

"You, too," Crockett said.

Both men accompanied him to the bulletproof window. "They're with me." Danny slid his DOJ badge through the recessed tray.

"I need to see your IDs, gentlemen," said the security clerk.

Crockett and Decker slipped their driver's licenses into the tray. Once the employee had entered the necessary information, she slid their IDs back through, along with temporary badges for Crockett and Decker.

"Wear those at all times," she said as both men clipped on the plastic visitor badge.

"I'll see you on the other side." Danny walked back through the employee entrance.

Similar to airport security, Crockett and Decker stepped over to a conveyer belt. They placed their laptops, cell phones, and Spy Flies into the plastic bin to be X-rayed. Then, both men stood in the "X" position while the security guard waved the wand over their bodies. Once cleared, they stepped through the metal detector and waited in front of a sliding glass door to one of three glass-enclosed isolation chambers.

When the door slid open, Crockett stepped into the space. The door closed behind him. Several seconds later, the glass door in front of him opened and he stepped into the FBI lobby.

After Crockett and Decker had retrieved their belongings, Danny led them to a large conference room. "They're on a brief break," Danny explained.

Based on the number of notebooks and tablets, they had a full house.

"How'd the previous demo go?" Crockett asked while Decker paired the two Flies with his phone.

"You know I can't get into the specifics," Danny replied.

"I didn't ask you anything specific."

"Yeah, right. It went fine. Unexpected, actually."

Knowing Lizzard, Crockett wasn't surprised she'd bring the *unexpected*. That seemed to be her strong suit of late.

Along with the three members from Round One of the source selection panel, four high-ranking individuals entered the room. They were the Chief Procurement Officer, Chief Technology Officer, Chief of Field Ops, and Chief of Surveillance Programs.

Between wheezy breaths, the Contracting Officer from Round One reiterated the agency's expectations per the solicitation, then turned the floor over to Crockett.

"Good morning and thank you for this opportunity." Crockett

glanced at each of the panel members. "Wilde Innovations is the industry leader in unmanned aerial vehicles. We are the eyes and ears during mission-critical operations for law enforcement, first responders and Special Forces. Our military-grade fleet of aircraft is designed to mimic birds of prey. Hovercraft drones, along with our larger craft, are used around the world with excellent results. Per your solicitation, today's demo will spotlight the two Spy Flies on the table. Black and Horse were designed to mimic the Black and Horse flies. Decker Daughtry, Wilde's Chief Innovator, will command each device via his phone, but they can also be flown using the handheld controller on the table. Please direct your attention to Black as we highlight its advanced maneuverability."

Using his phone, Decker guided the miniscule craft into the air. Based on yesterday's practice drills, Crockett had every confidence his equipment would exceed expectations. The Fly zoomed around the room before Decker landed it on the top of the projector hanging from the ceiling directly overhead. Then, he demonstrated how the tiny insect could hover in mid-air before landing on the table. After Decker directed it into the Chief Technology Officer's soft-shell tablet case, he buzzed it onto the Chief Procurement Officer's spiral-bound notebook.

"Nice," said the FBI employee.

And then, Decker's expression shifted. It was subtle, but his eyebrows puckered briefly. Acid churned in Crockett's guts. Black's demonstration still had another ninety seconds, but the insect hadn't budged. *Why isn't she moving?*

"As you can see, the equipment behaves like a common fly." Decker held Crockett's gaze for an extra second. "Please direct your attention to Horse. This insect is as maneuverable as Black, but we'd like you to pay special attention to the sound quality."

Horse rose in the air. Decker flew it around the table so the panel could hear the quiet humming of the insect. Then, the bug crashed belly up on the table.

"That's not good," mumbled the Chief Technology Officer.

The wheezy Contracting Officer's thick, mucous-filled cough made Decker flinch. Crockett's stomach dropped. He had to act quickly, so he slipped his hand into his suit pocket and pulled out his personal Moth. Not the device he'd used at the previous demo, but one he'd had for years and kept at home. As he flew it around the room, he let out a relieved breath.

Crockett operated the craft through a series of flawless maneuvers while Decker narrated. Though most stayed focused on Moth, several glanced at the catatonic Horse, still belly up on the table.

When the demo ended, Decker collected Horse and Black. A thin sheen of perspiration dotted his forehead. Though Crockett wanted to fling the tiny devices across the room and belt out a list of obscenities, he was too busy trying to come up with a plausible answer as to why both of his sixty-five thousand dollar pieces of equipment had failed in some form or another.

"What was the purpose of crash-landing the craft?" asked the Deputy Director of Field Operations.

The tech officer raised his eyebrows. "You did that on purpose?"

Leaning back, Crockett crossed his legs. "We build fail-safe behavior into the equipment to cover for human error or in the event the mission doesn't go as planned. The bug goes belly-up to fool the enemy into believing it's real. And it's dead."

"Very nice," said the Chief of Field Ops.

But Wilde Innovations's demonstration of their Spy Flies had been anything but. For the first time in his career, Crockett Wilde had failed.

Big time.

ALEXANDRA SPENT THE MORNING in production going over her *DC's Brightest Tech Star* segment with the editor. Pleased with the results, she hoped this feature story would open up more opportunities to cover the meatier ones. "Can I get a copy for my demo reel?"

Before the editor could respond, Stacy barged in. "I finally have a break in my super busy schedule. Max says I need mentoring."

"Oh, brother," mumbled the editor.

No small talk. No manners. "I'll make time when I get back from my interview. Plan on four o'clock."

As if hypnotized, Stacy stared at the monitor. "Hey, that's Tex. He's *super* hot. I let him know I'm *available*. What are you doing with him?"

Falling in love.

The production editor glared at her. "Quiet!"

Stacy turned on her heels. "I don't have time for this. See you at four, Al."

Alexandra cringed at the hideous nickname.

"I don't envy you," said the editor. "She's got the intelligence of a bobble head."

LATER THAT AFTERNOON, ALEXANDRA returned from interviewing the residents of Happy Day Retirement Village who were preparing for a 5K race. She had barely stowed her handbag beneath her desk when Stacy bombarded her.

"Let's get this mentor shit over with. I've got to get to happy hour."

"Why don't we start with your copy?" Alexandra asked, fighting the urge to roll her eyes.

Stacy plunked down several pieces of paper, then plopped into her desk chair and rolled next to her. After reading the first few copy sheets and leafing through the rest, Alexandra had her answer. Stacy Blunk couldn't write a basic news story. She didn't even cover the basic who, what, where, when and why. While her spelling was atrocious, that was nothing compared to the elementary way in which she approached an interview.

Max would risk the integrity of the news station and the reputation of the other excellent and qualified journalists on staff because he couldn't control his raging libido.

After Alexandra rewrote one of the stories, she slid her tablet around so Stacy could read it.

"Wait? What? You're done? That took you three minutes. How'd you do that? Never mind. I'll bring you what I've got every day. Those dumb neighborhood stories can't possibly keep you that busy. Plus, you'd be helping boost my popularity, which is your job as my mentor."

Over the years, Alexandra had mentored a number of fresh-faced journalists right out of college. It was something she loved doing. But Stacy had no interest in learning. Twenty minutes later, Alexandra wondered why she'd bothered to explain the basic structure of a news story. Stacy hadn't taken notes, but she'd checked her phone plenty.

"That was a handy lesson, the who-what-where-when-why. Did you make that up?"

Alexandra laughed. Stacy had a sense of humor, after all.

"What's so funny?"

No effin' way. "What did you study in school?"

"Boys, partying, like everyone else."

"Where did you cut your teeth?"

Stacy's lips twisted. "My teeth?"

"Where did you work before you came here? Which market? Or are you from print?"

Stacy's cheeks turned the color of her hair. "I worked in a men's clothing store."

"Nice." Alexandra tried to suffocate her sarcasm.

Puffing out her chest, Stacy said, "I was the number one rep three months in a row."

"Is that how you met Max?"

"He was my best customer! He bought an entire wardrobe while I worked there. My commissions were through the roof."

Max Buchard is such a pig.

"If we're finished, Max wants to see you." Stacy spun around at her desk and started texting.

Alexandra headed toward his office. *What could he want?* Max never gave her the time of day. While she hoped for the best, she was a realist. She was about to knock, when his door flew open.

Max reared back. "Christ, you scared the bejesus out of me."

Jumpy much?

"Come in," he said. When she did, he shut the door. "We have to re-do the interview for the winner of *DC's Brightest Tech Star*."

Her stomach roiled. "Why?"

"You have a conflict of interest." Hitching an eyebrow, he glared at her over his glasses. "Why didn't you tell me you were interviewing someone who'd done business with your brother? Damn waste of money and production time."

Her blood pressure spiked. "The fact that Mr. Wilde did business with my brother is irrelevant to the story. I use the name Reed. No one in this town even knows I'm a Mitus."

"My decision is final." He shuffled over to his desk and sorted through one of his many piles. After lifting a piece of paper, he held it out. "This is a good sort of story for you. The animal shelter in Falls Church is celebrating their grand re-opening."

Unable to control her anger, her cheeks grew hot. *This is absolute bullshit.* He was punishing her for something *he* did two years ago because he couldn't keep his dick in his pants then, either. "To whom did you reassign the story, Max?" The question was moot. She knew the answer.

"Stacy Blunk will contact the winner. As her mentor, help her prep."

"I conducted a solid interview," she said. "*Redoing* it is a waste of the station's money."

Max's smarmy smile left her feeling queasy. "Per usual, your self-serving needs come first. Shame on you, Alexandra. What about his poor sister?"

"Mr. Wilde discussed his sister because he trusted me."

"Instruct Stacy what questions to ask."

"You can't teach someone who doesn't want to learn." Alexandra shook her head. "I don't think Mr. Wilde will agree to another interview."

"Convince him." He opened the door. "Oh, and if you won't work with Stacy, I'll be forced to let you go for insubordination."

Her heart plummeted. Max had backed her into a corner.

After waddling into the hallway, he pivoted. His beady eyes drilled into her. "Maybe this time you'll learn your lesson, *honey*."

25

ALEXANDRA'S SUSPICIONS

ALEXANDRA WAITED IN Wilde's reception area, nibbling her fingernail. She would convince Crockett to redo the interview for Sophia's sake.

Crockett rounded the corner. "What a great surprise!" he said, but concern laced his eyes. "What brings you by?"

"I know you're busy. I need five minutes."

"You okay?"

"Absolutely."

"Let's talk in my office." The normally chatty workspace was eerily quiet, the atmosphere thick with tension. Had someone gotten fired?

The second they stepped inside his office, he said, "Make yourself comfortable. I'll be right back." Without waiting for her reply, he left.

Something is definitely wrong. She eased into the chair across from his desk and glanced around for a clue. Nothing was out of place.

A moment later, Crockett returned, deep worry lines etched between his eyebrows. "I'm all yours." His forced smile made her heart tighten. "Is it Kimberly?"

"She's fine, but you aren't. Talk to me."

"Just work. No big deal."

The push and pull continued. She asked him to confide in her. He told her he was happy to help her. She crossed her arms. "I'm not leaving until you spill. What's going on?"

Knock, knock, knock!

Decker burst into the room. "The bugs are performing perfectly. Like that freak fail never happened."

Alexandra whipped her head around. Crockett's phone rang. "I have to take this." He hit the talk key, pressed the phone to his ear. "Wilde."

As he listened, he pushed out of his chair and strode to the window. "I understand," he said. "What do you think?"

Decker sidled over to the conference table, removed his suit jacket and tossed it on the chair. His face was pale, he couldn't hold still. Jittery hands paired with darting eyes made for a very nervous Decker.

"Thanks for your honesty." Crockett hung up.

"Well?" Decker asked.

Crockett eyed her.

"This is where I'm supposed to leave," she said. "But I'm not. You two look like hell."

"Close my office door." Crockett waited for Decker to shut it. "That was Danny." A chill swept through the room. "Three of the attendees thought our demo was brilliant. They liked how we included the fail-safe."

"What about the others?" Decker asked, fiddling with his man-bun.

"Not so much. And one is convinced something went wrong. Danny isn't sure we'll make it to Round Three."

"Oh, no." Alexandra knew how important this was to Crockett. "What happened?"

Without getting into the weeds, Crockett told her about the Spy Fly failures during both FBI demos.

"You've never experienced anything like this before?" she asked.

"No." Both men responded in unison.

Crockett opened his top drawer and rifled through it. Then, he punched his phone console. "Ellen, I need aspirin, three coffees, and food."

The door flew open and Ellen set a bottle of pain relievers on his desk. She shot Alexandra a tight smile. "Be back shortly."

"I'd like to help," Alexandra said. "But I need more information. Can I ask you some questions?"

"She can be objective." Decker shoved his hands into his pockets. "I think we should tell her."

An hour later, the sandwiches had been devoured, the coffee long gone. Alexandra had learned enough to make a brash conclusion. "This reeks of foul play."

"I reviewed everything," Crockett said. "There's been no breach."

"I've double and triple checked," Decker said. "No one has hacked into our system."

"Who, here, would gain if Wilde failed?" Alexandra asked.

Up went Crockett's eyebrows. "No one."

Decker snickered. "That's absurd."

Alexandra pushed out of the chair and leaned against the windowsill. "If these incidents aren't coincidental—and it doesn't sound like they are—then someone wants you to fail."

Crockett's jaw ticked. "We've been so busy reacting, we haven't gone on the offense."

The color drained from Decker's cheeks. "Who would do something *that* vindictive?"

"Someone seeking revenge," Alexandra said. "Corporate sabotage is serious, which means the underlying cause is emotionally charged."

The two men stared at each other. Several seconds passed before Crockett turned his full attention to Alexandra. "Over the years I've terminated five—six employees at the most. Theft from the warehouse, poor performance, and falsifying a resume come to mind. Recently, I had an issue with one employee..."

Decker's eyebrows shot up. "You think?"

"It's possible," Crockett replied.

"She couldn't do it without help from someone on the inside," Decker said.

"Who?" Alexandra interrupted.

"Ruth Lizzard," Crockett bit out.

Alexandra hesitated. "Where have I heard that name before?"

"Larry Berry," Decker said.

"Tell me about them," she said.

"Not much to say," Crockett replied. "Ruth did a great job running QA. Larry was on her team. Last year, I had a VP slot open up. After Ruth's first interview, I eliminated her from the candidate pool. She wasn't the right fit. Then, she propositioned me in exchange for the promotion. I refused her. She tried a second time. And again, I refused her, this time documenting with HR."

"Then, she came after me next," Decker said. "And she threatened to blackmail me."

"Sounds intense." Alexandra crossed her arms.

"I terminated her," Crockett said. "She left and from what I've learned, she got a new job."

"With the competition," Decker added.

"I promoted Larry into her position." Crockett crossed his legs. "And that was the end of that."

"Not necessarily," Alexandra said. "What was his relationship with Ruth?"

Crockett shrugged. "They worked together. I didn't notice anything unusual, but I'm too busy to pay attention. Decker, thoughts?"

Decker scratched his head. "Ruth had a strong team. They all ate lunch together, but I never suspected anything between her and Larry."

"I'd like to do a little digging," she said. "Explore whether anyone you fired has motivation."

Crockett wasn't convinced a former employee would be involved in a scheme of this magnitude, but he was grateful for her help. "Absolutely. You can work with Ellen."

"I'd like to ask Larry a few questions," she said.

"You can't waltz in and say, 'Hey, Larry, can I ask you about your relationship with Ruth?'" Decker said.

"Crockett can let him know I need additional quotes for my tech story. I'll ask you and Natalie Floyd a few more questions, so he doesn't suspect anything."

Decker released a long sigh. "It might work."

"I like this plan." The frustration in Crockett's eyes subsided a little. "Thank you, Alexandra."

Suddenly, she didn't care that she'd lost her only decent story to a rookie journalist. What mattered was helping Crockett with his business. Crockett Wilde was the absolute best man she had ever known.

And he deserved *her* absolute best.

26

THE FIRE AND THE FIRING

That evening, Crockett and Alexandra pulled into the deserted parking garage of Incognito. The hair on the back of Crockett's neck stiffened. "Where is everyone?"

"There's a sign on the elevator," Alexandra said. He stopped at the curb so she could read it.

> We are closed due to a kitchen fire.
> Our apologies for the inconvenience.
> Check the website for updates. Thank you.

"We're not catching a damn break," he said.

"Hang in there, Sage," she said as Crockett drove out of the garage and into the night.

Ten minutes later, they entered his penthouse and he reached back to untie his mask, but she wrapped her arms around his neck and pressed her body into his. "I need you masked tonight." The fire in her eyes, paired with her raspy voice, turned him hard.

Her sudden kiss ripped through him, her breathy moan unleashing his need to bury himself inside her heat. He anchored one arm around her waist. With the other, he squeezed her ass.

She mewled and cemented herself against him. Her eyes, framed in the dark mask, blazed with passion.

In spite of everything they faced, desire consumed them. Stabbing pain pounded his side from the tournament injuries, but he pushed past and ground against her. He grabbed a chunk of her wig and tipped her face toward his. She groaned. He fastened his mouth to hers and pinned her against the wall.

"You...this," she gasped, fisting his hair. "I need wild and hard."

She needed Hunter and he would gladly oblige. Alexandra, in any form, was his sole desire.

Every time she shuddered and whimpered, a ripe stream of pleasure ripped through him. "You're mine," he murmured.

"Say it again."

He anchored a hand under her chin, kissed her sweet, sexy mouth and whispered, "You. Are. Mine."

"Yes, I am," she panted.

He unzipped and toed off his boots, stripped out of his sweater and pants. Dropped his underwear, tore off his socks. Her hand curled around his cock. Pleasure spiraled through him like cascading fireworks, but he kept his attention glued on her.

With her captive in his arms, he reached around, unzipped her dress and pulled it off her shoulders. The dress fell away, leaving her nude.

He kissed her neck, nibbled her ear and dotted kisses down to her shoulder. She responded with a coo or a whimper. She stroked his back with one hand, caressed his pulsating cock with the other. When his juices slickened his head, she murmured, "I need you in me."

Retreating into the bedroom, he returned, sheathed in a condom.

She jumped into his arms, locked her legs around his waist, and unleashed a torrent of energy. She kissed him hard, thrusting her tongue into his mouth.

He pinned her against the glass windows, speared her with his shaft. Her strangled cries crashed through the silence. He covered her mouth with his and devoured her raw, sexy sounds.

"Hard. Fuck me hard." Her guttural sound vibrated against his throat and he started moving inside her.

He thrust, again and again, until the mounting pleasure sent him hurtling toward a release. He broke from the kiss to warn her. "Too fast."

"Don't stop. Harder, *please*," she gasped. "I'm going to… oh…yes."

"Look at me. I want to see you when you come undone around me."

Shuddering and groaning through her orgasm, she stared into his eyes. Her intense beauty overcame him and he climaxed.

His mouth found hers and he kissed her. When she tightened her hold around his neck and melted into him, he murmured, "Alexandra, I love you, so damned much."

"Me, too."

Progress. She matched his loving smile with one of her own. Even with all the uncertainty they faced, he would love and protect her, *forever*. Of that he was certain.

THE FOLLOWING MORNING, CROCKETT and his innovation team sat huddled around the conference table in the Tank. Until he could get to the bottom of the suspected sabotage, it was business as usual at Wilde.

Quality Assurance had completed their analysis of Moth and Maverick's Eagle and those issues were considered closed to everyone, but Crockett. He hadn't divulged Charlie Bowen's crisis so Decker could work in secrecy, and no one besides Decker and Ellen knew about their epic fail during Round Two of the FBI demo. The less his employees knew, the better. He'd shouldered worse and he would manage through this, too. At least, that's what he kept telling himself.

All eyes were on the white board while Decker finished explaining the details of the plastics formula for their NVGs. Crockett's innovators and scientists had done the impossible and he welcomed the good news.

"On paper, this is fantastic," said Crockett. "Timeframe?"

"Manufacturing is going to knock out the prototype in two weeks," Decker said. "The plastic is definitely lighter than our initial calculations. Based on certain polymers and isotopes, we might be able to accommodate a few minor adjustments that would bring additional benefit to first responders and military personnel."

"Congratulations," Crockett said. "It's a huge improvement. But what's the damage?"

Ellen popped in. "Excuse me. Crockett, you have a visitor. She's driving Patty crazy with her incessant blather."

"Who is it?"

"A TV reporter. I've tried everything, but I can't get rid of her."

As Crockett approached reception, he bit out a grunt. The familiar redhead was talking ad nauseam, her hands flicking her hair and flying in the air for emphasis.

Stacy Blunk froze, mid-word. "*You're* Crockett *Wilde* of Wilde Innovations? I'm sure you remember me. Stacy B-L-U-N-K. I was hoping to hear from you."

"I'm in a meeting, Stacy. How can I help you?"

Thrusting out her chest, she shot him a gleeful smile. "I'm here to schedule your interview. You won some contest."

Crockett didn't have the time or the patience for shenanigans. "Ms. Reed completed the interview."

Stacy stepped close. The overpowering scent of her perfume stung his nose. "Did Al cover the who-what-where-when-and why? *Why* being the most important."

Patty, the receptionist, stifled a snicker.

This is a joke. He stepped toward the door, which he was two seconds from pushing open and shoving her through. "Did *Alexandra*—not Al—put you up to this?"

"Our boss, he shit-canned her story because of some conflict. So, can we set up the interview? I need to get to the POTUS."

His blood pressure kicked up. "What conflict?"

"Dunno. All I know is that I get to do this." She batted her lashes. "And with you, no less." She flicked her attention to Patty. "I was born under a lucky star."

"What's your boss' name?" Crockett asked.

"Max Buchard."

"Is he in today?"

"Yuppers."

He shoved open the glass door to his office suite. "I'm not redoing the interview." Her mouth dropped open. "If you'll excuse me, I have to get back to my meeting."

After stomping her foot, she stormed out.

"Please ask Ellen to get Max Buchard, Cable News Fifteen, on the phone," Crockett said to Patty.

"Yes, sir," said the receptionist.

As he powered down the hallway, he fisted his hands in frustration. Alex had done a phenomenal job interviewing him and his team. He popped back into the Tank, informed his team he needed to handle something, and paused at Ellen's desk.

"Buchard is on hold," Ellen said. "Private line."

Crockett entered his office and jabbed the speaker button. "Mr. Buchard, Crockett Wilde."

"Hello, Mr. Wilde. Stacy texted me quite upset. Any particular reason you're refusing to redo the interview?"

Seriously? "Why don't you tell me why the interview needs to be redone?"

"Conflict of interest. Alexandra Reed is a Mitus. You've done business with her brother. She should never have interviewed you in the first place. It shows bias."

Bullshit. "My business deal with Mr. Mitus had nothing to do with her story."

"I'd encourage you to reconsider, for your *poor* sister's sake."

Either Buchard was trying to incite him or play him for a fool. "I've met Ms. Blunk before. She doesn't strike me as someone who has the experience to realize my missing sister is the focal point of the story."

"Stacy is our most promising new on-air talent. With Alexandra as her mentor, she'll do just fine."

"Which circles back to my original statement. I see no reason to redo it." And then he realized Buchard's true motivation. His dick. Crockett's stomach soured.

"I'm sorry, Mr. Wilde. I have to adhere to the rules of journalistic integrity."

What integrity? "Even if I did agree to be interviewed again, I wouldn't discuss my sister with her. Please find another winner. Goodbye, Mr. Buchard." Crockett ended the call, then found Gavin's business card.

Gavin answered his cell. "Aviato."

"Hey, Gavin, Crockett Wilde. Wilde Innovations."

"How you doing?" His friendly voice was a godsend.

"I need your help."

ALEXANDRA'S HEART POUNDED WILDLY as she tapped the record button on her phone app just before entering Max's office. "You wanted to see me."

"Have a seat," Max said from behind his desk. When she did, he glared at her. "Mr. Wilde has refused to redo the interview."

Alexandra bit back a smile. "Run the story, Max. It stands on its own merit."

"I'll give you credit for one thing," he said. "The crux of that story *is* his missing sister. If the story doesn't run, there's *no* chance Sophia's abductors will ever be found."

Her cheeks flamed and she bit the inside of her lip. How dare he use Crockett's sister as leverage?

"I told you to convince him to change his mind," he continued. "You failed." She anticipated the worst and muscles running along her shoulders turned to stone.

"I hired you because the network forced my hand, but your services are no longer needed." He folded his hands over his paunch. "Before you go, give Stacy your interview questions for the Wilde story and rewrite her copy for whatever she's currently working on." With a satanic grin, he added, "That girl can't write her way out of a paper bag, but her other talents far outweigh her shortcomings."

What a pig.

Her head pounded. Though she could have unleashed a plethora of comments harking back to his indecent behavior at the California station, she rose and exited his office. On the way back to her desk, she stopped the recording.

"Employee list is ready," texted Crockett. "It stays in my office."

To her surprise, Gavin was waiting at her desk. "Let's grab a bite," he said.

Ten minutes later they were sipping sparkling water in a quaint Italian restaurant around the corner.

"I got canned." Alexandra told Gavin what had happened.

"I'm sorry." He covered her hand with his. "At least it's not because of anything you did wrong or didn't do right."

"True." Her expression fell. "Honestly, I don't understand how Max gets away with it time and time again."

Gavin drained his water glass. "Bad karma always catches up."

"Well, this is a slow-moving one."

He chuckled. "Crockett called me. Max infuriated the hell out of him." Gavin slid the thumb drive across the table. "He had the foresight to ask me for a copy of your interview. Honey, that man is a keeper."

Her heart bloomed. "He sure is."

After lunch, Alexandra headed over the 14th Street Bridge into Virginia. While relieved she no longer worked for Max, the sting from getting fired burned in her stomach.

Since her freshman year at USC, she'd always worked in a news station. Though she felt rudderless, she was certain she'd land another reporting gig. While she circulated her resume, she'd spend more time with her mom. And she'd help Crockett flush out the saboteur. He might not be convinced there was one, but she was.

She found parking in a nearby garage and hurried into the busy Crystal City building. When she entered Wilde Innovations, Larry Berry was speaking with the receptionist and a brunette.

"Hey, Alexandra, we got word you need more info for your story," Larry said.

"Did Crockett send out an email?"

"He sure did and I'm happy to comply. I like being in the spotlight." He grinned. "This is my wife, Roberta. This is Alexandra Reed, the reporter who interviewed me for the tech story."

Wife? Her thoughts flashed to Larry huddled on the coffee shop sofa with a blonde.

"Do you know when the show will be on?" Roberta asked.

"No air-date has been set," said Alexandra. "I'll make sure Crockett knows so he can get the word out."

"We're going to throw a party. I'm so proud of him." Smiling sweetly, she caressed Larry's shoulder.

Though Larry smiled, he leaned away from her. *Not into PDA? Or not into your wife?*

"Alright, honey, I've got to get to the airport," Roberta said. "I wish I didn't have to leave."

Larry said nothing.

How awkward. "Headed somewhere warm?" Alexandra asked, feeling like she should fill the silence.

"I've got a business meeting in Florida." She pouted. "I'm bummed Larry can't join me."

"You know I'm super busy here, Roberta," Larry said.

His wife rolled her eyes. "This guy's been burning the midnight oil. I had to arrange for my folks to take our kids for a few days."

"Next time," Larry said.

"Have a safe trip," Alexandra said. "Excuse me." She stepped over to reception.

"Walk me to the elevators," Roberta said and she and Larry left.

A moment later, Ellen bustled around the corner. "Crockett is at an off-site meeting, but we can get started without him."

Before leaving reception, Alexandra glanced over her shoulder as Larry pecked his wife's cheek before she scooted inside an elevator. As soon as the doors closed, Larry pulled his phone from his pocket, his thumbs flying over the keypad. *Who couldn't you wait to text, Larry?*

The two women entered Crockett's office and Ellen closed the door. "Before you begin, I'll need your signed consent."

"For what?"

After Ellen sat at the conference table, she opened one of two manila folders. "You'll have access to propriety information. By signing this form you agree to the following conditions: All documents are property of Wilde Innovations and remain in this office. You won't photograph anything. You can't discuss any of the information with anyone besides Crockett Wilde, Decker Daughtry and myself."

Alexandra tossed her coat and gloves on the sofa, sat next to Ellen, read the form and signed.

With a smile, Ellen handed her the second manila folder. "Your list. I anticipated you'd want to review personnel files of terminated employees, so I have those. You can see them one at a time. If you need to review a current employee's file, I can request it from HR." She rose. "Any questions?"

"No, thanks. I'm good."

"I'll be at my desk if you need me. Happy hunting."

Just before Ellen left, Alexandra said, "Actually, I do have a question. What can you tell me about Larry Berry?"

"You'll have to be more specific."

"Does he work late a lot?"

"Three days a week he picks up one of his children from child care. I know because we leave at the same time."

"How long has he worked here?"

Ellen paused. "A few years, at least. I can check with HR if you need specific dates. Crockett might know. He has a good memory for that sort of thing."

"Larry mentioned he was recently promoted," Alexandra said. "Would you consider him a satisfied employee?"

"I guess. Any reason you're asking?"

"Maybe. I'm not sure. Thanks for your help."

With a smile, Ellen left.

Alexandra flipped open the folder. Wilde Innovations employed over one hundred and fifty full-time salaried personnel and thirty part-timers. Over the past eight years, twelve resigned and five had been terminated.

Alexandra focused on the five terminated individuals. She jumped on the Internet and began her detailed search. The first employee had passed away over a year ago. The second had retired to Florida. The third was a government analyst by day and a local musician in the evenings. Alexandra didn't think the two living people had motivation to sabotage Wilde and crossed them off her suspect list.

The door opened. She expected to see Ellen. Instead, Crockett entered. His piercing baby blues bore into her and her heart skipped a beat. *So handsome. So sexy. So mine.*

The air grew thick. She had the strongest urge to run to him, throw her arms around him, and never, ever let go.

But in true Mitus form, she shot him a sultry smile. "May I help you?"

"Yes. You. Can." His deep voice sliced through the air, her insides clenched with desire. With his gaze pinned on her, he closed his office door, removed his overcoat.

She whistled. "Looking good." His tailored navy suit, white dress shirt and bold pink tie melded against his solid frame. While clothes may make the man, this one needed no additional assistance.

His swagger oozed confidence. His smile halted her breath, but it was the intensity in his eyes that confirmed she was his, in every way. She rose, eager to touch him, feel his mouth on hers, his arms holding her against him.

He closed the gap between them, drew her into his arms and kissed her. Her insides tingled all the way down to her toes. This man could undo her with the simplest touch. He kissed her once more before releasing his hold.

"How was your meeting?" she asked at the same time he asked, "Making any headway?"

Instead of sitting behind his desk and attending to emails, he sat next to her and gave her his undivided attention. "Good meeting." He hesitated. "I spoke with Max Buchard and refused to redo the interview. Did he tell you?"

"He fired me."

Anger clouded Crockett's sky blue eyes. "It's my fault. How can I fix—"

"The network forced him to bring me on board, but it wasn't working out." She fished the thumb drive from her handbag. "Gavin said you called him. Thank you for thinking of this."

"After speaking with Buchard, I had a feeling you'd need that."

"Reconsider doing the interview with Stacy, for Sophia's sake."

"You know how much I love and miss my sister, but I won't be manipulated into doing something. Max has no integrity. And doing a story about a girl who's been missing over a decade won't bring her home."

She caressed his arm. "Please don't dismiss anything."

Sadness shadowed his expression, but he redirected his attention to the open folder on the table. "I'll give it some thought." She didn't believe him, but didn't want to press the subject further.

"How's this going?" He spun the folder around. "Norris was a good man. Sadly, his drug addiction got in the way of his ability to do his job. I paid his rehab bill. Never heard from him again."

She closed Norris's folder. "I met Larry Berry's wife today."

"Roberta, right?"

"Yeah. If I touched you in public, how would you respond?"

"You're going to have to narrow that down. Are we at the movies? At dinner? At a work event?"

"Work event."

"Again, babe, it would depend."

She smiled. He'd called her 'babe'. "Let me explain. Larry Berry's wife was sweet and affectionate toward him, but he appeared uncomfortable."

"Maybe he's not into public affection. Some people are private. I kissed you in my office because we were alone. If you'd been in reception, I wouldn't have."

"Well, darn, I was hoping for the big make out scene right out there in the open."

He chuckled. "Do you think you're being overly suspicious?" He paused. "Never mind. Your hunch about the club was spot-on." Crockett's cell phone rang. "Excuse me. I've got to take this." He answered. "Hey, Danny."

After reviewing the roster, she grabbed the folder and left Crockett's office. Ellen was pulling on her gloves. "You ready for the fifth folder?"

"Please." They exchanged folders. "Please make sure you give Crockett that one before you leave."

"Will do. Thank you for your help."

"Of course." Ellen slung her handbag over her shoulder and headed down the corridor. On the way back into Crockett's office, she wondered if Larry would be staying late since he was too busy to take care of his own children. She dropped the folder on Crockett's desk, then rushed out. As she rounded the corner, she caught a glimpse of Larry hurrying toward the exit. As soon as he punched the elevator button, he began texting. Alexandra glanced at the time. Five thirty-five. *What's the rush, Larry?*

She returned to Crockett's office and stopped short. With his back to her, he stared out the window at the evening sky. He'd removed his suit jacket. She appreciated his broad shoulders, long torso, and that amazingly hot ass. Crockett Wilde was a whole lotta yummy.

"Not the news I wanted to hear, but I appreciate the heads up."

Feeling like she'd walked into a private conversation, she eased into the chair at the conference table and flipped open the HR folder.

"Yeah, dinner sometime sounds good. Give Allison my love." His hand dropped to his side. He didn't even bother hanging up. "Dammit. Dammit." He joined her at the table. Darkness tinged his bright eyes.

"What did he say?"

"Danny heard back from the source selection committee. The unofficial, off-the-record word is that they aren't going to recommend we advance to Round Three."

"I'm sorry." She squared her shoulders. "I'm not giving up. That means you aren't either."

"This is one fight I'm not going to win." He exhaled a harsh breath. "Why'd you run out?"

"Keeping an eye on Larry."

He eyed the open folder. "Making progress?"

She stared at Ruth Lizzard's photo ID stapled to the inside pocket. Her long brown hair and heavy bangs hung like a tarp, her expression deadpan.

"Damn," she muttered.

"What?"

"I spotted Larry at a coffee shop getting cozy with a blonde."

"So?"

"For starters, his wife is a brunette. I was hoping it was Lizzard, but this isn't the woman I saw with Larry."

Agitation swept over Crockett's face. He grabbed his laptop, banged something out, and swung the computer around. "Is that who you saw him with?"

Alexandra stared at the photo of the short-haired platinum blonde. Her big curls flowed up and back, the elegant style unforgettable.

"That's definitely the hair, but the woman had her back to me. I didn't see her face. Who is that?"

"Ruth Lizzard."

27

THE HOSPITAL VISIT

The following morning, Alexandra kissed her man goodbye before he left for work, checked in with her mom, and called her former boss in LA. While he was disappointed things didn't work out with the affiliate station, he wasn't surprised. She checked Incognito's website and her heart dropped. No change. The club was still closed.

She left the condo and drove to Wilde Innovations. While she had her money on Larry Berry, she needed to play this coy. She entered the suite, set her phone on Do Not Disturb, and asked the receptionist to contact Ellen. The ever-efficient assistant whisked her into Natalie Floyd's office for her first fake follow-up interview. When finished, Natalie dropped her off at Decker's office.

"C'mon in," he said.

She closed the door and sat across from him. "Is Ruth Lizzard's blackmail relevant to what's happening here?"

"It could be. I don't mind telling you. I'm bisexual. She saw me at a bar with a man and threatened to out me if I didn't convince Crockett to give her the Veep spot."

"So, she's super manipulative. Was she always like that?"

"No, about a year ago she underwent this major transformation. Clothing, hair. Her face, too." He shrugged. "She was on vacation for two weeks and returned to work a different person. She changed her long, dark hair to short blonde curls. Her clothing went from unremarkable to upscale. She dropped some weight, too. I don't usually pay attention to those things, but in this case, it was extreme. I remember her telling me she would do whatever necessary to land that VP spot."

"Do you think it's possible Larry's behind the recent product failures?"

"Our software's complexity would make that a challenge. I'm not sure Larry's got what it takes to override the code and then conceal his work. Ruth, however, could pull it off."

"Thank you, you've been super helpful."

"Crockett said your hunches are spot-on. I hope you're right. We can't afford any more failures. Let me know if you need anything else."

She rose. "And for the record, anything you tell me—"

"You have Crockett's back. I trust you now."

"Thank you for saying that, Decker. Can you take me to Larry's office, please?"

"You're welcome to go wherever you need. You don't need an escort."

"Which direction is it?"

He pointed. "Three doors down."

She opened his door. "Thanks for your time."

"You're the first journalist I actually trust. Don't prove me wrong."

On the way to Larry's office, she typed a text to her mom. "I'd like to take you to your next doc appt and we can have lunch together. I love you so much." She tapped on Larry's open door.

With a grin, Larry said, "C'mon in. I'm ready for my close-up."

She sent the text and relaxed into the chair across from his cluttered desk. "No cameras today. Just a few follow-up questions."

"You betcha. Whatever you need."

"What I need is a phenomenal memory." She set her phone on the table and pressed the record button on the app. "I'd like to record our conversation."

"I'm not comfortable with that."

"Standard procedure. Otherwise, I can't quote you. And I'd hate to cut you from the segment altogether."

His eyebrows flew up. "Oh, go ahead then."

After asking Larry to paint a picture of his career path at Wilde, she sat back and listened. His answers didn't interest her but his body language did. When he finished, she reminded him of his comment. "Ruth Lizzard is the brains behind Wilde's QA Division. Can you expand on that?"

At the mere mention of her name, he smiled and sat tall. "She's phenomenal."

"Tell me about her contributions."

In a heartbeat, Larry became animated and his face flushed like a teenager in love. He talked longer about her accomplishments than his own. Alexandra Reed had hit the mother lode.

"As a journalist, I'm always in search of my next story. I'd love an introduction."

He cleared his throat. "We don't keep in touch."

Sure you don't. "Well, darn. I'll have to call her office cold then. She sounds like someone I'd like to interview. A real take-charge kind of lady."

He beamed. "She sure is."

Alexandra rose. "Larry, you were the exact *oomph* the story needed."

On her way back to Crockett's office, Alexandra tapped off the recorder and checked Incognito's website for the second time that morning. Still closed. *Dammit.*

As soon as she swiped off the Do Not Disturb, her phone blew up with texts and missed calls. The first one was from Crockett. "I think this text was meant for Kimberly, but I'll respond. I don't have a doc appt, but my dental cleaning is coming up. You can take me to that. Lunch with you, anytime, babe. I love you, too. So much." Following his text was a big smiley face.

She burst out laughing. *I said it. No turning back now.*

The next text was from Colton. "Mom in hospital. She's OK. Left you a message. Talked to Crockett. See you soon." Adrenaline shot through her and she took off toward Crockett's office.

CROCKETT POWERED DOWN THE hallway with Alexandra's coat, handbag and gloves in hand. As they drew close, worry shadowed her beautiful face. "What happened?" she asked.

"She fell." He helped Alex on with her coat and handed her the gloves.

"How?"

"I'll tell you on the way."

At the elevator bank, he punched the down button. "Kimberly had difficulty getting out of bed and couldn't find her balance. They're doing a brain scan to check for recurring tumors."

Her shoulders sagged. "Oh, no."

The doors opened and they squeezed into the crowded elevator. Everyone else filed out at the lobby level, but they continued down to the underground parking.

"Thank you for dropping everything for me."

Pulling her close, he kissed her temple. "What kind of boyfriend would I be if I didn't?"

Her sad smile shredded him. Falling in love shouldn't be filled with so much angst. They climbed into his truck and he drove out of the parking garage. For several moments, they rode in silence while Vivaldi's *Four Seasons* played softly in the background. "We'll know more once we're there." He clasped her hand. "Would talking about your morning help distract you?"

Leaning over, she kissed his cheek. "Probably. I don't know. Maybe."

"Give it a try."

She gave his hand a little squeeze. "Larry thinks he's in love with Ruth Lizzard. He doesn't have motive, but she does."

"And you think she's behind my product failures?"

"It's a possibility. Decker is convinced Larry's not smart enough. But he thinks Ruth could have done it. Could Larry have given her access to the system?"

"Absolutely." He tightened his grip on the steering wheel. "This fucking pisses me off." He exited the G.W. parkway and merged onto the beltway, thick with traffic. She stroked his shoulder, alleviating some of his billowing anger.

"I'll call Ruth tomorrow for an interview and hope her ego takes the bait."

"Isn't that risky? You don't work for the cable station."

"She doesn't know that."

"If Ruth did orchestrate this, she's as crazy as she is dangerous. Please be careful."

They passed an accident, already moved to the shoulder. Moments later, they pulled into the Alexandria Hospital parking lot and rushed inside. Though Kimberly perked up when they entered the room, her sallow cheeks and glassy eyes were a definite sign she wasn't okay.

Colton rose from the chair next to her bed and hugged them both. "Thanks for getting here so quickly."

"Of course." After hugging her mom, Alexandra sat on the edge of the bed and held her hand. "What happened?"

"The doctor called it 'an episode'," Kimberly said.

Colton's phone rang. "It's the movers." Stepping toward the door, he answered. "Mitus."

Crockett kissed Kimberly's cheek, then sat in the chair Colton had just vacated. "What happened?"

"I stood and lost my balance. The nurse claims I was incoherent." She tossed a nod in the direction of a walker next to the bed. "My newest accessory. Colton's guesthouse is ready, so I'm moving."

"That's great news, Mom."

Colton walked back in. "Mom, I'm meeting the movers at your place."

"Thank you, son. When do I get out of here?"

"The doctor wants to keep you another day." Colton kissed his mother's cheek. "Don't worry about a thing. We've got this. Your job is to relax."

"Thanks for everything," Colton said to Crockett. "Alexandra, I'll call you later."

"I'll walk out with you," she said. "Be right back."

As soon as they left the room, Kimberly's smile fell. "I'm so tired. All the time."

Crockett sat on the bed next to her and clasped her hand. "What do you need? What can I do to help?"

Her rueful smile tugged at his heart. This woman was as much of a mom to him as his own. "Love my daughter and keep her safe when I'm..." Her voice cracked.

"I will. You have my word." He glanced over his shoulder. "While we're alone, I need to say a few things. First, thank you for forcing Alexandra's hand so she'd move in with me. I'll assume Colton was in on your scheme."

With a little smile, Kimberly nodded. "Of course. Desperate times call for desperate measures." She patted Crockett's hand. "That child of mine needed a swift boot in the derrière where you were concerned."

"Along those lines, I want to ask you something." He pulled out his phone. "Do you mind if I video our conversation?"

She frowned. "If you must."

He tapped the record button as she finished fluffing her hair.

"You look lovely. Not even a hospital stay can change that." He turned the lens on himself—flashed a grin—then switched it back to Kimberly. "I've given this a lot of thought...for a lot of years. You know how much I adore Alexandra."

"I do," she said, with a smile. "And I tried to help you out every time she came home. But my sweet girl can be strong-willed, too."

"She is and I love that about her." Crockett paused. "Kimberly, I'd like to ask you for Alexandra's hand in marriage. I'm waiting to pop the question, but I'd love your blessing."

Beaming, Kimberly said, "I've waited a long time for this."

"You and me both. I'm not sure she'll say yes."

"If she doesn't, she'll have to answer to me." They both laughed. "It means a lot that you asked me, Crockett."

"I've loved our Goth Girl for a long time. Even time and distance couldn't change that."

Kimberly patted his hand. "I know that, dear."

"You have my word I'll keep her safe and make sure she knows how much I love her—every day. I'll protect her and build a wonderful life with her."

Through the tears in her eyes, Kimberly smiled. "I wholeheartedly give you my blessing. But you've had it from the very beginning. I wish you both a lifetime of love and laughter. Be good to each other and you'll find that life is beautiful, even in the darkest times."

With the phone still recording, Crockett sat next to Kimberly, placed himself in the shot, and kissed her on the cheek.

"Ooooh, a selfie," Alexandra quipped as she breezed into the hospital room, but her red eyes were a clear indication she'd been crying. "What did I miss?"

"Crockett doing what he does best," Kimberly said. "Making me happy."

He flipped the camera on Alex. She blew him a kiss and he

stopped filming. Kimberly said she needed to rest. After Alexandra promised to visit the following day, they departed.

As soon as they entered the busy lobby, she pulled him out of the flow of foot traffic. "Colton answered my questions for the first time, ever. I have you to thank for that. So, thank you." After kissing his cheek, she stared into his eyes. "Her dying has become very real to me." She choked back a sob.

He pulled her close and hugged her, then kissed her forehead. "What really happened with your mom?"

"There are several new tumors. The radiation treatment didn't work. Neither did the chemo." Tears slid down her cheeks. "How will I survive without her?"

He cupped his hands on her shoulders and peered into her eyes. "Focus on the now. Because now is all we have."

EGOMANIAC

Just before seven in the morning, Alexandra helped Crockett into his overcoat. *"You.* Go to work."

"Are you sure?" he asked, caressing her bottom.

She dropped a light kiss on his lips. "Of course I want you to stay, but I've got to research No Man's Land before calling Ruth Lizzard."

"You'll do great." He stroked her arm. Even his simple caress sent tingles scurrying through her. "Her ego's too big to refuse the interview."

"I hope our plan works." They walked hand in hand to the front door of the condo. "I'll text you if there's a change to Incognito's website."

"You've been worried about Sage, haven't you?" He threw his laptop bag over his shoulder.

"How'd you know?"

He cupped her chin, kissed her. "You had a nightmare. Don't remember?"

"No." She'd hoped they'd gone away.

"Lock yourself in, babe. Good luck today."

After one more delicious kiss, she ushered him out. *I adore that man.*

With a lingering smile, she returned to the dining room and opened her laptop. Before beginning her research, she hopped over to Incognito's site and sighed. The club was still closed.

Two hours later, she'd learned enough about Ruth Lizzard and her new employer, Maryland-based No Man's Land, to feel confident enough to make the call.

"Good morning, No Man's Land," answered the perky receptionist. "How may I direct your call?"

"Ruth Lizzard, please."

"One moment."

Too easy.

"Ruth Lizzard's office. Cece speaking."

"Hello, Cece. This is Alexandra Reed. I'm a news reporter who recently interviewed employees at Wilde Innovations for a segment called *DC's Brightest Tech Star*. Larry Berry spoke highly of Ms. Lizzard. I'd like to speak with her about her contribution to Wilde Innovations before the segment airs. What's her availability?"

"Hold please."

For the first time in her career, Alexandra wasn't affiliated with a news station. She felt like she'd been stripped of her identity. *I'll find another job.* She cleared her throat.

"Ms. Lizzard's schedule is jammed. She can meet with you in two weeks."

"If I can't do the interview in the next day or two, the window for the segment closes. Any chance I can catch her during lunch or after work? I'm happy to accommodate her schedule."

"How long will this take?"

"Twenty minutes at the most."

"Hmm, she has a fifteen-minute window today at ten thirty. I'll check. Hold for me."

Alexandra paced on the hardwood. *C'mon. Say yes.*

"Hello?" asked Cece.

"I'm here."

"Is this for the segment?"

"Yes. Mr. Berry explained that much of Wilde Innovations's success is due to Ms. Lizzard's contributions." Alexandra sucked down a breath. She didn't want to push too hard. On the other hand, she wasn't taking no for an answer.

"What station did you say you were with?"

Alexandra's heart dipped. "The tech story is for News Cable Fifteen."

"One moment."

A few moments later, Cece returned. "Sorry, no can do. Try back in two weeks." The assistant hung up.

As a news reporter, Alexandra had become accustomed to doors being shut in her face, especially when she covered volatile issues. She hadn't expected Ruth would agree to be interviewed for a story about Wilde Innovations anyway.

After throwing on her coat, she grabbed her handbag, and left. Going at a snail's pace in rush hour traffic, she pulled into the parking lot of the three-story building just before ten. As Alexandra entered the first floor office suite, two women were busy raiding the candy bowl on the reception counter.

"Welcome to No Man's Land," said the cheery receptionist seated behind the counter.

"Hi. If Cece is available, I wanted to ask her a quick question."

"I'm Cece," said the other woman, tugging out a bite-size Snickers.

Alexandra smiled. "I'm Alexandra Reed."

Her friendly expression waned. "I told you, Ms. Lizzard isn't available."

"Yes, you did, but it's critical I have her input. I can't in good conscience report on a story without consulting all legitimate sources. I passed a coffee shop. What can I get you both?"

"We have coffee here." Cece's flat expression didn't deter Alexandra.

"Not like the coffee at Arnold's," whispered the receptionist.

"Why don't I buy all of you something from Arnold's?"

As Cece glanced at the other woman, her expression softened. "I could use a mocha with a double shot of espresso."

"I'd love a sweet drink with whipped cream," said the receptionist.

Alexandra smiled. "Done. What can I get Ms. Lizzard?"

"Large dark roast. Black," said Cece.

"Thank you," Alexandra said.

"I can't promise anything."

I'll camp here all week if I have to. "I understand," Alexandra said and strode out.

Fifteen minutes later, Alexandra handed Cece the hot cup. "One mocha with a double shot of espresso. And one caramel latte with whipped cream."

While sipping, Cece closed her eyes. "Chocolatey goodness with an energy boost." She took another sip. "You must really want to talk to Ruth."

"So much is riding on Ms. Lizzard." She handed Cece the black coffee for Ruth.

"Have a seat," Cece said. "I'll run this in to her."

Alexandra waited. *This is such a long shot.* If Ruth was up to something—and Alexandra believed she was—she'd never divulge her plan. But Alexandra wasn't there for a confession. She was there to determine if Ruth Lizzard was the puppet master and Larry her dutiful marionette.

Several moments later, Cece returned, this time with a friendly smile. "You're in luck. She respects women who make their own destiny. Plus, she likes her ego stroked."

After escorting Alexandra into an area filled with tall, gray cubicles, Cece sat behind her desk, located across from a closed office door. She gestured to a chair across from her desk. "Ruth will be out shortly. You can wait here."

With a smile, Alexandra eased into the chair. "Thanks again. You're a lifesaver. How long have you worked here?"

After discussing her job history at NML, Cece explained that she also worked for another executive. Then, she leaned across her desk and whispered, "I had it easy before Ruth came on board. My other boss is super laid-back. Ruth is obsessed with execution. Now now now! Several great employees have resigned since she started working here."

"It's a competitive market. Broadcast news is like that, too."

"If you're late to work, your dog had better be dead. No more midmorning dashes to Arnold's. And forget about having to leave early."

Several questions tumbled to the tip of Alexandra's tongue, but she bit it instead.

"I've circulated my resume," Cece whispered. "I can't work ten hours a day and be on call every weekend. I've got a life."

"I totally get it."

The office door opened and Cece rocketed out of her chair. Ruth Lizzard stepped out of her office in a whoosh of red, the Arnold's coffee cup in her manicured hand. Alexandra recognized her short, coiffed, platinum blonde hair from the cafe. Her chilly expression sent a shiver down Alexandra's spine. "Ruth Lizzard." She extended her hand.

Grateful she'd worn a couture suit herself, Alexandra smiled. "Alexandra Reed. Thank you for seeing me."

"You have ten minutes." Then, she flicked a finger in Cece's direction. "Hold my calls, unless Ray needs me." With that, she strutted back into her office.

Alexandra had done her homework. Ray Chavez was No Man's Land's wealthy, handsome and married CEO.

Ruth sank into her executive seat and clicked her long red fingernails on the shiny desktop. After explaining the reason for her visit, Alexandra tapped the record app and laid her phone on the desktop.

"What news station are you with again?"

"Wilde Innovations won *DC's Brightest Tech Star* competition on News Fifteen. Mr. Berry credited you with Wilde's success."

"I designed a system where nothing failed," she said with a smug smile. "I boasted a perfect run rate."

"What does that mean?"

"No downed vehicles. No rogue aircraft. 'Precision. Perfection. Pinnacle.' That was my motto and I did one hell of a job."

"Why did you leave?"

Anger flashed in her eyes. "I'd outgrown Wilde. Time for bigger challenges."

"To date, what is your greatest professional accomplishment?"

"I've become indispensible to Ray—Mr. Chavez. The CEO and I collaborate daily. His leadership style is invigorating and exciting." She paused long enough to hint at a smile. "Because of my efforts, we're on target to win a phenomenal opportunity with a very powerful three-letter agency. Ray is beyond excited." She exuded a radiant glow.

"The federal space is a big departure from the consumer market NML dominates. How did you achieve that in the six short weeks you've been on board?"

Ruth's perfectly tweezed eyebrow arched. "You did your homework."

"Absolutely." *C'mon, say something.* "Can you expand on that?"

"I push the envelope. I'm spearheading a project to launch a flock of small unmanned craft. Under my direction, NML will become the drone leader across all markets."

"Congratulations," Alexandra said, stroking Ruth's already massive ego. "Doesn't the creation of a new drone take years to develop?"

The executive hesitated. "I snatch shortcuts wherever possible."

"With this upcoming success, will you be recruiting members from your team at Wilde?"

"No reason. I've got a great group here."

Larry's going to get dumped for a bigger, richer fish.

"Let's switch tracks—"

Knock, knock, knock.

"Come in."

Cece stood in the doorway, her cheeks the color of ripened tomatoes. "Excuse me, Ruth. Mr. Chavez has an urgent question."

The company's CEO stood behind the short assistant. "Ruth, I need you."

Lizzard shot out of her seat. "Of course, Ray." Without so much as a backwards glance, she hurried out, though Alexandra believed she was rushing *toward* her next conquest. This maneater devoured them like candy.

After Ruth barked an order at Cece, the assistant scurried down the hallway. Ray strode in the opposite direction with Ruth heeling at his side.

Alone in the office, Alexandra stopped recording. While Ruth's comment about "snatching shortcuts" was suspect, it wasn't sufficient to point blame. Falling snow outside caught her attention and her guts churned. *Just my luck.* She stood and shrugged on her winter coat. Ruth's phone buzzed and Alexandra leaned over the desk to read it.

"Snagged you two more, baby," said a text from Larry Berry. "Slow going, but I'm getting it done for you. Trying to get you an Eagle. See you tonight. Can't wait."

Larry had sent a photo, too. She grabbed her phone, snapped two pictures of the message and stashed her cell in her coat pocket as Cece flew into the office.

"Ruth's morning just got hijacked," the assistant said, gasping for breath.

"I would imagine no one keeps Mr. Chavez waiting."

Cece escorted Alexandra to the lobby. "Ruth will want to know when the story airs. Please contact me."

Alexandra tugged on her gloves and hurried into the blustery morning, convinced Ruth was involved with the problems at Wilde.

As Crockett listened to the recording of Alexandra's conversation with Ruth, he strummed his fingers on the white Formica table in his Tank. Despite never having experienced this level of revenge and betrayal, relief washed over him. At least now they had something to go on. "Without question, she's guilty as hell, but without evidence we can't prove she's behind the sabotage."

"Ruth got called away and I snapped this." She showed Crockett and Decker the text. "I didn't want to forward this to you."

Decker studied the photo. "Looks like Spy Flies. How is Larry lifting these from inventory?"

Once again, Alexandra's suspicions had been spot-on. "First things first." Crockett scooped Alex's hands into his. "Thank you for doing this."

"Of course," she replied. "I'm happy to help you."

"We can't let Larry know we're onto him." Crockett let her hands go and leaned back in the chair. "Until we have something solid, it's business as usual. I'm pretty confident the answer to how he's hijacking control of the devices is in the code."

"My coding is rusty, but I'll check it," said Decker.

Alexandra rose. "I'll get out of your hair."

"Where are you headed?" Crockett asked.

"I'd like to visit my mom, but it depends on the snow."

"When did it start snowing?" Crockett asked.

"An hour ago, but it's not sticking to the roads."

After checking his phone, Decker pushed out of his chair. "Weather report says we can expect anywhere from a dusting to three inches."

"Decker, I know you're super busy...have you had a chance to search for rejuvenation?" Alexandra asked.

"I did a few searches. Haven't found anything," Decker replied. "With everything going on here—"

"It's okay," she replied.

"I'll make it a priority this week." Decker left, closing the door behind him.

Crockett rose. Peering into Alex's eyes helped assuage his anger. But the walls were closing in and his head pounded in his temples. "I'll drive you wherever you need to go."

She placed a soft hand on his shoulder. "Please stay and work. I'll text you when I get to Colton's. If the snow sticks, I'll stay."

He pulled her close and kissed her. The familiar zing of attraction brought the heat, but her inner strength and determination grounded him. "I won't be able to concentrate if I'm worried about you."

"Crockett, please. I'll drive slowly and I'll text you."

After pecking her forehead, he hugged her. "Most couples start with dating, then they go away for a weekend. They drink too much and screw all the time. We've had one crazy incident after another."

She cupped his unshaven cheeks and peered into his eyes. "I love every moment with you, even the painful ones." Her sweet smile made him smile. "And for the record, we're doing plenty of fooling around. This gal is one happy camper."

ALEXANDRA RAPPED ON COLTON'S guesthouse door, then stepped inside the warm foyer. "Mom?"

"In here, dear," called Kimberly.

As Alexandra walked into the cozy living room, her mom pushed herself into a sitting position on the sofa. Brigit's dog, Mojo, greeted her with a wagging tail and she petted the German Shepherd whose tail thumped on the floor.

"Your new home is beautiful." Alexandra hugged her mom.

"It is lovely and I'm relieved Colton is close by if I need help."

Brigit entered, set a serving tray on the coffee table, and offered her future sister-in-law a steaming hot mug of tea. "I'm glad you're here."

"It's good to see you." Alexandra took the drink and eased onto the sofa.

Brigit handed her future mother-in-law a small travel mug. "Kimberly, your tea is lukewarm. I didn't want you to burn yourself."

She closed her shaking hand around the plastic handle. "Thank you, Brigit."

After setting the plate of cookies on the table, Brigit snatched a wafer, broke it in half, and gave the larger piece to Mojo. "I'm going to give you two some time together."

"Please stay," Alexandra said. "I haven't seen you in forever."

Brigit hesitated. "I insist," Kimberly said.

With a sweet smile, Brigit sat on the ottoman and brought Alexandra up to speed with the move and the schedule going forward. "The night nurses will continue spending evenings with your mom."

"Thank you for taking care of that," Alexandra said.

"My pleasure," Brigit said. "How's your new job going?"

Alexandra didn't want to lie to her mom, but telling her she'd gotten fired would only upset her. "Settling in. Remembering there's no freeway. It's a *beltway*."

Kimberly laughed.

Twenty minutes into the visit, her mom's eyelids drooped and the plastic mug slipped from her hands. After rescuing it, Brigit set it on the tray.

"Would you like to rest for a bit, Mom?" Alexandra asked.

"I'm fine, honey."

Knock, knock.

The front door opened. "Anyone home?" Colton called.

"C'mon in, son," Kimberly replied.

Though Colton smiled, Alexandra could tell he was stressing. The V between his brows was more pronounced than usual. "My three favorite girls."

"Colton, I love the attention, but you were just here," Kimberly said.

"Do you remember Ashton Hott?"

"Of course I do," Kimberly replied with a smile.

"He's waiting outside."

Kimberly's eyebrows jutted up. "In the cold? Oh, for goodness sake, Colton, bring him in."

"I heard that," Maverick boomed. "Where's my Mama Mitus?" He entered the living room and threw out his arms, his contagious grin lighting up his face. "There sit three of the most gorgeous women this side of the Mississippi. Who wants a Hott hug?"

Kimberly laughed. "Oh, Maverick, honestly, you never did learn to use your inside voice."

Maverick's thunderous voice made Alexandra chuckle. After Maverick leaned down and tenderly kissed her mom's cheek, he bear-hugged Alexandra.

"Ashton!" she squealed.

"Hey, baby girl!" Maverick set Alexandra down. "How the hell are you?" He gave her the once over. "Damn glad Goth didn't make a comeback."

Kimberly laughed.

Alexandra tousled his blond mop. "You haven't changed a bit. And that's a good thing, too. Still a big ball of crazy?"

"Absolutely. Wouldn't have it any other way." Maverick eyed Brigit. "This must be the future Mrs. Mitus." With a sweep of his hand, Maverick bowed. "I am in awe. The *one* woman who could make this insane man fly right deserves my utmost respect."

Through her smile, Brigit shook her head. "Ashton Hott, the legend. Colton has told me some pretty crazy stories about *the wild bunch*. It's a wonder Harvard survived your escapades."

"The good old days," he said with a wink. His playful expression fell away and he sat next to Kimberly and clasped her hand. "I've been thinking about you. Wanted to tell you how much I appreciated you over the years."

Kimberly patted his hand with her other one. "Thank you." Her sad smile tore through Alexandra. "I'm glad I got to see you, Ashton. You were one of my favorites."

"You, too, Mama Mitus." Maverick kissed her cheek before clearing his throat. "You laughed at all of my lame jokes and always made sure I got something to eat whenever I'd stop by to see this guy. We had some good talks about life, you and I."

"Yes, we did," Kimberly said.

Alexandra had never seen this side of her brother's friend and she blinked back the tears.

Maverick gave Kimberly a gentle hug before he stood. "I need to borrow the golden man, if you lovely ladies can part with him."

"Mom, I'll be back to get you for dinner." Colton pecked her cheek. "I'm glad you're here."

"Me, too, dear," said Kimberly.

"Elliott is making beef Wellington," Brigit said. "Can you both stay?"

"You eat like a king, Mitus," Maverick said to Colton. "Count me in."

"I'll stay if it's still snowing," said Alexandra. "I don't like driving in it, especially since I had that little mishap."

Kimberly shot to attention. *"You had an accident?"*

Crap. She hadn't wanted her mom to find out. "It was nothing. Plus, Crockett was with me."

Relief washed over her as Kimberly settled back into the sofa cushion. "I love our Crockett."

Maverick laughed. "Everyone loves Crockett."

Me, most of all.

"Honey, I'm going to finish helping your mom unpack," Brigit said to Colton.

"Thanks for doing this, babe."

Rap, rap, rap!

As Brigit hurried toward the front door, she called over her shoulder, "Kimberly, I promise you'll get some rest."

"I love all the activity," Kimberly replied.

"What are you doing with yourself?" Alexandra asked Maverick.

Ashton Hott was one of her favorite people. Larger-than-life, he used to tease the hell out of her whenever he'd visit. Memories of her brother, Cain, were sparse, but she'd imagined he would have turned out like Maverick. Loud, funny, and with a headful of unkempt hair.

"Living *la vida loca,* baby girl. And keeping up my reputation as DC's biggest playboy."

She swatted his bulging bicep. "Seriously, Ashton, do you work?"

"I own a private security firm that provides protection to U.S. overseas interests."

"Like corporations?"

Maverick nodded. "You got it. Plus, military installations, private companies and individuals. I use *your* boy's unmanned aerial vehicles."

Her lips split into a grin. "What makes you think Crockett is mine?"

"Alexandra, please. I can't reveal my sources."

Kimberly laughed. Alexandra loved that Crockett had talked to one of his best friends about her in that way.

Maverick's phone rang and he lifted it from his pocket.

"Excuse me, ladies. I've got to take this. Kimberly, can I talk in your kitchen?"

"Of course." She glanced at Colton. "I'm in the hub of excitement."

"Something like that," Colton replied.

As he headed out, Maverick tapped his earbud. "What's the word?"

Brigit returned with Red, Colton's business manager.

"I'm a party crasher," said Red. "Your home is beautiful, Kimberly. Settling in okay?"

"Brigit is helping me unpack and I've had a string of delightful visitors."

"Hey, Alexandra," Red said. "Good to see you."

"You, too. How are you?" Alexandra asked.

"Living moment to moment." She tucked her short auburn hair behind her ear, revealing a diamond cuff. "I need your signature, boss. The fourth wireless carrier ordered ten thousand Crockett Boxes. The Francesco Company needs a parts order expedited."

"Did you read this?" Colton asked Brigit.

"Yes and I signed it," Brigit replied.

Colton scanned the contract. Using his finger, he signed on Red's tablet.

Maverick barreled into the room, his attention glued on Red. "Well, well, whom do we have here?"

Red plunked a hand on her hip. "Take a picture, hot shot. It'll last longer."

He laughed. "Great idea."

"This is my business manager, Red," Colton said. "And this is Maverick, one of my closest friends."

Instead of offering her hand, Red shielded herself with the tablet.

"I thought Vanessa was your biz manager." Maverick continued eyeing Red.

"Red took over that position three years ago," Colton said.

"I liked Vanessa," Maverick said. "Where'd she go?"

"Figures," Red blurted.

"Jail," Colton replied.

"What the hell, bro?"

"That's a whole different story for another day," Colton said.

"One I'd like to hear. Unfortunately, I've gotta fly—work crisis—but I need your help," Maverick said. "You know Senator George Internado, right?"

Colton tossed him a nod. "Need an introduction?"

He glanced at the women. "Can I speak freely?"

"You're in America, so I damn well hope so." Red rolled her eyes.

After resting his bum on the arm of the sofa, Maverick crossed his muscular arms over his broad chest. "Since Internado heads the Senate Select Committee on Intelligence, he's privy to covert operations within the CIA. Those players need my company's services."

"You're a cocky one," Red murmured.

Maverick shot her a wink. "In the sandbox where I play, you gotta be."

"Why now?" Colton asked.

"Rumor mill is hopping. Something big might be brewing."

Colton slid a hand into his pants pocket. "Red, please arrange a lunch—no, make that dinner in a private dining room at my golf club."

"Got it," she said.

"Babe, you want to join us?" Colton asked Brigit.

"No, thanks. I'll pass on Internado."

"No like?" Maverick asked.

"I managed his personal wealth, but things soured," Brigit replied.

"Red, include yourself," Colton said.

She whipped her head in his direction. "*Me?* What on earth for?"

"You know a lot of the players on the Hill, don't you?" Colton asked.

Her nonchalant shrug gave her away. *She sure does.* "What did you do before you worked here?" Alexandra asked.

"Lobbyist," Red said, then shot Maverick the evil eye. "And I took this job to get *away* from all of that."

"*Never* say *never*, doll."

Rolling her eyes, Red grunted.

While they were talking, Maverick's phone continued to ring. No sooner did he silence it than it would ring again. "Thanks for the intro, Colt. Gotta fly."

"Good riddance," murmured Red.

Maverick chuffed out a laugh. "Looks like you're stuck with me. Let the suffering begin."

29

NEVER LEAVE ME

"Dammit!" Crockett pounded his fist on the Formica table in his Tank and shoved out of the chair so hard, it banged against the back wall. He had reached his breaking point hours ago.

"Dude, go home," Decker said. "You're done."

Rubbing his neck did nothing to soothe his aching muscles. One thirty in the morning and they had nothing to show for their debugging efforts. "Something has got to give," Crockett muttered.

"I hear ya." Decker continued typing, the scrolling lines of code blurring together. "You want me to drive you home?"

"Thanks. I can manage."

"Text Alexandra."

"What for?"

"You talked to her at eleven. She asked you to text her when you leave."

"Right. Thanks for having my back." Crockett texted: "Leaving. Home in ten." Dots appeared. "Hell, she's up."

"She loves you, man. When you popping the question?"

"I'm working on that," Crockett replied.

"Success?" Alexandra texted.

"No," Crockett texted back.

"I'm outta here," Crockett said, opening the door of the Tank. "You coming?"

"That last pot o' coffee kicked in. I'll crash here."

"I've gotta give you a raise."

Decker tossed him a salute. "Mo' money."

Crockett drove home enveloped in silence. Fueled by the pressure to solve the problem, he'd expected they would find the bug in the code. But they'd uncovered nothing. Not even a breadcrumb of a clue that Larry Berry, or anyone else, had tampered with *anything*.

When Crockett rolled into his parking spot, exhaustion hovered like a storm cloud. His dress shoes echoed in the dead-quiet underground as he made his way to the elevator. When he stepped inside, the doors closed and he glanced at his reflection. *I look like hell.*

Knowing Alex would be waiting sent him powering down the quiet hallway toward home. Once inside, he hoped to find her curled up on the sofa, but the roaring gas fire was his only warm greeting. He dropped his computer bag and coat on the sofa, then poured himself a whiskey. The first mouthful burned a trail to his stomach, the second tasted like more.

Even at this ungodly hour, pent-up energy coursed through him as he tossed his noose-of-a-tie and suit jacket on the bar before dropping onto a stool. He wanted to unleash his fury on a punching bag, but the condo gym didn't have one and the karate studio had closed hours ago. *If I had a competition, I'd kick some serious ass.* His head had been throbbing all evening. Not even the three aspirins had offered him any relief.

"Hello, Huntah." Alex's sultry voice sliced through the demons raging in his head.

He turned. Wearing only a silver mask and stilettos, she sashayed over. A black mask dangled from her fingers.

Electra ignited his desire in a way that no one else could, not even Alex. A tornado of energy shot straight to his groin. He stood to receive her and to give his growing cock room in his boxers.

"Electra." She'd slicked her perfect breasts and pert nipples in oil, her shimmering skin illuminated by the flickering firelight.

When she pressed her naked body to his, heat infused his chest and a deep growl erupted from his throat. "I'm not sure even you can handle my anger and frustration tonight, baby."

Her already dark irises blackened with desire. "Yes, I can." She pressed her mouth to his and adrenaline spiked through him. Her fluttering lashes and big brown eyes stayed locked on his. One, two, three kisses against a backdrop of moans. "Give me all of you."

"I need you so badly."

"Mmm." She rubbed his crotch. "I need you, too."

When she ran her tongue over her lower lip, he wanted to shove his shaft into her mouth until she sucked him dry. As she got busy tying on his mask, he fondled her slippery breasts, thumbing her hard nipples. "I plan to bring you as much pleasure as you give me."

"I can't wait."

He placed his hand between her legs and fingered her slickened core. *She's soaked.*

Moments later, his clothes laid in a heap on the floor. His stiff dick jutted out, hungry to tunnel inside her. She lifted a condom packet from the bar, tore it open and rolled it onto him.

He grasped her hand. "From behind. By the window." He drained the glass before they headed across the room. "Hands on the glass," he growled. "Spread your legs."

"I'm so desperate for you." With her palms pressed against the window, she bent at the waist.

Though masked, Alex hadn't worn the blonde wig, so he fisted her hair into a ponytail and tugged, exposing her neck. He kissed her tender skin, biting his way from her nape to her earlobe before leaning around to claim her mouth.

Panting, she broke the kiss. "Take. Me. Now."

Arousal pounded through him. With the head of his cock poised at the opening to her core, he plunged inside.

Their cries of ecstasy filled the room as he tunneled to her end. She moved, ever so slightly, to accommodate his length and he was able to sink even further.

"Electra, I've missed you." He kissed her beautiful, bare shoulder. "So damn much."

Breathing hard, she groaned. "Pinch my nipples. Hard."

When he did, she clenched around his shaft. "Ah, yes," he bit out through gritted teeth.

"That…oh…oh…yes, like that." She pushed against his cock and the swell of arousal blurred his thoughts.

He smacked her ass. "Naughty, Electra."

His deep thrusts were met with her raw, throaty moans, the need building at a frenzying pace. He wanted to slow down, appreciate her, and the moment, but the deluge of pleasure overtook him. Again and again flesh slapped against flesh. In those moments, the intensity of their connection became his everything. Her body ebbed and bowed to his. Even so, he couldn't get enough of her.

"Huntah, you're gonna make me come." Her husky groan was his trigger.

A surge of euphoria pummeled through him and he anchored his hands on her hips and growled. The orgasm took hold, sending waves of ecstasy pouring from him. "Baby, I'm coming."

She tightened around his shaft, hissed out his name, and shuddered through her orgasm.

Still panting, he slowed his thrusting as he floated back to earth. His brain had shorted. For those several glorious seconds, she'd quieted his demons. He wrapped his arms around her and dotted a tender trail of kisses from one shoulder blade to her other. "I can't live without you."

She'd been moving gently on his shaft, but his words had stilled her. Had he said the wrong thing? Was the hard fucking still supposed to be void of emotion?

Moving slowly, he withdrew. Without hesitation, she turned to face him. Fiery brown eyes drilled into his. Then, she kissed him. He stroked her back while she kissed him breathless all over again. After removing her mask, she untied his, then cradled his face in her hands. "I'm afraid if I tell you how I feel, you'll leave me again."

He stroked her cheek with the back of his finger. "I've waited a long time for this. For you. For us. Telling me you loved me didn't end things back then. It won't now, either."

Her sweet smile touched his heart. But as he gazed into her eyes, she trembled. Running his hands down her arms and then her sides, she felt warm to his touch. *She's not cold. She's terrified.*

He wrapped his arms around her and held her tight. "That boy from Uvalde, Texas fell in love with you a long time ago. And he never fell out."

They climbed into bed and snuggled close. For a long moment, she stared into his eyes. "I love you, Crockett Wilde," she murmured. "Ever since I was fourteen, my heart, my soul have been yours."

And that's when her tears flowed.

"Please tell me those are happy tears," he murmured and kissed her forehead.

"Don't leave me again."

He framed her face in his hands and kissed her. "Never again. You. Are. Mine. And I am yours for as long as you'll have me."

One tender kiss erupted into an explosion of passion. Then, she unleashed a decade of bottled up emotion and he devoured everything she gave him. Crockett Wilde had finally gotten his Goth Girl.

In the aftermath, he wrapped her in his arms, stroked her back, kissed her. She draped her leg over his and ran her fingers over his chest. Peace settled over them.

"We've got a full plate," she said, breaking the long silence.

"We'll get through everything together," he murmured.

"It's a lot."

"Nothing we can't handle."

"The club is still closed." She sat up, snatched her phone from the night table, and tapped the screen.

"You're so worried about Sage," he said stroking her thigh.

"I can't help it. She's been on my mind."

"Honey, she's a grown woman. She can take care of herself." He propped his pillows and leaned against them.

"*Yes!*" she said. "The club is having a grand reopening this Friday. Black tie masquerade party. Reservations required."

Her fingers flew across the phone screen. "Reservations for two under Electra...in case you forget the name of your date." Her saucy grin fell away "I hope Decker finds time to hunt for rejuvenation this week."

"If he can, he will."

"Between that and your work, I feel like all we're doing is chasing ghosts."

"I know, babe. Chasing ghosts isn't gonna get us anywhere." He broke eye contact. *Chasing ghosts...ghosts...ghost code!* "Alex, that's it."

30

GHOST CODE

Though exhausted, Crockett knew he had to return to work, even if it was four o'clock in the damn morning.

Alexandra tossed off the blanket and rose. "C'mon, you can do it." She extended her hand. "A shower will wake you up."

With entwined fingers, he followed her into his bathroom. "You gotta join me."

She turned on the faucet. "I'd love to, but you don't have time to fool around."

"Like hell I don't." As the jets pummeled his aching back, he pulled her into his arms and smiled through the kiss.

On his way out, she handed him a plastic grocery bag. "Breakfast sandwiches for you and Decker. Good luck."

"Thank you for taking care of me." He kissed her. "I'll text you later. Bolt yourself in." He stepped into the hallway. She leaned out, kissed him and shut the door. He waited for her to flip the lock before striding toward the elevator.

After pulling out of the parking garage, he punched Decker's number on his phone.

"Hey," Decker rasped.

"You still in the office?"

"Fell asleep in the Tank."

"On my way back. I think I've got it." Crockett hung up and hit the gas.

Ten minutes later, he swiped his badge, entered his suite, and flipped on lights before powering down the deserted hallway.

When he opened the door to the Tank, Decker shifted his zombie-like gaze to Crockett. "Ugh."

"You look like hell." Crockett shut the door.

"You're not so pretty yourself."

After dropping into the chair, he slid two sandwiches over to Decker. "From Alexandra."

He lifted the egg, cheese and Canadian bacon sandwich. "Nice." They wolfed down their food in silence. When finished, Decker appeared more awake. "What did you dream up?"

"No dream, my friend. Two words. Ghost code."

"Hmm." Decker chewed his lower lip.

"We've ruled out the hardware. We checked and re-checked existing code. What we couldn't check was code we couldn't see."

"It would explain why the code in the devices mirrors what's in SDDS." Sitting tall, Decker tapped away on the keyboard.

Wilde Innovations utilized a proprietary Software Development and Deployment System—SDDS—that tracked the deployment of software to all surveillance devices.

Over the next hour, they re-examined the code and memory in each of the devices that had failures. While they couldn't find any remnant of ghost code, they did discover that the memory allocation significantly exceeded what was normally required.

"Holy hell," Decker said. "I think you figured it out."

"Credit goes to Alexandra. She got me thinking."

"The memory differential is almost a hundred meg. All I can see in the excess space is a bunch of zeros."

Energy rocketed through Crockett as he stared at the screen. "How can we see what isn't there?"

"I'm not sure we can," Decker said. "But this is consistent with what a programmer would see after ghost code erases itself."

Crockett reviewed the logs to determine the time frames when SDDS pushed software to each of the devices. "None of the dates are recent."

"Someone either connected to the devices directly or accessed them through the LAN." Decker rolled his chair back and crossed his ankle over his thigh. "It's too bad there's no way to track unauthorized connections."

"There might be," Crockett said. "When the multi-hub was installed, I instructed the network engineers to configure it to keep track of all connections, regardless of source."

Decker pulled the multi-hub log and reviewed it, line by line. "I'm going to either lose my sight or my mind."

"Look, there's a pattern." Crockett pointed. "Someone connected to each of the Spy Flies in question at two in the morning the night before the FBI demo." He swiveled to Decker. "Let's check Maverick's bird."

That, too, had been accessed the night before the surveillance craft had been shipped out.

"No way," Decker said. "This is the same IP address."

Crockett logged in and queried Wilde's IP database. "Gotcha!" Crockett said. "It's Larry Berry's computer."

"I want to jump up and down," Decker said. "But I have no energy."

Knock, knock.

Without waiting for a response, the door opened. "Oh, thank goodness." Ellen put a calming hand on her chest. "All the lights are on. I wasn't sure what I'd find."

"We live here," Decker said.

"Close the door," Crockett ordered.

Ellen's cheeks flamed and she started to leave.

Crockett chuckled. "No, Ellen, with you *in* the room."

"Oh." She shut the door and joined them at the table.

"We've found the breach," Crockett said. "I'm calling my cousin, Danny Strong. With any luck, he'll be here this morning. Until then, it's business as usual."

Concern laced Ellen's eyes. "Yes, sir." She glanced from one man to the other. "I'm glad you found it. I've been on pins and needles. Who?"

"Larry. I think Ruth Lizzard is involved. Text me when he arrives."

"He's here. We rode up together. Did you eat anything?"

"A few hours ago," Decker replied.

Ellen rose. "I'll make a Mimi's run."

"You're a saint," Decker said before she closed the door behind her.

Crockett dialed and with phone pressed to his ear, waited.

"Hey, Crockett," Danny said. "What's up?"

"I've got a work situation and need your professional opinion."

"Go."

"I have reason to believe one of my employees is sabotaging my products, including the ones I used during the FBI demo."

"Crockett, you gotta let this one go, buddy."

"Hell, no. Not when I have a mountain of evidence."

"Look, I can pass your message to the appropriate team."

Crockett's hand rolled into a fist. "Do not dismiss me."

"I know you're upset, but—"

"Dammit, Danny. We've pulled an all-nighter searching the code. It's all here, or in this case, it's not. Bring me a forensic software analyst who will hear me out."

"Crockett, agents aren't just sitting around waiting for a call. We've got full workloads."

Gritting his teeth, Crockett said nothing. *Hell can freeze over before I utter one more word.*

Danny broke the frosty silence. "I'll grab someone from the white collar crime division."

"When can I expect you?"

"By COB."

"Not good enough. We've got thousands of products in the market that *cannot* fail. I've no idea what additional surveillance devices my employee has tampered with."

"You're like a pit bull, you know that? You better have something concrete. I'll be by around noon."

"Thank you." He hung up before Danny could change his mind. *If I don't get to the dojo, I'm gonna punch my fist through a damn wall.*

"Nice job." Decker stood and stretched. "My ass is killing me. I'm working standing up today."

Ellen dropped off a cardboard tray of coffees and breakfast sandwiches. "Enjoy. I'll be at my desk if you need anything." She left.

"Regardless of how this goes down, I couldn't have done it without you," Crockett said.

Decker smiled. "You betcha."

Crockett collected his things and opened the door. "You staying in here?"

"Guarding the evidence."

"Door open or closed?"

"Open. The room is starting to have that asylum feel to it."

Crockett headed toward his office. After dropping his items, he sent Alexandra a text. "Danny swinging by later. How are you doing?"

No dots appeared on his screen, so he took off for his HR department. His Director, Daphne Johnson, was on the phone, but she waved him in. He closed the door and eased into the guest chair.

"Good morning," she said after hanging up.

"I'm here to discuss Decker Daughtry."

"What do you need to know?"

After discussing Decker's salary, bonus payout and opportunity for career growth, Crockett nominated him for the Wilde Employee of the Quarter Award.

"And I want to give him a salary bump, but no change in title."

Daphne glanced at him over her reading glasses. "You're being mighty generous today. You feel like spreading that Wilde wealth around?"

Chuckling, he said, "If you worked around-the-clock and slept here, I would certainly consider it."

After finishing up with HR, he returned to his office where he spent the remainder of the morning doing little more than pacing. Just after twelve-thirty, Ellen knocked on his doorframe. "Danny Strong."

Danny stepped in and Ellen asked, "Can I get either of you a beverage?"

"No, thanks, Ellen," Crockett said. "Danny, something to drink?"

He shifted from one foot to the next. "I'm good, thanks."

Ellen shut the door. Crockett rounded his desk and hugged his cousin. "Thanks for coming. Where's your white collar crime expert?"

"He asked me to vet your information. If there's anything solid, he'll swing by later."

On a huff, Crockett dragged his fingers over his unshaven face. "Let's get started."

The two men strode down the hall, through the lab, and into the Tank.

"Please record our conversation," Crockett said to Decker.

Decker fiddled with his phone. "Recording."

"I'd like to go on record that Crockett Wilde and Decker Daughtry have solid evidence that one of my employees, Lawrence Berry, has tampered with company products. Furthermore, we believe he's colluding with former employee,

Ruth Lizzard, who's currently Director of Software Development at No Man's Land. A competitor. We have reason to believe Mr. Berry has stolen surveillance devices that he provided to Ms. Lizzard for her to use during FBI product demos. And we also have reason to believe he's stolen two additional surveillance craft for Ms. Lizzard."

"And we're back to the FBI product demo," Danny said.

"Before you jump to any conclusions, listen to Crockett," Decker said. "The bags under my eyes are from getting zero sleep. We have proof."

Danny raised his hands. "Go ahead."

As Crockett and Decker began recounting everything in detail, Danny took notes on his tablet.

Over an hour later, Danny pushed back from the conference table and sighed. "You've certainly provided a thorough account. I need a brief break."

Decker stopped recording. "I'll grab a coffee. Any takers?"

"A double shot of espresso." Danny pulled out his wallet. "And something sweet."

"I've got it," Decker said.

"No," Crockett replied. "Take the money and pay for his items separately. Get the receipt. Danny's here on official business."

"Got it." Decker took the ten from Danny and left.

"Looks like you've got a solid case," Danny said. "I'll tell Agent Miles to get down here."

"Now we're getting somewhere," Crockett replied.

THE END OF THE workday brought a flurry of activity. Sitting around the conference room table in his office, Crockett recounted the events and presented their findings in a methodical manner. Special Agent Rupert Miles listened, asked poignant questions, and took copious notes.

"Based on your evidence this is an open and shut case...on

paper." Agent Miles stroked his close-cropped beard. "But people aren't neat like that. Their agendas are often convoluted and emotionally driven. Before I speak with Mr. Berry and possibly make an arrest, I'd like you to talk to him first."

"I'll use a Spy Fly." Crockett opened his safe and removed a tiny robot.

"I'll need to confiscate his equipment," said Miles.

"His computer is property of Wilde Innovations," Crockett said. "But he uses his personal cell phone."

"I'll get a warrant for you, Rupert," Danny said.

Crockett placed the creature on his head. "Fire her up, Decker."

Decker glanced over. "Is that Black?"

"Excuse me?" Agent Miles's eyes narrowed. "Should I take offense to that comment?"

"I hope not." Crockett lifted out the small robotic insect. "This surveillance device is modeled after the Black Fly. We call her Black."

"My mistake. I've heard some doozies over the years." Rupert pushed out of his chair and leaned against the windowsill. "You get Mr. Berry to confess, we'll arrest him."

Crockett tucked the tiny craft into his hair. "Sounds like a solid plan. Ruth Lizzard has an unknown number of my Spy Flies. At sixty-five thousand dollars apiece, I need those back."

"I'll note that, but we'll need to maintain possession of all equipment as part of the case," the agent explained. "We don't operate a carryout business."

The men laughed. "I reckon you don't," Crockett said.

"All set?" Agent Miles asked.

Crockett flipped his gaze to Decker. "Confirm."

"Video and audio confirmed. Good luck." Decker spun his tablet so both agents had a clean line-of-sight.

Crockett shut the door behind him. Adrenaline had carried him through the past twenty-four hours. But now, his heart beat a slow and steady rhythm as he made his way toward Larry's office. *This had better work.*

Before tapping on the open office door, he paused. Like any other day, Larry sat working at his desk. Crockett would never have guessed this long-term employee would be the triggerman in a scheme to undermine his business. *What a mind fuck.*

"Hey, Larry, got a minute?"

Larry jumped. "Sure, c'mon in."

Crockett closed the door and remained standing so Larry wouldn't spot Black. More importantly, it put him in a power position. This conversation mattered, so rather than rushing into anything, he suffered through a few minutes of small talk. When Crockett felt like he'd checked that box, he lost the pleasant smile and jovial tone.

"Larry, let's get serious for a moment."

"Okay." Larry swallowed.

"How many Spy Flies does Ruth Lizzard have?"

He steeled his spine. *"What?* How would I know? None, right?" he asked, his face flushing.

"Things might be easier for you if you'd cooperate."

After clearing his throat, Larry glanced at his screen. Crockett stepped forward, prepared to stop him if he tried deleting anything from his computer.

"Are you telling me NML is buying our devices and passing them off as their own? That's outrageous." He stroked his moustache while his beady eyes darted around the room.

"I would never authorize the competition purchasing our devices," Crockett said.

"Right. Of course not."

"I consider myself to be a reasonable man, wouldn't you agree, Larry?"

"Sure."

"Great. Let's try this again. My code has been tampered with.

Devices have failed at key times and the evidence points to you. What can you tell me about that?"

Larry leapt out of his chair. "I wouldn't do that."

"Sit down." When he did, Crockett continued. "Larry, you're digging yourself a hole you won't be able to climb out of."

Larry's back slumped. "I wanted to help her out."

"Who?"

"Ruth." He broke eye contact. "Ruth Lizzard."

He wanted Larry to spill his guts, so he softened his tone. "Why don't you tell me about it?"

"She hated being passed over for the promotion. It's all she talked about. After you fired her, we got close. When she started working at NML, she proposed a crazy plan, but I told her no." Larry wiped the perspiration from his brow. "She told me she loved me. Said she'd bring me onboard as soon as NML was awarded the FBI business. I'm leaving my wife for her. I gave her a couple of Spy Flies for the demo and a few since then. She encouraged me to tamper with the equipment to get even for what you did to her."

"So you did?"

"Yeah." Larry broke down. "She said we were invincible."

"You had a good thing here."

The QA Director wiped his eyes. "Are you going to have me arrested?"

"What would you do in my situation?"

"I'm so screwed."

Knock, knock.

After opening the door, Crockett addressed both agents. "Gentlemen, he's all yours."

31

BLACK TIE ONLY

ON FRIDAY AFTERNOON, CROCKETT entered the high-end jewelry store on Connecticut Avenue in northwest DC. A man in a tailored suit greeted him with a friendly smile. "Good day, sir."

"Crockett Wilde to see Mark Whitaker."

"Right this way, Mr. Wilde." The man escorted him into a private room. "Please have a seat. Mr. Whitaker will be right with you."

The elegant room housed two plush maroon velvet chairs separated by a small table covered in black linen.

Marriage hadn't crossed Crockett's mind until Alexandra had come back into his life. But as he waited for the owner of Tiny Jewel Box to present him with his custom engagement ring, he couldn't wait to make Alexandra his, forever.

His phone buzzed and he read the incoming text from Danny. "Congrats. Director impressed with your efforts. Wilde back in the running. Email from the Contracting Officer going out next week."

"Great news," he texted back. "Thanks for hearing me out."

"Pit bull," Danny texted back and Crockett laughed.

The owner of the upscale jewelry store entered the room. "Crockett, good afternoon."

"Good to see you, Mark." The two men shook hands.

"You're going to be delighted with the results." Mark sat, opened the ring box and presented it to Crockett. "Magnificent, isn't it?"

"It's stunning."

Mark handed the diamond ring to Crockett. "The four-carat radiant cut is flawless."

Crockett examined the ring from all sides. A halo of brilliant round diamonds surrounded the large, sparkling stone. "It's perfect. She'll love it."

ALEXANDRA WAS ANXIOUS TO get to Incognito. Her imagination had been running wild since she'd glimpsed the hidden room. Though she hadn't said anything to Crockett, she'd been obsessing over poor Sage.

As she struggled to zip her black sequined gown, her phone rang. Crockett had resurfaced. *Finally.*

"Hey, honey. On your way home?" She tossed her tiny clutch next to the black faux fur shawl coat.

"Hello, my love. I'm sorry I'm running late."

Her smile faded. "Still at work?"

"Stuck in DC. Traffic reporter said the President is traveling by motorcade. There are cops everywhere and traffic hasn't moved in ten minutes. It's a nightmare. If it's any consolation, I was picking up a little something for you."

"You smooth-talker, you. Why don't I bring your tux to the office and meet you at the club?"

"Thanks, babe. I'll text you when I'm—dammit. My battery is almost dead. Where the hell is my phone charger? I'll see you soon. I love—" The line went dead.

"I love you, too, Crockett," she said out loud to herself.

Tonight, she was determined to find Sage. Even if she had to confront Jase, she was not leaving without talking to her. If Sage refused help, Alexandra would walk away. But if Sage gave the slightest indication she was ready to make a break, Alexandra would help her in every way possible.

When she finished getting ready, she tucked Crockett's tuxedo and dress shirt with all the accessories into a garment bag. She placed his dress shoes and both masks into her carry bag. Feeling like a pack mule, she left.

Once she arrived at Wilde Innovations, Ellen showed her into Crockett's office.

"You look fantastic," Ellen said. "I love the wig. It's so fun. It's amazing how different you look as a blonde with bangs. I might have walked right by you in a crowded room."

Exactly what I'm going for. Alexandra smiled as she set down the bags. "Thanks. We're going to a masquerade party and I like keeping a low profile. With work and all."

"Oh, right. Well, make yourself at home. Can I get you coffee or a bottled water?"

"No thanks, I'm good."

"My family and friends are excited to watch *DC's Brightest Tech Star.* I am, too."

Alexandra's chest tightened. She didn't have the heart to disappoint Ellen with the bad news. "The show is in limbo until the station finalizes the schedule."

The assistant's shoulders drooped. "Oh, that's a shame."

"When the show airs, you'll be happy with your interview. You did a *great* job."

"You made it easy." Ellen headed toward the door. "Have a great night."

Alone in Crockett's office, Alexandra removed the tux and laid it and the white dress shirt over his sofa, along with the bow tie. She set his cufflinks and mask on his desk and placed his shoes on the floor. Eager to get to the club, she jotted a note and left it on his desk.

Can't wait to see you.
Alex

That's a little cold. She added a heart beside her name. It was almost six o'clock and she hoped her butterflies would settle down once she found Sage. She tied on her mask and hurried out.

The underground garage at the Silver Towers building was filled with cars, so she parked on the side near the business elevators and made her way toward the private elevators in the far corner. Several other masked clubbers waited, also dressed in formal wear. When the doors slid open, everyone squeezed in.

Instead of being greeted by the usual sultry sounds of jazz, rave music blasted through the wall speakers. Members shoved her out of the elevator and barreled into the lounge. She wanted Crockett to know she'd arrived, so she checked in via a tablet. She was greeted by a smiling server with a tray of flutes. She whisked off a glass and tossed back a sip of the crisp champagne. *I'll never find Sage in this crowd.*

The elevator delivered another boisterous group and she hoped her handsome man was among them. But he wasn't and her heart dipped. *Where is he?*

Francois, sporting a slick toupee, greeted guests like a politician running for reelection. "Good evening, Ms. Electra." His French accent sounded rusty. "Welcome back."

"You've got a fresh, new look." Her sweet southern accent rolled off her tongue. *"Très beau."*

His cheeks flushed. *"Merci."*

"This is quite a party."

"Glad you approve. Enjoy your evening." With a staged smile, he moved on.

Eager to find Sage, she walked down the hallway. As she

passed the alcove, she slowed, hoping Sage would burst out the door marked, "Private", but she didn't. Alexandra walked the entire floor with no luck. Coming full circle, she entered the lounge. Members were sandwiched into the bar, but she found a vacant table near the arched doorway and slipped into a chair.

Jase, wearing a tuxedo, sauntered in, scanned the room, and returned to the busy hallway to greet incoming guests.

Wendy bustled past. "Be right back, Electra," she called as she whizzed by.

Alexandra checked her phone for a text from Crockett, but there was nothing. Again, she scoured the crowd for Sage.

"Good evening and welcome to the insanity…er, I mean, Incognito," Wendy said.

Alexandra laughed. "Pretty crazy tonight."

"If Mr. Jase intended to recruit new members, this evening is a *whopping* success. Another champagne?"

"I'd love one," she said. "My friend, Huntah, should be here any minute, so I'll take two."

"Sure thing. Can I bring you a shrimp cocktail or exotic cheese and fruit platter?"

"I'll wait until Huntah arrives to order food."

With a quick smile, the server took off toward the bar. Alexandra slid her phone out of her clutch and checked for messages. Still nothing. *Where is he?*

When Wendy returned with the champagne, she set down a plate with four shrimp and a side of cocktail sauce. "On the house. Enjoy." Alexandra thanked her and the server scooted off.

As Jase greeted guests at the bar, a masked woman sidled next to him and tugged his tux sleeve. After she whispered something to him, he gripped her arm and headed down the hallway toward his office.

Sage! Alexandra hurried into the congested corridor. Determination powered her forward but Jase was moving too fast. She caught a glimpse as they passed his office and disappeared around the corner. When she rounded the bend, she crashed into two men. "Oh, excuse me."

"Hey, gorgeous. Join us for a threesome."

Alexandra darted around them and spied Jase standing in front of the alcove that housed the linen closet and the room marked "Private". He shoved Sage and she flew backwards. Seething with anger, Alexandra raced toward them. As she approached, she heard Jase's menacing warning.

"I *fucking* warned you, Sage. Now, I have to punish you."

"But he's sick and needs help," Sage replied.

Breathing hard, Alexandra blurted, "Don't you touch her."

Jase whipped his head around. He curled his lips into a joker-like grin.

Sage's cheeks were streaked with tears. But that was nothing compared with her black eye. Even the mask couldn't hide that.

Anger, pain, pity and rage fueled Alexandra. "He struck you, didn't he?"

As soon as Jase released his vise-grip on her arm, Sage rubbed it with a shaky hand. Her lower lip quivered while she peered at the floor.

Rising to his full stature, Jase stepped between the two women. "This is none of your business."

Her stomach roiled from his disgusting cigarette breath. "Come with me, Sage. I can help you. I want to help you. Please let me get you out of here and away from him before he kills you."

Jase growled. Staring into his eyes should have terrified her, but the image of her mother—no longer the faceless woman in her nightmares—along with the women at the homeless shelter bolstered her courage. If she didn't help this waif of a woman, no one would.

"You have the wrong idea." Jase had lowered his tone, but the pronounced pulse in his temple beat a fast rhythm. "Sage is fine, aren't you, Sage?"

"Like hell she's fine." Steeling her spine, Alexandra stepped around Jase to address Sage directly, but Sage refused to look at her. "I'm reporting him for abuse, either way, but I want you to leave with me. *Please*, Sage, let me help you."

Jase jabbed something against her side. The agonizing shock traveled through her like a lightning bolt. Crying out, she crumpled to the floor, immobilized. The onslaught of torture ripping through her rendered her paralyzed.

"Sage, open the door," Jase barked. "Now."

"Please don't—" Sage whispered.

"Open the fucking door, you little bitch, or I'll kill you both."

Alexandra lay there writhing in pain while Sage held open the door and Jase dragged her limp body through it. When Sage's eyes met Alexandra's, Sage murmured, "I'm sorry, Jase. I'll behave. Please don't hurt her."

CROCKETT YANKED OPEN THE heavy glass door to Wilde Innovations. Reception was empty as were the offices he powered past on his way toward his own. "Six thirty," he grumbled. As soon as he entered his office, he spied his tux on the sofa.

He dropped his phone in the rapid charger and smiled at Alexandra's note. After depositing the engagement ring in his safe, he hurried to dress. He wouldn't breathe easy until he could pull Alexandra into his arms and hold her close.

On his way out, he grabbed his charged phone and sent her a text. "On my way."

Knock, knock.

"Crockett, are you in there?" Decker asked.

The tightness in Decker's voice had Crockett flinging open the door.

Normally laid-back, deep worry lines puckered his brows. Decker brushed past him and set his laptop on the conference room table. "I need to show you something."

"What additional damage did Larry and Ruth do?"

"I finally got a hit on rejuvenation. You're not gonna believe this."

Two strides and Crockett stood beside him. After reading the online ad, his blood ran cold. "Oh, God, no."

32

REJUVENATION

Alarms sent Crockett powering out of his office. He broke several traffic laws and arrived at the club in seven minutes. Though he had no reason to believe Alexandra was in immediate danger, he needed to locate her and get her the hell out of there. Being at Incognito wasn't safe and it sure as hell wasn't smart. He'd alert the authorities and let them handle the situation.

According to the tablet in the greeting room, Alexandra had checked in forty five minutes earlier and would be waiting in the lounge. He strode across the hall, bumping into several clubbers as he pushed his way in.

"Good evening and welcome to Incognito's grand reopening." The familiar voice of the faux Frenchman boomed through the mic. "Time for our first drawing of the evening."

The spindly assistant stood on the bar sporting a microphone and a cheap toupee. *You'd think he was in Vegas.*

Crockett strode around the restaurant, but he couldn't find her. *Where the hell is she?*

Wendy hurried over. "You're Electra's friend, right?"

"Yes."

"I waited on her earlier and she—"

Francois announced the winner and the applauding partygoers drowned out what she said. "Say that again."

"Electra vanished."

Adrenaline shot through him. "What do you mean?"

"She ordered two glasses of champagne and told me she wanted to wait to order food until you arrived. I brought her the champagne, but when I checked on her, she was gone." Wendy held up the black clutch. "She left this."

Crockett opened the purse and retrieved her phone. When he pressed the home key, his unread text appeared on the screen. "When did you last see her?"

Wendy shrugged. "Maybe twenty minutes ago. I thought you'd arrived and you guys went into a suite. It's not like her to stiff me."

"Thanks for telling me." He pulled a Ben Franklin from his pocket and offered it to her.

Shaking her head, she threw up her hands. "I wasn't telling you for the money."

"I know that. Is Jase here?"

"Of course. It's a big night for the club." She bit her fingernail. "I'm worried something happened to her."

He dropped Alex's phone into his pants pocket, then shoved the money and the clutch at Wendy. "Keep these. I've got to find her."

Even if Crockett had access to every suite on the floor, he wouldn't check them. His gut told him she wasn't in any of those suites. Somehow she'd gotten into that hidden room behind the unmarked suite and couldn't escape.

Crockett's feet ate up the wood flooring as he strode down the hallway, his sights set on the room at the end of the hall. With adrenaline surging through him, he centered himself. Then, he inhaled a deep breath, aimed for just above the handle and kicked the door. The frame snapped and the door burst wide open, amber light glowing from the night table lamp. Three quick strides and he stood at the back wall. Desperate to get into the secret room, he couldn't find a handle or button to trigger the door, so he felt along the contours of the wall.

"Get out now or security will throw you out."

Crockett spun around.

Francois's ridiculous French accent had been replaced with a hissing, gritty voice.

"Open this door."

The squirrely assistant came at him with his arm raised. Years of karate training kept Crockett calm and in control. Just before Francois struck, Crockett grabbed his wrist, twisted his arm around and put him in a choke hold. Then he started counting. By the time he got to ten, Francois went limp.

He dragged him into the bathroom, took his cell phone, and left. Before continuing his exploration of the back wall, he tossed the phone on the sofa, then shoved it against the bathroom door ensuring Francois couldn't escape.

Several agonizing seconds passed before he located a lever near the floor. The panel slid open and he stepped into a dimly lit stairwell before the door slid closed behind him. After taking the steps three at a time, he yanked open the fire door and crossed the threshold.

The room he entered was an exact replica of the greeting room, though quiet and darker. And filled with children. At least ten teenagers—mostly girls—sat on the brown sofa as if they were posing for a photo shoot. Their subdued smiles couldn't mask the fear in their eyes. The hair on the back of his neck prickled. Three more kids leaned against the wall, also striking stilted poses. The girls wore makeup and provocative dresses; the boys were in button down shirts and skinny suits. Their vacant expressions reminded him of Sage's.

For several chilling seconds no one moved. No one spoke. Crockett's worst nightmare had been confirmed. The ad Decker had found offered sex with minors. His body stiffened as he fought to control his fury. The children resembled mannequins.

The emptiness in their eyes broke his heart. It was as if their innocent souls had been sucked from their bodies and their shells were all that remained.

A tall, rail-thin woman sailed around the corner. Unmasked, her sunken cheeks, melancholy eyes, and sallow skin struck a chord. Pain pounded his chest. It was Sage.

"Are you here for rejuvenation?" she asked.

Though desperate to find Alexandra, he didn't want to frighten her away. He removed his mask. "No, Sage, I'm not. I'm here to help you. Where's Electra?"

Her blank stare led him to think she didn't understand him.

"I'm here to help you *and* the children. But first, I need to find Electra. Take me to her."

As she studied his face, a deep line creased her brows. She appeared to be having trouble comprehending his words.

"Please." He kept his voice low and steady, though adrenaline pumped through him at a frenzying speed. "She's in a lot of danger. We need to hurry."

Fear flashed in her eyes. Sage flew down the hallway, her long wispy hair trailing like feathers in the wind. Though unsure if she was taking him to Alex or running him into a trap, Crockett had no choice but to follow.

He rounded the corner and almost bumped into Sage. With a haunting laugh, Jase pulled a door closed and headed toward them, a sardonic grin erupting over his face. "You're too late, pretty boy. Our little Electra is about to get the fuck of her life."

The rage that Crockett had fought for years to contain exploded from the depths of his soul. Jase surged toward him and Crockett's hands tightened into coiled fists.

Sage squeaked out, "He's got a stun gun," at the same time Jase yanked it from his pocket and sprinted toward Crockett.

With the weapon inches from reaching him, Crockett raised his knee to his chest and launched a punishing heel-stomp kick to Jase's sternum that send him flying backward and crying out in pain. He crashed to the floor, gasping for air. Fury clouded Crockett's thoughts. He wanted to wrap his hands around Jase's throat and choke the life out of him.

Instead, he grabbed the weapon, pressed it to Jase's shirt near his ribcage, and pulled the trigger. Again Jase cried out. His body went rigid. But the pain and incapacitation wouldn't last long, so Crockett landed a right hook squarely on Jase's jaw, knocking him out.

Crockett sprinted to the door, but it was locked. "Open this," he said to Sage.

Her hands trembled as she tapped the Silver Towers card to the keypad. The light blinked green and Crockett burst into the room.

Dracule stood beside the bed, unbuttoning his tuxedo shirt.

An unmasked Alexandra, wearing only her bra and panties, lay spread eagle on the bed, her wrists and ankles buckled into bands that were strapped to each bedpost. Her blonde wig was all that remained of her disguise. Her cheek was red and swollen. Dried blood clung to her arm from a gash on her shoulder. But it was the fear in her eyes that flipped his switch.

Crockett thundered toward him. "*No!*"

Dracule threw his arms in front of his face like an "X". Crockett delivered an uppercut to the solar plexus that brought Dracule's hands to his stomach. Then he wrapped his hands around Dracule's neck and body-slammed him against the wall so hard, the table lamp crashed to the floor. "I'll kill you, you son of a bitch."

Fear flashed in Dracule's eyes, his face turning bright red from lack of oxygen.

"Don't do it." Alexandra's voice snapped Crockett's head around.

"Sage," Crockett barked. "Free her."

Crouching in the corner, Sage rocked back and forth, repeating, "No more Payne, no more Payne…"

"Please, Sage, help me," Alexandra pleaded.

Sage stood, her body quaking.

"Unbuckle me so I can help you."

"What about the Littles?" Sage asked.

"The what?" Alexandra asked.

"Help Electra, then hide the Littles," Crockett ordered. *"Hurry."*

With tender steps, Sage approached the bed and unbuckled the wrist cuffs. Alexandra freed her ankle restraints as Sage ran from the room.

After throwing on her dress, Alexandra approached Dracule, hatred radiating from her eyes. But Crockett caught a glimpse of her true feelings. Perhaps she could conceal her terror from this monster, but not from him. If he'd arrived a few minutes later... *I could snap his neck like a twig.*

"Let me go and I won't press assault charges," Dracule rasped. "You have my word."

Crockett turned slowly toward Dracule. Pure evil stared back. Refusing to dignify that lie with a response, Crockett gritted his teeth and tightened his hold on Dracule's throat.

Alexandra brushed against Crockett's shoulder. "Tie him to the bed and I'll call the police."

Her soft touch, her soothing words, slowed his hammering heart. He'd arrived in time. She was safe.

After yanking off Dracule's mask, she fished her phone from Crockett's pants pocket and snapped a picture. "You sicken me." She slapped his face so hard his eyes watered.

Crockett threw him onto the bed and secured his wrists in the restraints.

"Let me go," Dracule begged. "I'll pay you, handsomely."

"Jase!" Alexandra screamed.

Crockett whipped around as Jase attacked with a six-inch knife, the blade inches from his neck. He blocked the strike but the knife slashed through his forearm, piercing his flesh and striking bone.

"Arrrghh!" Crockett cried.

Jase lunged at him again, the knife thrust at his abdomen. This time, Crockett's muscle memory kicked in. He deflected the weapon with a lower block, grasped Jase's wrist with one hand and jabbed his other, palm up, against the underside of Jase's chin.

Jase's head jerked back violently. The force of Crockett's blow sent him reeling back. Going on the offense, Crockett swept his foot under both of Jase's, knocking him to the floor with a thud, the back of his head hitting the bedpost.

"Ayyyyy!" Jase cried.

Crockett stomped his heel in Jase's armpit, keeping his weight on Jase. He cried out. Then Crockett grabbed Jase's arm and twisted, hard. As soon as Jase dropped the weapon, Crockett grabbed it and held the razor-sharp edge to his throat.

"I want to do this so badly," Crockett bit out, still breathing hard. Instead, he dragged Jase to the foot of the bed and pressed his full weight on Jase's legs to immobilize him. Alexandra rushed over and pulled one of the ankle restraints around. Crockett toss the knife out of Jase's reach, yanked up his arm, slapped the restraint around his wrist and buckled it on the tightest notch. They did the same for his other wrist.

And again, Crockett pressed the blade against Jase's throat.

"Do it," Jase said. "Kill a defenseless man."

Struggling to contain his fury, Crockett glared at him. Hatred boiled just below the surface.

"You've been stabbed," Alexandra said.

Crockett's hand was drenched in blood. He hadn't noticed, didn't care. Alexandra clasped his hand and rose. Jase yanked on the restraints, his legs flailing wildly in all directions. Crockett stood and moved her a safe distance away.

"Are you okay?" He searched her face, eyed the dried blood on her upper arm. "Where are you hurt?"

"I'm fine. Let's get your jacket off."

"I'll deal with this. Call the police."

Though her hands shook, Alexandra dialed. "I have an emergency. I'm at Incognito nightclub in Crystal City, Arlington. The GM attacked a guest. A member tried to sexually assault me. I need police and an ambulance." After a brief pause, she said, "My name is Alexandra Mitus."

Dracule's wail made Alexandra jump. "Oh, my God," Dracule cried. "No, no, it can't be. Oh, sweet Jesus, what have I done?"

In order to hear the emergency operator, Alexandra plugged her other ear with her finger.

"Shut up," Crockett yelled, but Dracule wouldn't stop blathering and crying.

"I'll meet the police in the lobby of the twelfth floor and bring them upstairs." After listening, she said, "We're on the thirteenth floor, but they won't be able to find us without my help."

She tapped a button and set the phone on the sofa arm. "You're on speaker and the attackers are in the room. My boyfriend was stabbed. I need to help him."

Alexandra yanked out a pillow from beneath Dracule, whipped off the case, and folded it. She hurried back to Crockett. "I'm going to remove your jacket."

When she slid it off him, his white sleeve was blood soaked. Alexandra folded the pillowcase in half, lengthwise, and wrapped the cotton around his arm. "Apply pressure where it's bleeding." She guided Crockett onto the sofa.

"The police have arrived at your location," said the dispatch operator.

"I kicked in the unmarked door," said Crockett. "Be careful. Francois should be trapped in that bathroom."

With her phone in hand, she gave Crockett a quick peck. "I'm on my way downstairs," she said to the operator before rushing out.

Applying pressure to the wound hurt, but Crockett didn't give a damn about himself. As he eyed Jase and Dracule, reality sank in.

He couldn't stand being in the same room with those two monsters, so he relocated to the quiet hallway. *Sage must have hidden the children.*

A few moments later, Alexandra hurried toward him with three police officers and four paramedics in tow, one pulling a gurney. While the female officer approached him, the two male officers entered the room.

"This is the man I was telling you about," said Alexandra.

With a hand on her hip, she eyed Crockett. "Mr. Wilde, I'm Officer Randolph. Can you tell me what happened?"

"We need to tend to his wound," said the paramedic. "Let's move him onto the sofa."

"I'm fine," Crockett said.

"Please, Crockett," Alexandra said. "You have a bad gash."

To appease her, he returned to the couch. While the paramedic tended to his knife wound and secured his arm in a sling, he spoke with the officers. "I feared for Alexandra's safety and forced my way upstairs. There's a man named Francois locked in a bathroom suite downstairs."

"We found him," said the officer.

"When I came upstairs, I saw several children waiting in reception," Crockett continued. "They were posed like mannequins and dressed like adults." A shiver ran through him. "Sickest thing I've ever seen."

"Ohmygod," Alexandra said. "It's much worse than I'd thought."

Before continuing, he nodded. "There's a young woman who works here. Her name is Sage and Alexandra has been concerned about her."

"Ms. Mitus told us," said the policewoman. "Where is she?"

"After she used her keycard to let me into this room, she ran to hide the children," Crockett said. "I found Alexandra strapped to the bed, in her underwear. I assumed by the man on the floor." A surge of fury rippled through him. "The other man—the one I've strapped in the bed—was removing his clothing."

"Aw, Christ," Jase moaned. "My head hurts like a motherfucking cocksucker."

The larger of the two male officers approached Jase. "I'm Officer Jones. What's your name, sir?"

"Jase Payne, GM. That member attacked me in my own club. I want to press charges."

"You keeping minors here against their will?" asked Officer Jones.

Jase's face reddened. "Jesus H. Christ. I run a club for *consenting* adults."

"Let's take a little ride." Officer Jones unbuckled Jase from the bed shackles while the second male officer stood nearby. "Face down. Hands behind your back."

Jase lay there while the officer threw a cuff around his wrist. But before he could attach the second cuff, Jase bolted up and swung his arm around, smacking the officer in the face with the metal bracket. Blood splattered from Jones's forehead as he tried to subdue Jase, but Jase unsnapped the officer's holstered weapon. As he yanked it out—

Bang! Bang! Bang! Bang! Bang!

Dracule screamed. Alexandra startled.

Jase hit the floor, blood gushing from his wounds, the unfired gun still in his hand. Officer Randolph stood, her weapon poised in her outstretched hands.

This is a hellish nightmare.

As the third officer pulled the weapon from Jase's hand, Officer Randolph radioed for backup while paramedics jumped into action. One tended to Jones's forehead gash while the other three tried to resuscitate Jase. Several tense minutes passed before one of the paramedics called it.

"No pulse," he said. They lifted Jase onto the stretcher and covered him with a sheet.

"Officer Randolph," said Crockett. "Jase has a master keycard. You're going to need that to check the rooms and locate Sage and the children."

Randolph spoke with the paramedic. After a quick search, they located the card. When Officer Jones unbuckled Dracule, Officer Randolph and the third policeman drew their weapons.

No longer full of bravado and big smiles, Dracule only whimpered. Officer Randolph ordered him to kneel on the floor while they cuffed him.

After Officer Jones read Dracule his rights, he paused in front of Alexandra. "Can you forgive me?" he asked.

Her upper lip curled into a snarl. "Monster."

With a firm grip on Dracule's shoulder, the officer nudged him forward.

Squaring her shoulders, Alexandra addressed the officer in charge. "I need to find Sage. She must be terrified."

Several clubbers had found their way upstairs and were lurking in the hallway. Officer Randolph ordered the two patrolmen to escort them downstairs and to remain outside the broken door on the twelfth floor. Then, she radioed for backup.

One by one, the policewoman tapped Jase's Silver Towers card against the keypads on the suite doors. The first two were empty. But in the third, a masked man and teenage girl crouched in the bathroom. Crockett's hands fisted when police led the pedophile and the child into the hallway.

"Call social services," Officer Randolph told her partner.

Alexandra sidled close. "This is way worse than even I suspected," she whispered. Eager to touch her, he stroked her back. Though anger blackened her eyes, he kept reminding himself that she was safe.

In the next room, there was a desk and a sixty-inch monitor hanging on the wall. The screen was split into eight squares that displayed public areas in the club along with what appeared to be private suites on that floor.

"That's how Sage must have found me in the club," Alexandra whispered to Crockett.

Three more men had been hiding in their respective suites with either a male or a female minor. When Randolph opened the door to a suite marked "Playpen", Crockett's chest tightened.

For several seconds, no one moved.

Several children huddled on two dilapidated sofas. Sage stood in the middle of the room, her eyes wild with fear; a small shepherd guarding her flock.

Unlike the posh suites, this decrepit room told the true story of their existence. Empty pizza boxes lay scattered across the floor. Dirty plates stacked in piles. Their only light—a floor lamp with a tattered shade—stood in the corner. Two racks of formal clothing were pushed against a wall. The surreal scene looked more like a horror movie than anything based in reality. These children lived worse than any pet he'd ever owned.

Some of the children gaped, their sad, hollow expressions void of emotion. The others peeked like caged animals too scared to make eye contact.

Crockett's heart broke. He couldn't begin to know the torture and abuse they'd suffered at the hands of Jase Payne.

Alexandra entered the room with Officer Randolph. "Thank you for helping me, Sage. I'd like to help you, now."

From the hallway, Officer Jones radioed that they'd need upwards of ten social workers to meet them at the hospital. "Looks like sex trafficking of minors. Approximately a dozen juveniles. Mostly female."

Sage gaped at the small crowd. "We heard gunshots," she said. "I have to protect the Littles."

"Hello, Sage. My name is Officer Randolph and I'm a police officer. I'd like to help you."

Sage stared from Alexandra to the officer before hugging herself.

"Can I get a blanket, please?" Alexandra called over her

shoulder. "Officer Randolph would like to help you *and* the Littles find your families."

Officer Jones handed Alexandra the blanket. After she draped it over Sage's shoulders, Sage murmured, "I'm scared. We're all so scared."

"I understand," said the policewoman. "Why don't we start with something simple? Can you tell me your name?"

Lowering her head, she whispered, "Sage."

"What's your last name?"

"He never gave me one."

"Who?" asked Officer Randolph.

"Papa bear."

"Who's papa bear?"

"Jase Payne." She clutched the blanket and started rocking. "No more Payne. No more Payne."

"What *was* your name?" Alexandra asked.

Terror radiated from her eyes. "I can't say or he'll beat the Littles. I'm Sage. *Just* Sage."

"He can't hurt you ever again," Alexandra whispered. "I promise. And I won't abandon you." Moving slowly, Alexandra removed her wig. "My real name is Alexandra Mitus. I've been concerned about you from the day we met. Do you remember meeting me in Jase's office?"

"Yes." Sage glanced toward the doorway. "You tried to help me."

"I did," Alexandra said. "I want to help you now, too."

Again, Sage looked past her to Crockett. "Is he your friend?"

"Yes, he helped me find you. Would you like to meet him?"

"Yes," Sage whispered.

Alexandra walked to the doorway. "Sage wants to meet you. She's terrified, so go easy."

When Crockett stepped into the room, the stench of body odor and rancid food permeated the air. Pity tore at his heart. The conditions were deplorable.

"Hello, Sage," he said. "Thank you for helping me. That was a brave thing to do."

Sage stared at him for several seconds before asking, "What's your name?"

"I'm Crockett. Crockett Wilde."

As she shuddered in a shaky breath, her eyes filled with tears. "From Uvalde?"

His heart rate jumped to the triple digits. "How do you know that?"

"Because that's where I'm from, too. I'm Sophia Lynn Wilde."

33

SOPHIA

Sobbing, Sophia threw her arms around Crockett. Tears spilled down his cheeks as he embraced his sister. Year after year, he'd hoped and prayed and screamed at the heavens for this moment. And now, he struggled to grasp the reality of the situation.

Crockett had never wished a man dead before, but as he held his sister in his arms, he knew that if the body of Jase Payne wasn't already on its way to the morgue, he would have killed him. And then faced the consequences for his actions.

She pulled away and stared into his eyes. "Mom and Dad?" she whispered, still shaking.

"Same house in Uvalde."

"Mr. Wilde, under the circumstances, I need to see your driver's license," said Officer Randolph. "We have to run a check."

Crockett handed it to her, then locked eyes with Alexandra. "Thank you."

Tears streamed down Alexandra's cheeks and she ran a tender hand down his back.

"I need someone to contact my—*our*—parents," Crockett said as he wiped his eyes. "Ron and Linda Wilde of Uvalde, Texas."

"We've arranged to take the minors to the hospital," said Officer Randolph.

Sophia's eyes widened and she broke away from Crockett. "I have to protect the children from Jase or he'll hurt them."

"Mr. Payne tried to hurt a policeman and I shot him," said the policewoman. "He's dead and he can't hurt you or the children anymore."

Sophia slid her gaze to Alexandra.

"It's true," Alexandra confirmed.

"What about Frank?" Sage asked.

"Who's that?" Alexandra asked.

"Francois," she replied.

"He was arrested and taken to the police station," Officer Randolph said.

Her eyes narrowed. "I hate him, too."

A warm smile touched the officer's eyes. "Miss Wilde, these children all have families, like you. The doctors need to check everyone's health. Jase hurt your brother and he's got to get stitches in his arm. Everyone's going to the hospital."

"Let me tell the Littles," said Sophia.

With the blanket still wrapped around her, she approached them. The children huddled around. She spoke quietly, pausing to look at each of them. When finished, some hugged each other. Several started crying. One boy knelt and prayed.

Crockett clasped Alexandra's hand. "I am indebted to you," he whispered before pressing a kiss to her temple.

She squeezed his hand. "Being able to do this for Sophia, for you, for your family..." Her voice cracked and she choked back the raw emotion teetering on the edge.

Sophia returned. "Okay, we're ready," she said and grasped Alexandra's hand. "Don't leave me."

Through the tears, Alexandra smiled. "I won't. I promise."

Choking back the swell of emotion, Crockett followed behind

his sister and Alexandra. Sophia led everyone to the elevator she'd never herself taken. The one that brought the rejuvenated men back down to the parking garage level. And out to freedom. Where she and the children were headed.

A police van waited inside the now empty parking garage.

Still clasping Sophia's hand, Alexandra waited for Crockett. "I'm going to ride with your sister," she said to him. "Find us after you see a doctor."

"Of course," he said before addressing his sister. "I'll arrange for Mom and Dad to travel here tomorrow. Can I hug you, Sophia?" Saying her name brought more tears to his eyes.

"Yes." Her sad smile ripped through his heart.

Crockett gave her a gentle squeeze with his free arm. "I've waited thirteen years for this moment. I love you, Soph. You're brave and strong."

Tears filled her eyes. "Thank you." She turned away, her frail shoulders quaking.

As Alexandra draped her arm around Sophia, she glanced back at Crockett and mouthed, "I love you."

If he spent the rest of his life showing her how much he adored her, it wouldn't be long enough.

When she attempted to board the van, an officer stopped her. "I'm sorry, ma'am, but you'll have to follow us in your vehicle."

"She rides with us," said Officer Randolph.

Officer Jones approached Crockett. "Sir, could I speak with you, please?" Crockett tossed Alexandra a nod before she followed Sophia into the van. "I've got your father, Ron Wilde, on the phone. He wants to speak with you."

Taking the phone, Crockett said, "Dad, I found her."

Aside from an occasional whisper between the teens,

Alexandra, Sophia and the children rode to the hospital in silence. The police van housed a row of seats on either side that faced each other. But most children cast their eyes downward, tears rolling down their cheeks.

Sophia had clasped Alexandra's hand so tightly it had fallen asleep. But she wasn't going to let go. Her heart broke for the shell of a woman sitting next to her. She couldn't begin to know the hell she'd endured.

"Thank you," Sophia whispered. "For years I'd been invisible to everyone. But not you."

In the darkened van their eyes met. Alexandra knew that no words could ever right this horrific injustice. She also knew that the road back would be a long one. "You will always matter to me, Sophia."

Even at one in the morning, the Arlington Hospital emergency room bustled with activity. But the group was ushered into a private waiting area away from the public. As triage rooms became available, physicians examined each of the minors.

Sophia jumped up when the first two children filed out after the nurse. "I need to stay with the Littles."

Alexandra rose. Her instinct was to place a hand on Sophia's shoulder, but she was so self-conscious about touching her. Instead, she offered a gentle smile. "The doctor needs to examine them. And then a social worker—someone who's trained to help each of the Littles find their family—will step in."

Fear sprang from Sophia's eyes. "Some of them ran away and were abducted. Not everyone has a family like I do. I'm all they have."

Alexandra worried that the truth could send Sophia into a panic, but she wouldn't lie to her.

"Once you've been examined and we meet your social worker, we can ask what's going to happen next."

"Are you leaving me?"

Alexandra's eyes grew moist with emotion. "I'm staying. Once Crockett is stitched up, he'll find us."

Sophia shuddered in a breath and sank back down into the chair. Alexandra joined her. Several moments later, a woman approached with a police detective.

"Hello, Sophia. I'm Tabitha Browning," she said. "I'm a special kind of social worker called a reunification specialist." With a warm smile, the woman pulled over an empty chair and sat down. "That's a lot of fancy words that mean I'm going to help you rejoin your family, for starters."

"What will happen to the Littles?" asked Sophia.

"We're going to start the search for their families. I understand you've already seen your brother."

Sophia released the vise grip on Alexandra's hand. "Yes. Crockett Wilde."

Tabitha explained that the police detective had questions and asked if Sophia was up to answering them. Her spine stiffened and her eyes chilled. "Some questions are okay. I don't like remembering back to the early years."

As Sophia's nightmare unfolded, Alexandra knew that her story needed to be told. And that she would be the one to tell it.

THE DOCTOR FINISHED SUTURING Crockett's arm. "You're lucky. No tendons were severed. I'll write you a physical therapy prescription for after the stitches come out. Do it. It will help ensure a full recovery, especially if you plan on continuing with martial arts."

After thanking the doctor, he inquired as to where he could find his sister. Before he headed down the corridor, he pulled his cell phone out of his pocket.

"Sorry to call so late," he said.

"What's going on?" Colton asked, his voice groggy.

"I need your help. Can you fly to Uvalde and bring back my mom and dad? Alexandra found my sister." Crockett gritted his teeth to keep from crying.

"Whatever you need," said Colton. "Text me their address and phone number. I'll update you when I get to Dulles. That's the best news." He hung up.

Crockett powered through the ER anxious to find his sister and Alexandra.

THE FOLLOWING MORNING, WHILE Crockett paced in the hospital lobby, his phone rang. It was Colton.

"Flight go okay?" Crockett asked.

"Smooth sailing," his best friend replied. "How are you doing? How's Sophia?"

"Good, I'm good. Sophia's so damned strong. Alexandra hasn't left her side. Thanks for flying my mom and dad here."

"Absolutely. A member of my security team is dropping them at the hospital. Should be there in the next few."

"I appreciate your help."

"You've waited a long time for this day. Try to enjoy it. I'll talk to you later." Colton hung up.

Relief and gratitude swept over Crockett. *I have waited a long time for this.* As soon as Colton's Bentley pulled up, Crockett's parents raced inside.

His mom hugged him. "This doesn't feel real."

Crockett hugged his dad. "You guys okay?"

"We're nervous, elated, in disbelief," Ron Wilde said. "How are you, son? How's Sophia?"

As Crockett guided them toward the elevator, he updated them. "She's got some health issues, so she was moved to a room."

Linda Wilde wiped her eyes with a soaked tissue.

"The physical ones she'll heal from," Crockett said. "The

emotional ones will take a long time. Be prepared. I didn't recognize her. It's a shock."

Linda grasped her husband's hand. "We'll get through everything *together*. Whatever it takes, for as long as it takes."

The elevator doors opened and they squeezed inside. When they arrived at Sophia's floor, Crockett hustled them down the hallway.

They stepped into the room to find Alexandra sitting at Sophia's bedside, holding her hand. When Sophia locked eyes with her mom and dad, she burst into tears. Though she had an IV in her arm, she pushed out of bed and into her mother's arms. Both sobbed while Linda clung to her child.

Crockett's dad, overcome with emotion, pulled Crockett into an embrace and cried. For the past thirteen years, Crockett had envisioned this moment hundreds of times, but the reality of the reunion was beyond the scope of his imagination.

Sophia broke from her mother's embrace to hug her father. "Daddy," Sophia said as he held his baby gently in his arms and wept.

Alexandra rose and inched toward the door, but Crockett slid an arm around her waist. "Please don't leave," he whispered.

"I don't want to interfere," she murmured. "This time is so precious and private."

"You're the reason for this miracle." When Crockett wrapped her in his arms, he could no longer contain himself. As the magnitude of what Alexandra had done for him, for Sophia, and for their entire family overtook him, he released thirteen years of pent-up pain and anger in a tidal wave of tears. When he pulled himself together, he kissed Alexandra's tear-streaked cheeks.

"Mom, Dad, you remember Alexandra Mitus," Crockett said.

"She risked everything to help me," Sophia said, clinging to her mom and dad.

With tears streaming down her cheeks, Linda embraced

Alexandra. "Thank you," she whispered. "Thank you for bringing our Sophia back to us."

"You've made our family whole again," Ron said before hugging Alexandra. "We're so grateful to you."

"Your strong, amazing daughter was worth the risk," Alexandra said. "But I didn't do it alone. Crockett was with me every step of the way."

For the first time in thirteen years, Crockett Wilde was happy. And through the tears, he smiled.

34

DREAM JOB

Four days later, Alexandra signed in at the network news affiliate in Arlington, Virginia, spoke briefly with the receptionist, and took a seat in the waiting room. Unlike her first meeting with Max, she couldn't wait to speak with Meryl Hastings, the TV station's news director.

No sooner had Alexandra sat down than Meryl walked into reception and greeted her with a bright smile and a firm handshake. The executive suggested they chat in her office.

"I just got off the phone with your boss, Rick Schwartz," said Meryl after relaxing into her desk chair. "I understand he's holding a spot on his investigative team for you."

"He is." Alexandra crossed her legs. "I'd planned on returning, but I'm hoping you'll make me an offer I can't refuse."

Meryl laughed. "Your email piqued my curiosity. Sounds like you've got one hell of a story. The local stations are still leading with that sex trafficking operation and it's been four days. Did you receive a tip while working at Cable Fifteen?"

Being out from under Max's thumb made her happy. "Working there wasn't the right fit. I found the story on my own, based on a hunch."

Meryl nodded. "Spoken like a true professional. For the record, I can't stand Max. His loss might be my gain." Leaning back, she crossed her legs. "Why investigative journalism? From what Rick told me, your news magazine show topped the ratings board every week."

"I loved hosting my show, but there's something deeply fulfilling about pursuing and uncovering the truth, especially if it brings value to someone else. Did you enjoy your investigative reporting career before seguing into management?"

"I loved it for the same reason. Working something from a simple hunch." She adjusted her black-rimmed glasses. "Pitch me your story."

Twenty minutes later, the color had faded from Meryl's cheeks. "Horrific. What's your working title for this piece?"

"*The Faces of Evil.*"

"I'd be a fool to let you leave my office without a verbal offer." Meryl extended her hand. "I'd like to bring you on board as an investigative reporter. I've got a midday anchor spot that's going to open up in late spring. That might be a good fit for you."

Alexandra beamed. "I would love that, Meryl." The two women shook hands.

CROCKETT STARED AT DANNY, sitting across from his desk. "Is this confirmed?"

"Unfortunately," said Danny. "I read the police report."

"This has got to be a mistake."

"It's accurate. You want to tell Alexandra or should I?"

"I'll do it," Crockett said.

"I was hoping my good news would overshadow this," Danny said.

"Justice was done when the FBI arrested Ruth Lizzard for corporate espionage and sabotage," Crockett said. "I'm thrilled the

FBI reinstated us as the front-runner for Round Two. My team deserves this win. But the bomb you just dropped upstages all of that."

Danny rose. "I hear you and I'm sorry."

"Thanks for making the trip to tell me in person." As Crockett walked his cousin out, Danny asked about Sophia.

"All things considered, she's doing well. Mom and Dad are moving to Virginia while she undergoes her initial treatment. The reunification specialist remains optimistic, but she's honest. It's going to take years, a lot of patience, and unconditional love."

"I'm here for whatever you need." After a hearty handshake, Danny heaved open the glass door and left.

Crockett told Ellen he'd be taking the rest of the afternoon off and to contact him for urgent matters only. On the way out, he texted Alexandra. "Headed home. See you there. ILY."

While driving, he called Colton. "Are you in town?"

"Had a meeting in DC. I'm heading over the bridge now."

"Swing by my place. I have some news."

"You want to tell me what this is about?"

"In person."

Crockett ended the call and gripped the steering wheel. *No way in hell will I manage this one alone.* His guts churned as he parked in his spot, then rode the elevator to his penthouse.

He went straight to his bar and tossed back a shot of whiskey, then poured one for Colton. After dropping his coat and computer bag on the sofa, he made a pot of coffee. Anything to keep busy.

Ten minutes later, Colton arrived. "Congratulations," he exclaimed, taking in the penthouse. "This is sensational. You've got a million dollar view."

"Thanks." He shot his best friend a tempered smile. His phone buzzed and he read the incoming text from Alex. "Be home soon. ILY2."

"I didn't buy that," said Colton. "You should be on top of the world. What's going on?"

"Alexandra is on her way." Crockett offered Colton the whiskey. "You're gonna need this."

Colton took the glass, but set it down on the coffee table before relaxing on the sofa.

Fueled by anger, Crockett paced. "A handful of scum was arrested the night we found Sophia. The sex club was a front for sex trafficking. It was deplorable."

"That's disgusting," Colton said.

"After Danny read the police report, he thought Alexandra should know the truth. She's due home any minute and I'm not doing this alone."

Colton furrowed his brow. "I'm not following."

"One club member was a serial pedophile. He was arrested the night we found Sophia." With clenched fists, Crockett stared out the window. "He also had a thing for Alexandra. That prick never laid his hands on her, but he came close."

"Jesus, what a sick bastard."

"I never knew his real name until today."

Colton stood beside him and Crockett felt his stare boring into him. "Who was it, Crockett?"

His guts burned, his head pounded. Crockett pivoted. "Wilson Montgomery."

On a growl, Colton's eyes blackened with hatred. "Fuck. No."

"You told me Wilson Montgomery was behind the hostile takeover," Crockett bit out. "What you failed to mention was his relationship to you."

"And said what, 'My father is trying to ruin me?'" Colton raked his hands through his unruly hair. "You brought me a phenomenal opportunity. I shouldered it and every damned thing that came with it. I wasn't going to fail you or the Francesco Company, and I sure as hell wasn't going to let that son of a bitch win."

"That pervert—Wilson Montgomery Mitus—would have sexually assaulted his own *daughter* if I hadn't gotten to the club in time."

"*Jesus*," Colton growled. "I'll kill him."

"Alexandra doesn't know and you've got to help me tell her."

35

TRUTH IS STRANGER THAN FICTION

Alexandra was bursting with the good news about her job offer, but when she entered the living room, the tension radiating off both men was palpable.

She rushed over to Colton. "It's Mom, isn't it? So much has happened in the past few days that I haven't—"

"Mom is fine," Colton said, cutting her off. "She's settled in and loves the constant attention. That's not why I'm here." He picked up a shot glass and downed its contents.

As she slipped off her winter coat, panic soared through her. "Did something happen to Sophia?" She'd visited Crockett's sister in the hospital every day and had become very attached to her.

Her brother paced in front of the window. The V between Crockett's brows wouldn't go away. Her chest tightened and she couldn't catch her breath. Lightheaded, she sat on the sofa. "Please, tell me. I feel like I'm going to pass out."

"I heard from Danny," Crockett began. "Jase Payne has been on the FBI's Most Wanted list for over a decade. His real name is Rodney James."

Alexandra swallowed. This couldn't possibly be the reason Crockett had summoned her brother. "Okay."

"Francois is Frank Robinson. No priors. Dracule is a man named Wilson Montgomery." Crockett flicked his gaze to Colton.

Colton sat on the coffee table across from Alexandra and clasped her hands. The pain in his eyes surprised her. "Last November, Wilson Montgomery attempted a hostile takeover of the Francesco Company. If he'd succeeded, Crockett and I would have lost the biggest deal of our careers. He wanted to ruin me professionally and he almost succeeded. I didn't know who he was until I met him."

"I'd never met Montgomery," Crockett said, turning from the window. "And Colton never told me who he was."

Eyeing the two most important men in her life, Alexandra vented her exasperation. "I'm not following. Who is this Montgomery guy and what does any of this have to do with me?"

"If I'd known, we never would have returned to Incognito."

Alexandra flew off the sofa and stormed over to him. "Then I wouldn't have found your sister! *What could be more important than that?*"

Colton rose, the anger rolling off him in waves.

"Tell her," Crockett bit out.

Her brother stared into her eyes while her heartbeat raced like a locomotive. "Wilson Montgomery is Wilson Montgomery Mitus. He's our father, Alexandra."

The air got sucked from her lungs. For several seconds, no one moved. Or spoke. Or breathed.

When she clutched the pillar for support, Crockett was by her side. Feeling like everything was happening in slow motion, she allowed him to guide her to the sofa. And there she tried to breathe. But she couldn't.

Dracule is a pedophile...and my father. The image of him removing his clothing popped into her consciousness. Her guts heaved and she choked back a gag. Little yellow stars blurred her vision. She slammed her eyes shut and pulled air into her lungs. Passing out was her way of *not* dealing with issues. This time she'd face it, no matter how difficult. She gobbled down a breath. And then another. Slowly, the nausea passed and she opened her eyes.

She had no idea how long they sat in silence, but eventually she found her voice. "He has a tattoo on his wrist. Cain's initials. He told me he lost a son." Colton's eyes blackened with hatred, but he said nothing. "I have questions about our childhood, Colton. And you have the answers."

"I'll give you two some time," Crockett said.

Alexandra clasped his hand. "I'd prefer you stay, if Colton doesn't mind."

Colton eyed his best friend. "I don't like talking about this, but I trust this conversation will stay between us."

"Of course," Crockett said. "You know that."

Colton poured a shot of whiskey, tossed it back. Then, he stared out the living room window for a long moment. Alexandra let go of Crockett, but her stomach was tied in knots. She'd waited a long time to learn about their past from him.

"Wilson adored you, Alexandra," Colton began, his back still to her. "Regardless of what he's become or the way he treated Mom and me, he was kind to you."

"Go on."

Colton turned, his eyes seething with hatred. "Even though Cain and I were inseparable, we were very different. He was loud and funny. I was quiet and shy. I developed a stammering problem. Instead of trying to help me, Wilson criticized and ridiculed me. So, I withdrew further. Kids bullied me, but Cain defended me. He'd beat the living hell out of anyone who dared tease me. Wilson stroked his ego and encouraged his aggression. But with me, he either poked fun or ignored me as if I didn't exist."

"Oh, Colton," Alexandra whispered.

"I don't remember much about you when you were first born, but as you got older, Wilson treasured you," Colton continued. "He would read to you and play with you. It was like he had three different personalities. Things got worse when Mom went back to work. He started bringing women into the house."

"Oh, my God," she said.

"Jesus." Crockett shook his head.

"I saw him with them," Colton continued. "It was messed up. You might have seen, too. I don't know. I think Mom knew, but she was trying to keep the family intact. They fought *a lot*. He was horrible to her. I tried confronting him, but he'd terrorize me and I'd retreat."

"I'm so sorry," Alexandra murmured. "I never knew."

"He got involved in some shady business dealings and couldn't pay the debts," Colton said. "Cain wasn't supposed to be home." His body stiffened and he turned away. "They killed him and I found him."

"Oh, Colton." She ran to him and threw her arms around her brother.

He kissed her forehead, tears in his eyes. "You couldn't know the truth. It was too horrible, too violent."

She sat on the arm of the sofa and dried her tear-streaked cheeks while Crockett held her hand and rubbed her back.

"Mom kicked Wilson out. That was the turning point for me, Mom, too. She never told me not to tell you anything, but I knew better. You were six, Alexandra, and so sad when Cain died. When Wilson left, you turned to me. I was ten and did the best I could."

As the sun dipped below the buildings and dusk cast its shadow over the day, Colton continued. He explained how the three of them had grown close. How he'd found his inner strength. How she'd helped him get over his stutter. Why he'd turned to kink. How falling in love with Brigit had changed him for the better. He'd never been so forthright; so honest. She admired and respected the man who had been more like a father to her than her own had been.

Crockett said very little. Wiped a few tears, stroked her back.

Offered tissues and hot coffee. She wondered if the information would scare him away. Mituses were anything but normal.

When Colton finished, the truth hung heavy. "I've said plenty," he said and rose from the leather chair. "I want to get home to Brigit and check on Mom."

She kissed his cheek. "Thank you," she said. "I love you so much."

"I love you," he replied, then he shifted his attention to Crockett. "You got an earful."

Crockett hugged him. "Nothing I can't handle. Still love you like a brother. Still think you need a haircut." He smiled. "Thanks for trusting me," he said and walked Colton out.

When he returned, he folded Alexandra into his arms and kissed her. "You are the love of my life, Alex. I'm here for you if you want to talk and it's okay if you don't."

Alexandra felt gutted, but also relieved. Learning the truth had finally freed her from the ghosts of her past. As she gazed into Crockett's soulful eyes, she felt certain of one thing. This amazing man loved her unconditionally and that, above all else, mattered most.

36

BEGINNINGS

CROCKETT STARED THROUGH THE glowing candelabras and across his elegantly set dining room table, appreciating Alexandra's beauty and grace. She'd wanted to throw a simple dinner party. But in true Mitus fashion, she'd created a culinary feast.

Roasted beet salad with arugula, preserved cherries, caramelized pecans and goat cheese. Filet mignon drizzled with balsamic glaze and served with spinach risotto. For Red, who didn't eat meat, she marinated sliced tempeh in minced garlic, lemon juice, olive oil and spices. Then, she baked the fermented tofu with the steaks.

At the opposite end of the table, Alexandra laughed with her mom, Brigit, Red and Gavin. He smiled. How could he not? He had his Goth Girl and his sweet sister was alive and safe.

The daily angst that haunted him had subsided. Sophia's road to health continued at a facility in Leesburg where equine therapy played a significant role in her recovery. His mom and dad had rented a cute house nearby. *Slow, steady steps.*

The following Friday, Colton would pilot their flight to California for a long weekend. Alexandra had insisted he and

Brigit join them. She was eager to put her LA home on the market, collect her belongings, and say goodbye to her former boss. Though her new job didn't start for a few weeks, she'd already jumped in, learning everything she could about the major players on Capitol Hill.

She turned in his direction. Her loving smile made his heart beat faster. He couldn't wait to make her his, forever.

"So, what do you think?" Colton asked.

"He's not paying any attention to us," Maverick said. "He's lost in love."

"About time," Danny said.

"From what I can tell, Alexandra is in the same love boat." Gavin winked at her.

With a chuckle, Maverick shook his head. "First Colton. Now Crockett. The law of averages is definitely working against me."

Red glared at Maverick. "From what I can tell, *you're* working against you."

The group broke into laughter.

"Red's got your number, Mav," Crockett said.

"I'm on the move," Maverick said. "No time to settle down."

"Find the right woman and you won't have to settle." Colton kissed Brigit's hand.

Beaming, Brigit pecked his cheek.

"Excuse me." Danny pushed out of his chair and walked into the kitchen.

Crockett followed. "I'm sorry Allison couldn't make it. Is she okay?"

"We found out Tuesday," he said, lifting his phone from his pocket. "She's pregnant."

Crockett smiled. "Congrats."

"She crashes the second she gets home from work. We're so damn excited. I'm gonna check in with her."

He slapped his cousin on the back. "Thanks for sharing your good news. Give her my best." Crockett extracted a bottle from his bar and returned to the dining room. "I'd like to propose a toast."

"Hennessy Eclipse," Maverick said. "That's the good stuff, bro."

After opening the cognac, Crockett poured a finger's worth into each brandy snifter. As he filled Alexandra's glass, she rose to kiss his cheek. Rather than returning to his seat, he slipped his hand around her waist and gave her a little squeeze.

Maverick raised a glass. "Here's to the two idiots I love like brothers and the women who make them better men."

"Charming," Red mumbled.

After the clinking of glasses and murmurs of delight at the luxury liquor, Crockett raised his glass. "To *my* Alex. My forever love."

"Oh, Crockett." She snuck a quick kiss. "Here's to the most amazing man I've ever known and will ever know."

"*Finally*," Kimberly said and the group laughed.

When Danny re-joined them, Crockett suggested they move into the living room. "I've got a short video I want ya'll to see. I'll throw it on the big screen."

Brigit got comfortable on the sofa. Colton sat next to her, pulled out his phone, and after a subtle nod from Crockett, started recording. Using her walker, Kimberly joined them. Gavin and Danny each grabbed a dining room chair to sit on. Red relaxed in the ergonomic chair and Maverick leaned against the pillar between the living and dining rooms.

"You can sit with us, Maverick," Brigit said. "I'll sit on Colton's lap."

"I thought Red would make room for me on her chair."

"Not happening," Red said. "Decker, you can sit with me."

Chuckling, Decker joined her.

Alexandra brushed against Crockett. He loved having her by his side and pulled her close.

"Mom, did Crockett wrangle home movies from you?"

With a twinkle in her eyes, Kimberly shrugged.

"No Goth Girl home videos, babe," Crockett replied. *This is it.* He tapped his phone. The television screen displayed Kimberly Mitus propped up in her hospital bed, fluffing her hair.

Kimberly choked back a sob, her eyes filling with tears.

"You okay, Mom?" Alexandra asked.

"Would you be if your hair looked like that?" Her mom pointed to the TV screen.

With a smile, Alexandra peered up at Crockett through her lashes. He tightened his grip and pecked her cheek.

"Okay, everyone, settle down." Crockett started the video.

"You look lovely," Crockett said. *"Not even a hospital stay can change that."* He turned the lens on himself—flashed a grin—then switched it back to Kimberly. *"I've given this a lot of thought...for a lot of years. You know how much I adore Alexandra."*

Kimberly smiled. *"I do. And I tried to help you out every time she came home. But my sweet girl can be strong-willed, too."*

"She is and I love that about her." Crockett paused. "Kimberly, I'd like to ask you for Alexandra's hand in marriage. I'm waiting to pop the question, but I'd love your blessing."

Alexandra's hand flew to her mouth. "Oh, Crockett."

"Ah hell, another one bites the dust," Maverick mumbled.

Beaming, Kimberly said, "I've waited a long time for this."

"You and me both. I'm not sure she'll say yes."

"If she doesn't, she'll have me to answer to," Kimberly replied.

The dinner party group burst into laughter.

"It means a lot that you asked me, Crockett."

"Me, too," Alexandra murmured and squeezed his hand.

"I've loved our Goth Girl for a long time," Crockett continued. *"Even time and distance couldn't change that."*

Kimberly patted his hand. *"I know that, dear."*

"You have my word that I'll keep her safe and make sure she knows how much I love her—every day. I'll protect her and build a wonderful life with her."

Alexandra swiped a tear while Red murmured, "So romantic."

Through the tears in her eyes, Kimberly smiled. "I wholeheartedly give you my blessing. You've had it from the very beginning. I wish you both a lifetime of love and laughter. Be good to each other and you'll find that life is beautiful, even in the darkest times."

Crockett sat next to Kimberly, placed himself in the shot, and kissed her cheek.

"Ooooh, a selfie," Alexandra quipped as she breezed into the hospital room. "What did I miss?"

"Crockett doing what he does best," Kimberly said. "Making me happy."

He flipped the camera on Alex. She blew him a kiss and he stopped filming.

The TV screen went dark. No one spoke. All eyes on Crockett. He'd waited a long time to get to *this* moment with *this* woman. And he couldn't wait to let the world know how much he adored her. And couldn't live without her.

Turning to face her, he pulled the ring box from his pants pocket. Then, he knelt. Alexandra's wide-eyed gaze followed his every movement.

"Breathe," he murmured and waited until she inhaled.

Her beautiful smile and sparkling eyes filled him with happiness. The intelligent, sexy, wild, gorgeous and insanely curious woman standing before him was everything he wanted in a life partner. If she would have him, he would cherish her for the rest of his life. He stared into her beautiful brown eyes.

"Alexandra Reed Mitus, I adore you." He opened the tiny box. "Marry me."

Her eyes slid from his to the jewelry. Then, her mouth dropped open. "Oh, Crockett." Beaming, she extended her trembling hand. "I cannot wait to be your wife. So, *yes, yes, yes,* I'll marry you."

He slipped on the dazzling ring and swept her into his arms. With her hands on either side of his face, they kissed as the room broke into applause.

"I love you," she murmured between kisses.

"I love you, too, my beautiful Goth Girl."

"Hallelujah," Kimberly exclaimed. "Only a decade in the making."

The group congregated around, offering hugs and congratulations.

"I hate to celebrate and run," Danny said when the string of congratulations and good wishes had come to an end.

"I've gotta get going, too," Decker said. "If anyone belongs together, it's you two."

Alexandra hugged both men. "Thank you for having Crockett's back and mine, too."

Gavin moseyed over. "Dinner was delicious and the engagement made me cry. You two are perfect together."

Alexandra hugged her friend. "I'm thrilled you were here. Give my love to Bruce."

"Being in the baby delivering business, he goes when the call comes in," Gavin said.

"We'll do dinner when I'm back from California," Alexandra said.

Hand in hand, the couple walked the men to the front door. "Thanks for being here," Crockett said. "It means a lot." He eyed Decker. "You're in charge while I'm gone."

"I think Ellen's in charge." Chuckling, Decker moseyed down the hallway toward the elevator.

"You deserve to be happy," Danny said.

"Best to Allison and congrats on the big news." Crockett said goodbye to his cousin.

Gavin shook Crockett's hand and hugged Alexandra. "This was a special night. Thanks for including me."

After closing the door, Crockett swept Alexandra into his arms and kissed her. "You've made me a very happy man."

Her adorable grin crinkled her nose. "You, happy?"

"It's a new concept, but I'm liking it." After he snagged another kiss, they returned to the living room.

Brigit and Red huddled around Alexandra while Kimberly watched her daughter's interview of Crockett and his team on his laptop. His future mother-in-law could not stop smiling. He sank down on the sofa beside her.

"You look like you're enjoying yourself," Crockett said.

She paused the video and smiled. "This is delightful." Her expression sobered. "I kept Sophia in my thoughts every day. Your family must be overjoyed."

"Overjoyed, stunned. You name it, we're feeling it."

"I'm sorry your parents couldn't make it, tonight."

"Under the circumstances, I didn't invite them, but I did tell them I was proposing. Once things level out with my sister, we'll celebrate with them."

"You're a good son, Crockett. My sweet Alexandra is a lucky girl."

He shifted his attention to Alexandra. "From where I sit, I'm the lucky one." With a smile, he pushed off the sofa, pausing to kiss his fiancée before joining Colton and Maverick.

The three men stood, shoulder-to-shoulder, staring out the living room windows at the twinkling city across the river. Maverick slung his arms around both men.

"It's good being around you guys," Maverick said. "Before you know it, you two idiots will be chasing babies in stinkpot diapers."

Crockett flashed a grin. "Bring it on."

"We're in no rush," Colton replied.

"I'm never getting married." Maverick leaned against the window to face them. "Time to talk shop."

"Now?" Crockett asked.

"He'll talk even if we don't listen," Colton said and they laughed.

"We've finished phase one beta testing of your pregnant Eagle," Maverick said to Crockett. "You're a genius to create a surveillance bird that carries a smaller device inside her. She's a beauty. I'm going to need half a dozen."

"You did the math on that, right?" Crockett asked.

"One point five mil." Maverick shot him a grin, then flipped his attention to Colton. "I need a silent investor."

"Colton's anything but *silent*," Crockett said. "And that's a good thing. He goes quiet on you and you've got a whole different problem on your hands."

"We'll talk," Colton said. "Did you hear back from Internado?"

"The good senator made a few calls," Maverick said. "He set up more meetings in the past week than I've had all year. It's like I've landed in Oz."

"Stay clear of the flying monkeys," Colton said. "Those things creep me out."

"I'd destroy those damned monkeys," Crockett said. "I don't trust that wizard hiding behind the curtain."

"My problem isn't with the monkeys or the old geezer," Maverick replied. "The Wicked Witch of the West scares the living hell out of me."

"Everyone has a price," Colton said. "Especially the senator. That job is just a launching pad for him. He's got his sights set much higher."

"You know better than anyone, Mav, there's no such thing as a free lunch," Crockett said. "Watch your back."

37

THE GIFT

After Crockett bowed, his little tykes bowed in return. Then, they scampered off the karate mats and over to their waiting parents. His yellow belts showed continued progression and he smiled. *Slow and steady.*

He couldn't spar until the sutures were removed and he completed the PT treatment, which meant he had to drop out of the karate competition. Minor setback. Gratitude filled his heart as he slipped into his shoes, said goodbye to Hannah and her dad, and left the dojo.

On his way home, he called Alexandra. "Hey, babe. Be there soon."

"Why, hello, Huntah. I haven't heard from you in a while."

Crockett smiled. *"Electra."*

"I've missed you. Are you available tonight?"

"For you, always."

"Your mask will be on the bar, along with a nightcap. Shed your karate *gi* unless you want to show me your hot moves."

Her sultry voice lured him home in record time. He entered his penthouse, expecting to see her waiting by the door. Instead, the rich, earthy timbre of Imelda May crooning, "How Bad Can a Good Girl Be" and the flickering candlelight and dancing flames in the fireplace greeted him. His Goth Girl was nowhere in sight.

He eyed the shot of whiskey she'd left for him on the bar. But he didn't want the burn of alcohol. He wanted the sweet taste of his woman. She'd left him a handwritten note beneath the bottle. "When you find me, you can have me."

Heat pounded through him. He stood alone in the master suite, the glowing embers casting soft shadows on the marble hearth. He stripped out of his karate uniform and continued his search. She wasn't in the guest room either. *Where is she?*

As he walked toward the kitchen, he spied a yoga-like chaise lounge chair covered in dark, rich leather next to the living room windows. A giant red bow rested on the larger of two humps that were separated by a valley. If Electra had anything to do with this, sex was involved. He couldn't help but smile, but his attention was diverted when Alexandra sauntered out of the shadows from the kitchen, wearing nothing but gold stilettos. His moan sounded like a growl as his gaze followed her supple curves. But it was the devilish gleam in her eyes and her beckoning smile that captured his heart.

"Hello, gorgeous." He drew her close and kissed her. "Where are our masks?"

She slipped her arms around him. "I changed my mind, handsome."

"No lovemaking?"

Caressing his cheek, she smiled. "That's *exactly* what we're going to do. I want *you*. No masks, no role-playing. Just love."

"I love the sound of that."

"There's something else...I'm on the Pill and I want us to be as intimate as possible."

"I like the sound of that, too." He nuzzled her neck, stroked her long back and curvy bottom.

She chuckled. "I didn't think you'd object."

Gazing into her eyes, he kissed her. "I adore you, Alex."

"I love you, so much." With their fingers interlaced, she led him to the curvy chair. "For the man who has everything, I bought you a Tantra chair."

"I do have everything," he murmured, wrapping her in his arms. "I have you."

Another Happily Ever After by
Stoni ALEXANDER

A NOTE FROM STONI

Thank you so much for reading THE WILDE TOUCH! Sign up for my newsletter on my website and I'll gift you a free steamy short story, only available to my Inner Circle.

Here's where you can follow me online. I look forward to connecting with you!

StoniAlexander.com
Amazon
BookBub
Facebook
Goodreads

Want to read more in The Touch Series? Here's Book Three...

THE LOVING TOUCH

Book Three of The Touch Series

Mirror, Mirror, on the Wall...

Taylor Hathaway—Mitus Conglomerate's sweet, timid event planner—has always played it safe. But when forced into the spotlight at a DC fundraiser and auctioned off to a gorgeous stranger from out of town, she makes a bold choice. No strings. No regrets. *And very little sleep...*

Hospitality Magnate Jagger Loving—sexy, bad boy of Loving Resorts—offers everything from exotic to erotic at his luxurious, couples-only properties. Days before the launch of his first US-based hotel, a sudden setback throws his world into chaos and the grand opening promises to be a colossal flop. In walks his short-term fix...the strikingly beautiful Taylor Hathaway. But he knows her as Raven. *And that's not all he remembers about her.*

Thrust together, they can't deny their powerful attraction. While Jagger is forced to confront past sins to save his empire, Taylor must conquer a lifetime of insecurities to ensure he succeeds.

THE WILDE TOUCH | 367

Everything hinges on trust...and the obstacles each must overcome to prove their love is eternal.

GRAB IT NOW or READ FREE ON KU!

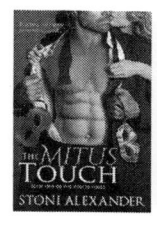

LOOKING FOR A SEXY STANDALONE?

GRAB IT NOW or READ FREE ON KU!

ACKNOWLEDGMENTS

A gigantic thanks to my husband, Johnny, who provided invaluable ideas as I birthed this plot. I'm grateful you're my first reader and, while I cringe at the abundance of red ink strewn throughout the manuscript, I appreciate your thorough edits. Being a renaissance man doesn't hurt, either.

Boundless love to my smart, funny, über-talented son for his love...and for *always* asking: "How's the writing going, Mom?"

Heartfelt appreciation to my critique group for their relevant edits and attention to detail. Thank you Magda Alexander, MC Vaughan, and Andy Palmer!

A special thank you to Cindy Maroni, LICSW, for her expertise in the field of social work and human behavior, especially in light of the delicate subject matter.

A big shout-out to Howard County Police Officer Patrick Gipe for taking the time to educate me on Tasers and for answering my many law enforcement-related questions.

Along the way, I've met some fantastic writers. I continue to be in awe of your talents. Your support and friendships mean the world to me. Thank you for your generosity and kindness.

To the wonderful, enthusiastic readers and bloggers who took their valuable time to read my debut novel, **THE MITUS TOUCH**. I am forever grateful for your encouraging words. The following lovely ladies deserve a special shout-out: Judy, Beca, Emma, Crystal, Kat, and Jenny. Thank you for my happy tears. Being a new author in an ocean of romance writers is an insane adventure, but you made me feel like I'm exactly where I'm supposed to be, doing exactly what my heart has always dreamed about.

ABOUT THE AUTHOR

Stoni Alexander writes sexy romantic suspense and contemporary romance about tortured alpha males and independent, strong-willed females. Her passion is creating love stories where the hero and heroine help each other through a crisis so that, in the end, they're equal partners in more ways than love alone.

In a previous life, she appeared in numerous television, film and stage productions before transitioning to a successful career in business. Stoni spent her childhood moving around the country and appreciates her deep-seated roots in the DC Metro area. She's married to the love of her life, is an über-proud football mom, and dreams of the day when her muse will inspire her at will.

Made in the USA
Middletown, DE
10 September 2020